D0408107

ALSO BY FRANK DELANEY

FICTION

Ireland

Tipperary

Shannon

NONFICTION

Simple Courage:
A True Story of Peril on the Sea

VENETIA KELLY'S TRAVELING SHOW

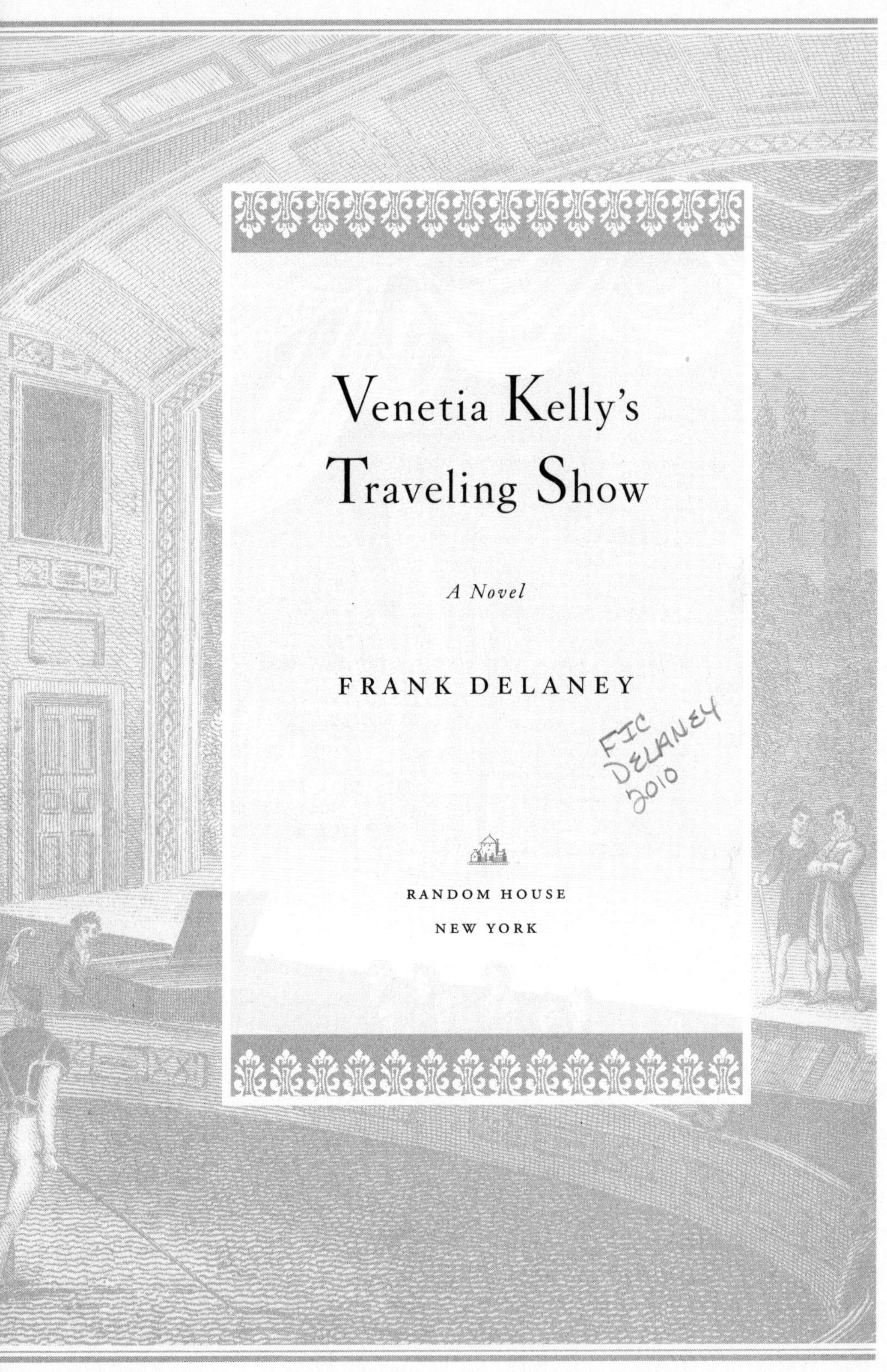

Venetia Kelly's Traveling Show

A Novel

FRANK DELANEY

RANDOM HOUSE
NEW YORK

Venetia Kelly's Traveling Show is a work of fiction. Names, characters, places, and incidents are the products of the author's imagination or are used fictitiously. Any resemblance to actual events, locales, or persons, living or dead, is entirely coincidental.

Published in the United States by Random House, an imprint of The Random House Publishing Group, a division of Random House, Inc., New York.

RANDOM HOUSE and colophon are registered trademarks of Random House, Inc.

LIBRARY OF CONGRESS CATALOGING-IN-PUBLICATION DATA

Delaney, Frank
Venetia Kelly's traveling show: a novel / Frank Delaney.
p. cm.
ISBN 978-1-4000-6783-1
eBook ISBN 978-1-5883-6973-4
1. Traveling theater—Fiction. 2. Ireland—Fiction.
3. Ireland—Politics and government—1922–1949—Fiction. I. Title.
PR6054.E396V46 2010 823'.914—dc22 2009028383

Printed in the United States of America on acid-free paper

www.atrandom.com

2 4 6 8 9 7 5 3 1

FIRST EDITION

Book design by Dana Leigh Blanchette

Author's Note

During the early twentieth century, Ireland began to practice a wonderful new dramatic form—politics. It was free, compelling, and wild, and the Irish, with their fondness for high intrigue and low comedy, embraced it with love. This was a natural fit. Though colonized for generations, and denied formal education, the Irish had retained in their race memory the innate culture of the oral tradition. Thus they were always prepared to come out for someone who would tell a good story, play a fine tune, or act a great part.

Extraordinary passions were stoked in this theater-for-all, as massive figures, of uneven character and temperament, opened up the nation's soul. The country became notorious for fiercely fought elections, fevered by noble intentions, instabilities, and greed. Some of the candidates believed that they had a destiny to lead; some proffered vision; some scarcely bothered to hide their predatory intent.

Idealism being the virginity of politics, the new nation burst at the seams with young zeal. But even the most idealistic discovered to their sorrow that freedom can also do harm to our values, because democracy, our "least worst" system, takes away even as it gives.

Innocence is the price of power.

VENETIA KELLY'S TRAVELING SHOW

She sprang from the womb and waved to the crowd. Then she smiled and took a bow. That's what her mother told me, and so did the midwife, Mrs. Haas. During the birth, the wind howled outside, and the snow whirled in a blizzard of frightful depth and terror. People died on the streets that evening, overwhelmed by the weather. When the blizzard cleared at around ten o'clock, the stars came out bright and brighter, salt grains and diamonds, high above New York. The wind had stacked up the snow in hefty, gleaming banks against the bases of the tall buildings. By then the infant was pink and asleep, tiny hands wrinkled and clenched. Venetia, her name was, chosen the instant she appeared, and she was born, her mother insisted, in mythic circumstances: "Moses"; "bulrushes"; "nativity"—she murmured those words, to herself as much as to me.

You are reading the story of Venetia Kelly, that "mythically" born baby. She became a young woman of remarkable talent and passion, and when she was thirty-two years old—the year I met her—she was drawn into a terrible intrigue that had a profound effect upon my parents and me.

I've waited a long time to write it down. My reasons for doing so at all? Simple: The story isn't over, and I'm telling it now to try to secure its ending. I'm aware that I'm like a man running after his hat in a high wind: I may never retrieve it; at moments I shall seem ridiculous; and finally the forces against me may deny me the result that I want. But there it is.

Venetia Kelly's story became my story too; it determined the direction I would take at one time, and has controlled how I've lived ever since. I can't say whether I might have had a different life if I'd never met her, but such has been her impact that I've never looked for anything else. In other words, the existence that I lead keeps me as close to her as I can get under the circumstances.

As you read, please know that I'm a man of mature years telling the story of himself when young, so forgive me if at times I make the young me seem and sound older than eighteen. In fact, I don't think I've changed that much; certainly I recognize myself easily. And I wasn't a complicated young man, but an only child is always a little different. My parents treated me almost as an equal, and I perhaps had more adult sensibilities than were good for me at that age.

I think that I might have found it easier to write about myself as a younger child—the small boy who dug for gold on the farm so that he could buy his parents gifts; who worried that they worked too hard; who bought his mother tinned pears for her birthday. At eighteen, some of that survived, but by then the sense of responsibility with which I am cursed had begun to grow all over me like an extra skin. I feel it every day, I feel it now; it too spurs me to try to put this account in your hands. But I'll endeavor to assemble all the reasons, as I think of them, and as they arise.

Tiny Digression (more Digressions later too): Is there an ideal age at which momentous events should happen to us? Is there a certain plateau we must reach before we're capable of taking on "big things"? I have no idea, and if anybody ought to know, I should.

2

As you'll see, I can't tell you this story without the detailed inclusion of the mother, Sarah Kelly, also an actress. Sarah, when telling me about Venetia's birth, flung about the word "auspicious." That afternoon, in an attempt to induce birth—Venetia was two days late—the mother sang something from Donizetti; she said that women in the theater had told her a high note could bring on labor.

As she hit the note, a horse in the street below neighed so loudly that the two expectant women, Sarah with her massive bump and Mrs. Haas with an armful of warm towels, went to the window and looked down. Sarah said, given the tricks of the light, that she thought she was "looking at a unicorn."

That same morning she had a letter from a school friend repaying an old debt.

"Auspicious," she said, waving a hand like a frond. "Wasn't it all auspicious?"

The father wasn't there that snowy night of the birth. Nor did he ever appear in Venetia's childhood. He did speak to me eventually (once the others had agreed to be interviewed), and he then, this unpleasant, aloof beanpole, tried to buy my silence. This was a fellow so measured that people said he never changed his clothes—always a black double-breasted suit, startling white shirt, dark red tie.

So: born out of wedlock, the daughter of a rich and prominent man and a glamorous and already renowned actress, a storm-tossed birth, a foot of snow in the streets, pedestrians hurled to the ground by winds of hurricane force, perhaps a unicorn, plus a recompense coming from afar. Was it mythic? It's tough to say no.

"We have myth to correspond with the great moments of life," Sarah Kelly said to me all those years later. She was prepared only to talk about such things as the birth or Venetia when young, and had condemned Mrs. Haas to the same restrictions. " 'When beggars die there are no comets seen; the heavens themselves blaze forth the death of princes.' And every mother knows the exact, the precise, the meticulous details of the birth of every child she has ever borne—that's her own, private little myth. So I can tell you—this was a birth from a legend. If you want proof, see how remarkable the child became."

Now, looking at my notes of that conversation, I can analyze what Sarah said. In essence, she linked the birth of her daughter to the birth of Jesus Christ, and she supported her thesis with an unattributed quotation from Shakespeare, the remark about beggars and comets, and so forth.

If you want to put yourself in good company, reach for the top. That was Sarah—dramatic, resplendent, with a long, elegant slope of a nose, and born without the gene of shyness. And that, in essence, was the level of sophistication we came up against, my family and I. Plus, not far away from Sarah, crookedness, thievery, danger, and death.

Nobody here in Ireland recalls snow that night, or planets crashing, or at the very least some thunder and lightning. I've made local inquiries, and I've checked the meteorological office records—rain here, frost there, fog somewhere else, temperatures between 28 and 48 degrees Fahrenheit, nothing abnormal.

Where Venetia Kelly was born, the weather also looked as though it would stay ordinary that day—a dry and sunny New Year in New York, the first of January, 1900. In fact, it was unseasonably warm on Park Avenue. And then, in a matter of hours, the blizzard swept down from the

Great Lakes faster than a rumor. No wonder Venetia often complained of the cold.

Sarah had to leave the house that night where she gave birth; she had to get out before the Andersons returned. That, apparently, was part of the deal. The conception of the baby had taken place in Mr. Anderson's study on Park Avenue—"on the desk," she told me. Sarah had always wanted to see his home, observe the things that comforted him; so, his wife away for Easter, Mr. Anderson had invited her over on the Sunday afternoon.

When she discovered that she was pregnant, Sarah then told him that she'd like the child to be born in the house in which it had been conceived, because she understood that great good luck attached to it.

"It's what the Chinese believe," she told me.

I myself have had the good fortune to know some Chinese folklore scholars, and none of them has ever told me—or confirmed or found for me—such a nostrum.

The blue-blooded wife knew nothing of their affair and its arrangements—although Mr. Anderson mused that if she had known, she might well have agreed; she possessed, he said, that kind of eccentric tolerance, she was an American WASP. But in any case Mr. Anderson maneuvered things so that, once he knew roughly the date, he would make sure that they would be in Connecticut for their annual Christmas sojourn.

"The arrangement was," said Sarah, "that I had to get out as soon as I felt able, no room at the inn, so to speak." After the birth, Mrs. Haas was to send a message to Mr. Anderson in Greenwich, using Sarah's code: "The workmen have left the house."

Everything turned out as planned, although Sarah said she could have done without the rush to her father's house on that cold night. Even so, she was to live there for eleven years until she came to Ireland.

Sarah Kelly eventually fetched up in Florida, retired and elegant, well cared for. She had spent most of her life in an ivy-covered house on the edge of Dublin, where I went to see her a number of times.

With her help (up to a point), and constant research and questioning, I've spent years trying to piece together this story. The decision to assemble it finally became a matter of inner peace. There had been so many days when I'd asked myself whether I'd really lived through it, whether it had actually happened. Over and over I've had to interrogate the plot. Not to mention the sense of loss.

And I've longed for—I still long for—any clues of any kind to Venetia's character, temperament, behavior, childhood, talent, anything. I want to know more and more and more about her; I never got enough of her.

Sarah didn't help much in supplying any of what I wanted because Sarah couldn't stop acting. After each and every meeting with her I spent so much time trying to determine how much was true, and how much performance. For example, as long as I knew her, she continued to give the impression of being airy, delicate, unknowing, and vague. She wasn't; she was as sharp as a tack and as smart as green paint. The proof is that she ended up unscathed by the entire incident, unmoved. And she died very rich.

Those peculiar visits to Sarah brought mixed pleasures. To begin with, I always caught my breath when I saw her, because it was like looking at an older incarnation of Venetia. She'd stand at the fireplace, looking regal. Or under the huge tree in the garden, beckoning to me, and looking mysterious. Then the hand on my arm, the sigh as she looked at me and shook her head as she murmured: "Adonis, still an Adonis."

Time was not the enemy of this beautiful woman; Sarah grew more beautiful. As she aged, she kept her figure splendidly, and—her actressy gifts—she constantly seemed to show it off to me, turning this way and that. Once or twice, I even thought she was giving me the old come-on. I never tested it, never did anything about it; I couldn't. More to the point, I *wouldn't.* But I often wonder if I should have; and then I think, *What if I had fallen for her?* I could have—the psychological conditions were in place. That was, of course, the trick; and she knew how to pull it off.

At the end of every visit, I came away cleft in twain by those mixed feelings: desire with distaste; liking with discomfort; warmth with repulsion. By the time of our last "appointment," as she called our meetings, I'd learned enough not to succumb, knew that I had to handle myself carefully.

Over the years, then, gliding about in her ivy-covered house, or walking like a stork in the garden, Sarah, still the grande dame of the Abbey

Theatre, told me her version of what happened on the night of Venetia's birth—how she turned up on her father's doorstep, infant in her arms, like a character from a melodrama.

"I was like Mary without Joseph. But elated, my dear. It was the first day of the week, the month, the New Year, and the new century, and there was I with a new life in my arms. I was so proud, and I felt vindicated in having her, even if she was technically illegitimate."

"Which is, I presume, why she bears the name Kelly and not Anderson?"

"I know, my dear Ben, that you have your own reservations about my father, the wonderful King. I understand. But that night—oh, my dear, he was supreme. He took his new granddaughter from my arms, carried her into the house, and sat by the fire, rocking her, crooning to her. He never reproached me, he never made a comment. Audrey was with me, and she adored my father."

The idea of Sarah's father being "supreme" is something you'll come up against as you read on. And by "Audrey" she meant, as you'll have gathered, Mrs. Haas, whose real name, Venetia told me, was not Audrey. She was Gretchen, Viennese-born. And she hated King Kelly—I mean true loathing.

Sarah called her Audrey after a character in *As You Like It.* Shakespeare gives the oaf, Touchstone, a girlfriend named Audrey, and she is described—by Touchstone—as "a foul slut." Mrs. Haas, so far as I could tell, never found out.

And that gave me another side of Sarah, not at all her managed demeanor of sweetness and light. The "Audrey" thing was amusing and tart, yes, and witty—and even ironic, given Mrs. Haas's efficiency and domestic flair. But it was bitchy and unjust, and it peels back a corner, just a tiny flap, of the other side of Sarah.

That sidelong detail gives me the appropriate moment to warn you of something. As I've already hinted, I'm prone to Digressions. Like my anger, it's a matter of character with me—meaning I have difficulty controlling it. I digress when I'm in conversation, I digress when I'm teaching, I digress—dammit—when I'm eating. If you can accept that about me without too much harsh judgment, you might even find me entertaining.

So, throughout this story you can expect three kinds of sidestep: Important Digression, which will usually be something to do with factual history; Relatively Important Digression, where a clarification needs facts and I will ferry them in from a side road; and—my favorite—Unimportant Digression, which can be about anything.

I ask your forgiveness in advance. We Irish do this digression stunt. We're so damn pleased with our ability to talk hind legs off donkeys, that we assume people like to listen.

And now, to drive home the point, here's one of those Unimportant Digressions; it's regarding Mrs. Haas and a peculiarity that puzzles me to this very day and for which I felt that I could never ask an explanation.

She was a lanky woman, and she wore "unusual" shoes—brightly colored, of shiny leather (I think she must have applied some kind of dye to them), and they always had high heels. The rest of her clothing leaned toward dull; I suppose that nobody in Sarah's orbit dared to dress outstandingly.

Anyway, when sitting down, Mrs. Haas used to kick off her high-heeled shoes—and then, and instantly, begin to scratch her behind. She often went to great lengths to achieve this, shifting in her chair and twisting this way and that. Off would come the shoes and the scratching would begin. Nobody paid a blind bit of notice.

And it was noisy scratching, as though she wore canvas underwear. When, with her feet, she fumbled her shoes back on, the hands would come out from under the backside and rest in her lap again. And she did it when alone. Standing by the kitchen table (as I watched secretly from a corridor), off came the shoes, down went the hands to the land of canvas, and scratch-scratch-scratch, all over her rear.

What was it? A reflex action of some kind? Or was there a relationship, an unseen nervous connection, between her shoes and her aft epidermis? I've never known, and because I never asked, I never found out.

How she didn't break her fingernails I'll never know—and I glanced at her hands whenever I could. She kept those nails as level as a hedge; obviously strong, they were like a good set of teeth on her fingertips; that woman had a gift of calcium. Perhaps the calcium had something to do with the scratching.

See? A Digression.

Back to Venetia's birth: Here are the true facts of that New Year's night, 1900. When Sarah arrived with her bundle in her arms, and Mrs. Haas panting behind her like a big, long dog, Sarah's father, baby or no baby, tried to slam the door in their faces.

But Sarah guessed that his poker game was up and running (she was right) and she told him that if he didn't let her in (in her shy way she said something like "If you don't take your daughter and your heiress in from the storm"), she'd tell the men there that her father had made love to most of their wives—which he had.

That version was given to me by Sarah's father, and I then challenged Sarah herself with the truth of it. She caved in—and added a little bonus.

"Yes, I did threaten him with that. I knew all their wives, and he had indeed connected with them. Except Dave Challoner's—but nobody had ever made love to Betty Challoner," Sarah said, "because Betty wouldn't have allowed them to." She paused. "Not even her own husband."

Sarah filled all her conversation with such asides, usually about people whose names meant nothing to me. Now and then a nugget like that flashed in the dirt from her life's riverbed; she could tell scandals of crimson. It was part of why I loved her company.

Of course, Sarah had her own personal mythology, so Venetia told me. She had lived with Mrs. Haas since infancy; Sarah's mother had disappeared when her child was no more than a few weeks old. Growing up, little Sarah had been told of her mother's tragic and dramatic death trying to rescue a puppy from a lake called Lough Gur in County Limerick. So, when it came to her turn to be a mother, Sarah held on to her own infant with what became her life's great passion, the drama that was her daughter.

Until I came along.

3

Let me tell you something now from the end of the story—to be more precise, from the beginning of the end. It's not one of my Digressions; I just want you to get a feeling of some of the forces that were ranged against me in that long-ago intrigue.

One day, I was asked in a serious and important way to go home to my parents' house. I agreed, and gave an indication of when I would arrive. When I got there, in the middle of the afternoon—I'm giving only the barest sketch here—I saw my father, my dear, maddening father, standing in the doorway of the cottage that we owned down by the river. He looked as though he was watching out for me. Close beside him stood a man whom I'd never seen before.

As I approached, the man ushered my father indoors. When I followed through the open door, an unseen person behind me wrapped an arm like a tentacle around my throat. I could smell the cigarette smoke on the sleeve. Straight ahead, in the middle of the room, my parents were sitting in chairs side by side. Above them stood two men pointing guns at my parents' heads. The year was 1932, and this was Ireland, this wasn't

Chicago. I managed to stay calm, or at least to appear so; I wet my pants, but only I knew.

After a moment the forearm at my throat relaxed. It became plain that neither parent was allowed to speak to me. I saw heartbreaking appeal in their eyes, but when my father began to say, "We had no way of warning you," one of the sentries clouted him across the head with a gun butt, and blood spurted from my father's ear.

Through the panic of my mind I thought, *This too is politics.* In the 1930s there was Fascism all over Europe; why should Ireland be any different? And all politics is local.

The situation shocked me all the more because at that moment I was living in a fairy tale, a wonderland of kindness and excitement and performance and beautiful language.

I'm locating this incident here, now, because I want you to understand the swing of the thing. Like the fastest and most exotic pendulum you've ever heard of, my life at that time swayed between magic and danger, between enchantment and death itself. And yes, that was the beginning of the end.

4

Let's stay for a moment in 1932, because that is the year central to all this, a Year of Destiny, it was called, and so it became for me. The incident in the cottage happened because in February we had a general election. Truly epoch-making, it altered the course of Irish history. What I want to say is this: The private events that so formed and perhaps distorted me occurred against a remarkable background.

Everything that year rang of passion. Where there's passion, deceit soon follows, and the major issue of the day, the general election, backdrop to my own drama, was, like all politics, characterized by passion and deceit. The entire country, including my parents—and myself—discussed politics more fervently than monks prayed. These events of ours were played out against that national fever. When I look back now, I think that everything must have been unstable, but we didn't know it.

I was so excited in those last months of 1931; I was on fire. And with good reason. Fierce winds of change were blowing across our little island, and the spores of turbulence were landing everywhere. We heard daily threats of Communism and Bolshevism and Fascism—all the public-life "isms" of the early twentieth century. One colossus, the tallest man in politics, was striding the national stage. His rivals in the government were attempting to close down his newspaper and haul the editor to a military tribunal. Not a few people, my parents included, feared that there might even be a gun-barrel coup d'état—by either side—before polling day.

That 1932 election finally settled the political definition of our country. It gave form to a structure that had begun to identify a nation—out of old clay, new shapes. At the same time we became a model of how democracies evolve, how a people can go forward hopefully while not abandoning their past. This was a battle between the fresh politics of the young state's first government, which had been in charge for ten years, versus forces that represented ancient and unquenchable warlike passions but hadn't been able to get their hands on the levers of power.

Of course it was all still being run by politicians. We have an old saying here: "No matter who you vote for, the government always gets in." My father, who had what he called a "flypaper mind," loved the writings of Ambrose Bierce and could quote at length from *The Devil's Dictionary,* one of his favorite books. And in this period of fierce shenanigans, Bierce's quotation defining politics rang through our house every day—"the conduct of public affairs for private advantage."

Mother and I became so used to it that whenever the words came from my father's lips, we chimed in like a satire's chorus. If we'd had a tune to it we could have sung it.

Moving from the general to the particular—I was guaranteed a ringside seat in the election. Even if matters hadn't suddenly assaulted us, even if my father hadn't done something so wild, so out of character, I'd have been in the thick of it all, because I already knew that I had an official job. At eighteen I was of age to serve as the clerk at our local polling booth in the village.

The day itself was memorable for a number of reasons. Our local teacher Mr. O'Dwyer acted as polling officer; he and I sat side by side at a table in the schoolhouse. As you'll see later on, I was there against all the odds, and, given everything that was going on, plus the possibility of wild embarrassment on the day itself, I think it was heroic of me to turn up.

My job was to supervise the Register of Electors, verifying the names and addresses of the people who came in and asked for a ballot paper. The pencil with which I did this task was specially provided, Mr.

O'Dwyer told me, by the government in Dublin—the "Mighty Pencil," he called it.

He mentioned one word over and over—"personation." Personation is an offense under the law—it should be called "impersonation"—and it involves entering a polling station, asking for a ballot paper under a name not your own, and then voting: in short, pretending to be another person. Already well known, it became a vogue word during that election; we, the Irish, loved the slogan "Vote early, vote often," and I saw it at first hand that day.

Polling was unusually heavy; we had a turnout in our area of 90 percent. Personation attempts also rose on that tide. Throughout the twelve hours, Mr. O'Dwyer challenged as many as twenty or so voters. The election fell on a Tuesday, 16 February, deliberately chosen as just an ordinary working day. Voting hours ran from nine in the morning until nine in the evening, and shortly after we opened the school door a tall gentleman strode in like a general, walked past Mr. O'Dwyer, and made straight for me.

"Name and address, please, sir?" I said, as instructed.

"Jeremiah Quinn, Ardkeeran, Mantlehill."

I looked up the letter *Q* on my thick sheaves of lists, and found the name and address. Just as I was about to brandish the Mighty Pencil, tick his name, and hand Mr. O'Dwyer the voting paper—which the polling officer had to validate with a little stamping machine—Mr. O'Dwyer said, "Is that Jim Kennedy I see before me?" He said it pleasantly and the man didn't move a muscle.

"Turn around, Jim, 'til we have a look at you," said the teacher.

Mr. "Quinn" or Mr. "Kennedy," or whatever his name was, marched out.

Shortly after that, a lady came in, older than my mother, a heavy woman in an old burgundy-colored coat like a bad carpet. She gave the polling officer a wary look—Mr. O'Dwyer had his head down at the time. But when she gave me the name and address, Mr. O'Dwyer raised his head and said, "Well, well. And the dead arose and appeared to many. I was at your funeral, Agnes. That was a good send-off."

She also walked out fast, and he muttered to me, "They'll be up out of their graves today."

He explained: Individuals from outside the district were coming to our village to vote. Hoping that we in the polling station wouldn't notice or know, they were giving us names they'd taken off headstones. And of course many of those names mightn't yet have been struck off my voting registers, which weren't always up to date.

Mr. O'Dwyer said, "Why don't they do the job right and hire actors? At least they'd be convincing." He added, "Wait 'til you see. Those two will be back here and they'll vote as themselves." Which they did.

The antics went on all day. Voters who had cast their ballots earlier came in late, in different clothes, giving different names.

Mr. O'Dwyer, cheery as ever, said, "Oh, John. Is it colder out? You were wearing no hat this morning." And he said, "D'you know what, Mrs. Glacken? You looked ten years younger this morning. Is it the headscarf?"

Once I had grasped what was going on, my antennae waved like a bug's. By the end of the day I was myself catching people who had already voted. The Mighty Pencil? I wielded it like a sword.

Did we get them all? I think so. The teacher was certainly very complimentary when he met Mother a few days later, and she told me that Mr. O'Dwyer said I'd make a very good detective. (That remark contributed to my burdens, and I'm afraid that Mother taunted me with it as the weeks went by.)

Prosecutions followed. We had a neighbor, Jack O'Donnell, an activist with a fierce political appetite. Convicted of voting twice in the election, he had to pay a large fine, and he will go to his grave known as "Jack O'Donnell–Jack O'Donnell."

Speaking of political tricksters, let me now unveil the father of Sarah Kelly, grandfather of Venetia. His full name, Thomas Aquinas Kelly, was a comic misnomer. The only moral inquiries this man ever made had to do with money—the inside track, the shortcut, the influence, the bribe, the pull, the means, typically foul, of getting what he wanted. He came out of the womb a criminal.

Everybody knew him by his nickname: "King" Kelly. I believe he gave it to himself. Out in Montana he told them that when he was growing up in Ireland he had been nicknamed King. When he came back to Ireland he told them that in Montana they'd christened him King. You can't dismantle a circular myth.

Like so many crooks, King Kelly had marvelous natural power. He wore check waistcoats and well-cut tailoring, but never learned that a brown suit says "Not a gentleman." His shoes, handmade by a cobbler in Dublin, came from exquisite leather, and when he wanted something from somebody he loomed in over them with his big frame and poked them with a finger as thick as a shillelagh.

Those who knew him—including myself—we admitted that we enjoyed King Kelly. There was guilt in the admission, but there was also pleasure. He was a gale of good company, and not a word from his mouth could be believed. He had a rich voice, full of Irish and with some American, and no better dinner companion have I known. But he was as crooked as a ram's horn; if King Kelly said he'd pray for you, you'd be sure of Hell.

He told me wonderful tales, mostly lies, but very entertaining, especially to somebody like me, who's interested in how tales are told. I wrote down this particular story; I ask you to remember it, see how illuminating it will become.

There was a man I knew one time [all King Kelly's stories began like that] when I was buying land in Galway, not so many years ago. And I was talking to this man when a lady approached me and said to me, "Are you the famous King Kelly?" I said I was, and she said to me, "I'd like a word with you, please, sir."

Before she drew me aside, the man I was with whispered in my ear, "Don't go near her—she's a fairy queen."

"She's a what?" I said, but by then it was too late.

Now I was worried, I'll admit to that, because there's strange people over there in Galway, people with purple eyes and jaws like horses, people who wear their hats upside down on their heads, and when they shake your hand you don't know whether they're trying to give you one of their fingers or take away one of yours.

So anyway I walk off a little bit with her and she says to me, "I don't want you to buy that land."

"What land?" says I, a bit baffled in myself, because I hadn't been talking to the man a bare ten minutes, and nobody else knew he was selling land.

"My family used to own it," she says. "Tell me you won't buy it and I'll grant you my favor."

She was a tidy-size woman, and she had a bosom as round as a brace of bells. In her right eye there was a hazel fleck in the gray, and she had lips so pursed and plump they could whistle by themselves. But land is land, and so I said to her, "My dear young woman, I don't know what you're talking about."

She looks at me and she lays a hand on my arm, and she says to me, "King Kelly, I offered you my favor and you said no! Well, now, here's my disfavor," and she tightened her grip on my arm.

It wasn't a tight grip, but all of a sudden my arm began to grow cold. And then it grew colder. And then it froze. And I looked down at my hand and it was as blue as the sea. And in front of me there was this woman standing like a proud little person, her silk blouse high at the neck, her face and the rest of her excited as a hen at a cockfight.

"Madam," I says to her, "is it that you're freezing my arm?"

She said, "That's the wintry blast of my disfavor."

Well, the arm got colder and colder, and then it began to hurt because the skin was beginning to shrink, and the tears came to my eyes, as the tears will do in the cold weather or when in pain. But here's the next thing I found: My tears were ice-cold. They were just above the point where water freezes and they were barely squeezing out of my eyes. Talk about bewildered—I didn't know whether it was Tuesday or Easter.

The little woman never took her eyes off mine. She stared into me, into my soul. Her face reddened a little at the cheeks, always a moment I find exciting in a lady. It was her left hand that lay on my arm, and next she took her right hand and placed it on my opposite hip. Oh, dear God. Instantly the bone froze.

"Madam," says I, my jaw slowing down as it froze. "I'll never buy land in this county again."

She released me and said, pretty as pie, "Thank you, King Kelly."

I said to her, "If that's what your disfavor is like, let me see your favor?"

But I never got an answer. She walked away from me and I turned around to my friend, the man I was going to buy the land from—but he was gone. And when I looked back at her, she was gone too, and we were out in the middle of the country with no place to hide, so she must have vanished up into the sky. I ran out of County Galway that night like a man escaping from his mother-in-law.

King Kelly told me that story, and many similar, while drinking big liquors and smoking great cigars, the veins in his strong cheeks like the lacy filaments of red leaves. He liked to talk forever, as did his daughter, Sarah, as did his granddaughter, Venetia, as did Mrs. Haas, whom King Kelly hated as much as she hated him; "Shark-face," he used to call her. So much for Sarah's insistence that they all adored one another. Those four people form the first half of the cast in this drama that took over my life when I was still in my tenderest years.

6

Here we meet the other main players—beginning with my father. Venetia Kelly said to me once, "Your father has the most beautiful skin of any man." When, sometime later, I repeated that observation to my mother—without, of course, attributing it to Venetia—Mother said, "Yes. It mirrors his dear mind." That she said it without a hint of bitterness told me a lot.

Forget the fashionable belief that sons never get to know their fathers; I came to know mine very well. I loved him, truly loved him, this tender man of great kindness and haphazard brilliance, this clever man who was as wise as an oracle and as stupid as a dribbling fool. I'm sure you've known people like him. We Irish have a lot of them—men who can be smarter than scientists and stupid as dolts.

There were times when I wondered was I, his only child, the only person who saw him fully, the one human being who knew that he wasn't at all what he appeared to be? Beneath the farmer's clothes, the muddy boots, the stained old tweed cap, the hands with the texture of wood and leather, the harsh instructions to lazy workers, the jovial talking to the cows as he milked them, I saw a different man. Deep inside, my father was loving, committed, sophisticated, and civilized, and with a vivid sense of humor.

Also, as I saw, he was mad when he wanted to be—stone mad, mad as a cut snake, writhing this way and that, convulsing with passion.

Sometimes Mother would surprise me with a gratifyingly accurate rendition of him, because for all her difficulties with him, she loved him more than she loved her own life. In a society where the word *love* had no above-the-surface currency, where sentimentality in relationships was a taboo, where couples circled around each other in duty and agreement rather than affection or caprice, she loved him more than she loved me, and I don't mind that.

So if in passing she gave me some insight into him, I would first inhale it like a drug, and then reel back in surprise at her perception.

"Your father is a century late," she said once. "He should have lived in Lord Byron's time, with all the other wild men."

Another time she said, "Your father is a useless card player. Everything shows in his face."

Mother was brisk and practical, or so I used to think, and didn't usually show much insight into people and things. And then she'd make a revealing observation about my father; or I'd go back and recall the Incident of the Animal.

The Incident of the Animal—I reach for it when I want to remind myself that Mother did have a true grasp of the world, and the way things are. She just lost it for a while. And I reach for the Incident because of the ultimate lesson it taught me—that when something is hurtling toward you, and you know it's frightening, and you know you're right about that, it may not always be frightening or dangerous in the way you think. But that doesn't reduce the fright or the danger. Sometimes its purpose is to bring foreboding—and foreboding can be a friend, but you must listen to it.

The Incident began when the Animal came hurtling down the hill in front of the house one September afternoon.

I have this belief, which I've held since a small boy, that I can see at a glance how the world evolved. The wheel? Easy—the rolling of a log suggested the idea, and then they cut a log into disks, and Eureka! Religion? Call on a bigger power to smite a big power—call on something bigger than the wind that's making such a noise in the leaves, or, more terrifying, thunder. And it also has to be a power that you can't see. So—invent it. Pray to it long enough and the thunder fades and the wind dies down. Sex? Easiest of all—make sure that the nerve endings in those crucial places are so exciting that we'll want to go there again and again. Trite? Obvious? Unoriginal? Perhaps—but not at twelve years old.

At any rate, I was standing in the porch, admiring the light again. Thanks to the sun pressing through the stained-glass windows, the floor seemed littered with colored petals. By turning my head just a little I could see how golden the world was outside, how russet and ocher the trees. The green bench under the large beech had just been freshly painted.

We had a white fence that ran all around the property like a priest's collar. It took years to erect; it came in from the main gate, broke away from the front of the house, and swayed up the hill in a parade of snowy rails. My father always said that as soon as the end of it had been painted it was time to start renewing it: "Like-like-like life itself," he used to say to me and I never knew what he meant; I do now.

The part of the fence that ran up the hill field had a foolish place on the farm. What was the need to split an already difficult acreage? Especially since we owned all the land? That fence gave us nothing; all it did was run right up through the middle.

That afternoon, though, the fence paid for itself—because its stark white graphic rails showed me the large black object that was galloping along beside it and heading down toward the house. What was it? A wild thing, and terrifying. The gate from the field to the forecourt—and therefore to the house and me—stood wide open. I stared and stared; I couldn't make out what it was. The thing had legs at the usual four corners; beyond that I couldn't say much by way of description.

"Mother!" I shouted loud.

Father had gone to Templemore to collect a clock being repaired there by a man whom he liked to meet; this clock maker was, by all accounts, the biggest liar in the county.

She came running—because, as she said later, the fear in my voice would have frightened God.

"What is it, Mother?"

"Well, it's an animal anyway," she said.

The Animal's front bulked twice as large as it should have, the head didn't sit on the shoulders in a normal manner, and from its chest protruded some massive, indefinable growth.

It had a basic shape—more horse than, say, rhinoceros; more donkey than, say, elephant—but it traveled like no horse or donkey I'd ever seen—or, for that matter, like no rhinoceros or elephant I'd ever imagined. And it seemed agitated—it swung its great lump of a head in all directions, and even at a distance of several hundred yards I could see the flecks of spume spraying from its nostrils. Also, it was huge—higher, broader, and thicker than any horse or cow we had on the farm or in the stables or had ever bred. And bulky as a cliff.

On and on it came, its speed getting up to a near-gallop, loping wildly along by the fence, crashing into the white rails, bouncing off them and smashing into them again; how they didn't shatter I'll never know. At any moment it would careen through the gate, pound onto the gravel of the forecourt, and perhaps head straight at the glass porch where we were standing.

My father's double-barreled shotgun stood in the corner of the porch. He often took a potshot at a juicy pheasant and then lamented the side of his nature that caused him to "Kill-kill-kill God's creatures." I looked at the gun, but I knew it would be too small to bring down this thundering black beast. My great-grandfather's elephant gun, a bell-mouthed blunderbuss, sat on a bracket over the fireplace in Mother's little study—but what ammunition could we use? My terror grew.

Mother stared as only she can, her eyes narrowing, her body a tall, slim cylinder of concentration. Hands on hips, she peered harder—and then walked out of the house and strode across the gravel to the open gate. Toward the creature!

On came the Animal and my heart came close to stopping. I didn't know what to do. The manly part of the boy fought the coward, the self-preserver. Should I help? And what assistance could I give? Shouldn't I be at Mother's side, indeed ahead of her—but who would run for help if the monster destroyed both of us?

I split the difference, as, when I can, I've learned to; I left the porch but didn't go as far as the gate. And, as I most certainly always do in life, I watched and watched.

The Animal slowed down and I heard its noises. Like a distressed asthmatic it wheezed and spluttered; and it seemed in agony. Explanations for its existence seared through my head: It had come from a family of prehistoric creatures long hidden in a land beneath the caves up in the mountains, and one of their number had now found a way into the outside world and was frightened at being unable to find its way home.

Or it had come from the next farm, the Treacys'. Mr. Treacy was a vet and a breeder, and his house was full of exotic stuffed animals. Maybe he had for years been experimenting at crossing ordinary breeds with exotic animals and this strange hybrid result had broken out of his sheds. Or maybe such a creature had indeed long existed in Borneo, known only to a few adventurers and zoologists. And it had at last been captured and, in circumstances of great secrecy, was being transported to England for a zoo there, but the ship had docked at Waterford to discharge cargo, and when the holds opened the Animal escaped.

I was soon answered. The Animal slowed down to a walk, still heaving its great head. I could hear Mother speaking to it, soothing and soft, "Yes, good boy, good old boy," and the Animal was responding. Now it had slowed to a saunter. Then it hung a hesitant mooch over toward the gate on which Mother leaned. The creature's great head drooped lower and lower; I thought it was probably abashed at its own foolish carry-on. And then it stopped, right at the gate. Another miracle from Mother! Whom I had seen juggle plates for a bet. Who could cast a dry fly into a salmon's mouth from Ballygriffin Bridge. Who could do coin tricks.

Cautious as a fish, I walked over. By the time I got there, and saw Mother stroking the creature's nose and forehead, and with her sleeve wiping away the foam from the mouth, the Animal had quieted.

Not a prehistoric fugitive from beneath a time-trapped lake in the Galtee Mountains; not a Frankensteinian crossbreed escaped from Mr. Treacy's sheds; not even an exotic capture from Borneo. This was a massive Clydesdale plow horse, twenty-one hands high if an inch. By way of comparison, our tallest three-quarter-bred was seventeen and a half hands.

Its head seemed distorted because it wore a large plowing collar that had come loose, worked its way around the back, and swung ever wilder the more the horse tried to shake it off, and it had forced the horse to carry its head awkwardly high to one side. As to the growth on the front, a large and decorative knee-length harness medallion had been hung on the horse's chest, but it got buckled in some collision suffered by the galloping animal, had worked its way up to the horse's face, and had begun to bite into its flesh, and was thus wedged.

Mother took command. In those days she had the gift of always being understood. She walked around to the horse's shoulder and began to pat it further. The poor creature accepted her affection so readily and eagerly that his nuzzling almost knocked her off her feet.

"Get Billy," she told me. "Tell him to bring a ladder. And go for Mr. Treacy."

Billy Moloney ran our farmyard, and was constitutionally unable to speak a sentence in the English language without, as Mother put it, "cursing like a sailor." She and I worked out a method by which I could report his conversation to her; every time he swore I would substitute my father's euphemism "flock."

I found him in the milking shed.

"What she want a flockin' ladder for?"

"A big horse," I said.

"Big flockin' horse to want a ladder."

"He's very big, Billy."

"Ah, flock it," he said. "I'll get the flockin' ladder. Jizz, God, you'd swear I do have nothing else to flockin' do, Jizz, flockin' wimmen, flock it."

Billy sometimes bisected words with a profanity: "cata-flockin'-gorically" and "un-flockin'-deniably." Sometimes he doubled down on his lexicon; my father claimed that he once heard Billy say "cata-flockin'-flockin'-gorically." As my father remarked, "Prob-prob-probably for emphasis."

While Billy fetched the ladder, I climbed on my bicycle and rode up the hillside path through our woods to find Mr. Treacy, who followed me down in his truck. He recognized the horse. It belonged to a plowing team that went all over the country giving demonstrations. A week later, when the horse was being collected, the plowing team told us that a rat had spooked the horse, and the horse had bolted. By the time the poor Clydesdale reached us he had traveled more than twenty miles.

That night, with the horse fast asleep in one of our loose boxes, Mother told the story to my father. She turned to me and said, "Why were you so frightened?"

"I didn't know what it was."

My father said, "Ask-ask-ask your mother for her lecture on seeing things."

Mother said, "In this world, there are two of everything. There's the thing that we see—like this sugar bowl on the table. And there's the thing we think we see. When the thing we see is the same as the thing we think we see—fine. If it's not—watch out for trouble."

She delivered this in that voice of hers that I grew up with—a voice that had no threat in it, a voice that up to then had never been raised at or against me. How could I have anticipated the ferocity, the persistence in this tall, capable woman with her boy's haircut, who had the most beautiful hands I have ever seen? And, as I'd find out, a capacity to make dreadful errors, and reap terrible harvests.

7

Most men have three lives, public, private, and secret. My father had four.

The world knew him as a successful general farmer who owned a horse or two. We had dairy, grain, and crops, held in place each season by this warm and well-liked man. When forking out a cowshed or clipping a hedge, he wore the big boots with the hobnails, and the "gaiters" made from the cutoff tops of Wellington rubber boots. He then wore tweed suits when he went to town, and red polka-dot pocket handkerchiefs, a man who was as comfortable with Billy flockin' Moloney as he was with Professor Fay and his sister, Miss Dora Fay, who came down from Dublin on weekends to the cottage we rented out to them, on the river at the bottom of the farm.

As to his private life, my father exuded kindness and good humor in our house. He had chivalry, even an old-fashioned, mannerly gallantry. In this he wasn't, I think, a typical Irish farmer—he had a sensibility that went beyond the ordinary male responses of his peers. I watched his care of Mother; I saw him waiting until she started to eat before he lifted his own knife and fork; I saw him racing to fetch things from upstairs that she had forgotten; I saw him clipping articles from newspapers, and leaving them on the desk in her little workroom in the alcove of the window; I saw him handing her more money than she asked for whenever she needed cash; I saw the tiny, myriad ways he expressed his respect and affection for her. For instance, if near at hand, he never let her lift or carry.

Often I saw him come in from the yard in the afternoon just to make her a cup of tea. And I heard them laugh and laugh behind the door of their bedroom at night—after he had made sure in the winter that a fire blazed in the grate there, and in the summer that all the windows were open, with the curtains blowing out like huge white kisses.

Did she behave as caringly to him? I want to say that she did, but the evidence wasn't abundant. Yet I have to bear in mind that she didn't have his demonstrative nature. To put it more simply, she seemed more head than heart, and he more heart than head.

Does this explain his actions that notorious night? And the long, anguished weeks afterward? I don't think so. It may mitigate some of his guilt in the matter, but it would be unfair to put that weight of blame on my mother's ordinary diffidence. She was, I think, generally blameless.

Blame it, to begin with, on the third life, as fast-flowing, mysterious, and powerful as a subterranean river, a force of which he wasn't completely in control.

He loved imagination. He loved possibility. He loved that the unexplained and the inexplicable could exist in the world and defy any reasoned argument. In this arena, he most loved human emotion and the means by which it got expressed.

I think now that he was a little ashamed of this part of himself and tried to hide it. But I always knew; I had seen what books he read; I knew that he loved the theater and acting, that his favorite play was that feast of rollicking possibility *A Midsummer Night's Dream*—and you could scarcely get a greater work of the imagination than that, with its magic world, its sprites called Cobweb and Mustardseed, its weaver turned into a donkey, and so forth. I'd take a strong bet that not another farmer's bedroom in the county had that—or much of anything else—as bedside reading.

Mother, from what I could see, didn't raise much of a glass to this, shall we say, *romantic* side of my father. She did, however, blush at a compliment from him, or grow tears in her eyes at a Christmas gift. There was a time when I thought this had caused the gulf between them—that he was too romantic and effusive, and she too practical and shy.

But no. That wasn't it. Wrapped inside this third life of my father's lay a fourth, the part of him that he couldn't see. In there, the trouble lay like a bomb that we never heard ticking.

8

Perhaps this is the moment to meet the Fays—Professor Cyril Fay and his sister, Miss Dora. Professor Fay was a historian who had a hunger for influence, and his sister a mathematician who loved words and language and stories. Acquainted with one of Mother's sisters, they began to rent the cottage on our farm for weekends, and then for stretches of the year during the long university vacations.

Both played their parts in this story. But how differently they affected me—even though they were twins and did many things together, and often very similarly. In many ways, they defined the term "unidentical twins"; he small and with no neck, she gooselike, thin as a knitting needle, and a good deal taller (though that wouldn't have been difficult). Only in one respect could a stranger tell that they were related—they walked identically. It was Mother who pointed it out—a fast pace, with a surge on every third step—one-two-*three,* one-two-*three.*

I can run my first memory of the Fays like a film. A Saturday afternoon in summer, I about eight years old; Mother and I walked down the fields to the river, and then along the riverbank path to the cottage; Mother carried a round Red Riding Hood wicker basket full of peas, gooseberries, new potatoes, and Lily Moloney's fresh soda bread hot from the oven. As we reached the cottage, Mother told me that we were going to meet "very clever people. It will do you well to know them. Very clever."

Miss Fay wore round tortoiseshell spectacles that gave her a surprised look. She sat close to the river on a chair that she'd taken from the cottage, reading so intently that her body bent to the chair's curve.

In the distance a man—"the professor," Mother whispered—walked away from us in a straight line. As I watched, he turned back and walked toward us just as briskly—and ignored us. Then he turned and walked again in the opposite direction at the same brisk pace, one-two-*three,* and then turned again and came back. I saw that as he approached us he was looking down and to his right—he had, we discovered, marked out with wooden pegs a distance of 110 yards.

"Sixteen of these makes a mile," he later told us.

Mother coughed, and the lady looked up from her book and blinked at the sun. Her warmth to Mother still comforts me.

"I know exactly who you are and I'm Miss Dora Fay and that's my brother over there; he's a big walker." When she shook hands with me she said, "If I have letters to post, or need milk, will you be my Mercury?"

I, because I had been raised quietly, nodded and said nothing, but Miss Fay asked, "Let me see your ankles."

She bent a little and peered—I was wearing sandals and no socks—and she straightened up, smiled, and said, "Yes, I can definitely see wings sprouting there."

She had prominent front teeth, Miss Dora Fay. She could, as they say, eat a banana through a tennis racket, and she was, I now think, my first true love. As first loves are capable of doing, she later inspired me, and gave me shelter and comfort.

When she died, an old lady, I was with her. I wept salt tears, and helped to carry her coffin to her grave. She bequeathed me all her books, and from time to time I find her lovely wide handwriting in the margin of something, always a thoughtful note, always inquiring, always seeking to expand knowledge, never judgmental.

I also have certain scientific instruments that she gave me; they saved my life; I keep them in a bank vault box, and I look at them every year.

She called her brother to meet us, but he waved her away and continued his walking. Miss Fay raised an eyebrow to Mother that said, "You and I understand these things."

It was only when I put together the many similarities between Miss Dora Fay and Mother that I grasped the cultural mixed-ness of my parents' marriage. The Fays came from an Anglo-Irish family, meaning not Catholics, and had roots in a society that originated in England, although their ancestors had been in Ireland for hundreds of years. They worshipped at the Church of Ireland, known elsewhere as Anglican or Episcopalian—what we have always in Ireland called "Protestants," even though the term properly refers to the Reform churches.

My mother, of Welsh stock, had also been a "Protestant," but converted to Catholicism in order to marry my father. His family can be traced back to the oldest of the Irish clans, and now I can survey where people might have seen certain differences between us and our farming neighbors.

We had that slight Protestant tinge—"English," if you will—that to some people seemed to set us apart. And to be apart is, if not dangerous, at least exotic. To my eyes, though, my parents never seemed different from anybody else's. I suppose if you've always been wrapped in wool, you don't know it's wool.

Mother had embraced Catholicism like a soldier takes orders—duty rather than passion, rote rather than inquiry. (My father once remarked to me, "She still has some of that Welsh Baptist wind in her pipes.") She left my religious education to my teachers, and faith played no part in our conversation.

In fact, other than the duty of Mass every Sunday, the only contact we had with the Catholic Church arose if Father Hogan asked my father to come with him when buying a horse; and sometimes they went to the races together.

The next day Professor Fay and Miss Dora Fay came to our house for lunch. Such talk! And all about politics. Up to that moment I'd never heard anything like it. The four adults conversed in gales; the winds of their conversation blew up and down the long table and out into the sunny Sunday afternoon. My parents thrilled to Professor Fay, who had all the latest news from Dublin. Miss Fay, when she wanted to make a point, swept the table in front of her with one hand and then the other.

That was June of 1922, the first summer of our new nation—which was why I'd never heard such talk. Intoxicating. Intoxicating even now to look back upon it, and I believe that's when my interest in politics first took hold.

A note here on Professor Fay: I didn't like him from the first. Being a small boy, I didn't quite know why I didn't like him. He had eyes like a bad-tempered pig and it grieved me to think so, because I loved our pigs. But we'd once had a bad-tempered sow who had often tried to bite me. Her name was Rita, and Professor Fay's little eyes reminded me of Rita's—mean-spirited, glinty eyes, sulky with malice. As it turned out, I was so right not to like him.

He also had an irritating habit of straightening his bow tie unreasonably often, and wetting his lips with his tongue, a darting little pink slink.

I did, however, enjoy the respect that he paid my parents, and how he said repeatedly to my father, "I perfectly agree with you, Mr. MacCarthy, I perfectly agree with you." But I adored Miss Fay, and I did indeed become her Mercury—letters to the postbox, the new milk from the cows every morning, butter when it was made, the hot soda bread, which she loved.

"You're always bringing me gifts," she said over and over. "So I must bring you gifts."

Consequently, Miss Dora Fay showed me how to do crosswords. She taught me rock, paper, scissors. And she arrived one time from Dublin with a five-thousand-piece jigsaw puzzle of *Moses Parts the Red Sea,* which we built together all summer.

"Let's do the sky first," she said. "The sky is always difficult."

She also gave me what is still my favorite possession—a red leather book named, in gold on the front cover, *Shakespeare.*

Almost more important, she said, "Don't feel that you have to know how to use it now," but she read passages to me and explained what was going on. She took *Macbeth* as the principal first lesson because, she said, "Boys like blood and gore and there's a lot of it in here."

Next summer she brought her own Shakespeare down from Dublin, the huge, new Yale edition, because her "happiest time," she said, had been at Yale. She described the university with longing in her voice—"the ivy, the statues." And she had me follow in my red leather book while she read *Hamlet* to me from her volume, and as we sat together she explained it as she went along. It remains my favorite play.

Those were the Fays, and throughout this story of the Kellys and my family, you'll meet them now and again. And they were there at the resolution—he disgraceful, she supreme.

9

Of the principal characters in this drama, I alone remain alive. In this I hope to be proven wrong—a factor that will become plain later on; and as to the issues, I believe that I've resolved all but one. Along the way, I've learned so much. For instance, whatever pain I've suffered, I've learned how to avoid disturbance. Nor will I ever again let people with power manipulate me as they did back then, and that's another reason for setting it all down: so that I can look at how they did it. And therefore I must begin with a good inspection of the sources whence came the trouble.

At the time of the romance that conceived her daughter, Venetia, Sarah Kelly, the Irish-American actress, strode New York like a child of the gods. She was twenty-two years old, and Mr. Anderson, the father, was in his late forties. Mother would have muttered, "There's no fool like an old fool."

Along with the house on Park Avenue, Mr. Anderson had inherited his father and uncle's law practice, specializing in shipping. He ran it very successfully, expanded the practice by opening offices in multiple ports, and elevated its reputation. At the peak of his success he also founded an insurance company. A dry man with a quick, disapproving glance, he said to me once, "You have an air of injury about you that I find weak"; then he turned his head away and didn't amplify. He had the habit of a wet sniffle.

But he possessed good judgment, it was said, when it came to hiring people—and indeed, whatever my own private reservations, when it came to choosing a mistress. I also came to learn that he washed his hands very frequently, and was at times white-faced and speechless in his passion for Sarah.

Their affair in its first, red-hot phase lasted two years—two idyllic years for them both, insofar as guilt would allow Mr. Anderson to relax. They met each week, often for lunch, in the Waldorf-Astoria hotel. I've been there to look—they had a bright set of private rooms, with a peaceful atmosphere and an aura expensive enough to make anybody feel good about himself.

Mr. Anderson had already been aware of her because he'd seen her in the theater. She was playing Rosalind in a new production of *As You Like It,* and when she first walked on he reacted so strongly that "I closed my eyes in some confusion," and he grew "so agitated" (Sarah added) that he feared his wife sitting beside him might notice.

It took him "several minutes," he then said, "to calm down." To his wife's surprise he broke a personal rule by leaving his seat at the interval. He didn't go to the restrooms as he had advertised; in his slow, nasal voice, he said, "I stepped out onto Forty-sixth Street and let the night air cool my face."

When I asked her why she thought Mr. Anderson had been particularly smitten by her, Sarah said that she'd been in four previous productions of the play, and because she knew the part so well, she felt completely relaxed. No nerves, no worries about forgetting lines; she could give all her attention, as she said, to "exuding. And I was lovely in those days. Very beautiful."

Then she told me how she had first noticed him—on Park Avenue. A blond woman, a well-groomed and rather beautiful New York lady, was walking a sleek bird dog on a leash. The dog suddenly leapt into the air and snaffled a low-flying pigeon. The owner seemed deeply embarrassed, and she began to admonish the dog, and to deal with its mouthful of feathers.

Mr. Anderson saw the incident. He walked over, began to pat the animal on the head and praise it. Then he took the bird gently from the hound's soft mouth, released the undamaged pigeon into the sky like, as Sarah remarked, "a priest releasing a soul to God," and said to the owner, "That's a wonderful dog, to stay true to its nature so far removed from its hunting grounds."

Sarah was walking nearby and, with her love of drama, had stopped to watch this freakish little event. Mr. Anderson raised his hat to the blond lady and walked on. At the next intersection Sarah caught up with him, and she commended his action. Mr. Anderson turned to look at her.

"It was as if," she said, "I had never before been looked at by a man."

He recognized her at once and raised his hat again; he said that he had been to see her on the stage. They parted and he almost went into shock. He walked to his office, booked a suite at the Waldorf-Astoria, wrote a note to Sarah, walked to the theater, and left the note at the stage door. The note suggested they meet at the hotel.

They loved each other; have no doubt about that. He said as much many years later, when I interviewed him, and although I found him impatient and contemptuously wary of me, I respected the ardor with which he spoke of Sarah. By then his original wife had died, and perhaps he felt free to use terms that he must have found so extravagant.

"It was like the *Arabian Nights,*" he said. "Sarah was Scheherazade." At which remark she strolled down the long drawing room, stroked his pointy bald head, and pinched his cheek.

He and she described their afternoons in that Waldorf suite. When she arrived, she'd close the door carefully behind her and secure the chain; the doorknob already wore its DO NOT DISTURB sign outside. Inside, Mr. Anderson would stand a little forward of the table, his hands clasped behind his back, stiff as a butler, his eyes locked on her. Then she'd turn and reveal herself, simply but dramatically, in the clothes she had worn to go there—almost certainly paid for by Mr. Anderson. He'd make a little bow to her, unclasp his hands, and stride forward to take her coat. She'd stand like the actress she was, head to one side, and wait. As he reached for the coat, she'd shrug out of it so that he could grasp it without touching her. He'd step aside and she'd walk forward to the chair, which he'd hold out for her. She would sit down and wait until he had hung her coat in the closet.

Then—as he did when they were finally living together; I saw it with my own eyes—he'd attend to her every moment, her every need, her every breath. He was her dog, tense and devoted. He'd bend to whisper in her ear. He'd touch her shoulder or upper arm with the reverence of a monk. Then he'd serve her; tea included tiny sandwiches, then scones with strawberry preserve and clotted cream, followed by what she called "gaudy little pastries." He had long-fingered, oblong hands the color of parchment, and a nervous, girlish smile, which I saw no more than twice in all the times I met him. Solicitous and intense, he'd ask, "Is your week being good to you, my dear?"

And Sarah would then keep her side of the bargain—she'd regale him with every detail of what had happened, almost hour by hour, since their last tea.

They may or may not have become lovers that first afternoon—but they soon did. When tea had ended, Sarah repaired to the drawing room of the suite and draped herself on the chaise. From there was the love affair conducted.

Week in, week out, watching the seasons change, they lay in each other's arms and gave to each other from their separate planets. Each devoured every word the other spoke as sunlight's bars slanted down the walls and across the carpeted floor. He began to teach her what he knew—money, banking, and the management of one's existence: "Practical Life" was, after all, the name of his insurance corporation.

When Mr. Anderson had said his short piece for the day, Sarah, by now, of course, naked and self-possessed in her beauty, began to speak the great parts that she had played around the country—in Chicago, San Francisco, Boston, New York. She transported him to the Venice of Othello and Portia and Shylock; to the Verona of Romeo and Juliet; to Prospero's "cloud-capp'd towers" and "gorgeous palaces." His feet, she said, scarcely touched the ground; "I was fabulous for him, I was like a fabled creature."

Whatever the mythology Sarah later spun in her account of the romance, both people were altered by knowing each other. The contradictions in them grew more pronounced. Mr. Anderson became a kinder man in the world, if more devious at home. Sarah grew into a more responsible girl, who now handled money astutely. Most compelling of all, she believed that this new sense of responsibility made her amenable to pregnancy.

"He was, believe it or not, my first gentleman," she said, "and I was too wild to think of caution. Now I was safe."

Her behavior in the affair seems to have been impeccable—at least Anderson said so. She said so too, but I take him to be the more reliable judge. When she found herself pregnant she asked for no money or extra attention; she merely said that she would like to continue meeting as usual; she hoped, she said, to include him in the experience of carrying a child.

She must indeed have been very beautiful. She was fifty-four when I first met her, and therefore ancient to my teenage eyes; I most remember her extraordinary poise. True to her profession, she possessed the ability to make herself look striking in any circumstance. When Anderson first brought her to the Waldorf in 1898 she was twenty—what else can she have been but gorgeous?

However, the looks took second place (in my view) to the personality. Well, not so much the personality as the attitude. Sarah Kelly had as great a gift of welcome as I've ever known.

By now in my life I've met many people in all sorts of conditions. Very often I meet them in what is potentially the place of their greatest welcome—their own homes. Most have shown enough warmth to make me want to stay. From the demeanor of some, you'd think they wanted me to come to live with them. That's how sincerely they greet me, that's how thoughtfully they care for me. But none of them has ever made me so regretful to part from them as Sarah Kelly.

That, I think, was her great gift; she made one want to stay near her, forever if possible. When I finally saw her on the stage, I understood that her audiences responded to this gift; they wanted as much of her as they could get.

And yet. And yet—her welcome was pallid compared to her daughter's. Venetia made you know that it was *you* and *only* you she had always been waiting for, the person she had always wanted to see. And in so doing, she became the only person you always wanted to see. Ever.

—

Before the birth, Sarah accepted Mr. Anderson's offer that he would maintain the child for life. Which he did. After the birth, Sarah's affair with Mr. Anderson began again, but not for some time, and it now took a very different form.

When he came back to New York in those early days of January, Mr. Anderson sent flowers to Sarah.

"A garden, my dear—he sent a garden. It was deep winter but he had his florist ransack the world. Jamaica, Uruguay, Borneo. We almost found hummingbirds in the blossoms." With hands flowing, Sarah made the shapes of flowers as she told me this.

She wrote to thank him, and asked when he wanted to see his daughter. To her wounded surprise, Mr. Anderson said he didn't, and wouldn't. She wrote again and expressed her hurt, and he said there was nothing he could do about it.

Sarah pressed and pressed; he refused and refused. A long standoff followed. Then one day he had a letter delivered to her in which he said that if they could talk face-to-face he might feel able to explain. And so, once more, they began to meet at the Waldorf suite; he had retained the rental in hope.

On the first afternoon they did not embrace; they sat to talk. Mr. Anderson seemed nervous and excited; he jumped up and down a lot, the long legs unfolding like a heron.

"Attending to me again," was how Sarah put it. "Tea, napery, milk, and sugar. Was my chair comfortable? How was my week? All of that."

She had considered surprising him by bringing the infant Venetia, but decided against it on account of the day's bitter coldness, with a wind coming off the Hudson that would, she said, "take the skin off the child's face."

Instead, she asked him directly and immediately, "Why won't you come to see your daughter?"

After a silence he said, "I'm unable. Incapable." And he said no more, and since she could find no way through, around, or past those words, she just accepted them.

They sat looking at each other. His passion for her seemed to have increased; he simply couldn't see enough of her face. After many long moments of silence he spoke.

"Shall we go on meeting again?"

"Yes."

"When? And how?"

"As often as you wish."

"Where?" he asked.

"Here," she said.

Again he fell silent and she waited, knowing what was coming.

"Shall we be—as before?"

"Not in the same way," she said. "Not until you bring your daughter into your life."

From that moment Sarah had eternal control over Mr. Anderson, and she used it. They began to meet in exactly the same way as they had done for the previous two years. She played Scheherazade again—with one exceptional difference: Sarah never allowed Mr. Anderson to touch her, not even a welcoming or parting embrace. Not until some months had passed after the birth (Sarah's wish for perfect appearance dominated everything), did she again lie naked for Mr. Anderson's endless admiration. Endless as it used to be, but now from a distance.

His eyes, she said, "became round and bright as he gazed at me." She enchanted him as before with her recitations. But as he sat there viewing that undraped body, with its breathtaking combination of lean and voluptuous, not once did she allow him to stroke her face or even to take her hand.

In that fashion, alongside her single parenting of Venetia, assisted and encouraged by Mrs. Haas, the lovers embarked upon celibacy. All of this Sarah Kelly told me herself, her grave face breaking into one of her planned and perfect smiles.

The contact between King Kelly and his daughter in those first years of the new century also casts light on what followed between him, his daughter, and his granddaughter in the years I knew them.

Talk about volatile! From the outside it looked as though Sarah loved and hated her father equally; she worshipped and despised him, she kissed him on the mouth and she slapped him in the face.

King Kelly adored his new granddaughter, no doubt about that. But, like all his responses, it was a love that considered his feelings, not anybody else's. For instance, one evening early in 1902 (this information comes from Mrs. Haas), King Kelly came home at about seven o'clock to the house in Brooklyn.

In his fashion—like a gale with musical accompaniment—he sang at the top of his voice as he swept into the hall. He called out to Sarah and Mrs. Haas that he was going out to dinner with some friends, who would come home with him later for a card game.

"And where's my little angel?" he shouted. "Where is she?"

"She's asleep," said Mrs. Haas. "Do not wake her. It took a while to make her sleep—she is tired and has new teeth."

"New teeth?" he roared. "Look who's talking about teeth—old Sharkface herself. I must see these new Kelly teeth. I, who have to wear other people's teeth, must see this."

He rampaged across the landing and into the nursery and switched on the bright gaslight. The child awoke, he picked her out of her cot and swung her high, and she began to shriek.

Drab Mrs. Haas, who was then in her mid-twenties, only a few years older than Sarah, ran up the stairs and Sarah came tearing after her. Little Venetia was now yelling in fear, and the big man was trying to soothe her by holding her cheek to his.

"But he hadn't shaved that morning and his beard hurt her," said Mrs. Haas—who took Venetia from him and began to calm her. (Venetia, by the way, claimed to remember every moment of this story, even though she was only twenty-four months old at the time.)

As King Kelly, in his brown suit, backed out of the nursery, protesting that he only wanted to see his little granddaughter, his angel, his jewel, Sarah reached the top of the stairs. She had been out walking that day and hadn't taken off her strong town shoes. When her father turned to greet her, she began to kick him. She landed her shoes on his shins, on his knees, every lower extremity within reach.

He grabbed her and held her at a distance, too far for her boots to connect with him. Then he spun her around, bent her over like a jackknife, and larruped her three, four, five times on the behind. The whacks echoed through the house. He pushed her away from him, made it to his bedroom, and locked himself in, while Sarah—who had almost fallen over when he dropped her—stormed up and down outside, screaming at him and kicking his door. Eventually Mrs. Haas prevailed upon her to calm down so that the child might get some peace.

Later that night, however, all through the card game, in which five of his cronies took part, Sarah sat right beside King Kelly, her thumb in her mouth, her head often leaning on his shoulder. During a break she sat on his knee, while he boasted about her to his pals: "My daughter, the great actress."

"I've never been conventional in my relationships," she often told me.

If I had known all those details, if I'd had any idea of what volatility they had survived between each other, I'd have understood better the bond between father and daughter, the seeming mismatch that so puzzled me later on.

10

Here I feel that I must balance things a little by telling you how different my own mother's life was in those days—such a contrast with the afternoon hours of Sarah Kelly in the Waldorf-Astoria hotel. Mother had been born a lean infant, wiry and long. By the time she was twelve she had acquired after-school and holiday work from a farmer who lived near her parents. When asked by the farmer what she'd like to do, Mother said, "The cows." All through her teenage years, she fetched them in the morning and evening for milking—a tall, thin young drover, appreciated by all who knew her.

"Handsome more than pretty," she herself said she was—but memorable even at twelve. And passionate about what she did. "Cows will do anything for you," she told me once, "if they like you. That's a good lesson, isn't it?"

When I discovered—I was about eight years old—this feeling she had for cows, I begged her for her stories. She remembered individual cows, creatures who would allow her and her alone to milk them. "There was a Friesian called Lucy who kicked everybody else. And Flicker, because she always caught you in the face with a flick of her tail."

She remembered settling them in their winter stalls, squeezing her slim body between their adjacent flanks. She remembered inspecting each cow for any ailment or injury once a week in case the vet had to be called. "When I was a child," she said, "I never got comfort. I was so bony. In the winter or when the east wind came in at the end of March, I felt the cold in every bone. The only place I ever felt really warm was with the cows."

She slept with cows about to calve—and she grieved if she lost either mother or calf. "A cow's grief is a real thing," she said to me once. "I'm not saying they cry salt tears—but you do weep if the calf comes out dead, and the mother can't lick it into life, and she lowers her head and looks away."

Her love of cows endured all her life. She talked to them, she represented their interests. Drovers famously carry sticks, long ash batons to steer and drive cattle. One lunchtime, I saw Mother rush out into the yard, where a drover, who had bought two heifers from us, was hammering on their backs to get them up on his cart. She grabbed the ashplant out of the man's hand and broke it across her knee.

" 'Twould serve you right," she snapped at him, "if they turned around and pucked you."

That day, though a little scared in case the drover, a rough fellow, might retaliate, I thought Mother was wonderful. Do I still think it? I do—and now much more so, despite everything, and I don't think it simply because of her love of cows. In time, she came to look a bit like them; as she aged, and once all her troubles were behind her, she too developed wrinkled and placid features.

No wonder I wanted to spoil her, make her life easy and easier. She had so many qualities that I liked—the quick movements, the fiddling with her hair, the laugh that, once it started, went right out of control.

11

All who know the Kelly family seem in agreement that Venetia's early years passed more or less sensibly, without agitation or unease. In the spring of 1901, and peacefully for mother and child, King Kelly had begun to travel a great deal in the United States. He was, he said, buying land, "investing in the New World." Thus, he impinged scarcely at all on the life of his daughter and granddaughter in New York. When he did, and when he overdid it, Mrs. Haas repelled his invasions.

The following year, 1902, brought a different pattern. King Kelly was in his forties, and by all accounts—and from the brown photographs—a sight to behold, with his elaborate waistcoat, distinctive hat, and silver-topped walking cane, not to mention the laugh that could crack a hillside. He'd been strutting about in New York, boasting about his daughter "the great actress," trying to make himself a gentleman among the posh clubs, and trying to avoid the Irish-Americans who might, he said, drag him down. As if he could find a lower place than his own morals.

At first he couldn't stay away from the Irish. They were too exciting and raunchy, and they were making money. So he played with them and he politicked with them. But then, mid-1902, he disappeared into the

West. In the now calmer house Sarah was able to devote herself completely, she said, to the care and attention of the infant.

A letter came in due course, in which King Kelly explained his absence, by saying that he had been elected mayor of Manhattan, Montana, "because of my unexpected and dramatic success at distributing land here in a fair and peaceable fashion." He was, said his daughter, "a savage when it came to acquiring land." Sarah had a way of resting her right elbow in her left hand as she spoke; for her, all the world truly was a stage.

By the time Sarah told me about Montana I'd come to know King Kelly too well to take anything at face value. In case it should prove useful, give me some clues, I decided at one stage to investigate this missing eighteen months of his life. I wrote a letter, "To the Editor, Local Newspaper, Manhattan, Montana," asking about the name "Kelly" and the 1902 land rush, and—"by great good fortune," as King Kelly himself might have said—back came a reply.

Dear Sir,

Reference to your inquiry, re: one Thomas Kelly, a.k.a. "The King." This gentleman did come to our town in 1902—it is thought he came here because we are famous for beer. He also did participate in the 1902 contest for town parcels. The contest was to be decided on "The race is to the swift"—meaning, also, "First come, first served." Regrettably the Kelly gentleman hired athletes to outpace all decent and honorable contestants. He also hired bullyboys with cudgels to crack the heads of legitimate entrants and slow down or halt their efforts. Also, he had by then opened a house of ill repute. For all this he received a jail sentence of seven years, which was commuted after eighteen months on condition that he quit Manhattan, Montana, and indeed also the state. He forfeited all parcels of land, properties that he once said he would "murder for."

Hoping that this reply satisfies your inquiry. Glad to be of assistance. One is always warmed by a letter from the Old Country.

Yours truly,

Cyrus Murphy, Editor.

In King Kelly's absence, Sarah returned to the theater. Despite her great status as an actress and a beauty, she found herself limited in what was available—because she refused to tour plays, a normal practice in those days. She overcame this by straightforward talent, and landed a number of good parts.

The New York stage at that time had great energy. Big names and bold works made headlines every day. As did Sarah, in *Nathan Hale,* as the mischievous and tender Alice Adams, and what she herself termed a "famous" performance as Roxanne in the new play *Cyrano de Bergerac.*

Her career, insofar as she told me, and insofar as I've been able to trace it, seems to have been shrewdly managed. She received the respect of her peers and her public without the "star" label and its problems—because although she worked in prestigious houses, she didn't let herself get strangled by the big owners. Even though chagrin pierced her when the occasional impresario ignored her and brought on actress after actress, she held out against being owned by managements—and it seems not to have damaged her career.

Nor did she become the plaything of a Diamond Jim Brady or any of the other Irish flashmen who strutted across the skyline of New York like rakish giants.

"I had enough of that at home," she said, "and I didn't need more of it. Also, I had Mr. Anderson's heart, and I simply loved my work. I got plenty of both and I had my lovely baby daughter."

Whatever Mr. Anderson's role, her world turned around Venetia and the theater, the theater and Venetia. With Mrs. Haas in attendance, she conducted her household quietly and with efficiency. And she steadied her life—helped considerably, she acknowledged, by the guiding (but not touching) hand of the tall, nasal Mr. Anderson.

It was a good existence. Society accepted her because of her talent. In this, she said, she was lucky.

"Try to imagine," she remarked to me, "what New York in those days was like for us. We were Irish-Americans with the look of money, and therefore considered somewhat vulgar. It was assumed that we were Catholics, and so we were still reviled by the ruling classes of New York. If we'd been poor we'd have been a lot farther down the social ladder. A lot closer to the bottom-of-the-heap Irish coming in off Ellis Island."

The idea of socially acceptable Irish in nineteenth-century New York—call that an oxymoron. No matter their wealth, the new Irish-Americans had a tough haul. Any status they achieved came mostly through politics—where they weren't trusted anyway. Or the Church, still tarred as "Papist."

I was to learn that Sarah didn't play that "bottom-of-the-heap Irish" harp too loudly. But she did inherit—and passed on to her daughter—ferocious ambition to succeed.

13

By now I've made clear that I'm assembling this material—from notebooks, jotters, backs of envelopes—so that I can survey and judge—so forgive me if I sometimes come across as jumpy. And I also want to grasp and analyze what I myself did in those crucial times. I know that, at the end of it all, I did some remarkable things, far beyond the reach of a man of my age. We've all heard stories of great sportsmen or performers who, in one moment above all, reached the sublime—and then couldn't say whether they knew beforehand that they could do it. They just hoped that they could do it again. That somewhat defines my position, though only in part; so I'm also writing all this down to see whether I can find in me the qualities I exhibited at that time—power, love, care, daring—because I need them all the time.

But I've learned much else—in particular how to read signs. You see, I realize now that I could and should have anticipated some of the unpredictable fires that broke loose and almost burnt the house down. After all I was a secret witness to what I call the Prizefight. Mother never knew about it, and only at a sharp moment in our relationship did I tell my father that I'd been there.

The Prizefight took place on a Good Friday. When you grow up alone you learn how to acquire knowledge secretly. If you're an only child, you think that most of the whispered conversations between your parents are about you. Or so you have to believe in order to survive.

Thus, at an early age I learned to hide in order to listen. I knew how to skulk around the property, pretending to play my wild and solitary games, but in essence watching everything. The ancient structure of the house, with its nooks and crannies, gave substantial cover. So did the trees and the gardens, and I could spy on people indoors and out, and I did all the time. This continued into my early teens. You learn a great deal about people when you can observe them from hiding. The first thing you learn is that they behave differently when they're alone and think nobody's looking.

Spring had come. We had a late Easter that year and the air had begun to hum and sing. At the top of one section in the home garden, rows of currant bushes, dense as a little green city, ran along the brick walls. When I came into the garden through the gray wooden gate, I saw my father and Ned Ryan, our yard worker, in conversation with another man. As I watched, a rough argument broke out, unusual to see in my life.

I recognized the other man; he scared me. His name was Thomas Kane—the principal in the next village's school. A tall, burly man, he'd been a gunman out in the fields during the War of Independence, and had laid some claim to being called a hero. I've since learned that he was also considered a bully, and I think I must have known it at the time because I was afraid for my father. Mr. Kane's pretty wife, a small, brown-eyed woman whom he married some years later, became one of Mother's "warm acquaintances," as she called those who hadn't quite made it into the inner ring of friendship.

As little Ned Ryan bounced up and down between them trying to make peace, Mr. Kane poked his finger into my father's chest. Then he rapped his knuckles hard on my father's head.

Brushing the hand away, my father whipped off his jacket, a rust-colored Harris Tweed of which I was fond. Ned Ryan took the jacket—and next accepted Mr. Kane's coat, who then squared off toward my father. And he shouted something that I couldn't quite hear, though it smacked, I felt, of Billy Moloney's "flockin' " lingo.

My father stripped naked to the waist; Mr. Kane didn't. The two men walked to a small patch of clear and level ground. Ned Ryan followed, fussy as a hen.

Now my father held up his fists like a pugilist of old, and said something—to which Mr. Kane replied with a punch. It seemed to me that my father allowed the punch to hit him—on the side of the head—and then the fight began in earnest.

My feelings, I remember, twisted my heart like twine. On the one hand I felt afraid that my father might get hurt; on the other hand I was watching a trial of strength and ferocity between two men of the parish. I didn't seriously think that my father might lose—or was that just hope?

The punches flew. Mr. Kane had a longer reach and he jarred my father several times, set him back on his heels. All the birds stopped singing. The dogs lay in the grass, noses down, eyes narrowed, uncomfortable, whining. And the fight swung back and forth along a wide grass path between the vegetable beds.

I see it all so clearly, still: two big men in their thirties, my father's torso whiter than dough, and now reddening here and there as punches landed. Mr. Kane had black hair, and eyebrows that met in the middle; the sun caught my father's wavy red hair.

It became a brawl. The classy pugilism went out of it when Mr. Kane suddenly delivered a kick. Ned Ryan shouted, "Foul blow, foul blow."

The kick was meant for my father's groin, but he spun and took it on his thigh. He rocked right back at the force of the great boot. For a moment he dropped his fists and I almost rushed out of my hiding place. And then my father ignited: He said something. Again I didn't hear the actual words, but it inflamed the other man, who drove forward.

They grappled and wrestled, untidy and roiling about. They fell to the ground, they rose again. Once more they grappled, looking for a grip here or there. My father grabbed Mr. Kane's jacket and tried to swing him around; Mr. Kane took a fistful of my father's hair and twisted; my father somehow wriggled away.

The fight ended at that moment. With one clean punch my father lowered him. I heard the crack and saw my father wince and pull back his hand as Mr. Kane staggered, half-slipped, and fell. I thought his head rolled a little.

He lay on the earthen seed drills; Ned Ryan came forward to inspect my father's hand. My father flapped the hand vigorously and nursed it; he bent at the waist, raised one knee in his wincing, and sucked at his knuckles. Soon, garment by garment, he began to take his clothes as Ned Ryan offered them.

By the time he had dressed again—undershirt, shirt, waistcoat, jacket—the man on the ground was sitting up. He looked at nobody and I felt half a pang of sorrow for him. I expected my father to reach down and offer him a helping hand but he did no such thing.

Turning his back, he beckoned Ned Ryan, who carefully laid Mr. Kane's coat on the ground and followed my father out of the garden by the far gate. My father finished tucking in his shirttails as he walked, and he sucked his knuckles again. His force, so unexpected, so brutal, roasted me; even from that distance I felt my face burn.

Mr. Kane sat there for several minutes. *Will he catch cold,* I thought, *on the wet grass?* Then he clambered to his feet, spread his hands like a doctor all about his face, searched his head and torso, picked up his coat, and put it on. He stood for long moments, then walked straight toward where I hid. I watched from the bushes as he strode within a few feet of me, his face angry. He muttered under his breath. Then I heard his great boots crunch the gravel, and he had gone.

Sometimes when I try to understand what my father was truly like, I recall that day. I see him as a sturdy prizefighter, stripped to the waist, old-fashioned pose, arms out like big commas.

I see a ruthlessness too, in this man from whom I'd never received anything but tenderness and warmth. Of what was the ruthlessness born? What was it that he kept hidden for so much of his life? I suppose that he, more than anybody, had always known what might happen if he ever broke out of control.

14

At this point I want to share an old silent film with you—*The Courage of Esmeralda.* A lanky youth named Liam dug it up for me in a Dublin archive. He had no idea why I sat weeping after this seven minutes of crackling, hissing flicker.

Esmeralda, in a dress of many frills, is walking by the shining river gathering pretty flowers, when she hears a cry.

The word "Hark" appears on the screen, and we see Esmeralda halt her flower-gathering. She cups a tiny hand to her shell-like ear. Now the urgent white words prompt her to mouth, "Where, oh where can that voice be coming from?"

She looks all around—and then she sees. On the road that runs along by the river, a horse, pulling a cart, is rearing and bucking. A man and a boy sit on the cart; the man is trying in vain to halt the horse with the reins. Now it begins to gallop!

Esmeralda puts aside her posy of flowers—she rests them with delicate care on the little roadside stone wall, and she looks in fear and apprehension at the oncoming, galloping juggernaut.

"What am I to do? I am so small!"

The horse's head is rearing, his nostrils flare, his eyes are wide. He flings his head here and there. The reins fly from the man's hands, and he cowers on the cart. He clutches to his chest the boy, the dark-eyed boy with the long eyelashes. Esmeralda holds a hand to her little breast in fear. She looks this way and that, hoping for help.

"Is there nobody near? Is there nobody to help me?"

Now Esmeralda's eyelashes flutter—but there's no help at hand.

Finally, she takes a deep breath and the screen says, "I must do it alone."

Esmeralda steps out into the roadway and holds up a hand. Now the screen says, "Mr. Horse—stop. At once!"

The horse comes tearing on. Esmeralda holds up a hand again. The screen says, "Stop, I say, Mr. Horse. This instant!"

And the horse sees Esmeralda. He shakes his huge head like a mad beast. But he skids to a halt, and Esmeralda walks over to him. She pats his nose. The screen tells us what she says: "Nice Mr. Horse. Good Mr. Horse. Now have some grass."

The grateful father and the adoring boy climb down. They walk over to Esmeralda.

"You saved our lives!" shouts the black screen in its white curly words. "How can we ever thank you enough?"

Through my tears I reflected that I could have told Esmeralda a thing or two about bolting horses.

Here's the background. In August 1910, a gentleman named Sidney Olcott crossed the Atlantic by steamer and arrived in Cork. His employers had spun a globe of the world in front of him and asked where he'd next like to work. He chose Ireland, the land of his mother's birth.

Sidney Olcott was a film director, one of the first, and one of the most famous of his day. Since infancy, and having listened to his Irish mother's tales and reminiscences, he had revered Ireland, and the notion thereof. It's a not uncommon malady.

The Kalem Company—"K" for George Kleine, "L" for Samuel Long, and "M" for Frank Marion—was founded in 1907, and generated myriad films in the United States. When he landed, Mr. Olcott took long reconnaissance tours all over his mother's motherland and settled—unsurprisingly—in beautiful Killarney.

His first film there, *A Lad from Old Ireland,* packed theaters back in the United States, a box-office sensation, because every Irish immigrant, and all people of Irish descent, wanted and needed wonderful images of home.

In 1911, riding the magic carpet of his success, Mr. Olcott came back and set up a permanent company in the village of Beaufort near Killarney. He invited leading male and female actors from all over the world to work with him there, in films such as *Conway, the Kerry Dancer; The Colleen Bawn; Rory O'More;* and dozens more. All told, the Kalem Company made more than a hundred films in Ireland back then, many in and around Killarney.

Sarah Kelly had known Mr. Olcott slightly since New York days; he knew her work thoroughly; he sent out a call for her, and she answered.

They sailed excellently, despite some choppy seas. Venetia remembered it well, and described it to me one afternoon twenty-one years later. She said that she couldn't be torn away from the rail, where she wanted to stare at the ocean all day. They didn't get seasick, and the ship also delighted Mrs. Haas. Always a bonus—the lifting of that frown.

For Sarah, the voyage became a social whirl. Her fame had begun to cross the Atlantic with her; man after man pursued her.

"My dear Ben, I dined at a different table every night," she said to me.

Of Mr. Anderson not a word was mentioned. Sarah hadn't told him of her decision. On the day of sailing she simply failed to turn up at the Waldorf. He went there every afternoon for two weeks and waited for her. Eventually, when no reply came to his letters, he found a way to inquire discreetly, and that was the first Mr. Anderson knew of Sarah Kelly's departure. She had turned her back on him—and his money. But she knew, she told me, that he'd follow her one day.

Beaufort lies some miles from the town of Killarney. Once settled in the Great Southern Hotel, Sarah hired a sidecar with a driver, called a "jarvey." They told her in Beaufort that Mr. Olcott had gone elsewhere with his actors to shoot some scenes for the production under way. Mr. Olcott's chief assistant, "a girl named Mae," said Sarah, "with blond bangs reaching down into her eyes, and lips tight and red as a new rose, wrote out very carefully, in very large handwriting, the directions."

Mr. Olcott was "most anxious," Mae said, to meet his new leading lady.

The jarvey didn't even look at the piece of paper. "They're out at Moll's Gap," he said, and cracked his long whip. The horse, he said, knew the way.

Whatever the ancient feelings coursing through her, Sarah looked every inch an American: prosperous, helpful, charming. She enchanted all she met, including the jarvey.

She asked him to repeat the names of the places through which they passed, and while telling me she rolled them on her tongue. Tullig; Kilgobnet; Suanavalla; Coolcummisk; Dunloe; and finally Gortacollopa, where they found Mr. Olcott. Wearing a white peaked cap and check knickerbockers, he was standing in the middle of the road beckoning to somebody. And then they saw two people, obviously his actors, walk swiftly across a field to a gate, which they climbed, and upon which they sat and batted heavy eyelids at each other.

In the fashion that would become iconic, Mr. Olcott shouted, "Cut!" He turned to greet Sarah, kissed her hands, and offered her an engagement that would last, on and off, for as long as he stayed in Ireland.

She went to work on the following Monday, in a film called *Rosaleen's Return,* about an Irish emigrant girl who comes home to her birthplace and restores her family cottage. From a ruined hovel with the thatched roof falling in, she makes a white-painted haven with picket fence and rambling rose. A "sow's ear to silk purse" plot—how could she lose?

Sarah, with very few lines to mouth, gleamed and soared. The camera loved her, full-face and profiles, which Mr. Olcott pronounced "very unique." Those eyelashes, that rosebud mouth, that sloping nose—he lost part of his heart to her, and then lost most of the rest to her daughter.

"What is your name?" said Mr. Olcott, to the child swinging her legs from the garden gate.

"Venetia Kelly, and my profession is that of actor. And you, sir?"

He professed himself "swoony for that kid" and that night wrote a film for her. He called it *The Courage of Esmeralda.*

15

In Killarney the last bolt of this Kelly family preamble slides home—because a major character now appears, brought there in a cardboard box by King Kelly. A man who made every room turbulent upon his entrance, whenever King Kelly held out his arms, it became a race between Sarah and Venetia. That day Sarah won, as she would for the rest of her father's life. Venetia wrapped her arms around his beef of a leg and held on, until he prized her away and lifted her up to be kissed.

He had no luggage; he said it would arrive later, and that the railway company had lost it. Who could ever believe him? Sarah had to go out and buy him clothes. Out of his copious pockets, however, he began to pull things—sticks of barley sugar, a chocolate bear, a tiny bottle of scent, a lace handkerchief. On the floor beside him he had already deposited a large box.

"Tell me a story, tell me a story," Venetia cried, and King Kelly, with the child still in his arms, found the sofa and sat down.

"What kind of a story would you like?" he said. "You know that for the whole year you're eleven years old you can have any story in the world because eleven is a magic number."

"You said that too when I was ten," said Venetia. "And when I was nine. And eight, and seven. What's in the box? Is it for me?"

"Venetia, honey," said her mother, but the warning of good manners faded in the gale of laughter.

"I'll tell you the story first," said King Kelly, "and then I'll open the box and you'll see why I told you the story."

With Venetia settled on the arm of the chair from where he could look straight into her face, he began to tell his tale. I'm repeating the story here as Venetia told it to me many years later, and I'm repeating it because it formed such a fundamental influence in the early making of Venetia Kelly's Traveling Show—and in the management of Venetia's life.

There's a man I know, and I know him well. He's living up in the north of Ireland, and he's a very unusual man—because he had a very unusual teacher. His teacher taught this man something that nobody else ever knew—how to talk to animals. He understands everything that animals say, even to one another. Because, as you know, animals and all creatures have their own language.

If this man hears the crows out in the field and they're cawing and jawing, he knows they're discussing where the next best bit of food might be. And if he sees the cows coming in to be milked, he hears them saying to each other, I hope there isn't anybody milking us tonight who has cold fingers. He told me that himself. And every time the dog barks or the cat meows, he knows perfectly well what they're saying—because his teacher taught him every animal language he needed to know. When he was a young lad, he tried to tell his family but they laughed at him.

One day, he was going off to his aunt's house with his father and mother, and they were driving in a lovely painted pony trap drawn by their own horse on the farm, and the horse's name was Myko.

Now my friend had conducted many secret conversations with Myko the horse. As he had had many secret conversations with the dog, Ted, and with the two pigs, Betty and Buster, and the cat, Chester, posh cat it was, name like that. All these chats were secret, you understand, because the animals didn't want to get my friend into trouble with his parents, and he certainly didn't want to get them into trouble.

Well, they were belting along with Myko in great rapid form, and the sun shining, and suddenly Myko gives a big whinnying neigh out of him and my friend jumps up off his nice leather seat and says, "Stop, stop."

His father looks at him and says, "I'll do no such of a thing," and my friend says, "Stop, you have to stop—one of the shafts is going to break."

Well, against his better judgment, his father looks out over the front of the trap and sure enough he sees that the shaft has a big crack in it, and he draws the reins slowly tight until Myko the horse comes to a gentle standstill. They all get down and inspect the damage and as they do so the shaft finally breaks off and falls down like a dying thing.

If they'd all been still aboard when that happened, they'd be as dead as doornails. The father scratches his head in puzzlement, and the horse lets out another whinny.

"Tell him you heard a crack," says the horse to the boy. And the boy says, "I heard a crack."

"Back there on the bridge," whinnies the horse.

"Back there on the bridge," says the boy.

"I suppose," says the father, with a snigger as big as a curse, "the horse told you."

The boy said nothing. And now he felt worse than ever, because the animals were talking to him in their language and they didn't know any of his language. So he decided to teach them. That night, when they were all home safely, Ted the dog came up into his bedroom as he always did and snuck into the bed with him. He said to my friend, "Myko told me about today and the broken shaft."

My friend said, "Ted, I feel awful bad. Because I know how to speak in dog and horse and cat and pig, and you don't know any of my language."

Ted the dog said to him, "Why don't you teach us?"

And so my friend started off teaching the dog to say "Hello" and "How are you" and "Please" and "Thank you."

In no time, all the animals in the farmyard were speaking the boy's language. And then they hit a snag—and it could have had very bad repercussions.

One day, the boy and his father were mucking out the pigsty and the father said to the boy, "These two will soon be ready for the table."

The boy said, "What does that mean?"

The father said, "It means the same as it always meant. We're going to kill them and eat them."

Now Betty and Buster understood exactly what he'd said, because of course they now spoke English, and Buster said out loud, "Oh, no, I don't want to be killed."

"Who said that?" said the father, turning around in great surprise.

"I did," said my friend, quick as a wink, and he went over to Buster, squatted down beside him, whispered, "Say it again," and when Buster said it again the boy moved his lips.

"How did you do that?" said the father, amazed out of his head.

"I read about it," said my friend. "They call it throwing your voice. Vent—something."

And thereafter, if one of the animals spoke in English, the boy pretended it was him, and he had them all warned not to say a word in English unless he was nearby.

"Did they kill the pigs?" Venetia asked.

"No, that's the thing," said King Kelly. "The father was so amazed that he invited people over, and he made bets with them that the pigs could talk. And he won all his bets."

Venetia remembered how the room exhaled when the story ended. Then she made King Kelly reach for the box. He opened it and took out a big doll.

"Now," he said to Venetia, "I'm going to show you how to teach this doll to talk."

He had brought her a gift almost as big as herself, a ventriloquist's doll or dummy, and it wore dungarees and a plaid shirt. It looked like an Irish farmer—to be more accurate, it looked like the American doll manufacturer's impression of an Irish farmer.

"We have to give the doll a name; he can't go 'round the place without a name," said King Kelly. "What'll we call him?"

Quick as a flash, tongue sharpened to a point, Venetia said, "There's only one name for him."

They all looked at her, and she said, "Blarney."

And what of my own parents at this time? While the Kellys were climbing into their firmament, where did my family stand in the world? What comparison could I make that would connect us?

Nothing. Nothing at all. Each of them had lived among people whom their people had always known; other Irish farmers and their farm laborers and their countryside society never touched anything like the wilder lives I'm describing.

When Venetia Kelly was born, on the first day of the new century, Mother was eighteen—as was my father; they'd been born a few months apart in 1882. Harry MacCarthy, my compelling father, had finished school at seventeen, and was just about to read for a liberal arts degree in Dublin when a stroke killed his father. The farm at that time didn't generate enough money to hire a manager, so Harry, bright, sparky, and keen to be a man of the world, had to stay at home and run the place for his mother, my grandmother.

As for Mother—she'd always wanted to be a farmer's wife, which wasn't what her family wanted at all. They'd hoped, given some of the Hopkins family connections, that she'd marry a public figure, such as a judge who came from a good family, or a young man who would inherit commerce, shipping, or banking—because although she was shy, she certainly had enough by way of looks and quiet style to land such a catch.

Mother, however, showed little interest in much beyond her cows—and other animals, and harvests, and all farm and country things, and she went through her young life as shy as a maiden, unsocial and living at home, without as much as a suitor or a swain, until Harry, with the red hair, and the polka-dot pocket handkerchief, and the merry grin, and the slight speech hesitation and three hundred acres, dropped by in 1910, when she too was twenty-eight years old. Everything, it seems, happened in 1910. Until everything else happened in 1932.

17

Here's another—in the circumstances, very significant—fact about my family. My father, in his mid-teens, made a journey to visit an uncle in the west of Ireland, and found himself being invited with said uncle to Coole Park, the home of Ireland's most famous widow, Lady Augusta Gregory.

Whenever my father spoke of education he expressed his disappointment at how he had been denied. "A lost opportunity," he'd say, "is like uneaten fruit. It rots." I never quite got what he meant; I do now. But in Coole Park, under the famous copper beech tree, he had sat on the grass, at a picnic, and heard Lady Gregory, this cultural powerhouse, in her widow's weeds, discussing the setting-up of a national Irish theater. Her partner, not present, would be her "dear friend" the poet Mr. Yeats. Yeats had said to her, "As with the voice the spirit," suggesting that "only an Irish actor can convey the Irish spirit, since words are the clothing of the soul."

My father came away from that meeting quivering with thrills. He told me of it over and over again. They'd talked all day about acting.

Someone did an illustration, a character sketch from Shakespeare—the moment when King Richard III wakes from his dream and faces his conscience: "The lights burn blue. It was now dead midnight."

"You-you-you could see it," said my father. "You could see the anguish in this actor's face. He was the murdering king, he-he-he was shifty and regretful and everything."

On the way home from Coole Park, his heart had "caught fire," he said, at the notion of "being" another person as an actor must be, of "writing" with his own face and voice and body and actions the story of a completely other person.

My father told me that ever after that picnic, when he was out in the yard, or the fields, climbing the stairs to bed at night, aching in every bone after hours of labor, or bounding down the stairs next morning, the thought never left him—and he said that he studied people thereafter as though he were compiling an album. "All-all-all their shapes. And-and-and their actions and voices."

Indeed he became and remained a good mimic; for a man with a mild stammer, he was amazing with nuance and shade.

"I missed my vocation," he once said to me. "I should have been an actor."

Which was, after all, the life of Sarah Kelly. She took role after role by storm, and all the early playwrights of that period, including Mr. Yeats himself, insisted that she appear in their works.

Sarah sailed into Dublin society as a lovely ship glides into home port. Thereafter—and for the rest of her days—she lived in some style. In the beginning, she was aided by an aunt, King Kelly's sister, Gretta. Though her married name was Monahan, Gretta was never called anything but "Miss Kelly." Mr. Monahan had quit the scene after two years of marriage, departing with some suddenness; he crashed headfirst from his horse into a stone wall during a foxhunt.

His widow said, "He was on a big gray horse and three quarters of a bottle of port."

In this merry widow's household now dwelt this glamorous single mother from New York, already a bright light on Broadway, a new star in the motion pictures, and about to become one of the great figures of the

Abbey Theatre—and her daughter, Venetia, a winsome and lively child. Plus Mrs. Haas.

For Aunt Kelly, Heaven had come to earth. She set up a social round for her beautiful niece. Every Sunday she held what she called her "Dublin lunch," a salon, in effect, and she invited the great and famous—"the cream of the city," she said, "rich and thick."

18

Now the cast is more or less assembled—the main characters in this, my story. My life was irretrievably and fundamentally altered and shaped by them: by my dear father, an ordinary Irish farmer who worked harder than any man he hired; by Mother, a farmer's wife, with recipes, account books, cows to be milked, chickens to be fed; by King Kelly, a bruiser dripping with charms; by his daughter, Sarah Kelly, and above all by her daughter, Venetia, whose life, whatever it was, has defined mine.

Other characters will come, go, or stay, as players must do: Mrs. Haas; Billy Flock and his wife, Large Lily, our housekeeper; and hosts of others—acrobats, egotists, storytellers, politicians, actors.

And Blarney, the ventriloquist's doll, who mesmerized an entire country; Professor Fay, who believed that he knew everything; and his sister, the adorable Dora. Through her, one other—and major—character walked onstage.

I had often heard her mention "a dear friend who knows everything in the world." She kept saying that I must meet him one day. And I did meet him, as you soon will too. James Clare was his name, and he did know everything in the world. He wore black; he had a placid face with a nose like an owl's; he taught me about time and self-respect, and the connection between the two.

Shall I count myself a player too? I must. The fact that I'm the storyteller here, that I'm the narrator, the observer of these people, should neither absolve nor exclude me. Whether I had an effect on them even remotely proportional to the way they influenced me—how can I tell? Can you see yourself accurately? Even when we look in the mirror, isn't everything reversed?

Forgive me if I've taken too long to introduce them to you. I promise that it will all prove relevant. As people are, so shall they be, except for the fact that those few of us who were changed—well, we were truly changed.

And so we come to what Mother ever afterward referred to, in a whisper, as the "Catastrophe." I should have been ready for it. Hindsight, I know, but I now understand that a mood of apprehension had fallen over me like an invisible net. As it turned out, I had good cause.

One Sunday in January 1932, we had a guest for lunch—"Missy Casey" she called herself, Julia Casey, from two farms away. Imagine a duck in a fitted tweed coat and laced brown shoes; that's what she looked like.

Missy Casey was a neighbor who also insisted that she was "an intimate friend." She demanded more attention than triplets, or so Mother said. Everything she did drew notice to herself; for instance, she sent Dinny, her frequently mad laborer, over that Sunday morning at seven o'clock to say that Missy Casey would be fifteen minutes late—for lunch six hours later. She hadn't been to our house for two or three years, probably because she was so irritating.

When she arrived, she sat on the bench in the porch to get her breath back—though we saw no sign of panting. After all she'd arrived in a trap driven to our very door by Dinny the Madman. She fluttered her eyelashes—I mean a true flipping and fluttering—when my father appeared, and after several minutes in which Mother, my father, and I stood in a semicircle around her, she declared herself ready for lunch.

Which began badly. Missy Casey looked across the table at me as though she had never seen me before.

"Louise," she said, her face reddening, "where have you been hiding him? Ben, stand up, let me look at you. My heaven"—as I stood—"you're six feet three. Louise, lock him up."

My father, sensing my loathing of such attention, said, "We-we-we feed him oats. He has his own nose bag."

Missy Casey stared and stared at me, then looked down at her plate, shaking her head. "I wish I were twenty again," she said.

Mother looked at my father and shook her head, a warning to say nothing. We all began to eat. Then came the next grenade: Missy Casey began a conversation about Saint Valentine.

"I'm so looking forward to his feast day," she said. "It falls on a Sunday this year. D'you think Father Hogan will say anything about it at Mass? Wouldn't you think he'd want to preach on someone as important as Saint Valentine?"

"Important?" said my father. "How so?"

This old trout had another technique for retaining attention. After making some opening statement, she'd take a mouthful of food, and then lay three demure fingers to her closed lips. We, of course, had to wait until she'd finished chewing, and I've seen cows quicker with cud; even mild Mother said Missy Casey was "an arch-ruminant."

"Harry MacCarthy, you're just like Father Hogan," said Missy Casey, after a swig of milk from her glass, which frosted her mustache. "Why did Father Hogan say nothing about Saint Valentine? I'll tell you. He's afraid of love. Like all men. He's—simply—afraid—of love." She looked at my mother. "Isn't that true, Louise? Men are afraid of love, aren't they?"

Mother said, without thinking, "That's true indeed."

I knew that Mother didn't mean what she said. She was agreeing with this irritating dame for the sake of moving on to the next topic. But my father coughed in that hard way he had when he was irked. He took a drink of water and coughed again, and I saw him decide to say nothing.

"Maybe I'm being extreme," said Missy Casey. "Maybe I am. Because—" And she took another mouthful of food. Again we waited. When she unfastened the clasp of her fingers from her lips she said, "Now where have I put my bag?"

All three of us, Mother, my father, and I, we rose from the table and began to look for the bag; Mother found it in the porch, where Missy Casey had recovered her breath.

"Because," she continued, "I received this last year. In the post. Anonymously. I carry it around with me."

This spinster, older than a stone, dry as a shrub, nostrils like gun barrels, drew out a large pink envelope and flourished it.

"See? See?"

Mother reached for it, took out the card within, and read the words aloud, "Be. My. Valentine."

My father had said nothing since the remark about men and love. He reached for the card and the envelope. Missy Casey watched his scrutinies.

"Harry, don't tell me," she said, "you recognize the handwriting?"

"Can-can-can you do copperplate too?" he asked.

Mother saw the knife coming out of the sheath. She said, with her voice in a hurry, "D'you know, I never heard of Valentine cards down here in the country. We're getting very modern altogether."

My father handed the card and the envelope back to Missy Casey.

"Well, that's-that's-that's a love you can be sure of," he said. I knew he was angry. "You can tell a lot from handwriting."

"Don't tell me it's yours?" she said like a girl.

He let a silence rise. Then he said, "I-I-I think it's yours."

Such an outburst as we then had.

"Ohhh!" Missy Casey grasped the edge of the table, dragging the cloth. "Ohhh!" she said again, a tortured wail.

My father looked at me and winked.

Bang! Bang! Bang! Missy Casey thumped the table, and crockery hopped, and cutlery rattled.

"That's a terrible thing to say. That I'd send a Valentine card to myself. Ohhh!"

She rose from her chair and staggered from the table, reaching for the wall. Mother raised fierce eyebrows at my father, who nodded as though to say, "She did, she did." He looked at me and winked again.

Mother followed Missy Casey, and that was the last we saw of her. Next we heard the pony trap rattle away, with Dinny the Madman screaming prayers at the horse.

When Mother came back in, she said to my father, "That was uncalled for."

"She-she-she asked for it."

"How so?"

"That remark about men—she's always doing that. And anyway she did send the card to herself."

Mother said, "And where's the harm if she did?"

My father shook his head impatiently and I got Missy Casey's untouched and spurned dessert.

But a chill had fallen between my parents, a rare occurrence in our house. Its very unusualness was the kind of thing I should more closely have observed.

19

After lunch, to escape the house's mood, I went outdoors. Fog had come in. From the yard I went on a long looping walk that I'd worked out since the first days I was allowed to roam the fields alone. I was six years old then, and imagine what the woods looked like. Thrilling—a mysterious forest, especially in fog, when all branches took on new shapes. I saw caves that didn't exist, and the ghosts of animals long extinct—a fog in the woodlands is a work of ever-changing magic. Even now, though I was a dozen years older, and they seemed less populated by the supernatural, the woods served me well.

The well stands away from the woods, its mound like a green breast out in the fields. As you approach you hear the water burble faintly against the pleasant and orderly walls. Those stones have lined the well for centuries. This is the best, the freshest drink that you can have.

When I emerged from the trees, I saw an old woman by the well; she stood still, and she was looking toward me. Nothing unusual in that; the local people, from the cottages and from one or two of the smaller farms, drew buckets from here. Miss Fay often came with me as I fetched a pail of water for them; going back to the cottage she always made the same joke about how we were Jack and Jill.

Still, I thought that I knew everybody who used this well, and I'd never seen this tall crone. Nor the garment she wore—except in paintings; she had an ankle-length black Kinsale cloak. As I drew closer I could see that it was lined with bright, shining green fabric, probably silk. The Kinsale cloak billows out into the world; it's from another century; it has ruffles. You don't see it much in the countryside, as it's mainly worn by rich city women on classy occasions.

To add to the mystery, this creature also carried something I'd never seen except in storybooks—a wooden pail. All our buckets were enamel or galvanized metal.

I stopped and, unusually for me, I didn't speak a greeting. The woman, much older than Mother or Missy Casey, beckoned me forward. She had an urgent air of command. I walked forward, picking my steps.

She waited, still beckoning. Beside the dark pool of the well the fog lay thickest, a gray blanket, swirling and dense. On and on she beckoned me until I stood no more than some feet from her. Now I could see that the cloak obscured the lower half of her face.

She felt strange in the way only a total stranger can. I knew I'd never seen her before—and I had been a boy who rode his bicycle like a hero all around these roads. She had a gray face, and her cloak's hood also covered her head so that I couldn't say what color hair she had—or indeed if she had any. Her high cheekbones—from what I could glimpse of them—suggested that once upon a time she might have been a beauty. Now she seemed tired, maybe exhausted.

I could have reached out and touched her face, as she could mine. Neither of us moved; I, frightened, held my hands by my sides. I felt the damp fog on my face, saw my breath on the air. She held the wooden pail in her hand. Her eyes searched me, every square inch, head to foot.

"Look at you," she said.

A statement, one with no emotion in it, no kindness, no threat, no criticism, no praise. I kept my eyes down. Her creaking, slightly uncouth tones gave no identification. An Irish voice? Perhaps, but I couldn't say whence.

"Look at you," she said again.

Somewhere in the woods behind me a bird swore, harsh and high. The fog thickened.

"I've something to say to you, young lad," she announced. "And you'll remember it many times."

Fear is what I remember. Of what, I didn't know. Fear of having no control? Or fear that a stranger could presume to have an influence upon me, make an observation of me? As she now did, and this is what she said.

"You're going to be given a shock, young lad."

I found my voice. "Where are you from?"

She eyed me. "You're thinking, 'Is she real, or a witch or something?' Aren't you? And you're thinking, 'She looks like a witch, don't she?' That's what you're thinking."

As indeed I was—those exact thoughts.

"I can tell a lot about you," she said. "Just from looking at you, just from the light you give off. We all give off a light, and you're thinking now, 'If that's the case, her light is gray.' Isn't that what you just thought?"

Again—exactly.

She said, "Now you know you can trust what I'm telling you. And I've one piece of advice that you'll have to remember. You won't know the truth about what came from the sea for many, many years, but keep away from it. Good-bye now."

She turned her back, stooped to half-fill her wooden pail, and walked away into the fog. I thought, *She looks like something out of my book of* Grimm's Fairy Tales. And then she called out over her shoulder, "Oh, I'm real enough, young lad."

The truth about what came from the sea? But what had come from the sea?

After a few minutes I followed the path that she'd taken, which leads to the road. Although she was a good deal older than me and carrying a pail of water, and I was young and a quick walker, I never saw her, never caught up with her.

You should find our well one day, you should go there, try to make it in winter, and stand there and try to imagine how eerie it felt. Had I been old I might have died of fright.

That path leads to the Fourpenny Road, but not a sign of her did I see there. I halted in the gateway of Mr. Thompson's house and looked up the driveway. On slightly higher ground now, the fog had thinned, and I could see right up to the front door—but not a person walked or stood anywhere. Except myself, puzzled and afraid in the fog and knowing somehow that I must tell nobody.

What was the truth of that encounter? Did I dream it? Or did I actually meet the old hag? Did I invent the story, my own mythology to prepare me for what was about to happen? Or to justify it?

I went home. In from the fog. I made myself some ham sandwiches. Mother appeared and had a cup of tea, and then Father arrived. We all sat at the kitchen table; she didn't look at him. Missy Casey wasn't mentioned—but she might have been in the room. I said nothing about the woman at the well.

A frost as stiff as this had fallen once before in our house, when my father was a day late coming home from the Galway races. No telegram, no message, and neighbors whom he'd met there had dropped by, asking if he was home yet.

This irked Mother, who then ripped into him when he did return, and the ice between them chilled everything for an unpleasant week. Since then all had been more or less sweet.

But this afternoon, he chatted to me more than usual, and in a louder voice. Mother read the newspaper, head down; she was hunched and a touch remote.

Except when he asked me, "Tonight'll be great, won't it?"

That's when Mother looked up—at me. I answered her unspoken question.

"Venetia Kelly's Traveling Show," I said. "She's coming to Cashel."

Mother looked at my father; he avoided her eyes. Then she folded the newspaper very slowly and said, "I see."

Rising from her chair, she walked from the room, passing behind his chair but not mine. Normally she patted his shoulder, or stroked his head, or mock-throttled him. That afternoon—nothing.

Walking very slowly, she reached the door, which she opened ceremoniously. She left the room like a queen—and then slammed the door so hard that the doorknob fell off. It had always been loose. My father rose, retrieved the white porcelain oval, and gingerly slid the knob back on again.

We reached the hall in Cashel an hour before the performance—my father had insisted. With nobody else there, we sat side by side in the empty, freezing place. I should have known, but then hindsight is despicable; it mainly tells us how stupid we've been. Father chattered like a monkey that night. I had rarely seen him so animated. His face had reddened slightly, as it did when we had company or he'd had a few swift whiskies. And he did this anxious thing with his hands, tenting and interlacing his fingers back and forth, over and over. He also shifted in his seat like a man with bad hemorrhoids.

I think we went in early because he'd hoped that we'd see some of the performers setting up the show. We didn't—but we heard them. Behind the crooked hangings that passed for a stage curtain they shuffled and shoved, laughing and sending out little hollers to one another. At each sound my father put a hand to his ear like a hunter, and said, "Whisht!"—even if I hadn't been speaking. From time to time he sat forward and clasped the back of the chair in front of him.

Time stays infamously slow in the countryside. The poster outside said 8:00 SHARP, but not until a quarter past did people drift in. By half past eight the hall had filled, but untidily so; men stood at the back and chatted; banter rattled back and forth; people left their seats to greet newcomers or to surprise a neighbor whom they had just seen three rows ahead, and so on. My father grew ever more impatient.

At twenty minutes before nine an imperfect drumroll came from behind the curtains. It started hard and high and stayed that way until the audience quieted, and then a man pranced out, a tall man, naked to the waist, thin as an orphan, torso white as a sick fish. He wore the skintight pants of a troubadour, wide red and yellow stripes, and he turned two somersaults in the narrow space between the curtains and the edge of the stage.

My father whispered to me, "He's Michael. He's one of the leading actors."

Michael turned two more somersaults, took a bow, and disappeared behind the curtains. The drumroll began again, and a male voice called out, "Ladies and gentlemen, we present Miss Venetia Kelly in the famous Trial of Shylock by William Shakespeare."

Part of the trick for this traveling company was to offer excerpts from plays in the school curriculum. This guaranteed attendance. Our teachers always said we missed a great deal by not seeing a performance of the play we were studying; that night, much of the audience consisted of boys and girls a little younger than me. In fact, *The Merchant of Venice* had formed part of my own English studies and I knew the play by heart.

The curtain drew open and revealed a row of chairs set up so that their backs formed a kind of hedge. This was evidently the front of the dock. On one chair knelt an elderly man facing the audience—clearly Antonio, because he looked so miserable. At the back of the stage, on a high stool, sat another old man, wearing a black robe and a judge's long wig; he was the Duke.

The acrobat Michael reappeared. He now wore a short black velvet jacket, but his height meant that a gap of his flesh appeared between the hem of the jacket and the waistband of his striped pants. I could tell that he was playing Bassanio, because he walked up and down in a fret, and rubbed his hands together in an anguished way. Once or twice he gave us the benefit of a swift somersault. It had nothing to do with Shakespeare, but the audience loved it.

On a chair nearby, whetting an ugly knife on the sole of a shoe, sat

Shylock, a small, extremely fat man with no neck. His front teeth reminded me of a rabbit's.

Somewhere offstage the drum rolled again. Michael, i.e., Bassanio, turned another swift somersault and got another cheer. As the drumroll stopped, everybody onstage stood up and stepped aside, making way.

That was the moment when I first saw Venetia Kelly. Even now, as I write it, all these years later, I need time to digest it.

Let me tell you instead that my father had been disappearing throughout the year. He went at random intervals, and in odd but always consistent ways. Midafternoon he'd leave the fields or the yard or wherever he was working, go into the house, change into his best clothes, and drive away. I often saw Mother frown as, half hidden, she watched from the porch or a window or behind a garden hedge.

His return always woke me up. Sometimes he got back before midnight, sometimes an hour later. Soon, from far away, came distant noises of argument in the suspended night.

What had he been doing? I suddenly knew. He had been making journeys of different lengths, to different towns, to see these traveling players. As the evening wore on I knew it more and more; he not only knew the name of every performer on the stage, he could murmur their ad-lib lines.

I too began to mouth lines as he did—Antonio's "the weakest kind of fruit / Drops earliest to the ground." They had taken some liberties with the text, and I soon understood why—the piece had been rearranged to create an entrance for Portia.

What is it about what we call today a star? What quality, what dimension? Is it an inner burn that transmits itself to us whether he or she knows about it or not? Venetia Kelly made no dramatic stride into the center of the stage; she didn't leap or pounce. She kind of slouched on, a slow walk, shoulders taut, like somebody wondering whether to be wary. She looked all around the stage, taking in everything, and then came far enough downstage to be seen by the entire audience—which at once fell quiet.

Beside me, my father reacted so hard that he made the bones of his chair creak. He pulled back his hands, tightened them into fists, and held them in front of him like a man containing himself.

She wore, neck to foot, a black gown of a light velveteen material with a pattern like a faint Venetian brocade, and she wore small, pointed, black velvet shoes. No jewelry, no ornament shone anywhere. From my father's throat came the noise of a small animal. I was barely able to take my eyes from this actress, and yet I had to look at him. Had I not known better I should have said he was in pain.

You could hear a feather drop in that shabby old hall. We weren't in Cashel—we were in old Venice. A step at a time, Portia looked to right, to left, her head turning like a lamp. Maybe I imagined it, but it seemed to me that each actor quickened when she looked at him, then stood or sat at greater attention.

And still, as I tell you this, I marvel that she was, as yet, barely past thirty years old. And still I marvel, as I feel again the pain of the memory, that she was perfect. The first time I ever heard that voice, it was speaking a perfect rendition of Shakespeare's iambic meter, five-notes-to-the-bar.

"Which is the merchant here, and which the Jew?"

Antonio and Shylock identified themselves to her. My father leaned forward, and leaned back again. Then he bent down, bent double almost, as today's aircraft passengers are instructed to do in a crash. He put his head in his hands. For a moment I thought that he'd been taken ill, and I turned to look at him. He had become inaccessible; no part of his face showed; I could see only his thick mane of bushy red hair.

"Are you all right?" I whispered.

He shook his head and came out of his dive, raising himself slowly. His eyes were still closed tight, and he bit so hard on his lip that I expected blood. He opened his eyes, turned them on me like lamps, and whispered these words:

"Ben, I'm not coming home with you tonight."

"Why?" I whispered back.

When we ask the most important questions we already know the answer. *How ill am I, Doctor? Is my business ruined? Am I as inadequate as I think I am? Do you love me?*

Such was the case here.

My father said, "I'm going to join Venetia Kelly's Traveling Show."

21

Things had been going so well in my life. No complications yet—no girls, I didn't smoke or drink, and I didn't gamble. I didn't even swear, not out loud. When I looked ahead, life promised well too; my achievements in school told me that next year I'd enjoy college; I liked our farm, the horses, the dog, the cat, my parents, the neighbors, the people who came and went.

My days were lovely—from the clatterings of the sparrows every morning, to the bats fooling around in the evening. I had known no threatening difficulties; I'd had a good ride of eighteen years. Now, though, somebody was creeping up behind me with a hammer, and that somebody was my own father.

How did I react when he made his announcement to me? I don't fully recall. For certain I frowned, because that's what I do when I'm hit by a thump I'm not expecting. Also, I waited, because I have a slow emotional metabolism and I always need to digest things in order to cope with them, especially if there are strong feelings attached. In my house there wasn't much training in matters of emotion. So I'm surmising that I sat there, instantly woolly in my brain, with big lights flashing the thought *What does he mean? What does he mean? What does he mean?*

I do recall an immediate worry about driving the car at night because I'd never done that. And I do recall trying to figure whether there was a moon to help light the way. I remember also thinking, *Oh, well, it has good headlamps.* Other than that, I can't bring any reaction back to mind.

Here are the words again—"I'm going to join Venetia Kelly's Traveling Show."

I hadn't mistaken it; that's what he said. He had the eyes of a child when he spoke; he was innocent, relying on me, and thinking only of the world to which he was going.

When Portia declaimed, "The quality of mercy is not *strain'd,*" the slight emphasis made my father shudder. "It droppeth as the gentle rain from heaven / Upon the place beneath"—and I could hear, like leaves rustling on a tree, the whisper of fifty teenage voices murmuring the words. "It is twice bless'd / It blesseth him that gives and him that takes: / 'Tis mightiest in the mightiest."

Now I too began to whisper—"it becomes / The throned monarch better than his crown"—and I felt a tight grip on my arm: my father's hand. He seized me so hard that I looked at him and saw that he had closed his eyes; tears oozed down.

"Shhh," he said gently.

I subsided, his grip eased, and I sat back to listen.

They had cut short or cut out almost every other part. Shylock got a few sentences to say; the Duke of Venice interjected only once. And when Portia had finished, Bassanio cheered and did another somersault. Many years later Miss Fay smiled at this detail.

"A loose interpretation," she said.

Bassanio's handstands gave the audience a cue. They yelled and applauded and Venetia Kelly withdrew from the stage as gracefully and silently as she had entered. My father sat up, whipped his red polka-dot handkerchief out from his breast pocket, and mopped his face and brow. The crowd cheered on. Portia, still gowned in black, came to the front of the curtain and took a bow. My father stood and whistled on his fingers. He was fifty-two years old.

The show continued as a series of sketches. Somebody from each wing got behind the curtain and dragged it toward the center to prepare the stage for the next act of the evening.

No more Shakespeare; Michael (not Bassanio now, but in the same costume) sang a mournful song about "How Can You Buy Killaaaaaarney." The fat, neckless fellow who'd played Shylock and a girl we hadn't previously seen came on as a lovelorn comedy duo—he a rustic swain, she a milkmaid with a wooden pail, a bantering and slightly blue act.

"Why are you holding my bottom in your hand, kind sir?"

"Oh, pretty miss, is it not a lovely and beautiful and useful thing to hold in my hand?"

"No, kind sir, not useful."

"Not useful, pretty miss? What do you mean?"

"Well, kind sir, what use would it be in a fight?"

The crowd loved it.

Three men in white tie and tails (Michael was one of them) sang and danced—as they juggled. The old man, the judge, waddled on in a troubadour's costume; he looked like the joker in a pack of cards, and he played an indiscernible tune on a tuba, and it made him red in the face.

Venetia Kelly reappeared and once again the hall grew so quiet that a passerby would have thought it empty. Wearing a long white opaque shift, she stood on the edge of the stage and spoke. " 'I fear thee, ancient Mariner! / I fear thy skinny hand! / And thou art long, and lank, and brown, / As is the ribbed sea-sand.' "

My father now sat out on the edge of his chair, so far forward that his breath must have hawed on the neck of the man in front of him. I sat transfixed, as this woman burned herself into us.

"Oh, God," whispered my father. "Oh, Jesus God."

I can remember every detail of that show, but I choose not to bother with its mishmash now: the long passage from *The Rime of the Ancient Mariner,* with the line that the audience was waiting for—"As idle as a painted ship / Upon a painted ocean"; some more songs; a "funny" recitation about brown bread and onions by the old tuba player; handstands, somersaults, and juggling tricks from Michael and the others. They were all, each act, less distinguished by a good margin than Venetia, who performed like an actress from the classics; but the unevenness didn't matter to that audience, which was standing room only.

And then came the finale.

The curtains drew back some of the way to reveal tall black screens, making a small three-sided space. On strolled Venetia Kelly, calm as a stork. She wore a lady's cream blouse with a cameo brooch at the high, maidenly throat. Over lilac tights she wore a purple froufrou skirt, bigger than a huge tutu; she wore a wig of bobbed yellow hair and had round splotches of red on her cheekbones like a rouged clown-ette: *Had this been Portia?*

She folded her hands, primped her froufrous, and cleared her throat with a little cough. Looking up at the audience, she prepared to speak, but an indignant and hurt voice rang out offstage.

"You forgot me!"

From the wings an unseen hand thrust forward a ventriloquist's dummy.

Venetia Kelly said, "I'm sorry, Blarney," took the dummy into her embrace, and began to console it. Blarney wore dungarees, a little tweed vest, and a farmer's shirt with no collar. He had sticking-up hair and thick, worried eyebrows.

"You should be sorry," he said, "and the price of eggs."

He sat in her lap and the routine began.

"How are you, Blarney?"

"Fine."

"Is that all you have to say, Blarney?"

"That depends on you."

This drew a huge laugh from the audience—and my father. He whispered to me, "This fellow's great!"

"What have you been doing, Blarney?" She behaved cautiously with him, as with a volatile lover.

"Not enough."

"Oh? Why not?"

"Your fault."

"My fault?"

"Yes."

Every time he spoke he turned his head, with its glittering blue eyes, to the audience, and then twisted back again to hear her next question. He disturbed me.

"Why is it my fault?" she said.

"Because I can't get rid of you." And Blarney swiveled his head. The audience roared again.

"Well, what would you like to do?"

"I'll tell you."

"Tell me, Blarney."

"I'll tell you."

"Tell me."

"I said—I'll tell you."

Silence. Then Venetia Kelly said, "I'm waiting."

"For what?"

"For you to tell me."

"Tell you what?" He had a mouth as red as scandal, and his squared-off cheekbones were born of a carpenter's knife.

Venetia said, "You told me that you'd tell me—"

"D'you want to hear a joke?" Blarney interrupted.

"Yes, Blarney."

"A man went into a shop and he said to the shopkeeper, 'Do you keep shovels?' And the shopkeeper said, 'I certainly do.' And the man said, 'Why don't you sell them instead of keeping them? You'll never make money that way.' "

My father laughed at this joke, laughed and laughed, almost into hernia country. Blarney watched with his glittering blue eyes as the crowd's laughter subsided.

"D'you want to hear another joke?"

She—and we—waited.

As did Blarney. Then he swiveled his head at her. "Do you?"

Venetia Kelly started and said, "Yes, yes of course." She looked at the audience and raised her eyebrows at his cantankerousness.

Blarney said, "A horse walked into a bar and the barman said, 'Why the long face?' "

I had always known that my father had a sense of humor, but I'd never seen him guffaw like this. Again, Blarney waited; he knew about timing.

"A man walked into a butcher's shop."

"Yes, Blarney."

"Yes, what?"

"Just—yes, Blarney."

He looked up at Venetia, looked at the audience, and shook his head in pity.

"A man walked into a butcher's shop."

This time she didn't interrupt. Every time I looked at this doll, this wooden dummy, he seemed to be looking straight at me.

"He said to the butcher, 'By any chance do you have crubeens?' " By which he meant pig's feet, a delicacy in the south of Ireland.

" 'I do,' says the butcher. 'Tell me,' says the man, d'you find it very hard to walk?' "

They cheered and whistled, they laughed, they cheered again. Standing at the side, near the front, leaning against the wall, one man laughed louder than any other, a tall, heavy man in a brown suit and a check waistcoat. How I remember that sighting.

When he—and the audience—had stopped laughing, Blarney said, quite tenderly, "Venetia?"

"Yes, Blarney."

"You were lovely tonight. As Portia. That was a great performance."

The audience released a large "Awww!"

"Thank you, Blarney. Would you like to be an actor?"

Blarney grew coy. He tucked his head into Venetia Kelly's upper arm. We waited.

"Would you?" Her voice had grown soft but we could hear every word.

Blarney, his head still hidden, nodded like a shy child.

"Blarney, we can arrange that."

He shook his head, waited, slowly emerged, and looked up at her.

"Blarney, I'm puzzled."

Blarney looked at the audience and held a silence.

"Would you or wouldn't you like to be an actor?"

Swinging his head like a lamp to include all the audience, Blarney orated a little rhyme.

"The House of Success is great and wide. Its rooms are always full.

And some go in by the door marked 'Push.' And some by the door marked 'Pull.' "

The audience laughed again; everybody in that hall knew the value of "pull," and many had almost certainly complained that they couldn't get anywhere in life because they didn't have enough of it. Indeed my father often groused, "Low influence in high places. That's my problem."

And then Blarney delivered the coup that set the nation talking—and laughing.

Venetia Kelly commented, "That was a nice little joke, Blarney, and it went down very well. But we were talking about you wanting to be an actor, weren't we?"

Blarney, top of the bill, sitting on his mistress's knee, said, "Yes, Venetia. That's what I'm talking about too."

"Good. This is exciting. What role do you want to play, Blarney?"

"I want to be a candidate in this election. With all the other dummies."

22

We waited. After the applause had died down, and when all the audience had sloped out into the night, my father and I rose from our chairs, stiff as tired workmen. Outside, a few people chatted here and there, still laughing. My father strode away around the side of the building to the rear of the hall. I hung back, agitated and uncertain. Then I followed him, walking fast.

What did I have in mind to do? I don't know. Stop him, perhaps? I don't think so; and nobody could have.

By the time I rounded the corner of the building he was surging like a powerboat. Already dismayed, I stopped and watched him.

For weeks afterward the first image in my head at each morning's awakening remained the same; when I reach for it now, I feel its haunting mood. My father is striding away from me; he may as well be wearing a sign saying PURPOSE. He reaches the upright rectangle of a dimly lit open doorway. Now he is standing between two tall and elegant women who have come out to greet him. They draw him by the arms toward the door. He frees one hand to turn and half-wave at me, he surrenders that arm to them again. Then he turns and walks through the doorway with them. For a moment he looks back over his shoulder at me. The door is closed.

Many years later I saw the play *Oedipus at Colonus.* At the moment when the blind king was flanked by his daughters as he was about to leave them and die, I alarmed myself by beginning to weep. Nothing could have been farther from my life than Sophocles and ancient Greece. Yet I wept, and my memory told me that those women, Sarah and Venetia Kelly, had been escorting my father into his next world.

Like a photograph, I still see that moment whenever I reach for it, or when it comes back unbidden. But to the day she died I never told Mother, never described that incident to her. For one thing it seemed to say that my father was indeed being taken away by forces too powerful for us to counter.

For another, I sensed a possessiveness that offended me, even if I couldn't have put that into such words at the time. And I reasoned that if it offended me, it would have seared her.

So I stood there, watching. My breath offered a small cloud up to the night. The door closed and now everybody had gone and I was alone. Soon, they must come out of that hall and I would know what to do next. They didn't come out and I didn't know what to do. The few lights of the town dimmed and began to die as people went to bed.

At two o'clock in the morning I was still there, afflicted. More than once I went over to the closed door but I never knocked on it. I slunk along the walls under the windows of the hall; from inside I heard laughter and loud convivial noise, so at odds with how I was feeling.

My father's voice rose and fell and I knew that he was regaling them with his delightful stories. At the sound of his voice so merry I could also hear the pieces breaking off my heart, like bits of a cliff falling into the sea. I made the hard decision and turned for home.

23

No matter what I've told you so far, I can't overstate it. I can't exaggerate the gulf between the life my father had been living and the world into which he now threw himself. The strangeness of it all, the unlikeliness—could it have been any more extreme? When things went boxy for any of us, or for the world at large—a typhoon, an earthquake, a shipwreck—my father had a saying, "Ah, it could happen to a bishop."

In this case I doubt it. My father's voice wasn't rough, but it never pealed like bells. The collars of his working shirts got no ironing; they crumpled like wings. He didn't use the word "manicure"; how could he when at any moment he might be forking out manure alongside "Flockin' Billy Flock," as he often called him?

And here he was now, about to travel with people whose voices rang like chimes, who probably ironed their clothes day and night, who certainly spent hours of each morning attending to their intense faces and hands.

Did I know all that when he turned to me and made his announcement? Maybe not in detail, but I knew that he had leapt across a ravine and hadn't once looked at the rocks and waters below.

—

If we had regulations governing licenses for cars or drivers in 1932, I don't recall them. Most of my driving had taken place around the farm, and when my father and I went on the public roads I often took the wheel; he was prepared to say that he was teaching me. In short, I'd had plenty of experience.

How was the night? Fine for a time. Sometimes chaos is followed by a hiatus, which brings a respite, a little protective quiet.

That twisting, winding road from Cashel to our house—I knew it so well, the steep hills and sharp dips. My mind checked off the names of the houses—Murnane, Ryan, Baragry, Carroll, Magner, Mahony, Gleeson.

The headlights poked yellow tubes into the night, dark and still. I had a moment of fright; the acid greenish-yellowish eyes of a goat caught me from his grazing post at the roadside. Otherwise I had the cold and clammy world to myself.

No lights shone in our house, not a candle, not a lamp. I put the car in the barn—same as my father did when he came home late. In the dark yard I stood and listened to the silence. I remember the thought *Well, this is the time for spells. Has someone cast a spell on us? On this place?*

In the kitchen I organized some bread and marmalade, and a glass of milk, and tiptoed up the back stairs to my room. The wood-smoke aroma from the living room still floated through the house. Mother must have been sitting up late: It was now three o'clock in the morning.

My room was as cold as my spirit; I listened like a thief, but I heard not a sound. Nor did I sleep, not at all. When five o'clock came, I lit my little oil lamp and began to read. Futile; I couldn't concentrate because I was waiting for Mother, for her footstep, her voice. But I must have fallen asleep, because at half past eight I woke with a start at morning's mighty noise from Large Lily rattling about in the kitchen below, a slow train with a vast, clanking engine.

I blinked my eyes, sore from that image of my father, and his two women, and the dimly lit open door like a cave, and I rose, washed, dressed, and went down.

How do you tell a woman that her husband has left her? And if the woman is your mother?

24

We had a breakfast room in that house, with, seasonally, a fire. The round table accommodated four; usually we were three. That morning we were two—and terribly so.

I heard her footsteps on the stairs. Mother was always of a quick, light step—but that morning she trod like a convict. When she reached the door of the breakfast room I turned, unable not to, and saw her as I had never seen her before.

She hadn't yet dressed in her day clothes; she wore a long gray cardigan wrapped as tightly around her nightdress as a shroud. Her hair, usually smooth and shiny as a blackbird, flew out in alarm from all sides of her head. Unprecedented. And her face, white as death, had two red holes—the rims of her eyes.

"Where is he?" she said.

I shook my head and began to stand up.

"Where is he?" Her tone of voice roamed between fear and menace.

"He said—he said—"

"What—" she snapped, and then almost wailed. "What did he say?"

I was slow, and she caught me.

"His exact words, please. Ben? His exact words."

And still no sound got out of my mouth.

"Repeat what he said. No matter what it is. Quote him. Say what he said."

Mother had now advanced into the room and, terrible-eyed, had come around the table to look me up close in the face.

"What were the words?"

I know that I lowered my head. Knives of feeling slashed at me. And then I wilted under a sense of protectiveness toward my father. And bent further under a dreadful, impossible desire to protect Mother. Too much, all this, too much for a schoolboy.

I remember thinking, *Get it all out in a rush, then it'll be over. Like an excuse at school.*

"He said—he said he wasn't coming home, that he was going to join Venetia Kelly's Traveling Show."

Mother sat down, heavy as a dropped rock; her chair almost cracked. The yellow cat, Miss Kennedy, jumped from the windowsill and ran out of the room. A bad sign; Miss Kennedy didn't yield to anyone or anything.

"Go after him. Bring him back."

"What?"

"Go now. Now. Eat your breakfast and go."

She locked her hands behind her head and began to rock back and forth in her chair.

"Mother—what can I do?"

Do you know that feeling when alarm makes you suck in your breath? And a red color gets in behind your eyes?

"He's your father. Go after him and bring him back."

"He's—he's going on somewhere."

"You drove the car home. At least I presume that was you driving it. It didn't leave again. You can drive out now and bring him back."

She'd heard me return and had lain awake listening for—she hoped—two pairs of footsteps.

"It was a desperately cold night."

"Yes. That's it. You go after him and bring him home. You know where he is. He'll listen to you, Ben. You know full well that you're the sun in his life."

"Mother—"

"Yes, you are. Ben, you are."

"Mother, I'm only eighteen."

Did tears form in my eyes? I can't remember.

"Yes. I know. This is man's work, Ben. But you're well on your way to being a man. Everybody calls you a young man."

No. Not going to do it. Not going to tug my father's sleeve outside some ramshackle village hall and beg him to come home with me. And yelp when he prizes my arm from his sleeve and walks away.

"I can't interfere, Mother. I'm not up to that."

On fire now, she got up from her chair, went to the wall, and, trembling all over, leaned her forehead against it, her arms spread like a crucifix. She steadied and the trembling ceased; then she came over to me and leaned closer.

"I knew this was going to happen. He's been after her for ages. But we need your father here. We can't run this farm without him."

"But Billy needs a hand today, and I said I'd help—"

"Buts are for goats"—a favorite saying of hers; at least some of her wit had begun to return.

I said, trying to be firm, "We'll run the place fine. We've Ned. And Billy. And Lily. And me. And you're great at things. We'll run it 'til he comes home. And he will."

She strengthened. "I need him. Is that clear? I need him. Go and get him for me. Bring him back here. That's your job."

"Maybe he's only going for a few days—"

"He won't come home. I know him. He won't. Tell him I'll be ruined without him, tell him I'll have no one to talk to."

Large Lily steamed into the room with her big tray and her broad tongue; " 'Tis that cold out there you'd need to grow fur."

Mother preempted any nosy questions.

"Lily, the boss isn't here for breakfast, he's away for a day or two." Her precise speech returned for just that moment. "Set the table for Ben and me."

Large Lily spread her wares, turned like a marching soldier, and clattered back to the kitchen. My father said that Large Lily had a dispensation from the Pope to wear her legs upside down.

Mother left the room too; "I'll be back," she said.

Much as my father always did, I shook out the huge folds of the newspaper. I thought, *My God, I'm already behaving like him,* and I wanted to drop the paper to the floor—notwithstanding the irresistible headlines: ELECTION SPEECHES FROM PLATFORMS OF ALL PARTIES.

That morning, the first of my life's true struggles began. Mother advanced on me like an army. Her feelings tugged me this way, hauled me that way. She pleaded and she pressed and I knew she'd bring me grief. And in time she did.

While I ate breakfast, and before she came back, I began—my father's great dictum—trying to "think rather than feel."

"Use-use-use mental skill," he used to say. "Think your way through it. Forget what you feel." Over and over he'd say, "Skill, not emotion." Hah! The irony!

Well, thinking about this business told me that it was, to say the least, a startling matter: I heard my mind say, *I mean, look at it. Your father has run away from home with an actress. How's that for a ball of wax?*

But my thought process collapsed at once, new feelings swept in, and I began to miss my father with actual pain, a pain in my heart, a pain in my stomach. I was so fond of him. From as early as I could remember I went everywhere with him—on his short errands to town, or into the village, or to spend time at the blacksmith's. I'd had difficulty settling down in school because I was no longer free to be with my father about the place, and I was lonely for him every hour of the day.

And now what was to become of him? He couldn't act, he couldn't dance, he couldn't sing. Perhaps, I consoled myself, he needed to get this thing out of his system. But my father didn't have fads or passing fancies; he was a farmer, he was slow to take up things. Yet—and here was the warning shot—if he took them up he truly embraced them, and made them part of his life forever.

Then, on that bleak morning with my breakfast and my newspaper, in rode the most chilling reflection. I looked out at the wooden gray sky and said, "Golly O'Connor."

Golly O'Connor, a mad, obsessive character, was my father's favorite teacher. He'd been in the British army, and when something surprised him he said, "Golly!"

Golly loved the classics, and spat Greek and Latin quotations like other men did tobacco.

"Remember Heraclitus, boys," he used to cry. "Character is destiny."

That was my father's most beloved remark—"Character is destiny." Thinking of it, I felt less hopeful and very unsure.

When I look back now and see myself there, that Monday morning, I see the early fogs of 1932 boiling soft and slow, mists of damp, gray wool muffling the hill field. Through the other window, I look into the gray stone yard, and there's a horse dipping and swooping its great head as it's being marched in from a gallop. That's Bobbie Boy, a young hunter that my father bought up the country last year, and loved so much he'd never let anyone else touch him. *When will Bobbie Boy begin to miss him? When will the yard begin to know that the boss isn't going to be here anymore? When will Bobbie Boy rear up and kick somebody?* I'm certain I began to talk out loud to myself; that's one of the things I do under severe duress.

Which brings me to Mother's pressure upon me. When she returned to breakfast she rapped a knuckle on the table.

"Ben, listen to me. Let me put this as clearly as I can. I want you to get in the car, go out and find your father, and bring him home. For me."

She didn't say, "Bring him back," she said, "Bring him home." And she didn't wrap it in some vague domestic reason—she said, "For me." Plain as day. And there, plain as an egg on a slate, sat the challenge. And my mind translated her words: *I'm your mother. Go out and bring back the man I love. My husband. Your father. Restore him to my life, to our ordinary life.*

Then she attacked harder: "After all, you were with him when he ran off. You could have stopped him." As though it had been my fault.

I ate my breakfast, and then I went into the kitchen and retrieved my father's breakfast and ate it too. When in doubt, eat. In my mind's rampages did I come up with any cohesive, useful thoughts? I don't remember, but I don't think so. Except one—I wasn't going to get in the car and go searching for Venetia Kelly's Traveling Show or Blarney the parliamentary candidate or my father or anybody.

Standing up in the kitchen, I devoured the food meant for my father, felt surprisingly good about doing it, and headed for the yard. All day I kept out of Mother's way, because I knew that she was looking for me. I headed down the fields, I lingered in the woods, I came back and lurked about the yard—but it was winter and there wasn't much to do. Ned

Ryan had gone off somewhere, Billy Moloney was in one of his "flock off" moods, and eventually, caving in to hunger, I had to go back into the house.

Mother stood in the hallway, leaning against the doorway into the porch. I saw her from behind—tall as a stake, but hunched and bunched. Her folded arms kept out the world and protected her bruised heart. As I watched from the kitchen door, she moved from one foot to the other and back again like a wounded stork.

When she turned around and saw me, she began her next attack. And for two more days she gave me no peace. She assailed me in all sorts of ways, with pleadings and recriminations and, from time to time, utter charm. She woke me up in the morning, she came to my room last thing at night, she rose from the table at every meal and came around to where I sat and leaned in over me, she pulled a chair up beside mine. The Welsh, as a people, have determination when they need it, and if Mother wanted to make a point she knew how to do it.

"He won't listen to me, Ben. For reasons I'm not prepared to go into."

"Are you surprised, Mother?"

"You could have him back here by midnight."

"Are you surprised that he did what he did?"

"You went out with him. You should have seen to it that you came back with him."

All Monday, all Tuesday, I fought her off, still refusing this embarrassing, unseemly task. On Wednesday morning she came to the breakfast table with a face as gray as the fog outside, as bleak as the stone in the walls of the yard. In her arms she cradled like a baby the "Big Ledger"—the farm accounts.

"Now you have to bring him home," she said, and tears rolled down her face. "Ben? Ben?"

Mother didn't cry; she wasn't that kind of woman. And I don't think I'd ever had the thought of what she might look like if she wept. I know, however, that I wouldn't have expected the sheets of water that I now saw, the helpless crumple.

"We. Have. No. Money," she said.

"What?"

"Gone," she said.

"Where?"

"Hundreds. Over months and months. Hundreds—and thousands."

Like God handing Moses the Ten Commandments, she gave me the Big Ledger. For months, my father had been writing checks, all payable to "Cash," and he—or somebody—had been drawing the money from the bank.

"But you keep the accounts?" I said.

"I only keep track of what we earn and sell; your father does the banking, he writes the checks—I have no permission."

And I knew this to be true; not for decades afterward were Irishwomen allowed bank accounts without the written permission of their husbands, and many, including Mother, didn't bother.

She sat now and said, "You have to bring him back. Ben, you have to."

It was—and remains so in my memory—an awful moment.

25

She came to my room with me after breakfast and we planned my clothing. With a notebook and a pencil, making lists of things I'd need, she sat on the bed and fought with herself to give out an aura of calm. Never had I encountered such worry, and it cut into me. This, what an irony, needed my father—he alone could cope with her. She talked as though steam-driven.

"Every time you see him—and there will be a number of times, because I don't expect him to say yes immediately—I want you to look your best."

But I had my feelings too, and they burst out.

"Mother, I'm too young for this."

"I wonder if I should give you some clothes for him. But of course he won't need them if he comes home with you."

It's so difficult for an only child to be his real age. My parents treated me as almost an equal. And I looked mature quite early; I'd grown fast and I had broad shoulders. Inside me, however, at that moment, I was no older than twelve.

"What is your job?" Mother asked me.

She'd coached me, and I had to say, "I am in search. Of my father. To bring him home."

"What is your job?" Mother asked me again.

And I had to repeat it. "I'm in search of my father and I have to bring him home."

At ten o'clock in the morning I drove out through our gates. She said that she would expect me that night or the following night, but certainly no later than Friday, "with your father in tow," as she put it.

This gave me a picture of walking into our house, holding my father's hand, dragging him along behind me. *Yes, very likely,* I thought.

My first destination had to be Cashel, to ask where the traveling show had gone since Sunday. It took me three hours to find anybody connected to the hall, and the man with no teeth who had been on the door on Sunday night told me that the show had gone to Mitchelstown for two nights. Then he told me that it was coming back to Cashel "in a few weeks."

This delighted me and I drove the few miles home again to tell Mother.

"Now," I said, "we can wait. And we'll both go and talk to him."

"No," she said. "No."

Off I went again.

At five o'clock in the afternoon, the sky over Mitchelstown had begun to darken. On wet roads, the brakes slipped a little down the hills. Obeying Mother's orders, I found a bed-and-breakfast place, and a woman with warts on her hands asked whether my parents would be staying too.

It occurred to me to inquire whether other people had booked in; a cattleman from up north was staying, she said, and a couple back from England visiting the wife's family. But no traveling actors.

"We'd never let them in," said the woman. "They're rakes, they've no morals, and they run off without paying."

She might as well have pinched my skin. Was this what my father had joined?

I paid in advance, she said no more, and I went to the room. It felt strange and not at all as good as home; I had never stayed away by myself before.

—

The show didn't even have a curtain in Mitchelstown; while setting up for the performance they blocked off the audience's view with a pile of chairs.

As to the acts they presented, nothing much had changed since Cashel on Sunday night. We still had Michael and his somersaults; we still had *The Merchant of Venice.* I trembled as I sat there, afraid that my father would somehow appear onstage. That, to use a well-plied word of Mother's, would have been "mortifying." But he didn't.

One thing had changed—Blarney, Venetia Kelly's ventriloquism doll, had a new script. Tonight he made what he called "a political speech."

"Ladies and gentlemen and citizens of Mitchelstown." He paused. "D'you get that? Ladies. And gentlemen. *And* citizens of Mitchelstown."

The audience laughed obediently at the insult.

"You'll all be voting for blarney, won't you? Oh, you will. You'll be voting for all kinds of blarney. Isn't that what you voted for before? For the last four elections you voted for blarney. And you got it. But I'm giving you a chance to vote for the real thing—the real Blarney. And I'll be elected. And do you know why I'll be elected? Because I'm very promising. Blarney's the name, Blarney's the game."

The audience lapped it up. I laughed too—but he made me shudder, with his carved cheeks and the lewd red scar of his wooden mouth, and most of all the way he sat on Venetia Kelly's knee, leered up at her, and then leered out at the audience.

Not yet did I begin to think of her as the voice behind Blarney; not yet did I begin to discern the layers of cleverness and quiet rebellion and truth-telling that lay beneath her ventriloquism. For the moment I took Blarney almost as a real living person. And so, it seemed, did everybody else.

After the show—and this had also happened in Cashel—the audience left the hall slowly. They chatted to one another in the rows of chairs; they sauntered out, sure sign of a good experience. I dawdled, putting off the difficult hour. The night air hit me like a wet sheet; my heart climbed up my body and into my mouth.

Again the tall rectangle of light from an open door; again the flashed image of the two women from some nights ago.

Men stood in that doorway; Michael, the semi-naked acrobat, leaned there, smoking a cigarette, which he held between his ring finger and his pinkie. He looked at me as a cat looks at a dog, wary and yet dismissive. The man with no neck peered 'round Michael, looked me up and down, gave a little whistle, and saluted me as though I were a soldier. They both stepped back into the hall, and one of them closed the door.

I moved away and waited. Twenty yards from the hall I paced, back and forth, like an anxious young policeman, swinging my arms against the cold air; it was so dank.

In about fifteen minutes my father came out alone. Straightaway, he saw me. I moved toward him and he froze. He held his palms out flat in front of him as a man might ward off a bear. I opened my mouth to speak—but no words did I have. With the backs of both hands, he flapped a gesture at me that said, "Go away, go away"—not a harsh dismissal, a frightened one, and he stepped backward.

Michael the acrobat arrived, looked at the scene, and took my father's arm. The two of them stepped a wide arc around me and walked down the street into a pub.

I followed, my heart wincing. If I could have clutched his arm, his leg, his coat, hung on to him somehow—I would have done so. At the door of the pub I lost my nerve and the failure clashed with my concern for him. The concern won. I thought, *Next time, I'll bring some warm clothes for him, and his gloves. He looks as though he's cold.*

26

Now—in order to rest from that painful moment, which still wounds me, here's an Important, if Short, Digression. I've already made the point that there's an argument linking the emotions in my parents to the hubbub and hurly-burly of the country. At this point in my story, it all becomes intertwined. So I need to step back a little, and give the context, a nutshell of Irish politics.

Except for some lingering skirmishes, and some dreadful incidents, the Irish Civil War came to an end effectively in the summer of 1923. I, though still a child, knew enough to feel relief.

For my family it had so often been local. In one incident, four antitreaty men—"Irregulars" they were called—abducted a man from the village, a young soldier in the new, official army, and took him to a shed in our fields. They'd begun to torture him with razor blades when Billy Moloney heard the screams, ran out there, and stopped them. He brought the soldier up to the house, and my father took the man to the doctor to have the long slashes on his legs bandaged. I well recall the appalled look on Mother's face.

Politically, we'd all had almost a decade to settle down since the last shot was fired. After the treaty of 1921, the same two broad factions, divided and bitter, had remained: those conservatives who still favored the treaty, which partitioned the country, and the republicans, who wanted England's boots off every scrap of Irish soil. To this day the ideological descendants of these opposing sides in the Civil War face each other in the Irish Parliament. Although much has mutated since then, bitter feelings continued for a long time.

It's not surprising that the divide continued; Irish memory is a long thing, as elaborate as a comet, and with as many tails and trails and glowing flares. What interests me, though, is how the politics of my time also identified, and indeed defined, a cultural divide.

Those who wanted the treaty tended to come from merchant and urban societies, people with second- and third-level education, professionals, old money, of "good" families. In the 1922 general election, led by a gentleman named William Cosgrave, they'd gained the first power of the new Irish state. Mr. Cosgrave had fought in the Easter Rising of 1916, enabling him to say that he had as much right to be called "patriot" as any man. He and his colleagues had accepted the treaty because they felt that was the best they'd get, that England would never sell the million and more Protestants into a predominantly Catholic united Ireland. By 1932, they'd been the largest party in no fewer than four elections, and in order to govern they'd formed coalitions with smaller parties, and could also rely on some maverick independents.

By law there has to be a general election in Ireland every five years, although an election can be called by the prime minister inside that period, or the government can fall at any moment if it can't get the numbers to fight off a vote of "no confidence." Our last election had been in 1927 and another had long been expected.

The government's opponents, the republicans, were led by a more famous 1916 warrior, Eamon de Valera, who, all his life, wanted Ireland united, and hated settling for anything short of that. His followers came mainly from the fields and the hills, farmers, farm laborers, men of the earth, and, unable for ten years to win enough votes to become the largest party, they sat on the back benches and smoldered.

Embers, if not doused, can catch fire again. And they did. In the rural parishes like ours, in the villages and country towns, with their pubs and chattering street corners, in the summer meadows by the riverbanks, on the mountainsides and along the lanes, at morning creameries with their lines of carts, during afternoon harvests, on long Sunday after-church talk with pipes and tobacco, republican passion, stoked by Mr. de Valera and a number of fiery henchmen, built and built. They called themselves the "Warriors of Destiny," and by the winter of 1931, nobody, friend or foe, was immune to their fervor.

That's my nutshell—a nutshell that any day, we felt, could once more fill up with blood. Today, I liken the tension in the country at that time to those photographs of cities at night, when the camera's flash turns the neon into streaks and colored streamers. No wonder we all went a little mad.

On the night my father and I had gone to Cashel, Sunday, 31 January 1932, we discussed in the car how the Parliament had been dissolved the previous day. And on Monday morning, after he had gone, I sat at breakfast, as I've said, and opened his newspaper. The election campaign had well and truly begun.

In those days, the front page never carried news, only advertisements and some legal and public notices. The thrust of the paper came inside, and that Monday morning the headlines on page eight shouted about Mr. Cosgrave's "whirlwind tour," and his "enthusiastic welcomes escorted by motors," and his "big audiences."

We took the *Irish Independent* daily, largely because it had the biggest circulation and therefore the widest coverage, and—not insignificant—because it sided with the government, the pro-treaty faction. This gave my father reason to hate the newspaper, and disagree with everything it said, and though not a hate-filled man, nor disagreeable, he liked to have something to loathe.

I remember hoping that he read a paper that morning. How he'd have bridled at Mr. Cosgrave saying, "We are against Russian methods here. We are against Communism. The State will not submit to either Russianism or Communism."

My father's voice echoed across the breakfast table in my mind, "Nobody-nobody-nobody's asking him to. Who ever remarked it but himself, the old goose?"

I found no mention that day of Blarney's entry into the election campaign; perhaps the news hadn't yet traveled the hundred miles from

Cashel to Dublin. Having looked for all the things my father would have read aloud to us—especially the weather forecast, with its anti-cyclones and "this-this-this is tricky; troughs of low pressure over Norway"—I did find a snippet on another page that gave me an acute pang, because it was just the sort of item my father relished.

The "Social and Personal" column reported that "King Boris the Third of Bulgaria is 38." That would have sent my father off about the place singing in his cracked voice, "Happy birthday to you, Happy birthday to you, Happy birthday, dear King Boris the Third of Bulgaria, Happy birthday to you."

Election turmoil, then, was the background against which I had gone out into the Irish countryside to find my suddenly wayward father. The arguments wouldn't change, with the Cosgrave government attempting to paint the de Valera people as gunmen and Communists, and the republicans retorting with their pressure, telling us to stop being puppets dangling from England's strings.

When my father walked away from me that night, I left Mitchelstown. Took my clothes from that flophouse and left. Deep hurt to confusion to anger—everybody knows that path. Against Mother's wishes, I drove home. In the kitchen I broke a glass because I gripped it too hard; blood and milk everywhere.

Mother had heard me arrive. Not expecting me, yet expecting me with terrifying hope, she assumed that if I'd come home, he had come too. When I walked into the kitchen and she saw that he wasn't with me, her anticipation turned to rage. Two of us—enraged, on fire. She shouted at me, Mother who never raised her voice.

"Oh, God, why can't you do as I ask? Why? Why? Did you ask him? Did you ask him to come home? You didn't, did you?"

That's when I squeezed the glass.

"He waved me away."

"Did you talk to him, did you?"

"There were people."

"You didn't ask him, did you?"

I dropped the broken glass and threw my arms up. Mother frenzied; she came around the table and caught my shoulder.

"How was he looking? Was his shirt dirty?"
"Mother, it was dark."
"But did he look as if he was all right?"

The upshot? I was sent out next day with new marching orders: *Stay near him. Follow wherever he goes. And don't come home without him.*

I'll never forget that first period of pursuit, that awful rough, damp time of February days, bad food and worse beds, cold journeys, hours of waiting outside decrepit halls and shabby pubs. Worst of all was the nonstop sense of pain and failure. I'd have given anything to be somebody else—or at least to be somewhere else. How could I succeed? You see, I still lived according to a boy's fast, racing imagination, an adolescent's need to be in the other world, the existence that has nothing to do yet with Life or Reality. I still hoped that I'd one day learn to fly, and swoop down on our yard, back from some foreign place where great birds as black as malice sat on stones high above the sandy desert. I still hoped that I'd one day go to some warrior school and learn swordcraft, and then stride through my own country, dealing out justice and avenging wrongs.

On good days, I sometimes consider that horrid task the greatest compliment I've ever been paid. Mother kept on saying that she knew I was up to it, and I can see now that, even at the age of eighteen, I knew things. Epic things. Mysterious things. I don't know how I came to know and understand them—all that solitude as a boy, I suppose.

Was that how I came to grasp while still a schoolboy that my own country was in an epic moment? It had all the trappings, plus something that all epics need—a mysterious giant. He was the tallest man in politics, an epic figure if ever there were one, the difficult, opinion-splitting Eamon de Valera. Bear with me while I give you his background; you're about to see him up close.

God, monster, or both, Eamon de Valera dominated the country. He'd raised his image with care—the scholar-warrior, the soldier-intellectual.

Control is the essence of power. De Valera measured every step he took, pondered every word he spoke. He allowed a brief pause before he answered a question. He had a frown as deep as the silence of Buddha. He stood head and shoulders above most people; it was said that his closest allies were chosen from men no more than five feet ten inches tall, so that his six feet and several inches could seem further heightened.

They were the men who also nurtured his mythology. They called him "Dev," but never to his face: They addressed him as "Chief" even before he won office. They said he understood the theory of relativity. They whispered that he had, in his soldier days, a beautiful and rich mistress from the upper reaches of his enemies, the English aristocracy.

An entire mythology surrounded his birth. I've heard many versions, and depending on who told me the story, they ranged from immaculate conception to the whore with the heart of gold.

One man swore to me, "Dev is the child of a Protestant mathematics genius from New England and a wild, beautiful dancer from Mexico." Another man in the group said, "No, no—he was born in a Florida cathouse."

Here's the version that my father told me.

Edward—originally George—de Valera was the child of a girl from Bruree, a wooded part of County Limerick. Catherine or Kate Coll went into the service of an Episcopalian or Anglican clergyman down in the southwest of Ireland, and fell pregnant to the son of the house. To evade scandal the clergyman and his wife paid Kate's passage to New York.

Onboard ship, as her condition became more and more noticeable, the captain told her that without a named father for her child she wouldn't get into the United States.

He, as ship captains are empowered to do, entered her into a marriage of convenience. On deck on a sunny morning, a day out from the Hudson, Kate Coll married a Spanish gentleman by name of Juan Vivión de Valeros. He's recorded in the birth details an "artist"; some people insist that he was a sailor on the crew of the ship.

The child was born in New York some weeks later, registered on 10 November 1882 at a foundling home in midtown Manhattan. Senõr de Valeros is said to have died. The mother, who was to remarry a gentleman named Wheelwright, had no place in her new life for her barely legitimate son. She sent him back to County Limerick to be raised by her relatives.

That's the story as I've pieced it together, and some of it at least must be true, because it's a fact of history that in 1916 Mr. de Valera had been able to prove to the British military authorities that he was American-born, and that's why he wasn't executed with the other rebel leaders.

When the 1921 treaty was signed, Mr. de Valera used his fierce opposition to it as his power base. But half the country's population blamed him for the civil war that broke out.

His standing took another hammering when his former rebel ally and now chief rival, Michael Collins, the new nation's army chief, and the country's unequivocally beloved hero, died in an ambush. Dev's enemies said that if he didn't pull the trigger himself, he knew it was going to be pulled, and he could have stopped it. He could have issued an order to his men decreeing the absolute exemption of Collins from all and any assassination threats.

My father, a fair-minded man in his conscious thoughts, worshipped Collins—yet he voted for Dev. He said that the Civil War and the death of Collins left Dev no place to go except deeper into a stance for the unity of Ireland. If Dev diluted his position, then the voices asking why Collins had needed to die would have forced Dev out of politics completely.

As it was, Dev's republican, united-Ireland stance cost him four elections and threatened to keep him out of power for all time. He, however, drove on, drawing huge crowds every time he made a speech. Soon, as he built his legend, the rural Irish people saw him as almost a mystic, as a leader whom they would follow over a cliff.

Year by year, that power built up, and it cut both ways. Those who loved him would die for him—and many did. Those who hated him wanted to kill "the Long Fellow," as they called him. In fact, were Dev to look like winning this election, said the rumors, the sitting government would stage an armed coup to keep him from getting power.

And thus I, while searching for my father, came to observe a living myth at first hand, and in time drew him into my life.

Never have I seen rain come down so vertically. It leaked into the car as I drove; when I halted under a tree, the wind blew the branches so hard that the rain tipped down on the roof in slews and slobs. I thought about turning back—until I imagined Mother's face when I arrived home alone.

The show was advertised to appear in Kilmallock that night. Blarney's candidacy had by now made all the newspaper headlines—IT'S ALL BLARNEY ANYWAY and HOW APPROPRIATE and ANOTHER DUMMY IN THE RACE. A big crowd would surely turn up—but there was an even greater attraction. The town was about to see a larger audience than any hall in the county could hold, thousands of people. Driving rain wasn't going to stop them.

By the time I reached the outskirts of Kilmallock, the windshield had misted over on the inside; rain washed diagonally across the glass outside. I could scarcely see, nor could I peer out of the side window and look ahead. My speed came down to about five miles an hour; a donkey could have passed me.

I asked a man sheltering in a doorway where the traveling show was to be.

He said, " 'Twon't be 'til very late—the Long Fella is giving a speech here."

"In the town?" I'd been so preoccupied I hadn't noticed.

"I hope he gets pneumonia."

I said, "Well, we have the weather for it," and drove on.

The Chief was known to let nothing stop him. Were the weather to turn biblical, the rally would still go ahead—his crowds were already on the march. By arriving so early I secured a place front and center. My eyes would be level with the speakers' feet. Above me, I'd get the closest view of their faces. Looking behind me, I'd be able to see the entourage approach.

Also, in this position I'd be able to turn to see the heckling when it started—if it started. Mr. de Valera represented the biggest prize among all the election hecklers, but his henchmen had a robust attitude toward interruptions.

The crowd thickened early and soon began to press around me. My raincoat and sou'wester hat proved equal to the weather and I stayed dry as flour. Judging from the pressing forward, the crowd was going to get even bigger than expected. I held firm, my hands against the backs of the barricade. A man behind me said, "Pity you're not a girl I'm that close to you."

Within minutes I saw a familiar face—my uncle Denny, married to my father's sister. We often visited their house; my father and my aunt had a close and friendly relationship, and my father dearly liked his brother-in-law. That night I knew I mustn't meet him; Mother had warned me to avoid all contact with everybody we knew: "Don't talk to anybody until your father comes home again."

Which meant I had to slink around the countryside like a spy. But from the depths of the crowd and muffled in my raingear, I could look at my uncle without him seeing me—and I didn't like what I saw.

This decent, happy man had changed for the worse. Always round and jolly, he now sagged, gray in the face and with a lonely air. His coat hung from his shoulders like an empty sail, and he stared ahead, unseeing and alone. That told me how ill he was, this famously gregarious host, who kept a most genial public house at the far end of the street.

I looked away and looked back again, to confirm my first impression.

The second look gave me a worse result, and I wondered if my father had seen him lately. This could help me; this could draw my father back into the fold.

But I didn't have time to dwell on it. A moment later I felt a sudden surge of pressure at my back as newcomers piled forward. A chatter sprinkled though the crowd, a buzz of fever.

"He's here," said voices around me, rising in excitement. "He's here."

I heard pipe music and I turned around.

In the distance of the dark night, down the hill of Sarsfield Street, which had been kept empty, a wide and long rectangle of lights moved forward at a steady pace. These were lines of men holding up pitchforks, on which sat flaming bricks of gasoline-soaked peat. I counted ten men across and twenty deep. Under the poor street lighting, they marched in slow step, a triumphal and stately advance guard. Their flames soared and flickered up into the night, lighting their faces, and those faces were as rustic as the burning peat, and as fierce as the fire they carried.

Many yards behind them, in a wide open space all to himself, stepped a piper, with a set of bagpipes as big as a sheep. He played one of those Irish tunes that are called a "march," but they're a slow march, and they stir the blood with their deliberate power.

Behind the piper marched twelve more torchbearers, six on either side of a great white horse. On the horse rode a tall man wrapped in a massive black cloak. Dev had arrived, the Chief, the leader of the "Soldiers of the Legion of the Rearguard," as the republicans now called themselves, the Warriors of Destiny. This was politics as theater—and how we loved it.

The site of the speech had also been chosen for dramatic reasons—the medieval stone arch at the foot of the hill. Under its ancient curve sat a truck whose wooden flatbed had been set with chairs. The torchbearers arrived at the arch and formed two columns of honor guard; within moments the campaign team arrived. Six men ascended the platform by a short wooden ladder, and stood, three by three, to face the crowd.

And then came the seventh man, the One. Sedate and competent, he slid from his horse and walked a slow pace forward. The round spectacles on a beaked nose glinted in the light. With a steady climb he ascended to the truck flatbed and stepped forward for the crowd to see him. Had I been standing farther back I'd have seen how he'd arranged for the arch to frame him. The crowd began to applaud—and then to cheer, and to cheer, and to cheer. Eamon de Valera bowed with a swirl of his wide black cloak, looked behind him to find his chair, and sat down.

The early speakers had little to say: land sales, dairy prices, and a hot national potato—wage increases for the police. Their warm-up act didn't last long, and then the Chief stood up.

He pushed back the hood of his cloak and stood bare-headed, so far forward from under the arch's edge that the rain poured down his long face. He would be fifty the coming October, and he looked older than the mountains. The great black cloak stayed wrapped around him; the glass circles of his spectacles shone. His head turned like a lighthouse, for five, ten, fifteen seconds, scanning the crowd, giving them his beam. Then he threw open the cloak, held out his long white hands, and pronounced, "My beloved people."

Everything about him—the torchbearers, the white horse (or was it winged Pegasus?), the black cloak, the defiance of the elements: mythic. Even as I watched, he seemed to grow taller.

And the voice completed the fabled presence—a wide, rich accent, with a growl when needed, and above all a clarity. Though he seemed never to enunciate, you could hear every word he spoke. He'd been a teacher, I knew; and his experience of a classroom's authority had translated itself upward to the political stage. This man stood there as if rooted—unassailable and fierce. As Large Lily would have said, "He was like something you'd write away for."

The content of de Valera's speech took second place to its form; the meaning of his words mattered less than the impression. At first he didn't seem a spectacular orator—little fire, less brimstone; but as his speech continued I began to feel hypnotized.

Remember—I wasn't there to fall under anybody's spell. Yet I found myself unable to stay outside this experience, to watch as a mere observer. Whether I liked it or not, I was being drawn into the mood of the night.

Epic? Yes—without question, especially to somebody like me, who even at that age was drawn to the legendary and the fabled. Here, though, wasn't I watching that most dangerous of things—a myth being deliberately built? Of course I was! Politics has always reached for whatever it can to secure the hearts and minds of the voters—promises, theatrics, blandishments, snake oil.

It's to my credit and discredit that I went along with it—and perhaps as a boy of eighteen I should have done. I felt the crowd's excitement. I looked up at this man and was awe-stricken. I saw the weather of Ireland on him, the rain falling on his head and flowing down his face, and I felt that he was part of those elements, that he was in some way from the gods.

That's what he wanted me to feel, I know. And yes, he did grow taller as his speech went on, but it was a rising to the occasion that lifted him higher. And the cadences of his voice grew warmer, but it was the warmth of fire. And he became more reassuring, but it was the reassurance of a man who felt that he was about to be confirmed as the most powerful figure in the land.

"Since we got our freedom," he intoned, "the freedom we struggled for, the freedom we roamed the mountains and hills fighting for, the freedom we spilled our blood for. Since we got that freedom, we have been seeing the beginnings of a new slavery. Taxation. The government has paid its members and its friends handsomely. Taxation. Out of our money. Taxation. They drive big cars. Taxation. They live in fine houses. Taxation. What has happened to freedom? Taxation. What have they done to man's most precious possession, the gift of liberty? Taxation."

Not once did he wipe the rain from his face. Not once did he flinch as a fresh February squall swept over him. Not once did he falter, hesitate, stumble, or halt.

And I doubt that any of his three thousand listeners flinched either—I certainly never wiped my face. I stood directly beneath him and next day I had a crick in my neck, because I'd never once ceased to look up at him. If that's not a mesmeric effect, what is?

The words he spoke told us nothing new. We were a proud nation, with an ancient history; we had the resources and the international friendships to go it alone; we deserved our total independence, but we wouldn't have that independence until all the vestiges of a foreign power had been expelled from our rich and storied island.

He'd said it all before; he'd say it all again; this was a man who rode to power on the white horse of his own vision. And made us see that white horse too, and wish we owned it.

Mr. de Valera didn't stay for the adulation; he'd have been there all night. He turned away, descended, didn't look right or left, didn't shake hands—and vanished into the dark of Sarsfield Street. I saw the hawk face in profile one last time and it wasn't made of flesh, it was carved from stone.

Somebody near me asked, "How long was the speech?"

A few voices answered, "Just over the hour."

In the rain, on a cold evening, this man as aloof as a hermit had made us forget for sixty minutes where we were, and made us think only of where we might go. Under his leadership—and he said so—we could go anywhere, be anything, be free.

The crowd began to thin out, and I looked across to see my uncle Denny. He didn't move when the others did; he stood there, silent, head bowed, rain dripping from his hat. His hand rested on a lamppost—I soon realized that he needed its support. He looked dreadfully ill, and it wasn't just the peculiar light from the lamp above his head. I waited until he began to walk, and then I followed him to make sure that he reached his home or someplace that looked safe.

He could have taken a number of shortcuts, but he stayed on the same long, climbing street. I saw him clearly all the way, ten yards ahead. He walked very slowly. Many people hurried past him; nobody stopped him to greet, to talk. They say that when a man knows he's going to die, he'll let nobody recognize him.

With me now twenty yards or so behind, my uncle reached his house, climbed the steps, and paused. He was so weak, trembling and shaking his head. At last he opened the door to his house and went in, slow as a funeral. I never saw him again.

29

"My beloved people," began another political speech that night, "I love you because you're going to vote for me. Since we got our freedom, the freedom we hid under the beds for, the freedom we ran away for, the freedom we spilled other people's blood for—since we got that freedom, we're slaves. But I want you to be *my* slaves. I want you to stop paying your taxes to the government and pay them to *me.* I want a big car out of *your* money. I want to buy myself a fine house out of your money. That's what your money can do for me. That's why I want you to vote for *me*—I want you to elect me as the best man to take your money. I'll buy a bigger car than anyone. I'll buy a better house than anyone."

You can probably guess who the speaker was—but I hadn't a hope of getting into the hall. It seemed as though de Valera's entire audience had simply turned around and gone to hear Blarney.

In front of the doors they milled about like bees at a hive. Many snuck down each side to see if they could get in at the back, but the single rear entrance had been firmly bolted. The big van and the two cars that the show used stood nearby, also locked and protected, with planks leaning against and all around them.

Eventually, one of the wide front doors opened a crack, and a man I had never seen before slipped out and faced us. He closed the door behind him, stood with his back to it, and made an announcement in a strong English accent; he had long greasy hair tied in a ponytail.

"Ladies and gentlemen. My name is Crawford." Though he said *Cwawfod.* "I'm a member of the company and I want to help as many of you to see the show as we can fit into the hall. Now we've assessed the accommodation, and first of all we want you to form a nice orderly queue, two people side by side in a long line."

The people of County Limerick did as Cwawfod asked. It took perhaps five or six minutes, with much good-natured shoving and jostling, and then Cwawfod went down the line, counting. Nobody knew whether they'd get in—until he bisected the queue and said, "That's as many as we can fit. I'm so sowwy, ladies and gentlemen."

Those for whom there hadn't been enough room went away, somewhat reluctantly but in very good humor. They yelled slogans: "Vote for Blarney" and "Up Blarney." The others waited until the doors opened, and Cwawfod started taking the money for the tickets. Cwawfod's eyes, however, were bigger than his belly; many of us were left standing outside the open doors, looking in.

Cwawfod's face impressed me; he looked worn and tired, a lonely man. Or so I thought. Maybe through Cwawfod I'd get to my father—without telling him who I was.

The rain had ceased; the bitter cold had gone from the night. As I looked in and watched the antics on the stage I could see matters a little more objectively. Without question, this traveling show, which was tawdry in many ways, and awkward and goofy, had some magic ingredient. Why else did the audience respond so wildly?

Venetia Kelly was the magic. I know that now; I've known it for a long time. Her presence infused each show, she lifted it above what it seemed to be. That night, she was dressed neck to toe in a long crimson gown that folded about her as though she were a Roman empress. She again spoke a long passage of verse, not from *The Rime of the Ancient Mariner,* but from Tennyson's poem about the death of King Arthur—also a school text.

The silence indoors enfolded us outside; a cough would have echoed around the hills. My eyes never left her. I stood straighter as she came to the moment when the truth is told, when the knight of the Round Table, Sir Bedivere, hurls the sword out into the lake for the third time. He's been cheating, hiding the sword, not doing as the dying king directed.

Looking to the door, she spoke the line of the arm rising from the lake waters to grasp Excalibur as it whirls through the night sky, a woman's arm, "Clothed in white samite, mystic, wonderful."

I shivered; people near me made small murmuring noises. Inside the hall, they closed their eyes in wonder and emotion. And I swear that none of us, inside or out, moved or breathed until she'd reached the fading words "And on the mere the wailing died away."

She was fourteen years older than me and from a different civilization, another world. My mind, my soul, left that drab patch of scrabby ground in front of the church hall and watched as the three "black-stoled, black-hooded" queens placed the dying King Arthur in the barge, "dark as a funeral scarf from stem to stern," and took him off to the Heaven of Avalon. Glorious! But—I wanted to be the only one listening to her. With a reluctance that hurt, I began to understand my father's actions, even if I was being demented by them.

I wondered again that night who chose the order of the show's program. Directly after the dramatic poem, we had more songs, more tumblings, more chasing of maidens (a barmaid this time), and the flockin' tuba. And then came the top of the bill. This time he arrived onstage with Venetia Kelly; she pushed him in a perambulator, and then lifted him out and held him on her knee as she sat on a high stool.

He told jokes again.

"D'you want to hear about my friend MacInerney?"

"Yes, Blarney."

"My friend MacInerney—he had a dog that everyone in the pub knew. For years and years, here comes MacInerney, here comes the dog. Then one day MacInerney arrives into the pub by himself. Alone.

" 'Hah, where's the dog?' says the barman.

" 'Ah, sure I had to put him down,' says MacInerney.

" 'You had to put him down? Was he mad?'

" 'Well,' says MacInerney, 'I can't say he was too pleased.' "

I recognized it—one of my father's favorite jokes. Had he provided it? Was he now finding his feet in the land he'd always longed to travel?

Then came the politics. At first the audience seemed unsure; many of them had just heard similar words from Mr. de Valera. As Blarney warmed, however, they tasted the satire and went with it.

"We're a great country," he declared. "We can do anything. We can drink all day and sleep all night. We can go to Mass every Sunday, and on Monday morning backbite our next-door neighbor."

The audience went, "Ooooooooooh!"

He looked at them, this little wooden doll dressed now in a dark suit and a shirt and tie, he looked all around the hall at them, and I could have sworn that his eye had grown malevolent, and his mouth mean.

"And look at how great we are at having children. Put your hands up any man here who has fathered more than six children."

A small forest of hands rose.

"You see! And we love our children, we love them so much we send them off to England and America. Vote for me and I'll send them off younger, take 'em off your hands."

The edge didn't bother the audience; Blarney brought the house down. When he waved good-bye, he said, "I have to go now—there's a dirty old donkey waiting for me outside, and a widow with a harmonica, and two fellas with flashlamps to guide me."

People streamed away, animated, satisfied. I waited, reasoning that somebody would have to close the doors of the hall. As I hoped, it was Cwawfod.

"Yeh?"

"I enjoyed the performance," I said.

He looked at me suspiciously. "It's only a woadshow."

"I like watching acting," I said.

He softened. "Ahhh," he said, wistful as a girl. "You stagestwuck?"

"Would you like a drink?" I asked, almost saying "dwink."

We walked together like old friends to the first pub we could find. He wore pants so tight I could see the muscles in his legs. The success of the evening had tinged him—he glowed a rose color.

"It's wonderful being part of a box-office success," he said. Two vans, some curtains, a singing acrobat, a tuba player with asthma, and a wooden dummy—and Cwawfod said fondly, "Bwoadway's where you find it."

The pub proved as thronged as the show. We forced a way in; Cwawfod was recognized from his performance with the tickets at the door, and they hailed him as a star. I bought him no drink, never got the chance; the adherents of Kilmallock buried him in liquor—pints, short whiskies, rum, gin—and Cwawfod downed them all like a drinking machine.

A moment came when I could ask him a question.

"Where's everybody else?"

"You gonna follow us? You can come with me in the wagon."

"Do you get new people often? I mean, could I join the show?"

"Oho, that could be twouble, mate. Geezer just joined us, 'arry's his name, and now he's gone, vanished."

"What did he do, get tired and go home?"

"No, mate, vewy mystewious. He's gone. Into thin air. Disappeared. We're askin' no questions."

Before I could press him, and as a cold tide flowed down my spine, some farmer grabbed him, and soon Cwawfod was telling them about his "gweat woles" in the West End of London.

Cwawfod dismissed me—simple as that. He next found a lady, began to chat to her, and waved me off. Her name was Philomena and he exulted (mystifying to me in those days), "Oh, I'm going to have my Phil."

The chill of it, the bewildering confusion. What had he told me—that my father had disappeared? *Disappeared?* In obviously strange circumstances? Should I go to the police?

There's a noise I make to myself, a sort of "nnnngg" sound, when I'm frightened, and I heard it now. In that crowded pub I began to make that sound—so I fled to the street, the wet, shining street, and heard myself in the night go on and on in that whimpering sound.

I don't recall doing it, but I went to the car, started it, and drove out of that town. Nor did I recall parking it sometime later in a woodland lane, off the road and out of sight, and going to sleep. Yet somewhere along the road between Kilmallock and our home at Goldenfields, I went to sleep in the car. When I awoke I knew that I'd been dreaming of the strange hawklike face of Eamon de Valera, and of a white-sleeved arm reaching up from a dark lake. I believe that I slept for no more than an hour. I hadn't eaten, and in the deeps of the night, panic dropped a rock on my chest and woke me up.

30

Where—and how—do you begin to search for a missing parent? I huddled in the car, in my coat, not able to see a thing in the dark. The trees took their turn at raining; each drip from a bough hit the roof of the car like a hammer. It seems to me that I waited—for what, I can't say. Perhaps for the morning light, because it certainly knocked some sense into me. Though now thoroughly frightened, I sat, and thought, and compiled in my head a little calendar of events. It's how I regroup my life to this day.

Friday, 29 January 1932: In Dublin, a hundred miles away, the Dáil (pronounced *daw-il,* it means "parliament" or "forum") is dissolved.

Saturday, 30 January: We hear the news and are delighted that a general election will be held; we hope the government will be thrown out of office. My father goes about the place chanting, "The conduct of public affairs for private advantage."

Sunday, 31 January: Missy Casey and her Valentine card to herself. Frost between my parents. My father and I discuss the election as we drive to see Venetia Kelly's Traveling Show in Cashel. He decides he's not coming home. I go back alone.

Monday, 1 February: I break the news to Mother. She asks me to pursue my father and fetch him home. I refuse.

Tuesday, 2 February: I refuse again.

Wednesday, 3 February: I refuse a third time, until Mother discovers that all our money is missing. I set off to pick up the trail, discover they're coming back to Cashel, and try to get out of it all that way. Mother dismisses my argument that we should wait and see.

Thursday, 4 February: I go to Mitchelstown, see my father, but never get to have a word with him. I go back home and Mother shouts at me.

Friday, 5 February: They play Doneraile; my father ignores and evades me.

Saturday, 6 February: They play Buttevant; again, my father won't speak to me.

(Unimportant and Very Brief Digression: The first steeplechase in the world is alleged to have been run from the church steeple of Doneraile to the church steeple of Buttevant and back again in 1752; hence the term "point-to-point.")

Sunday, 7 February: Kilmallock and de Valera's rally, and Cwawfod; I don't see my father; he doesn't come out of the hall. He has, I'm told, vanished into thin air.

Afraid to go home empty-handed again, I sleep in the car, wake up lonely and cold, and find myself more or less in shock.

Now I had to go home—what else could I do? The news not only shocked Mother, it reduced her. In front of my eyes she aged. She sat down and stared at me—just stared into my eyes, diminished in the space of minutes. Was it fear that had darkened her own eyes? Or, if the eyes are the windows of the soul, had her soul just left her body?

I had to speak. "Mother, you don't think he's dead, do you?"

"It's worse than that." Her voice had become as dull as a slack drum.

"What should I do?"

She didn't answer.

"Should we be making inquiries?"

Not a word came back—nothing but defeated silence. I had the bizarre thought *Is this how soldiers are when they lose a battle?*

"Mother, if . . . if there was something I knew to do . . ."

I sat down beside her. The trap, as I could see, was constructed of discretion and scandal; whom could I ask at all?

When a wind fills my sails, I go where it takes me—and often with some force. And I've been doing it since that morning. I eased myself from Mother's beaten and mute presence and tore into the kitchen.

Under Lily's amazed eyes, I grabbed food of all kinds, slammed it into boxes and bags. Upstairs, I took extra clothes, spare boots and shoes. I raided my own cashbox; I rarely spent money and had several hundred stashed away. From the yard I hauled a five-gallon carboy to fill with gasoline and carry as a spare. Moving silently and with enraged speed, I stowed the car until I figured that I had enough provisions to last me weeks.

Dashing back into the kitchen, I wrote a note—*Dear Mother, I'll find him*—and drove away faster than a rocket. I had a week and one day before my job in the village on polling day.

Five miles along, the steam went out of me. I pulled the car over to the side of the road by an old stone quarry, and climbed out. I had no plan. Where in God's name could I begin to look? Not the police. Nor did the show know where he was. And I didn't want to ask them. Had he left the country? If he'd gone from the area, then there was no point in looking for him.

We have limestone as our bedrock; it gives the horses good bones. Staring at the winter-gray striations and white rock faces in that old limestone quarry gave me nothing back but misery. Sometimes out of misery—because you have to climb out of it—ideas come.

So I reckoned that since he'd run away to join the circus, he'd likely stay somewhere within the orbit of the circus. Why would he distance himself from the people he had just so passionately joined?

Unless he'd had a row with one of them, which was the only reason I could think of for his disappearance. Cwawfod's "mysterious" reference would suggest some difficulty, wouldn't it? And if so, my father's habit was to let things cool down and then reenter. That gave me the first idea of a plan.

Second, I began to put together the things my father liked to do. He liked to socialize and had a lot of friends, including some who would probably ask no questions if he dropped in and asked for a bed for the night. At this thought, some comfort enrobed me—until the next consideration hit me like a chisel to the chest.

What if he'd fallen ill? What if they'd taken him to some hospital, because they couldn't cope with him on the road? And, not sure of their responsibility for him, had just left him there? I can tell you now, and it's useful for you to know this—those were the moments when I learned how to keep panic at bay.

I filled the next several days with extraordinary activity. I behaved like "a red-bottomed bee," to quote Mother. I roamed all over, and as I did so, a kind of guidance began to emerge, like a finger pointing from the clouds.

Get a map. You couldn't buy a local map in those days; it had to be a map of the country. *In any case maps don't show which towns have hospitals and which don't. But I need a map to follow the show. In other words, go looking for him loose and tight, search among hospitals and his friends, and shadow the show every alternate night.*

And so my thoughts went; and so my search began. I hopped back into the car and headed for the city of Limerick.

More rain; I half-slipped on the wet steps of Barringtons Hospital. At the booth inside the door I made my inquiry.

"We do," said the porter. "We do have him. He's up in the General Ward. Go up the stairs and he's down the corridor, second last door on the left."

I went back out and bought a bag of apples from the woman at the stall. She looked at me with pity.

"If he's dying, apples is no good to him."

Inside again, I established the "second last door on the left" by finding the last door on the left and turning back. A nurse with a great white bonnet like a sail said, "You don't look sick at all."

"I'm looking for Mr. Harry MacCarthy."

"Thank God! Take him home with you, it'd give us peace and ease. He's down there, that far bed."

The relief! The exhaled, gasping relief!

"Is he all right?"

"The leg'll mend but he won't." She answered my puzzled expression by saying, "People are born that way."

And so he was—Harry MacCarthy, a man with a small face and a shock of vertical black hair. Isn't there a religion somewhere in which the men grow a topknot so that God can lift them up to Heaven?

"Who are you?" He took sourness to new heights.

I said, "I have the wrong man."

"Do you smoke?"

I shook my head.

"What use are you, so?"

That wasn't all he said. If language makes kinship he was Billy Flock's brother. I said, "What happened to you anyway?"

"Flockin' pony. Couldn't jump the flockin' wire."

I said, "They have to be trained to jump wire."

"How the flock would you know?"

"Would you like an apple, Mr. MacCarthy?"

"Ah, flock off with yourself."

Which I did, my nostrils filled with disinfectant, my heart with disappointment.

The nurse with the great bonnet did me a kindness. I told her I was traveling through, that I'd heard a friend of my father's was in a hospital in the area; where else might he be? She wrote a list of hospitals and I thanked her.

As I walked away, she said, "And when you find your father, give him an earful for not telling you where he is."

31

I searched every hospital I could find. I met nuns and nurses and patients and porters. At last I took a nun into my confidence; she had an accent thick as a bog and the pointed face of a medieval aristocrat. She told me that they had strict rules about notifying next of kin. My father would have had to tell the hospital whom they should contact.

But if he was unconscious?

"Then we'd find out who he was, and we'd tell the guards and they'd tell the family."

By the time I had that conversation, at the end of my first day, I'd been to seven hospitals in all, some big, some small, all redeemingly calm. In the Glentworth Hotel, I ate a steak. That night I slept longer than an infant.

I'd ascertained from Cwawfod that the show would play a series of different towns, some one-night stands, some two and some three nights, circling back finally to Cashel after the election. On the map, when you trace those weeks, their travels form two loose circles; I see them now as twin breast-shaped loops.

Here's another little calendar of events:

Sunday night, 7 February (actually the small hours of Monday morning): I go home; Mother berates me even though she sees that I'm shivering and shaking—and very hungry. I tell her about the disappearance and she folds like a cloth.

Monday, 8 February: I leave the house, mad with intent, I buy a map of Ireland, I stride those hospital corridors, and I'm like a ravening hound, I'm hell-bent on finding him.

Tuesday, 9 February: Early, I arrive in Dromcolloher, find the hall, meet Cwawfod again, give him some food from home, and tack myself onto his coattails. Each night, Cwawfod tells me, they have a full house. On some days they've been giving two performances; in Buttevant, they'd given a third—they played it early in the day, because people were flocking to hear Blarney and his political speeches.

They'd have played Dromcolloher three times, Cwawfod said, and packed the house every time, but the priest who controlled the hall hated all theatricals. When he heard of Blarney's satire on Mr. de Valera's speech, the priest came down to the hall next morning as they loaded and ranted at them.

In Dromcolloher too, I get myself a room in a bed and breakfast. Cwawfod's coy about the members of the cast and where they're staying. I ask about "the man who vanished" and he shakes his head.

That night I can't bear to go to the show, but I hang around afterward and I see Venetia Kelly and her mother climb into a magnificent car—that's the only word for it, *magnificent*—and drive away without a glance toward me. I think about following them but it's night and they'll see my lights, and instead I go to the door, but once again they close the door on me, and I hear it being bolted from the inside.

I wait, hiding in a place where I can see what happens next. But nothing happens next; the company is obviously going to sleep in the hall, because at around one o'clock in the morning the last dim light of a candle, lamp, or flashlight goes out and I'm alone in the dark and cold—again. No sign of my father.

Which is when the shadowing of the show began.

Never too far away from me, and often within sight, seen in the distance at the top or bottom of some long hill out in the countryside—that's how I saw the caravanserai, such as it was, whenever it set forth into the morning air. From town to village we went, the vans led by two cars, packed with people, and I in the distance, behind them.

Slowly, I began to enforce a routine upon myself. I'd follow them to the hall, make sure I could find it again, and then establish a place to stay for the night. Then I'd hang around, peering here and there. Ask questions in the town as to where the people from the traveling show were staying. Inspect each house, each bed-and-breakfast place, and try to guess where my father might be making his bed for the night—that is, if he had come back and I hadn't been told. You see? I was already suspicious that something was rotten in this particular little state.

In the evening, I'd arrive at least an hour before they were due to begin their show. I'd buy my ticket and sit near the back, looking around me all the time in case my father came into the hall. Then I'd move out before the show ended, go around to the back of the hall, and wait until the performers came out.

This proved the most difficult part. I'm not good at lurking shadily, nor am I easy to hide. Furthermore, I looked very like my father. So there I'd stand, at the back door to some whitewashed, ratty old building, and hear the distant laughter of the audience, still delighted, always chattering, as they walked away. I'd feel lower and lower and then the light would begin to go dim inside the hall, as the company doused the lamps and candles, and turned off the rare electricity.

Night after night I played that scene. And night after night it refused to develop as I wished. In fact, it always played out more or less in exactly the same way.

First of all, the various company people appeared at the back door of the hall. They stood there and debated whether to load the truck that night or wait until the morning. If they were going to another town for accommodation, Cwawfod made them load there and then; if not they often came back in the morning. In either case they stood around, with me a little distance away in half-shadow but within earshot, and waited until "the ladies," as they called them, appeared.

Much later, I discovered that they'd been told to behave as though I were some strange sort of hanger-on, a pest, a kind of shy Stage-Door

Johnnie. Some of them, especially Cwawfod, felt very bad about that when they eventually came to know me.

And finally, the two ladies. Tall and mysterious, they climbed into the wonderful, ghostly car. The ghostly car that never seemed to park anywhere near the hall, the ghostly, ethereal limousine that I couldn't find in any of those towns.

32

It wasn't going so well, was it? Two days trawling through hospitals, three days pursuing the show, not a trace of my father. He was, among many other things, a stubborn man; if he'd had a row, he could have walked out, and felt too proud to come home. In which case he'd have gone to a house that he knew and where he felt safe. When I thought about that, I knew another world in which to look for him, because my father and his friends had one abiding love in common—horses.

Where I grew up, every pub knew when the local hunt met. In season, which included February, men and women went hunting, sometimes twice, three times a week. My father loved it. Even if we didn't have a hunter that was ready or right, he borrowed a horse or followed in the car along the small roads.

That week, if he'd gone to a friend's house, he'd surely be attending a hunt meet in the village of Knockainey. The hunt alone didn't dictate my choice; ten years earlier, I'd roamed Knockainey with my father. Few places in Ireland have more history. Even the goddess Anne lived there: "Knock" means a hill, and "ainey" means "of Anne."

We went there more than once—enchanting days, poking at the

mounds and peering at the stones. He and I searched the long grass, trying to find the door to the Underworld, my father encouraging me to believe that one day we'd find gold. And we'd stop and stand still, listening for fairy music from beneath the ground. We never heard any—which simply meant, he said, that we hadn't gone there on a good day for music.

The Scarteens are one of the oldest foxhunts in the world, and my father had often ridden to them. Their history compelled him; the Ryans had owned this pack for centuries. He loved the family's colorful nature, and told everybody the story of the Requiem Mass.

It was being held for a member of the family lost in the Great War when a man burst into the church and interrupted the ceremony by shouting, "The master is saved, the master is saved!" A guard on the mail train passing nearby had sorted a postcard from a German officer, which said that "Mr. Ryan is taken prisoner but quite well—unwounded." As the train spooled through countryside near the Ryan household, the guard wrote, *The master is saved,* on strips of paper, which he then threw out the window of the caboose.

Seventy, maybe eighty people gathered that morning in Knockainey. Only a few wore the red coats, the "hunting pink." My father never did, so I looked for a man in a tweed jacket and jodhpurs and found plenty, but he wasn't one of them.

Foxhounds stand tall; they're friendly dogs. The Scarteen hounds are black and tan in color and it's a tribute to the affection felt for the hunt that even though they're known as the Scarteen Black and Tans, they never got confused with the British forces in Ireland during the War of Independence, in their hated black tunics and their khaki pants.

I rode in the hunt that morning. As I stood caressing the hounds' heads and talking to the whipper-in, and knowing from the way he asked about my family that he hadn't seen my father and hadn't heard of our scandal, another man walked over and said, "Aren't you young MacCarthy?"

He couldn't ride, he'd hurt his hip; he was a friend of my father's. The man who was supposed to ride his horse hadn't turned up, he said, and he wanted the horse to have a good outing before running him in a steeplechase the following week, and he wanted to know if I'd try on the pair of riding trousers he had in the car?

I rode for four hours.

Today, older and more thoughtful, I know why I did it: I was hunting for my father. In some mad fit I thought I might see him. I remember thinking, *He might be out there, at the edge of some grove of trees, or standing on top of a hill, and he'll wave to me as I ride by, and I'll wheel around and ride back to him, and I'll steady the horse while he swings up behind me.*

Have you ever hunted? On a horse, a big horse? Across fields and over ditches and stone walls? You should try it—not for the pursuit of the fox; I never liked that part, and I always reined back if a kill looked likely. I loved it for the sheer thrill of the ride. I'll try to describe it to you, because it'll tell you something about me that will explain—or help you to understand better—some of what's to come, some of what I did, the nerve I showed.

First of all, a high horse is a big horse. You climb up, and the ground is a long way down, especially if you're tall. That morning I mounted an animal eighteen hands high, that's six feet tall at the withers, where the front of the saddle sits, meaning my head was more than twelve feet off the ground. Second, a big horse is a wide horse, and since so much of your work involves talking to the horse with your knees, you have a job of work to do. Third, you don't know until the horse moves off what kind of mover she is. Lady Limerick, gray and high, was seven years old and had more than a bit of a dancer in her.

But, fourth and finally, wait until you're flat out across a field. I could hardly hold her—it took a good ten minutes to get her under my hands; after that, Paradise. I had no hat that day, which is how I preferred to ride, and the wind touched every root of every hair on my head. Lady Limerick was so strong that I stood in the stirrups for a lot of the time, "listening" to my legs and holding her down as much as I could with my hands.

In the etiquette of hunting, you mustn't overtake the master. More than once I almost had to wheel her out of the pack. Eventually, I took her over to one side and rode on the fringes, ready to wheel away until I knew I had her under control. And when she knew I had taken full command, then she allowed me to ride her as I wanted.

If you ever do ride, watch out for the moment when you take a wall or a ditch at full speed. The faint riders slow down; I, my father's son in some respects, rode faster. When Lady Limerick lunged up into the sky at our first wall, I lay forward on her, feeling her huge shoulders under me, and excited enough for heart failure. And when she came down out of the sky and I hadn't fallen, and I leaned back onto her, I almost laughed out loud.

I didn't see my father that day with that hunt. I saw many other things but not a red-haired man standing by some wall somewhere watching the rise and fall of the riders going over and being startled to see his son among them.

I saw the wild surge of the hounds as they "found" a scent and took off with the sound of the huntsman's heavenly choir, the baying of a pack, but I never saw a red-haired man leaning against a tree at the outer edge of a copse and holding out his arms in delight as the hunt streamed down the hill.

And I saw the fox go to ground, into a covert on the side of a small hill, a den of furze and limestone and the hounds wheeling, jawing, and pawing outside, but I never saw a red-haired man on top of that hill looking down and nodding his agreement as the master and the whipper-in withdrew in the knowledge that the fox had won the day.

"Hunting," said my father, "was invented by-by-by the gods so that Man could feel what it's like to be a god once in a while."

But the old gods of Knockainey didn't give me my father when I hunted for him. That night, however, the show was to play a nearby town called Charleville—where, once again, everything changed.

33

By now I knew that I wasn't doing this solely for Mother. I missed my father. I missed him every moment of every day. When I awoke in the morning, my heart sank at the thought that once again he wouldn't be at the breakfast table. And therefore couldn't ask me, as he often did on some farm matter or other, "What-what-what would you advise?"

Although I know now that he was teaching me, training me, I didn't feel that at the time. Instead I felt that I was part of the place and its systems, that I wasn't there merely to eat, drink, go to school, come home, eat and drink again, and go to sleep—I felt useful. Now that he was gone, that was gone.

And I missed the sound of his voice, and the way it filled the places he inhabited. By that, I don't mean that he was loud and overbearing; it's just that he seemed to be the natural sound for the places in which I saw him—as natural as a rushing noise from a river, a wind in the trees.

I missed too his interplay with Mother, the responses she drew from him, his earnest intent to answer every question she asked, his desire to please her, his evident wish to give her credit for everything that happened every day, including the rising of the sun. Yes, I know that a coolness had seemed to exist between them now and then, but they were a natural couple, buck and doe.

For instance, Mother had always lived in general from one lift of her spirits to the next. In between, she trod what my father called "the vale of melancholy," often not raising her eyes for almost a full day.

"Your mother's in the vale of melancholy," he'd say when I was a little boy. "We'll leave her by herself for a bit and then we'll go and cheer her up."

I had visions of some dark cleft in some high brooding mountains, like the engravings in the old books that we had. To be fair, she never ruled people with her moods; she tried to keep them to herself, but they leaked from her, leaked all over the household.

My father was her elixir—he and he alone knew how to break such a run, how to race down into her glen of despair, grab her, and hustle her out of there and up into the sunshine. I couldn't do it; as a boy I tried, with stories, with impersonations. Once or twice I shook her into laughter with a description of a neighbor or a reenacted scene from the forge or a fracas from one of the village shops, but only my father could make the restoration last.

He did it by generating good news, usually with a compliment thrown in. In the evening he'd say, "You-you-you have an admirer."

Unable not to be curious, she'd raise her head from the sewing or darning and look at him, her eyes, but not her lips, speaking the question "Who?"

My father would then mention the name of somebody they had met, some dashing man, married, or a bachelor known to be exciting, a rake, maybe, and Mother would say, "Oh?"

To which my father would then say, "He-he-he needn't go sloping around here, that's for sure, if he knows what's good for him. And anyway I think he's partly a lunatic. They-they-they say you can see him lurching up the hills and through the woods when there's a full moon."

That always got her—the full moon; she'd go against her own mood and laugh. Now, of course, she realized that if my father truly had run away with this actress, he had taken her elixir with him and somebody else was drinking it.

As for me—I missed above all the sudden little things that happened so often, that moment in which he would call or beckon and say, when I reached him, "I've-I've-I've something to show you." And it would be a new and much lighter model of horseshoe that he'd picked up at the forge, or a quotation that he'd found in the newspaper or one of his books and had scribbled down on the back of an envelope.

I didn't know how much I loved these things until I no longer had them, which is an echo of a saying Mother now uttered every day: "You never miss the water 'til the well runs dry."

In Charleville, the town named for King Charles II, the well wasn't dry—but it did feel fouled at first. Not because my father reappeared, which he did. Normal as the night, he stood at the door to the hall, taking the money and handing out the tickets—and a new pain began.

I hung back, waiting until the last tickets were sold; then I could grab a word with him. As people approached the door and saw him, they nudged one another and pointed him out. I overheard their first remarks: "That's the fella that ran away from his wife and farm"; and, "Him selling the tickets—is he the dirty oul' fella ran off after the woman in the show?"

My father had acquired a notoriety; my family was being marked as scandalous; perhaps audiences were larger because they wanted to see his paramour; this invoiced feelings of deep, deep shame.

I stepped back farther into the shadows, so as not to be seen—and to watch more closely. Yes, the people of Charleville were indeed pointing him out, and yes, they were indeed sniggering. Under my clothes, I felt the slime of chagrin pour down my body, from my head and neck down my shoulders and rib cage, down my stomach and thighs.

When it seemed as if all the people had entered the hall and I came forward to buy my ticket, my father ran. He ducked away from me, raced around the side of the hall, and disappeared. I got in free, but that wasn't the bonus I had sought.

That night, Blarney made much of what he called "the politician's promises." The country rang with them and Blarney capitalized. He seemed to know which politician was making the most outrageous promises and he lampooned them without mercy.

Each evening, his performance began with the words "I'm the most promising politician in Ireland—I'll promise you anything." The audience was laughing already. With no reference to the fact that he sat on Venetia Kelly's knee, he looked out over the audience, his red mouth opening and closing slowly in chunks as he launched into his satirical tirade.

"I'll promise you anything. I'll get wives for men with no teeth. I'll get husbands for women with bandy legs. I'll give every man, woman, and child here money. Cash. Into your hand. For free. There'll be a barrel of drink at every crossroads and a tube sticking out of it and all you'll have to do is suck on it. Free for every man, woman, and child. But the clergy'll have to pay."

Venetia Kelly, serene as the moon, sat and looked on and Blarney ranted, his words driving spikes into the national spirit.

"How many farmers are here tonight? Put up your hands."

As hands rose all over the hall, he peered across their ranks.

"Too many. Now I'm going to work a miracle. I'm going to please the farmers!" and everybody roared with laughter. Admiration too for the shrewdness of the satire; every politician outside the big cities knew that the farmers carried the key to the election, and they'd been notorious for complaining about everything.

"In fact," he went on, "I'm going to start by fixing the weather. Every year, July and August are going to be fine, and the harvest'll be great."

More laughter.

"And September'll always be lovely. For the other ten months of the year, I'm going to give ye all grants. Money. Into the heels of yer fists. So that ye never have to work again. Isn't that what ye've always wanted?"

Loud cheers rang out. He paused and looked all around, whispered something to Venetia. When she nodded, Blarney turned to the audience again.

"But that mightn't be a great idea. Because what'll the farmers have to complain about then? I call it—soothing the baby."

How they howled as he filleted them. He judged it with a fine touch, and he seemed to know that his darts would become the currency of the next day's local conversation.

Sometimes he played games with the audience.

"Ask me for a wish," he'd say. "Come on, ask me for a wish and I'll grant you a wish."

Some foolish person would call out, "I'd like a wish, Blarney."

"What's your wish?"

"I wish for money, a ton of it."

"Your wish is granted. When you go home tonight your house'll be burned down and you'll get a ton of money from the insurance company."

That night in Charleville, Blarney came out and asked, "How many people in this audience trust either Mr. de Valera or Mr. Cosgrave?"

Many hands went up.

"What would you trust them with?"

Nobody answered.

Blarney pressed. "Would you trust them with your money?"

They laughed—some uneasily, I felt. And nobody answered.

"Would you trust them with a gun?"

Like the sound of some massive snake, the intake of breath hissed through the hall.

"I suppose," said Blarney, "you could trust them with your womenfolk." Laughter. "And God knows you could trust your womenfolk with them." Much more laughter.

Then he delivered the punch. "But could you trust them with your children's future?"

Nobody laughed.

34

Blarney's parting shot made an uncomfortable night worse. While waiting for the show to begin, I'd heard more criticism of my father. "What kind of a fool is he? Hasn't he a big farm over near Cashel?" And, "Ah, he's off with this young one outta the show, you'll see her in a bit." And, "Four hundred acres nearly, and he walked away from the whole thing. Something dirty there." When Venetia Kelly first appeared as Portia, two people behind me sniggered and one said, "That's her, that's the bike the oul' fella is ridin'."

After the show, I heard it too. "What did you think of her?" And, "Jaysus, if I saw her first, that oul' fella wouldn't get a look in." And, "You could ride her in the Grand National."

I cringed. I wanted to ream them, but I didn't have the courage. And when they'd gone from the hall, which was up a lane, I followed them down the slope to the street, walking behind one group and then another, trying to hear their comments. Mostly, they were laughing—which also felt filthy and awful.

And then my life changed forever. Altered for all time by a single gesture.

When we look back in wonder at the moments when Fate shows itself, it's never that things might not have happened; it's that they might have happened differently, that one might have been inserted into a particular orbit at a different angle and consequently have taken different actions, producing a different outcome.

I turned away from the sneering mockers and stumbled in the dark, almost falling over Charleville's high double curb. As I steadied myself I saw a movement, a flash of light across the street. I looked over at a wide, elegant house, and saw the movement again. A hand in a white sleeve was waving, beckoning. Was it waving at me? I looked all around; nobody stood near.

Now both hands, both white arms, came through the door and—no question—they were waving in my direction. Up and down they went, like a semaphore.

I walked toward the house. If the arms didn't belong to somebody who knew me, at least their gesture showed enough quirkiness to be worth investigating. As I approached, one arm withdrew, and the other changed its movement; it stopped waving and beckoned. Behind me, I couldn't see a soul—therefore the beckoning had to be for me. From the open door came a glorious female voice singing something that sounded like Italian opera.

A bright lamp lit the hallway. I approached, peering forward, feeling my way, looking for details. The hand beckoned again and now that I'd come within a yard or two of the open door I could see into the hallway. The upper half of the walls had a lemon paper on them, with faint and lovely trees. Below a rail at waist height spread a firm anaglypta paper, chocolate-colored, with geometric patterns. Somebody with taste and a sense of color lived here.

The arms had disappeared but the voice kept singing. I ventured fully into the doorway, wondering what to do next, and now I stood in the empty hall. Should I follow the siren call?

But the voice was fading as though the singer were moving far away; they do that in legends to draw the hero farther in. And then the voice grew strong again and she appeared. I had never seen this woman close up but I knew who she was—the older of the two who had led my father through the lit doorway that night in Cashel, that night that now seemed so long ago, but was less than two weeks past.

Graceful and smooth, she walked to me in a glide. I stood there, not knowing what to do. Next she held out both of her hands, palms down, to take both of mine.

"I," she said, with a pause, "am Sarah Kelly. The actress."

As distinct, I thought out of nowhere, *from Sarah Kelly the Pope. Or the train driver.*

That was how we met; we would know each other until she died, many, many years later.

She continued, "And you're Ben. Without a shadow of doubt. You're so like him. Let me have a look at you. Oh, my—you're so big, so handsome. You look so refined!"

Since Missy Casey doesn't count, this was the first compliment I'd ever had from a real woman. My mind lurched. *How much of this can I ever tell Mother?*

But my second thought slammed in like a ramrod: *Where's my father?*

She guessed it and said, "He's in here. We had to take him out of circulation for a while. Do you like my new home?"

I began to say, "Is he all right?" but she interrupted my effort and said, "Look."

Holding on to me with one hand, she lifted the lamp from the hall table and led me into the nearest room. Her hand was as soft as a glove.

I had an impression of robin's-egg-blue walls, turquoise armchairs, paintings of mountains. On a dark piano sat rows of photographs. The raised lamp drew me to look at them—mostly posed shots of Sarah Kelly, and some of Venetia when an infant and a child, though none of Venetia as an adult. One by one Sarah held up the photographs and told me each narrative:

"This is me in *As You Like It.* And this is me in *The Well of the Saints.* Mr. Yeats especially likes that picture. And this is me with Mr. Yeats. His wife was quite jealous of me."

Sarah had a number of stratagems for getting attention, most obviously a low tone, so that one had to lean in to hear her, and—even more effective—she had an upward inflection at the end of each sentence, suggesting that she always wanted an answer. I perceived this only many years later; I was too young that night, and too afraid, and I hadn't yet learned how to observe people and make mental notes of how they behaved.

I know that I've already described Sarah as she was earlier in her life, as she narrated it to me, and then later in life, how she was in the years I visited her near Dublin. However, so that you can fix her in your own mind—and you should—let me recall her at that moment in Charleville.

To begin with, I've always been accustomed to tall women—Mother, Miss Fay, Large Lily, who was not only tall but, well, large. Their tallness and Sarah's differed, and the difference came from two factors—the way Sarah held herself, and the way she moved.

James Clare told me you should always dance as if there were nobody watching you, and you should always sing as if there were nobody listening to you. Sarah carried herself as though onstage all the time. When she came into a room—that was an entrance. Every time she left—that was an exit. And if she sat, rose, or made a gesture, she seemed upstage of everybody else—unless she wanted to be downstage.

In the first few minutes of that meeting, she walked about the place like a character in a Russian play—all demeanor and no force, all mood and no challenge.

She kept her voice low, she looked directly into my eyes, and from time to time she touched my arm—not a grip, not a slap, a feather's touch, an inclusion. I had no consciousness of people's age in those days; forty, sixty, eighty—it meant nothing to me, it never does to the young; people were old or they weren't, and Sarah was old. But young-old, not ancient; she was within reach, like an aunt.

And she was exquisite, what would later be called "movie-star beautiful." She tossed her hair back frequently, she freed my hand from hers and groomed her tresses. Notwithstanding my anxiety of the moment, I stole a look at her face and her figure when I could.

Also, and to my surprise, I liked her so much. For some reason that I hadn't yet defined, I was prepared for two-way hostility. It never happened; she defused that possibility with an attitude kinder than comfort.

She used her hands a great deal—even the hand carrying the lamp waved about, casting shadows on the walls, and making these rich little rooms into alluring caves. I glimpsed a few more oil paintings on the walls, tall, serious portraits, and some more mountains, and lavish drapes hung from floor to ceiling, and I walked by a chair of brilliant yellow. Sarah talked on and on in that voice to which I could—and eventually did—listen all day.

If I had to sum up my impression of Sarah Kelly as I saw her in the first few minutes of that meeting, I'd say: tall, not a bone out of place, by which I mean, not angular or awkward; a sweeter face than one could imagine, so gentle close up that I can't believe it translated to an audience at the back of a theater; and yet—power. Power in the way you know steel is strong just by looking at it. Power like a big cat who doesn't have to hurry, because the kill will be there when wanted.

I have to say, though, that I found her thrilling to be near because of the attention she exuded; nobody else had ever made me feel like that. And she was kind to me, smiling, touching my arm, thoughtful, almost loving, as when she smiled at me and said, "I'll take you into the living room now."

35

She led, I followed—and there he sat. My father. Close up in this light, he looked tired. Apart from the punched brogue shoes, I didn't recognize his clothes—a thin check shirt, a jacket that I'd never seen, gabardine pants. At the door of the hall he'd worn his overcoat; he'd had it with him since Cashel. Yet I have to say that he seemed peaceful—so peaceful and natural that once again the nature of the circumstances seemed impossible to believe.

Sarah hovered at the door, then stepped out of sight with a little wave to me, though I'm certain she stayed within earshot.

We imagine in advance, don't we, the feelings that will surface at such moments? I had long anticipated what it might be like when I confronted him for the first time—affection, tears, maybe. The imaginings had escalated when I first learned that he had "disappeared," and I thought only of the relief I'd feel if and when I found him.

This meeting didn't go like that: Fear stuck its nose in, as fear so often does. And as we all know, fear often turns to anger in order to speak what it must.

I said, and I know I was rough in my tone, "Why'd you run away from me tonight?"

"Here. Sit-sit-sit down." He patted the couch.

"D'you want to come home with me? I have the car here."

"How-how-how are you?"

"Will we go, so?"

He shifted on the sofa.

A lovely room—I observed that much. Beige flock wallpaper, butter-colored cushions. How many rooms did this house have?

"Will we go?" I insisted.

Constitutionally my father had little ability to refuse any request from anybody. Which, I suppose, is why and how we all found ourselves in this situation.

"How-how-how's the car?"

Nothing about this—nothing—made sense. But in the ordinary scheme of everyday life, nothing made sense of the Great War or the 1916 Rebellion or the guerrillas in the hills or the wild arguments over the treaty or the Civil War or the fellow from the village with the razor-blade slashes up and down his legs. Nothing on any scale makes sense if you're enmeshed in something senseless. As this was.

My father said, "Did-did-did you get something to eat?"

I decided to change tack. If I got off the subject of his possible homecoming, I might find out something useful about the life he was living.

I said, "Where are you traveling next?"

"Isn't it a pity-pity-pity you haven't a vote yet?"

You know that moment when a piece of metal breaks loose from something, and it screams as it comes in contact at speed with other metal? That's how the questions screamed through my mind—high shrieks, with little or no control attached. I wanted to ask: *Where do you sleep at night? What kind of bed? Is there somebody else in it with you?*

Shaving was my father's ritual, his High Mass, a time of mountainous lather and walrus grunts, a cry of delight or calamity now and then, and at the end wild praise for his results.

"Isn't that marvelous?" he'd say over and over, his hand fingering his chin like a housewife buying a cauliflower. Stroking the flourishing mustache, he'd sometimes add, "I've great growth in me."

I'd seen this ritual for as long as I could remember, perched beside him and reveling in the mighty importance. Now I wondered if he'd shaved at all in the past two days. And his mouth was twisted in a kind of ruined, unhappy line.

I also wanted to ask: *Who's feeding you? What kind of food are you eating? Are you eating enough?* My father loved his food more than a gourmand, and he loved Mother's cooking—and not just to eat it, but to talk about it. "The Nobel Prize for carrots was awarded today," he'd begin, or the Nobel Prize for mashed potatoes, or the Nobel Prize for chicken broth. Or he'd cry out, "The Nobel Prize for cooking was shared this year among the following nominees; Louise MacCarthy for her baked parsnips; Mamzelle Louise Hopkins for her leg of pork; Mrs. Harry MacCarthy for her apple tart."

To my eye this didn't look like a man who had awarded a Nobel Prize recently.

But I didn't ask any food questions or shaving questions or indeed any more questions. Instead, my shrewd intentions collapsed and I sat there and told him, in a voice like a mad fellow's, what I felt.

"I've been looking for you everywhere. I've seen the show so many nights, I was always in the hall or very near at hand, and I've stood there freezing and often in the rain until nearly the dawn watching the lamps in so many bed-and-breakfast places finally go out, sometimes at three o'clock in the morning, wondering if you were the fellow in that room, behind that window. And all you could do was run away from me." I stopped—and added, "And I'd rather go hungry than do without you anymore."

He listened, sitting right beside me, so close that I could feel the warmth of his heavy torso beside me, and the heave of his breathing, so close that I could tell him all this in a low voice, so close that I could have reached out and touched him—but I wasn't able to, I just couldn't do it.

And so close that I saw the tear trickling down the side of his profile that was turned to me. I couldn't see him full face on, and I regretted that, and he didn't turn to me, not even when he asked, "How-how-how is your mother?"

No chance to answer—we were interrupted. He heard the footsteps before I did, and he quickened, wiped his face, sat up, and began to rise. I knew who it was before she came in.

At least as tall as her mother, she wore a towel around her head and a mask of white cream on her face, and she too entered a room as though walking onstage. She wore a blue ankle-length robe of some kind, not unlike a djellaba, with a hood. The entire effect, the hood, the death-white mask, the elongated stance—they all created a wild, unsettling combination of great force and total anonymity.

I rose as my father did, and he began to introduce me.

"This-this-this is Ben—"

She didn't glance at me; to my father she pointed out the fact that with cream plastered like dough all over her face and lips, she couldn't speak; and she pointed a finger to the ceiling, meaning, I supposed, upstairs.

He nodded, and said, "Good-good-good night, so, I'll be up later."

How those words, how that moment, came back in the months ahead, came back to haunt me and hurt me—hurt me so hard for him, for his sake.

He yearned toward her but didn't follow—he was like a man in a skit whose boots were nailed to the floor; he leaned far forward and then sprang back. And I saw something in him at that moment that I'd never seen before—I saw a longing, a desperation. It's the attitude you see in a dog that deserves praise but so far hasn't received it, that willing eagerness, and if the master is withholding, that disappointment. My father subsided.

Sarah reappeared. "Has Venetia retired?"

My father nodded and turned to me.

"Will-will-will you be all right going home?"

"No, no, Harry, it's much too late. This is glass-of-milk-and-spare-room time. Audrey!"

And that's how I first met Mrs. Haas, scratching Mrs. Haas, my eventual guardian angel. She came into the room, not like a human, but like a goose, a long inquiring neck jutting forward; in different circumstances my father would have called her "a peninsula—which is a long neck sticking out to see."

"Audrey, this is Harry's wonderful son, Ben. Food, don't you think? And the spare room?"

Mrs. Haas looked at me, blinked, and clapped her hands.

"Yes, I know," said Sarah. "Gorgeous, isn't he?"

Then Mrs. Haas spoke: "Come vith me."

She and her spiky teeth beamed at me; it was like being smiled at by a saw. I liked her immediately. Now she was about to feed and house me under the same roof as my father. Was she leading me to a scaffold? No matter. I would have followed.

36

I've never seen a cleaner kitchen. Don't get me wrong—at home we didn't have chickens jumping on the tablecloth. But our kitchen wasn't a clinic. This was. The stone flags on the floor shone like mirrors; fine china twinkled on high shelves like the stars; copper pots hung from hooks, each a bronze sun. Everything felt so new—which it was, but I didn't learn that for some time.

To say that Mrs. Haas made sandwiches is to say that Rembrandt dabbled. She was a painter who preferred the knife to the brush, and she plastered butter on tiles of bread. On the bread she slammed down slabs of beef and onion slices as big as saucers, and then oiled the lot with runny chutney. As to milk, she poured not a glass but a vase.

I think my hunger must have shown because she made me a second flagstone of a sandwich, and then a third. The sight of a man eating must have held some significant if undivined appeal for Mrs. Haas, because she looked like a woman touched by the gods. And she fed me that night as though I were a god.

She talked to me too, all the time. In the beginning I never heard or understood a word because she muttered in an undertone, a happy noise, not unlike a baby, with lots of breath and highs and lows, and she did so in a language I had never heard and didn't understand.

In later years I discovered that when excited or very happy, she spoke a dialect of Austro-German from the province of Carinthia, which is why I didn't understand it. But I liked its humming noises; the merry little ululations reminded me of Father Christmas in his workshop with his elves—I have no idea why.

As I ate, so many questions rode across my mind like horse soldiers. *Who owns this house? Who could be so rich in Charleville as to have a house like this? And it seems to go on and on*—Mrs. Haas had led me down a passageway, a long, winding corridor. *And how do Sarah and Venetia Kelly happen to live here? What is their relationship with my father? Who is this strange woman with the pointy teeth, the long legs, and the thick accent, who keeps smiling at me as though I were her bridegroom, and who then proceeds to scratch her behind so energetically when she sits down that I have to look away and chew my sandwich extra hard so as not to hear the noise?*

When I had finished my "big fnack," as Mrs. Haas called it, she beckoned me, and I followed on this night of beckoning and not yet reckoning. Upstairs, with a lamp that she'd taken from a corridor table, she showed me into yet another pretty room, with a single bed. It had a bathroom attached and—something we didn't have at home—running water, hot and cold. And all the while I was editing, editing in my mind what I could or would tell Mother.

Mrs. Haas made a wide gesture with her hand, indicating that I must enjoy the place. Then she bowed—bowed! To me!—and withdrew. I sat on the bed, bewildered—replete, yet anxious; cared for, yet bereft. I washed my face, took off my clothes, and put on the nightshirt that had been laid out; long and white, it made me look like a young Druid.

With the lamp extinguished, and no streetlights through the window, a peaceful darkness settled. Such a comfortable bed; from the sheets issued a perfume of sweet orange; I closed my eyes.

Now came the sounds of the stillness. This is when the mice can be heard, their little scratches and pattering runs. This is when the foxes can be heard, barking clear and cold on the distant hills. This is when you hear the spit and yowl of fighting cats, tearing at themselves and the night.

I heard none of those sounds in that Charleville room—instead I heard something else. From somewhere nearby, not next door but perhaps in the room beyond that, I heard voices. One rose and fell, as though reciting, as though entertaining or even imploring, declaiming even, with speeches of great drama and romance.

I got up, and like a prowler I stood at my door and listened harder. From the show, I soon recognized Venetia Kelly's voice, so much younger, lower, and fuller than her mother's. The other voice could be heard but rarely, and not continuously; it uttered only interjections, sounds of appreciation. And that was my father's voice.

When I was six years old, I fell quite ill. Dr. Hassett diagnosed pleurisy—"Like thorns inside your lungs," he said. The pleurisy had been no more than the scout; the entire troop then followed in the shape of pneumonia, both lungs.

In those pre-penicillin days they called the telling moment in pneumonia the "Crisis," when the patient either turned the corner or didn't. Notwithstanding fever and incoherence, I recall it so clearly.

My parents took turns with nurses to sit in my room, watching to take me through the Crisis. They behaved so differently. Mother, practical, patted my forehead with cool flannel every few minutes. My father sat and read to me, and every so often he animated his reading with enthusiastic punctuations. He'd say, "Oh, this-this-this is great!" or "Very good, very good!"

Through that wall that night I was now hearing both—the rise and fall of Venetia's narrative drama, punctuated by his appreciation.

When those noises ceased, I went to sleep. I believe that I slept soundly, yet I had the distinct impression that sometime after dawn, when there was a little early light, somebody came into my room. Whoever it was came to my bed and peered down at me, then went as quietly as they'd entered. The feeling they left behind had nothing in it but warmth.

Nowadays I'm good in strange houses. For instance, I know what to do at that most difficult time for a houseguest—the morning. That's in part because I've had a lot of practice—but often when I come down to breakfast in somebody's house I remember that morning in Charleville.

Perhaps I was exhausted; I never moved a bone until nine o'clock. But I knew where I was the moment I opened my eyes, and I lay for a while and listened for the noises of the house.

That's one of the pleasures of visiting a new place—hearing the morning sounds. Farms are delightful—the clop of horses, the cluckings in the yard. In 1932, Irish towns and cities were still mostly hooves and footsteps, and had barely begun to hear the noise of machinery—for years I rushed to the nearest window if an engine clanked.

In Charleville that morning I heard a dog bark somewhere in the town. I heard two people on the street talking loudly—and when they stopped I heard the rise and fall of conversation very close by. Listening at my door again, I figured that the talk came from downstairs, and I got ready very fast.

A dining-room table had been laid for three people, and two already sat there—Sarah and my father. Sarah smiled and pointed to the empty chair as she might have pointed to a treasure-chest onstage, and I sat down. She touched my arm again.

"Good morning, Ben."

I nodded, not yet educated sufficiently to know the practices of sophisticated people. At home nobody said, "Good morning." The day began with somebody's thought process, my father saying something like, "Unless he gets an overall majority, and I doubt it," or Mother saying, "I don't know at all. By this time last year I had four litters." In both cases their conversations had already begun with the world, if only inside their own heads. Therefore, I wasn't used to "Good morning," so I half-nodded and said nothing.

My father had shaved—and shaved well; the mustache had been trimmed, thank God. His eyes had red rims, and he wore the same clothes as yesterday.

And once again I knew that I had no true clue as to what was going on. If I'd stabbed a guess at it, I'd have said that some crazy passion was up and running, but it might be nothing like anybody could imagine.

"Did you sleep well?" Sarah said. "I slept wonderfully." She wasn't waiting for an answer from me. "I sleep so well in these country towns."

Mrs. Haas blew in, making that "fffsss" noise with her teeth; I had heard it last night and wondered whether she had something wrong with her, some minor body complaint. I would learn that she made that noise if she felt about to embark upon an important task. She saw me, gave me a wide smile, and clapped her hands.

"Food. Lots of it!" and she turned on her heel and marched out, going, "Fffsss."

"Audrey's smitten," Sarah said to my father and me.

In those days I didn't know what "smitten" meant, and I didn't ask.

It's difficult to look at people when you desperately want to look at them; there's a danger, especially at such close quarters as a breakfast table, that you'll stare. I needed to see Sarah in the morning light, and above all I wanted to look at my father.

"My hands look wonderful today," said Sarah, holding them out like a priest. "Don't they?"

My father and I nodded.

"It's the water down here," she said. "Is the water different from Dublin? It was very different in Killarney."

"There's a lot of limestone around here," said my father. "Great for the bones."

Had his voice changed? Less hearty? Or was he merely deferring to this exotic woman across the table from him? No—he was subdued. I watched him for the next few minutes, chitchatting with Sarah about this and that, mostly about Sarah, and he was definitely less ebullient than the man I knew.

Mrs. Haas came back with a breakfast for three laborers and planked it down in front of me. Sarah laughed; significantly, my father said nothing. This was strange because he never failed to comment on the size of the meals I consumed—"We'll be seeing more of you" being his favorite remark.

Sarah reached a finger to my plate and took off a small fried mushroom.

"I simply must have a taste," she said, and chewed it as though eating something dainty and arcane.

The expression on my face must have showed—I wanted to cut off her hand at the wrist for taking my food—because she said, "Oh. Perhaps you don't share food." She patted my arm again. "Sorry, Ben."

That smile melted the laces in my boots.

—

I ate; they chatted—no, Sarah chatted and my father made agreeing noises. Mrs. Haas steamed in and out, checking that I had enough. I ate whatever she brought.

When I'd finished, Sarah said, "Now I expect you two will want to talk," and she rose from the table. My father looked disturbed. He stood, then sat down as she swept from the room. That house was freezing cold; over a long dress Sarah wore an ankle-length coat of brocade, purple, cream, and gray.

We didn't move; now I could see my father, look at him full in the face, inspect him; I had more courage than the previous night.

"How are you, Daddy?"

He looked away, then back at me. Not a word did he manage; his lips didn't move.

I persisted. "Are they looking after you all right? What about your clothes? Do you need gloves?"

Now he couldn't take his eyes from mine. He sat there, looking full on at me, straight into my eyes, in silence. At the edge of my field of vision I kept seeing the polka-dot handkerchief in his breast pocket.

Neither of us stirred, and I never broke the eye contact. Months later, James Clare suggested to me that my behavior—no matter what had happened afterward—had probably saved my father's life.

"Not every bit of love has to be spoken," James said. "Often the unspoken piece says most."

Well, it certainly was largely unspoken that morning. We had very few exchanges after that.

I said, "We all miss you."

Then I said, "Where are you going to vote?"

And finally, "Daddy, every day, I'm going to be just behind you. Wherever you're going."

To each of these remarks my father said nothing. He lowered his eyes, took out the handkerchief, wiped the palms of his hands, stowed the handkerchief again, and sat quietly, his hands in his lap. He looked like a man waiting for a frightening diagnosis.

I felt a breeze, and a door opened from another part of the house. In came Venetia Kelly, in a white floor-length coat, tall and straight as a

Roman column. She had drawn a scarf across most of her face, and this gave her a swathed look head to foot. My father stood up as she entered, and, taught to do so for a lady, I stood too.

She glanced at me, fleeting, piercing. With the scarf across her face and the vivid, glowing eyes, it was a look of a woman in some Eastern bazaar. Then, with a sweep of her hand, she indicated the world outdoors—and she was gone.

My father didn't sit again. He fidgeted, and I knew it was time to go. As I went to the door he followed me and said, "Give-give-give your mother my best, my very-very-very best regards."

The crack in his voice twanged like a dirge.

37

Blinking in the weak sunlight, I stumbled out into the street and found emotional refreshment. Against all this private drama of ours, the election campaign ran like a film sound track or an opera recitative. Every town had a rally, every village had posters. Through some parishes went men on bicycles, with crude bullhorns, and in Charleville that morning I saw again my favorite candidate.

I can't give you his name, because he was—believe it or not—elected, and he went on to serve in Parliament for the rest of his life, and we have to respect the dead. He was my parents' favorite candidate too, and he'd already given us great entertainment; we'd watched his career since we'd first seen him, at a rally in Cashel in the 1927 election.

Now, this morning, his face had grown redder, but he wore the same remarkable headgear; shaped like a flowerpot, it came straight from a nineteenth-century stage-Irish cartoon—it even had a buckle on the front like a leprechaun's hat. He stood with a megaphone on a parked farmer's cart, the horse swishing its tail now and then. He wore tall boots, tied at the top with harvesting twine. He had a medically compelling wealth of saliva. Here, roughly, is what I heard him say.

"Ladies and gentlemen, yes. I come before you, yes. To stand beside you. And to stand behind you as you go forward, yes. And as we look ahead, we will have no turning back. This country is at a standstill, yes. Sideways at a crossroads, that's where we are. Which road will you take? Ask yourself that, yes. That crossroads can have only the one road. Which road will I take, yes? Answer came there none. I'm here to guide you down that one road. 'Tisn't the road to rack and ruin. But you already know that; otherwise you wouldn't be at a standstill, at the crossroads, not knowing which way to turn. And 'tisn't the road to pestilence, famine, and decay. You know that for a fact. Every farmer should be getting a better price for your milk. Your local creamery should be paying you more money. I'm here to guide you down the crossroads."

A heckler shouted, "Come down here and look at yourself up there," and the dozen people listening laughed.

Perhaps he would be successful and get elected because nobody could make out a blind thing he was saying. And in that he wasn't alone.

Our candidate's confused oratory mimicked my thoughts. I came home from Charleville reeling and tumbling, my mind full of the wide, stylish house and all of that conflicting experience. And—I had done as I'd said I would; I had found him. As I drove I grappled with what to tell Mother, how much to divulge, and how to phrase it. How should I control the delight that I genuinely felt? Such a pleasure, seeing my father and speaking to him again.

Nor could I say how much I'd enjoyed the company of Sarah Kelly. I'd seen Venetia only twice, once to be introduced, and once fleetingly as she passed through the house; on neither occasion did she acknowledge me. As I neared home I understood that the good, positive news of having found my father would distract Mother sufficiently, and I'd never have to give my own reactions.

She'd heard the car, and she'd come to the back door to intercept me.

"Did you—?" She let the question hang.

"I found him. After much searching." I was able to smile. "And I had two long talks with him."

"When is he coming home?"

"One thing at a time."

She caught my sleeve, a new habit. "How is he?"

"The best thing to do, Mother, is for us to sit down and I'll tell you everything."

Her eyes filled with tears. "Oh, thank God. Thank God."

She walked with me into the house; I could see Large Lily peering at us through the window.

Mother said, "We'll go upstairs," meaning a private talk sitting on the couch in my parents' bedroom.

"Now. Tell me everything." She sat no more than two feet from me; her fingernails went to her mouth to be chewed.

"Well—"

Mother interrupted. "Did he ask for me?"

"I said that you were fine, but you miss him; he asked twice."

"That I'm fine. But I miss him." She often did this, repeated somebody's words so that she could think aloud. "I'm not that fine, but I do miss him, so that bit is true. When is he coming home—did you ask him?"

"I'm working on a plan," I said. "It's based on what I saw." I lied—or did I? Sometimes we know what we're going to do before we know it.

"Oh!" She clapped her hands. "That means he'll come home. Oh, good man, Ben. I knew I could depend on you. What did he say about the money, did you mention the money?"

I now had two dilemmas in one moment. How could I tell her that he seemed to have no intention of coming home? And that I'd had no discussion that could solve the money problem?

Luck helped me. Large Lily called up the stairs to say that we had a visitor.

"The professor, ma'am."

Mother flung a casual preen at the mirror, and ran down.

As she left, I said, "Do I have to meet him?"

She didn't answer, so I wandered along the landing to my own room and sat there on the window seat looking out. From the voices I knew that the professor had arrived alone; had Miss Fay been with him I would certainly have gone down to meet her.

The conversation lasted so long that I almost fell asleep. When eventually I heard the professor huff and puff his way out of the front door, I came downstairs. Mother greeted me.

"I have good news," she said. "We have somebody who wants to stay in the cottage for a couple of months and he's going to pay me in advance today. We'll be meeting him later."

Distracted, she dropped for the moment any further inquiries about my father, and I had a peaceful few hours.

38

At three o'clock Mother called me, told me to put on my coat and come with her. We walked in lemon sunshine down to the river and along to the cottage. A pony trap stood there, and some hubbub seemed under way. As we approached, a man in rough clothes came out, fetched a large valise, and hauled it into the cottage. He came out again and took another trunk.

"It looks as though our tenant means to stay for a while," muttered Mother; she seemed excited and I felt grateful.

The man in the rough clothes came out once more, walking half backward, and thanking an unseen person within. He clambered into the pony trap, hupped the horse, and clattered away. Mother knocked on the door and called out a demure "Hello?"

A great voice hollered back: "Come in, come in."

I stayed behind, watching some waterfowl scurrying on the river and wondering why they seemed never to feel the cold, and speculating whether, if the river were ever to freeze, their legs would get caught in the ice.

Voices came from the cottage—the large booming tone, now in conversation but scarcely less powerful, and then, to my delight, the sound of Mother laughing, something I hadn't heard in the previous two weeks. Next, she appeared in the doorway and said over her shoulder to the—as yet unseen—gentleman inside, "And my son is here with me. Ben?"

I remember him most by my first impression—the eyebrows. We have an insect we call a "Hairy Molly," a kind of centipede; farmers anticipate the winter's chills by the color of the fur. These eyebrows looked just like that—thick, waggling stripes of fur, brown principally, but with a bizarre tinge of a tan color here and there. The face had cheeks that reminded me of a pippin apple—red-veined and crackled, and then came the waistcoat, the yellow check vest, half-gambler, half-frog. And that was my first encounter with Thomas Aquinas Kelly, better known as King.

Neither Mother nor I guessed the connection, nor would we know for some time. All we understood at first was that we had met a man by name Thomas A. Kelly; "a most distinguished businessman," Professor Fay had said to Mother, "who made all his money in the States and is back home in the land he loves." Professor Fay could and should have said "rogue" and "crook" and "Fascist," but he didn't.

Instead we saw this flashy man with heavy charm. Ponderous as a bull, he breathed as if he had asthma. He smiled a vast mouthful of teeth, he shook my hand like a returned emigrant—and we never heard the pillars of the temple cracking.

Had my father been there, he'd have said as he did about all dodgy characters: "Put a coat over that fellow's head."

But my father wasn't there and I was the one who—in an entirely different context—recognized this Mr. Kelly; I was the one who got excited, and whispered, "Mother!" I'd heard the name and seen the photographs; he was running for the government in North Cork. Now Professor Fay appeared, peering over those heavy black spectacles.

"He needs a place away from the hurly-burly," Professor Fay said.

We should have been more suspicious; King Kelly bent over Mother's hand and kissed it. Then he stood in the doorway of the cottage with Professor Fay and made admiring comments.

"This is the best thatched house I've seen in a long while," he said.

Mother said to him, "And Professor Fay tells me you're from not far away."

"The broad fields of North Cork," he said. "But the wider world sent for me when I was young."

Other than the help around the farm, Mother had avoided meeting anybody since my father's departure. She wore a look of shame most of the time, and it pierced my heart when I saw her. And, in some respects, that hurting embarrassment was what pushed me as far as I eventually went.

That morning I could see how she struggled; I could see how she battled to keep the humiliation from her face.

"Terms?" asked King Kelly.

"Pardon me?" asked Mother, in her politest voice.

"Rent?"

Professor Fay said, "I've taken the liberty of telling Mr. Kelly the rent we pay. Is it acceptable if he pays the same amount? For every month, of course, and every portion of every month that he's here in the cottage, not just a few months of the year. And he'll pay in advance."

"What about you and Miss Fay?" said Mother.

"I travel a great deal," said Mr. Kelly. "And if I'm lucky I'll be spending much of my time in Dublin. This will be a quiet base for me."

"We're very fond of Miss Fay," said Mother, piping like a bird.

King Kelly rapped a wall. "Solid, these old walls. We know things, we Irish, don't we, Cyril?"

"Vernacular building, vernacular building," said Professor Fay, once more saying the same thing twice.

"We'll knock twenty percent off the rent, won't we?" said King Kelly to nobody.

I should have guessed then that he knew all about us and was taking advantage.

She agreed, weak as water. Then Mother insisted that she go off and organize a drink.

"Now, how old are you?" King Kelly asked me.

"Ben's eighteen," said Professor Fay who, as his sister said once, answered for everybody and to nobody.

"Perfect age," said Mr. Kelly, and smiled at Professor Fay.

Mother returned with the tray. I can cut this part short; the conversation offered nothing strange or startling, other than a check handed by Mr. Kelly to Mother, who blushed like a bride.

"Isn't he loud?" she said to me later.

As we left, with many farewells and mutual jabberings, King Kelly said to me, "Come down tomorrow morning for a cup of tea."

Mother whispered, "Say yes."

"Yes," I said.

Would I have done anyway? I might have, because I was by now intrigued as to why he seemed familiar to me, why something about him rapped at my mind, but I couldn't get the door open to let it in. Not yet did I place him as the man I'd seen laughing so hard at the show one night. Just as well. If I'd put that connection together earlier, I might have refused to go to see him; I might have avoided him altogether. And then I'd never have acquired the cruel knowledge that made the final difference.

39

When we'd walked out of sight on our way back to the farm, Mother took my arm.

"We'll go home and sit down," she said. "I'm feathered out," her term for emotionally fraught.

She looked tired beyond words. In two weeks several shades of gray had spread across her face. The furrows on her forehead had grown deeper and new lines had opened. Her hair no longer received the attention she'd always given it, and she was chewing her fingernails to the skin.

"Tell me about your father. Tell me everything."

I said, "We talked for ages."

"About coming home?"

"He's looking well, Mother."

"What about his clothes?"

"We met at a house in Charleville. He was indoors all the time, and he was eating well."

I realized that since the moment of his departure we had discussed him as though he had gone off to war or had been sequestered in a clinic.

We reached the house and she headed for her most comfortable chair, by the fire in the parlor.

"Did he give you any money?"

As I answered her, she began to sit back; she closed her eyes. I thought that she looked defeated in every way; her collapse down to this level seemed to have come very fast.

Trying not to seem evasive, but not answering her questions too closely, I think I rendered as good an account of our Charleville meeting as I could manage. Mother never said a word. Maybe I was boring, maybe my voice droned, because quite soon I saw that she fell asleep. I never mentioned the Kelly actresses.

For some time I sat there, in case her sleep proved no more than a brief nodding-off. But she went deeper into it, so I fetched a rug from the back of the sofa, draped it carefully over her, added some wood to the fire, and tiptoed from the room. I looked in every fifteen minutes or so; four hours later, five hours and then six, she was still in a deep sleep.

Large Lily and I took it in turns to watch for Mother awakening.

"She didn't sleep any night, no," said Large Lily. "Not an eye shut. So we'll let her sleep on—she'll wake up out of her own accord. And when she does won't she be fine?"

My father always said that Large Lily, every time she opened her mouth, spoke for two people—but he could never make out who the other person was.

I sat up until midnight, then I piled the fire with logs, arranged the fire screen carefully, and went to bed. When I rose at eight o'clock, Mother was still asleep, and by the time she finally awoke, she had slept twelve hours in that chair.

Even now, I think constantly of Mother as she was during all that time. This great blow fell upon her in the winter, bleak weather for a bleak time in her life. A hardy woman always, and often seen on the chilliest mornings fetching the cows from the lower fields with neither a coat nor a scarf, she now wrapped herself up as never before. As tall as my father, she'd always "borrowed" his shirts, as she well could; they shared the same major dimensions; she was one of the tallest women in the parish. Now she wore his coats and jackets in his absence.

If I look back through the years, I can see her now, walking up the lane to the house in the late afternoon. She's been out somewhere, probably in the woods. All through those gray days, when the fog seems never to quit the farm, she's blanketed by her own mists too. She's talking to herself even more than usual. She's wrapped in one of my father's old greatcoats and when I see how her shoulders sag I can't tell whether it's the weight of the coat or the weight of the grief.

No, I'm sure it was the grief. She changed her habits; she went to Mass on Sundays in different churches, farther and farther away. And she stopped doing her shopping in the village, and had Billy Moloney (when I was absent) drive her in the pony trap to places where she had a better chance of not being asked questions—no matter how innocent—about the boss.

On many days of that February, I came across her when I least expected to—sitting on a bench inside the kitchen garden, looking bleakly at the empty and cold ground. I also found her in the woods, on the walk up toward Mr. Treacy's house, leaning against a tree that she loved, her shoulders squared back against the trunk. Once I found her with her face pressed to the bark, and it left a green mark on her cheek.

One day, when I came back to the house to get fresh clothes, I saw that she was wearing one of my father's hats. I'd never seen her do that before; Mother, for all her insistence on practicality, had a wide feminine streak and would never dream of allowing herself to meet people without what she called "titivating" herself.

My father's hat made her look like one of the squaws whose photographs I saw in *National Geographic,* from a North American tribe such as the Creek or the Apache; she lacked only the feather.

She must have known how little the hat became her—a battered old brown trilby, with a line of black sweat marks near the hatband. Indeed I'd often heard her chastise my father for wearing it, and he'd reply that he was so fond of it he was now going to wear it in bed.

I now see the hat for what it was—my quite austere Mother, wearing her grief as publicly as she could, and at the same time displaying her wish to remain as close as possible to her missing husband. The weather stayed dank and unremitting; we matched its gray mood. I assumed that she was sad—but I so often found her so fierce that it was difficult to imagine she could get back down to sadness within a short time, so high was the peak of her anger. Ireland being Ireland, balmy days began to replace the fog, and Mother went with the weather's mood. She eased up;

she calmed down. The new rent income must have helped. She began to chat about her farm life and make plans, although I did once or twice find her in tears, again in remote places away from view.

But when she accepted the cottage's new tenant, Mother didn't know either the bargain or the devil with whom she'd struck it. At first sight you may think that Professor Fay and King Kelly sought to exploit a vulnerable woman. You'd be right, and you'd think, "That was bad," because she gave King Kelly the cottage at a bargain rent. I wouldn't have given a virus to that crook.

I need to think it all out before I can write it down for you. Also, my own part in it wasn't too edifying—I can best describe myself as innocent to begin with, and then savage, and I'll divulge that too; just give me a little time. Therefore, and while I remember it, here comes an Unimportant Digression, a brief dissertation on the word *blarney.*

Dictionaries always call it "lying," and "shameless flattery." Oh, but it is much wider than that in its reach and warm embrace. First, there is an actual place, Blarney—I've been there many times—a small and sweet village not far from the city of Cork. They'll tell you there that halfway up the tower of the old castle there's a memorial triangle of cut stone inserted in a wall, with, if the light is good, an inscription visible. The words are CORMAC MACCARTHY—FORTIS ME FIERI FECIT. AD 1446. This Latin idiom is a bit loopy, as though composed by a local poet or priest who wasn't quite up to the job, but my translation works fine: "Cormac MacCarthy built me for strength"—meaning (I think) that Cormac MacCarthy set up this castle to be a fortress.

So far as I've been able to trace, we're not descended from this branch of the MacCarthys. By the way, according to some experts, the name MacCarthy means "beloved"—an irony on which I've been impaled for a long time now.

The stone with the Latin inscription isn't the one kissed by tourists seeking the gift of the gab, the Stone of Eloquence, as it used to be called. The locals chose another slab in the wall, one that's just accessible enough; they figured that if they hung the seekers of eloquence (or shameless flattery) upside down and held them by the ankles, they'd remember kissing the Blarney Stone. I like the available metaphor—eloquence turns everything on its head.

As to the original connection between blarney and eloquence, here are some versions, beginning with the oldest, which James Clare gave me.

Long, long ago, Blarney was a wild place, and it had a magical grove, atmospheric in mood, with haunting light, a place where Druids met at dawn on Midsummer Day. When the sun had cleared the horizon, it shone a finger of light into the heart of this grove. The ray came to rest on the ground in a golden triangle, from which a stone rose out of the earth, the same shape and color as the golden sunbeam.

Each Druid who stepped forward and kissed this stone found his eloquence increased. When the sunbeam retreated, the gold triangle of stone sank down into the earth again, and the Druids went off about their business, which was mostly talking.

One of the Druids was a MacCarthy, and one year he lied to the other Druids—he told them the solstice was a few days later that year. On the true morning, he stood there alone and when the golden triangle rose from the earth, he reached down, snatched it from the ground, and ran away home with it and became the chieftain of the tribe. That's the stone on the wall of the castle, and that's why everybody who kissed it grew eloquent. All this, you understand, is the gospel truth.

A later tale says that more recently a witch sauntered out of the mists one day and handed MacCarthy More, the Big MacCarthy, a heavy triangular stone.

"This," she said, "will be the cornerstone of your family." (They also say that she herself was a MacCarthy.)

They lived in wooden castles then, but obviously had the foresight to say, "Listen, boys, a day will come when we'll build stone houses, so let's hang on to this rock and use it later as a cornerstone."

It took centuries more for the family to build stone walls, but the triangle was passed down the generations. When the time came to embed it in the wall of their castle, the famous Cormac decided that he'd trace the stone's origins, and when he searched for the witch, he was told that she came from Tara, the province of the High King of Ireland, and that the slab was originally part of the Stone of Destiny that sat on Tara's hill.

This stone formed a crucial part of prehistoric Ireland's governance, because it identified impostors and pretenders. Every would-be king had to sit on the Stone of Destiny. If he was a fraud, a silence would fall; but when a rightful heir to a throne sat on it, the stone shrieked like a wild thing with joy at the new monarch.

One day, when the true High King was found, a bolt of lightning accompanied the shriek; it broke off a corner of the stone, and that was the triangle given to the MacCarthys by the witch. All this, you understand, is also true.

As to the origin of the word *blarney,* taken to mean lies and shameless flattery, that came from Queen Elizabeth I of England. (Her sobriquet the "virgin" queen might itself belong in the realms of blarney, by all accounts.) She'd ordered her envoy—who was also her lover—to acquire the loyalty and the lands of the MacCarthys. Every time the good ambassador tried to negotiate with the MacCarthys, they flattered him with a banquet in his honor, where they sang his praises and talked him out of his plan. To explain himself, his reports to the queen were long and wordy, and she said, referring to the MacCarthys, "This is all Blarney"—which in a sense it was.

End of Digression; now back to my own story, which, as it developed, had more than its share of blarney—the flattery that kills.

41

Looking back, I now think that I grew up with the country. First, the rowdy infancy—we'd had a revolution in 1916, and a two-year guerrilla war that began in 1919. Then the age of reason, with agreements and treaties. Next, the first noisy childhood of the new state—and we certainly knew all about that. Then, the adolescent fights with parents and siblings—the Civil War.

When it ended, there was a sort of settling-down into a system, a maturing. In politics, as in life, those who want to be successful see the writing on the wall and, unless they want to be permanently unemployed and powerless, they get themselves organized.

Where democracy is an option, that pattern is familiar all over the world. Ireland still provides a tidy case history, because we modeled that pattern more or less exactly. Having at first thrown into turmoil the post-treaty debates about how we should govern ourselves, Mr. de Valera's republicans strengthened and rallied voters behind them.

All through the 1920s, noisy and aggressive, they began to give the governing party of Mr. Cosgrave a run for its money—Dev even had fringe elements still threatening armed struggle. The government countered, shouting the word "sedition," wondering aloud about an armed coup, striking fear. Mr. de Valera grew stronger and stronger in parliamentary and local polling, and in late 1931, he seemed at his strongest. And here was I, also fledgling, trying to grow up very fast, too fast. That, you understand, is hindsight again.

Now, given that interest in politics, you can imagine, can't you, how excited I was to meet an actual parliamentary candidate? At that first meeting in the cottage, no alarm bells rang—or at least I was deliberately deaf to them, and a little overwhelmed by King Kelly. Therefore, despite how uneasy I was about the rental transaction—I thought he'd bullied Mother—I couldn't wait to get to the cottage next day.

At ten o'clock in the morning, I set off. By then, as had become my habit when at home, I had checked Mother's general condition, found out what was happening everywhere on the farm, eaten breakfast, read the paper, and done some more thinking about the "situation."

I had plenty to think about: *The Kelly women, they've left some kind of mark on me. I've never met their like—they're mysterious.* And I knew that they were exotic—I gathered from her photographs that Sarah had sparkled in the brilliance of New York, and I guessed that she and Venetia had outclassed the new style of Dublin. Can you imagine how they looked in the small towns of Munster, where fleas still hopped, where milk went sour when the sun came out?

My father, though, he doesn't look happy; that was my next thought. *Is he unhappy because he hasn't got his familiar things around him? Or is he unhappy because he's trying to put on a kind of new personality? He looked cold in his bones, and I don't think he's enjoying his food. I didn't sense much nourishment in his life. Those clothes, they didn't look right on him—or is that because I've never seen them before?*

And that affable certainty that was his hallmark—that was gone. He seemed more hesitant, not exactly timorous, but he had less assurance about him, and he conducted himself, his hands, his face, his general expression and demeanor, as though struck by a kind of permanent half-shyness. *That smile—it had an embarrassed tinge to it.*

My thoughts kept switching between him and the two women: Which of them had captivated him? A blind man could have figured that they were mother and daughter—the same walk, the carriage of the head, the neck. But whereas I'd been entertained, so to speak, by Sarah, and she'd engaged in conversation with me very fully and generously, I had no clue as to Venetia's personality.

As I finished breakfast and prepared to walk down to the cottage, I thought again of the face behind the scarf. And I stepped back like a man scalded. *Of course! Of course! It all hangs together!*

How is it that a fraction often tells the whole story? Synecdoche—the part represents the whole. How is it that a sliver of light illuminates a whole room? From no more than the glimpse of the person behind the scarf, I somehow knew that she with her eyes glowing at me, and her mother with the soft touch and deep welcome—they were King Kelly's blood.

Would this man, therefore, if indeed he were connected to the people with whom my father had run away—would he be any good in getting my father to come home to us?

The innocence that I had then. Oh, the innocence.

42

Those weren't just trees in our woods, they were friends of mine. I loved our woodland, and I knew all the residents—they stood there, one-legged, cold in the winter, anxious in the damp and mists. In the coming summer I'd see them relaxed and so pleased with themselves in their new leaves. How often I visited them, just rambling, placing a hand on a trunk here, swinging from a branch there. I often helped them by clearing away their old bark and fallen debris, but I never ripped off a branch until I knew it to be truly dead. If I saw fungus I made sure to scrape it away—nasty stuff, and damaging, full of disease. (I met the human version that very morning.) If you'd dropped me blindfolded into that wood I could tell you where I'd landed, and I'd make my way simply by caressing tree after tree. We didn't have woodpeckers, and I'd have hated it if we had—those beaks piercing the sweet bark.

The sun had emerged, that primrose sun we get along the river in winter, mild as a lamp shining in daylight. I came out of the trees and, despite the wet grasses, ignored the path and went straight across the fields to approach the cottage from the rear.

It had a small fence all around the front, enclosing a little garden, where Mother grew zinnias. There was a lilac tree to one side, large enough to give Miss Fay shade when she read out of doors in the summer. The rear of the cottage was reached abruptly—no fence, just the grass of the field running straight up to the wall and the back door, which was usually closed in winter but opened in the summer to let a breeze blow straight through the house.

As I skirted the corner I glanced in through the living-room window—and stopped. King Kelly was standing in the middle of the floor holding a gun. Next to him, with another rifle, stood a stranger, a man whose kind I'd never seen—stocky, very swarthy, hair gleaming black. I walked on past the window, pretending not to have seen, halted, didn't know what to do, half-turned back, stopped.

A gun? Well, maybe the man—and Mr. Kelly—had come here for the shooting, for the abundant pheasants.

When I knocked on the closed door, I heard some quick shuffling from within. I waited, then knocked again. King Kelly opened the door and greeted me like a gale—he greeted bigger than anybody I've ever known.

"Come in! The very man I want to see! I was just sitting here thinking about you and our little appointment. Come in!"

He led the way into the empty living room; the gentleman with the oily black hair had disappeared.

"Sit down, sit down! Are you Benedict or Benjamin?"

"Benedict, sir."

"Of course you are. The most distinguished name in the church. Did you know that Saint Benedict founded the most arduous order of monks ever seen? Oh, yes. I have great devotion to him myself. One of my favorite books is the account Saint Patrick wrote of Saint Benedict's life. Oh, yes, I've even been to Rome to visit Saint Benedict's first monastery; they've his body preserved there. God, he was a hard man, he was as hard as Hell's doorstep. He used to flog his monks to within an inch of their lives—did you know that? And then pray with them, for he was a very devout man. That's a great name you have, Benedict, a great name. And he was a wonderful athlete; by all accounts, he could run like the wind."

Every word of this was a lie. One of my teachers was a devout man called Willie Dalton. "He prays like a flockin' engine," Billy Moloney said, because he used to approach the altar on Sundays and say, "Jesus, Willie is here." My father observed, "And there was probably a voice from Heaven saying, 'Jesus, I hope not.' "

Mr. Dalton often narrated to us the lives of the saints for whom we were named. Saint Benedict was one of his favorites. And I had visited with my parents the Benedictine Abbey of Glenstal in County Limerick, where we were given a tour by the abbot, who was the son of Mother's cousin.

(The genealogical term for such a relative is "a first cousin once removed." Every time the abbot's name was mentioned, my father said, "A first-first-first cousin once removed is very difficult to replace." Again, one of his oldest and most threadbare jokes.)

Therefore I knew that the order of Benedict—actually, there isn't an "order"; there's a Benedictine Rule—wasn't in the same league as, say, the hair-shirted and silent Trappists; that Saint Patrick didn't write the life of Benedict because Saint Patrick was dead long years before Benedict was born—it was Pope Gregory who wrote it; that Benedict was a quiet and thoughtful man who never raised a hand to anybody; that his first monastery (as such) wasn't in Rome but farther south in Monte Cassino; and that his body wasn't preserved.

From an early age I knew the name of every saint whose body was preserved anywhere in the world, and I knew the state of preservation, whether bones, leathery skin, or parchment. Call it a morbid interest if you like, but there it is.

And I'd never heard a word about Benedict being an athlete.

Knowing that I had just listened to a pack of lies from an adult, I sat down as bidden. King Kelly sat directly opposite me. From his pocket he took a cigar bigger than a rocket to the moon, and offered it to me. I didn't know what to do, so I said, "I don't smoke, thank you, sir."

With silver cutters and elaborate match work, and more ceremony than you'd see from a priest saying Mass, he fiddled the cigar into life, blew a bonfire-size plume of smoke to the ceiling, bent forward, and looked straight into my eyes.

"Would you be prepared, Ben, to become a leader of men?"

I said, "I don't know, sir." And I added, "I'm very busy just at the moment."

"If you want something done," he said, "ask a busy man. This is a serious question."

"I suppose, sir," I said, "I'd have to know a little bit more before I could answer such a question honestly."

"Hah!" He slapped his thigh hard. "There's the word I was hoping for. 'Honestly.' Where would I be lucky enough to find a young man today who has that word in his vocabulary? 'Honestly.' Hah!"

James Clare told me something interesting one day; he said, "Whenever you hear somebody saying, 'To be perfectly honest with you'—you can be sure they're lying." I wish I'd known it then, it would have helped me with this man facing me, a man who applauded needlessly my casual use of the word "honestly," a man who looked like a huge toad with black hair in his ears.

Next, King Kelly said, "Ben, would you be prepared to die for your country?" He said it with the gravity of ages; he might have been reading the words from a stone tablet. "Ben, there are serious times coming. Serious times. A group of us, all like-minded men—we're looking to be ahead of these times. And we're looking for a young leader—a handsome, striking young man. He'll be our standard-bearer."

When I'm in difficulty I want to close my eyes. In fact, I feel them closing and it takes an extraordinary effort to keep them open. It began to happen at that moment—and what kept them open was a different physical reaction, the response I now know as fear.

The insides of my bones, where the marrow is, grew cold. My thighs chilled; so did my forearms under my sleeves; so did my neck. I ran my tongue against the back of my upper teeth; I felt my toes clench.

King Kelly reached forward and put a hand on my knee. My father had told me long ago, "There's no-no-no need for any man anywhere to put his hand on your knee or connected regions, and if some fellow does, you should politely leave the room and say you have to see a man about a horse." (This was much in keeping with my father's style. When I asked him where babies came from, he told me this and only this: "It depends on the weather and the condition of the roads.")

I sat back a little, not able to move my knee on account of the tightness with which it was now gripped. Apart from the prizefight in the garden, I had no experience of physical violence; school had been peaceful; my size had helped.

Keeping his hand on my knee, King Kelly said, "I won't sing, but I'll recite to you the words of a famous song about an ancestor of mine." He arranged his face into what I assumed he considered a look of nobility, and said, "Tell me, who is that giant with gold curling hair, he who rides at the head of our band? Seven feet is his height with some inches to spare, and he looks like a king in command."

Naturally I recognized it, as everybody in Ireland would have done: "Kelly of Killane," a famous ballad about one of the Wexford leaders in the 1798 rebellion.

"Ben, listen to me. John Kelly of Killane was my great-grandfather."

This too, I reckoned, must be a lie; John Kelly was executed before he was twenty and, as every schoolboy knew, the yeomen soldiers of England used his head as a football in the streets of Wexford.

King Kelly squeezed my knee harder, and released me.

"The world, Ben," he said, "is often a dark place, and into that darkness we have to bring light. Do you understand me?"

"Yes, sir."

"And it's given, Ben, to only a few to be the bearers of that light. Do you understand me?"

"Yes, sir."

"A true leader has to be a big man. Big. Strong. Kind. Moral. A man of decency." King Kelly pushed back his chair, stood up, and began to pace the floor. "Like you, Ben. You're a big, strong, kind young man. You'll make a great leader. Like my great-grandfather, John Kelly of Killane."

I rose from my chair and said, "Sir, I only came down to tell you that I couldn't stay long."

He looked at me with an eye so calculating and dangerous that I felt the first reaches of a vomiting impulse.

"Come over here to me," he said, standing in the middle of the room, his chest puffed out like a vile monarch's, his pale eyes glittering like a seagull's.

I didn't go over to him; I made a little feeble wave, said, "Good-bye, sir," got to the door and out into the air, and didn't calm down until I reached my lovely, familiar wood and was able to hug my friends the trees.

Within an hour I went back on the road. My quest to bring my father home suddenly felt even more urgent.

Once again, I had no plan. My general feeling was that I should head to Charleville. Assuming that he'd still be there, what could I say to him, what would we talk about? Suppose I didn't talk to him about the "situation"? Suppose we talked only about politics?

Back at the house, Mother had asked nothing about my visit to King Kelly. Anyway I had made up my mind to lie, say he wanted to know about milk and eggs and such things—and I wasn't going to say a word about my belief that he had a connection to the traveling show. How I loathed deceiving her!

In Charleville, I saw my father on the street. The sight arrested me—not because he was doing anything wrong or awkward, but because he was sitting on a bench reading the newspaper, and he looked as though he might have been doing this all his life—gone out in the morning, bought the paper, and read it on this same bench.

In those days people still came out of their houses to look at a motorcar. A small crowd had gathered by the time I'd parked. Over his pages my father looked at me and the car and the half-dozen people and didn't move, and I knew that he wouldn't. I sensed that he wasn't necessarily waiting for me to go sit beside him.

When all the questions had been answered, and the people and the children had dispersed, I walked to where he sat.

"Were they looking for the handlebars?" he said.

I laughed; this was a spark of him as he used to be.

"How are you?" I said to him.

"D'you know," he said, "that you can make your teeth three shades whiter in three days?" He showed me an advertisement for a toothpaste called Kolynos. "I suppose that'd be a shade a day."

"Where's the show tonight?" I said.

He said, "Here's good news," and read an advertisement. " 'Switzers' millinery buyer has returned and a lovely selection of new spring hats is now ready in their millinery department, including a large variety of sports and afternoon models, some of which are quite inexpensive.' "

He began to fold the newspaper; then he turned to me. *I hope he doesn't cry again,* was my thought.

"Ben." About to say something, he stopped himself. "I have to go now." He touched my hand for a split second.

I sat while he rose. From the bench I watched him as he made his way down the street and crossed to the house where he was staying, where I had stayed. There's a lot you can tell about a man from his rear view, and my father that morning had as large a burden on his shoulders as I had ever seen him or anybody have to bear.

Feeling that I'd see him again soon, I waited. Once again I was hit hard with the thought *Nothing about this makes sense.* Not at that moment in my life anyway, when I as yet had no knowledge of blinding passion, the kind that makes you feel as though you've gone red behind the eyes. No, it didn't make sense because I'd observed my parents with the acute focus of an only child.

Through all the phases of early childhood, puberty, and adolescence I'd watched them consciously and unconsciously. Since the Catastrophe, I'd been reviewing what I'd seen. And I knew—or thought I did—a great deal about their relationship, how fond they were of each other. No decent man speculates aloud on what happens in his parents' marriage bed, so I shan't. But their banter gave a clue as to their deep affection.

As small children do, I asked my father one evening, "Did you propose to Mother?"

"I did," he said. "I went down on one knee so often that I have a bad leg."

Turning to her, I said, "And did you say yes immediately?"

My father interrupted. "She did not. She turned me down like a bedspread."

Mother laughed, and I went away from the exchange so encouraged by my ability to please them both that I often asked thereafter about their early life and courtship.

"Did you bring her flowers?"

"Yes. Her father's goat ate them."

More laughter from Mother.

"Did you bring her chocolates?"

"Yes," he said, "and I was gentleman enough to point out that the hard ones were the ones with the teeth marks."

"Is that true, Mother?"

She'd shake her head, still laughing, and say, "Not quite—but I always counted them when I opened the box."

As I sat there on that street bench, disturbed not so much by these memories as by the contrast with them that I had now been witnessing, I saw Mrs. Haas. She was walking backward out of a shop that was half bar and half grocery. A bald man in an apron walked out too. She was facing him and remonstrating; he was spreading his hands in helpless appeal, and she moved back in toward the door and stabbed him in the chest with her finger. I swear that I saw him wince.

He went back inside, reappeared, and like a man with a peace offering handed Mrs. Haas a glass bowl of eggs. Mrs. Haas took them and flounced away back along the street toward the house to which my father had gone. Although she seemed agitated, she too looked as if she belonged here. I was the one who felt out of place.

My father had a saying: "When you have nothing to do—do nothing. It's often good for you." That morning, I can't say that I had nothing to do; in fact I had the biggest task of my life facing me. But I couldn't do much, other than wait and watch.

In the cold beginnings of 1932, sitting on a bench in the middle of a small town in Ireland felt like sitting and watching the surface of a pond.

Interesting things were hinted at on the surface, but nothing much moved. Now and then a blurt of activity broke out—a woman emptying a bucket of water into the street, a man wearing a tweed cap cycling past.

If this is humankind, what did the Creator have in mind? That this place too, these people, should have a reckoning on the Last Day? Very difficult, I often think, to reconcile a Grand Universal Plan with the almost imperceptible life of a small town in Ireland.

Fifteen minutes or so after Mrs. Haas went into the house, a traveling-show truck appeared around from the lane beside the house, with my father alone at the wheel. I guessed that he'd enjoy that. He didn't drive past me; he headed out of town, and I followed. It's open countryside; some of the roads have hills; the trees were bare; I could easily keep track; and I stayed back as far as I could to avoid being detected by him.

We reached the town of Croom without seeing another human being. I soon understood the reason. A crowd had gathered on the main street for an election rally. At this time of day? Rallies usually took place in the evening or on Sunday mornings outside church gates. I should have guessed; this was a Blarney rally.

They had turned out in hundreds. All week the newspapers had been hailing him: DUMMY IS BEST CANDIDATE, SAY VOTERS, and WE'LL VOTE FOR THE DUMMY, and ELECT THE DUMMY—YOU WON'T NOTICE THE DIFFERENCE, and COSGRAVE, DE VALERA, BLARNEY—WHICH ONE'S THE DUMMY?

Blarney himself reveled in it. He sat on Venetia's knee and glittered at the crowd, his mouth a red slash in the sunlight, his hat askew, his eyes wicked. I pushed to the side of the gathering, as near as I could to the farm cart on which Venetia sat; no sign of my father.

"Tell me now," Blarney was saying. "Would you vote for a man as dull as Cosgrave? Or as tall as de Valera? I mean voting for a dull man could give you indigestion—he'd be hard and lumpy to swallow. Voting for a tall man is a bad thing. They're only useful if you want something down off a high shelf. A tall man will always talk down to you. Which is worse—a dull man or a tall man?"

They loved it; they lapped it up. Blarney's head swiveled this way and that, smiling, smiling.

A heckler spoke up. "Better than a dummy."

"Who said that?" said Blarney.

I could see the heckler and I thought he'd made a mistake; never get smart with a comedian. The man had a large, bulbous nose, fodder for a cartoonist.

"Well, now," said Blarney to him, "aren't you the smart man? Well, Mr. Smart Man, I'm going to give you a nickname that'll stick to you for the rest of your life."

Nothing can be more enjoyable to an Irishman than the objective spectacle of malice; meaning, as long as we're not the butt of it, we love it. The crowd murmured a collective gloat, and Blarney glittered at the unfortunate heckler.

"What's your real name?" Blarney asked. The man didn't answer.

Naturally, somebody answered for him; "He's Mick O'Brien."

"Hey-ho, Mr. Mick O'Brien. I'm looking at your nose now—" And Blarney stared, then turned to the crowd and started to laugh. He laughed so infectiously that the entire crowd joined in. I watched Mr. O'Brien, and he didn't laugh.

"The nose!" said Blarney, wheezing through his helpless laughter. "The nose! Did you ever see anything like it?" He paused, collected himself, and said, "A nose like that didn't come from a father. A nose like that didn't come from a mother. A nose like that came from"—he paused—"a nose like that came from a distillery!"

The crowd laughed and laughed.

"And so, Mr. Smart Man Mick O'Brien, I here and now and hereby and thereby name you Bottle O'Brien."

As many as thirty years later, staying in Charleville one night, I heard that story retold in a public house. The name had lived as long as the man.

44

For the moment, and in that election, that was the last I heard of Blarney's campaigning. He made an appearance that night in Croom, and again, by all accounts, they packed the hall. I didn't go there. That afternoon, I followed my father on foot to the show, and hung around waiting for him to come out. Venetia had disappeared in their car after Blarney's "campaign rally," and as I saw her go I fancied that this gave me a chance for some time alone with my father.

He reappeared, and I walked to greet him. But as I did so he once again held both hands in front of him like a man fending off an attack and ran back into the hall. Chagrined beyond words, I retreated to the car.

When I recovered, I made up my mind to get firmer about this entire matter. I drove back to Charleville and went straight to the house where I'd stayed, where I'd met Sarah Kelly, where I'd breakfasted with my father. Now I would wait for him there and bring this matter to a head.

Mrs. Haas answered the door and greeted me as though I were a man she hoped to marry. She didn't know that I had questions to ask.

"Come in! Come in! Ve're all alone, they haff flown, they haff flown away to anywhere!"

She led the way into the kitchen and began at once to prepare food.

"You must be hungry; all big strong young men are hungry; if I had a son, he vould be as fat as the balloon."

For my first ten minutes there she talked all the time—the energy in her speech, the sheer vigor. I, however, felt a little apprehensive, as though I'd burgled somebody's house—and I had no plans in place to explain myself should Sarah or Venetia return. My father, I figured, would stay in that hall until the show had performed, packed up, and moved on.

Mrs. Haas told me that Sarah and "Wenetia" loved each other "like the twins." They wore each other's clothes, they rehearsed each other's lines. When one had a pain, the other had it too: "Miles apart they haff the pain, not that they are ever too many miles apart." They ate the same food, used the same soap, disliked the same people. "Disliking is a better guide than liking," said Mrs. Haas, as she cooked the best eggs that I've ever eaten. "Nutmeg," she told me, "just a little; it fights with the salt of the ham in the mixedy-up eggs."

She brought the food to the table—the eggs, the long strips of fried potato, the hot apple bread, of which I ate so much that I felt disgraceful. Suddenly I was strengthened—less defeated, stronger than at any time in the wretched few weeks since this business had begun.

"Is Mr. Kelly—King Kelly—is he the father of, is he the grandfather—"

Before I could finish she turned on me. "No! Ve vill not talk about him. Not him."

And then, in one burst of speech, Mrs. Haas changed the subject—and at the same time energized me and altered my plan of the day.

"Oh, tomorrow vill be such a furious day," she said. "It vill begin furious, and go on furious, and end furious, they vill all be furious. The father, he must go to wote. And your own father, he must be taken to your place to wote. And my Sarah has to go to Dublin to wote and with her my Wenetia and that vill take many hours. I must make the food for the car."

Whew! I sat back. Point by point I walked her through it. Yes, it was Mr. Thomas A. Kelly, and yes, he had rented a cottage not too far away, and he is "Sarah's father and little Wenetia's grandfather," and my father would be back in our village at ten o'clock in the morning, because the plan was to go to the polling booth at Charleville to see King Kelly vote, and to see Blarney there too, and urge people to vote for him, then drive my father to vote, and then go to Dublin in time to vote before the polls closed at nine o'clock in the evening.

And yes, yes! Mr. Thomas A. Kelly was running against the ventriloquist's doll Blarney. What on earth was going on in that family?

As I was hearing all this information, I heard the noise, as of fingernails, rapidly on canvas. By now Mrs. Haas had finished cooking and had come to the table, where she sat opposite me. She kicked off her shoes and away she went, scratching like a truffle hound.

45

Synecdoche: taking the part for the entire. I will now use synecdoche because I want you to know the kind of country, in particular the social culture of the Irish countryside, that came out to vote in that election. It was homogeneous and undramatic. Here I can kill a number of birds with one stone. That's a dry epithet, you'll see, because to describe the general I'm going to tell you about three women in particular: Mother's friends Mollie May Holmes, Joan Hogan, and Kitty Cleary.

As well as typifying the population on whom our democracy was built, they were the kind of people Mother couldn't face in this new shame. She couldn't face their strength—which lay in their ordinariness. They all belonged to a world where this kind of thing didn't happen.

Mollie May Holmes lived four miles away, also a farmer's wife. She and Mother met every few months, usually after an exchange of letters through the post, blue envelopes with, in Mollie May's case, even bluer ink.

In winter they met in town, a cup of tea and some seedcake, at Kiely's bakery on a Friday afternoon. On summer Sunday afternoons, they met on the riverbank at a point two miles from Mollie May's house and two miles from ours. There, on the grass, they had a picnic and what they both called "a good old chat."

They'd been to school together since the age of four; each held back only the secrets that would embarrass the other. They cooked for their families, they knitted, they darned socks and the elbows of sweaters; they looked after elderly parents, if need be, and never complained. Their husbands also knew each other, cordially but not well. My father liked Joe Holmes but never thought much about him.

Joan Hogan lived nearer and shared a birthday with Mother, not that birthdays received much attention. Mrs. Hogan wore "the worst clothes in the county," according to Mother, but she "baked like an angel." She also had a laugh that made all others laugh, a kind of helpless whoop that she couldn't stop once it started.

Unlike Mollie May Holmes, Joan Hogan hadn't been schooled beyond the age of fourteen. She always came to our house, Mother never went to hers, and so far as I know they never met in town. It strikes me now that Mother might have been ashamed to meet Joan Hogan in public, with her stringy hair, her thick glasses, and always a hem of slip or petticoat dragging and dipping below her skirt.

I liked best the third friend of Mother's, the one my father called "the Cherub." Her name was Kitty Cleary. From a family as poor as any we knew, she had a round, pretty face and a good heart, which took her up a significant notch socially—she married into a strong farm.

"Not, of course, as strong as ours," Mother would say when telling the tale of Kitty's courtship, "but a good deal better than what she came from." Her clothes didn't come from fashion plates either.

These three women came to know one another through having Mother in common. The mutual understanding of all four never had to be spoken, with their sensible shoes (on their farms they wore rubber boots most of the time), their undramatic (to put it kindly) dress sense, and their shared concerns—family, farmwork, placation and management of husband, and launching of children into the world as safely as possible.

Their responsibilities occupied their entire lives. They never spent time on themselves; they had little vanity and few cosmetics. For entertainment they had neighbors' visits, to and fro, with perhaps once or twice a year a dance in the local hall or a picnic by the river.

Tragedy came by in its casual way. Joan Hogan and Kitty Cleary had both suffered stillborn infants, as did Mother; Mollie May Holmes's mother-in-law, who lived with them, had been an interfering harridan. She then went mad overnight, but the son wouldn't let his mother be taken into an institution, so Mollie May Holmes's red hair turned an astonishing shade of white almost in a week from coping with the mad old woman.

Also, and so important, these women voted. They *were* the electorate.

James Clare had a friend, Patrick Kavanagh, a poet from County Monaghan, whose name is now famous. Kavanagh was about ten years older than me, and after a slow and disbelieved beginning he eventually acquired a fine reputation.

An awkward man, with a harsh voice and a dire lack of hygiene, he had a morose air. Since he was a consumptive, it was said that his days in a tuberculosis clinic had made him morbid. But I know the countryside up there in the north whence he hailed. He himself called it "stony, gray soil"; it's a hard territory, poor land, that part of Monaghan, and a man who came from farming stock there was born into disappointment.

Behind that grumpy and unhygienic exterior hummed a soul as strong and sweet-sounding as a good engine. When I first met him, and for many years afterward, I assumed—and others made the same mistake—that Kavanagh was a "provincial," that is to say, he was a regional poet, not much above the level of gravestone verse for local newspapers. What I didn't yet know—being too callow then—was that his poetic spirit had the power of the ancients.

And here's the point. Kavanagh became a voice for those who knew the essence of small things. One poem above all states his thesis. "I have lived," he wrote, "in important places, times / When great events were decided."

His "great events" had to do with quarrels over half-acres of land, quarrels that became fights, family feuds, tiny local wars over the ownership of "half a rood of rock, a no-man's land." He saw these men with their "pitchfork-armed claims" as Homeric, as great and tragic as the Greeks, and he described how Homer's ghost whispered to him, and told him that Homer "made the *Iliad* from such a local row."

Kavanagh called the poem, all fourteen lines of it, "Epic," and once I had heard the sonnet from James Clare and then read it—and it was one of those days when you remembered everything about the moment, where you were, who was nearby, what you were eating, what clothes you wore—I felt something powerful and relieving. In the small, the poem said, is also the great.

What, therefore, would the poet Kavanagh have made of Mother's friends? What would Shakespeare have made of them? Probably what Shakespeare made of similar country people in rural England.

Mrs. Haas's information led me to a decision. I set out in the car after I had eaten. Before going home to prepare for my job next day as polling clerk, I called upon each of Mother's friends.

"Delicate" is the word; that's how they were with me. None broached the subject until I did—yet each began by asking, "And how's your mother?" They knew—but they didn't say so. Nobody spoke out of turn—by which I mean none of them criticized my father, or passed judgment. I'd been afraid—especially of Joan Hogan, who had a lacerating tongue; yet she proved almost the kindest.

My time with them varied; Mollie May Holmes had responsibilities. Her husband and their help had gone over to Callan to buy a wheel rake and they weren't expected back until very late, so she had calves to feed and some cows to milk—not all had gone winter-dry. Joan Hogan seemed keenest to talk, but held back bravely the gossipy questions that I sensed she'd have liked to ask. The Cherub, Kitty Cleary, blushed when she looked at me (she always did that); she was the youngest of the three and the one who insisted that I eat something.

All heard my story with respect. I told it plainly—that my father had suddenly left home, that he had run away with a road show of actors, that my mother's state slipped lower and lower on a daily basis, and that I'd been sent to bring my father home and had had no success. Tomorrow, I told them, he would be at the school at around ten o'clock in the morning. If they were going to vote anyway, could they please vote around ten o'clock, be there when my father arrived, and see whether they could hold any sway over him?

All agreed, even though all asked the same question: "Will your mother be there?" I told them that as yet I hadn't decided to tell her and that I'd ask her to vote much later. All said, "Good."

46

One election looks and feels much like another—or so goes the assumption.

Not in 1932. We knew we were in an election the way a dog knows he's in a fight. The comings and goings in the schoolyard, the last-minute canvassing, the posters, the handbills, the handshakes. Inside the school, the air crackled around our heads. Excited about the event, but nervous as a kitten, afraid of what was about to happen, I sat there—but I did my job.

I hadn't slept well. My mind raced with a sense that I'd gone to her friends behind Mother's back—and yet I felt that if she knew my father was coming into the village, there could be only two possibilities. Either she'd be there and confront him, and cause a scene that would later make her shrink into deeper embarrassment, or she wouldn't come out to vote, and she'd seclude herself so far down in her "vale of melancholy" that it would take me days to dig her out.

I knew that I was gambling—gambling that she wouldn't hear that my father had come back to vote. There was no doubt in my mind that the parish knew the story by now and talked of little else. Someone might tell her—or might not.

When I boiled it down in the small hours of the morning, my bigger fear, therefore, was the possibility of a scene—a scene with bystanders. And that was a chance I simply couldn't take; I couldn't risk exposing her—and, in truth, him—to any spontaneous histrionics.

Plus, the Kelly women would be sitting there waiting for him in their elegant, shining car. This could explode.

Always early for everything all my life, I reached the school at half past eight. I was as tense as a wire but luckily we had some setting up to do. The individual polling booths had arrived and needed to be arranged—six of them, on tables and large desks, tall, folding, oblong three-sided boxes, each with a cloth curtain. Voters would reach head and shoulders through this curtain and, thus shaded from view, fill in the ballot paper with the pencils we had chained to the booths.

Our system was and remains a multi-seat constituency—every county elects a number of representatives to the Parliament in Dublin. Some counties, according to size, are classified as three-seaters, some four, some five; we were three.

This voting, based on proportional representation, gave people a choice—one, two, and three, in the order of your choice. When the first candidate was elected, his remaining number-one votes were then distributed to the next most popular, and so on, until the seats were filled.

To foreigners this has always seemed complicated. To a population accustomed to working out bets on horse and dog races—the complicated mathematics of doubles, cross trebles, bets, and accumulators—child's play.

For the first hour my heart filled my mouth. Then—and I should have known his promptness—my father arrived at precisely ten o'clock. I heard the car, which he must have loved; by now I knew the model—a Daimler, high as a church, smooth as a priest. From where I sat I could see through the porch window into the yard. And I could hear loud talk—some canvasser greeted him and got an equally hearty reply.

He came to the door—and froze. When he saw me he put his hand to his mouth like a man about to swear but stopping himself, turned on his heel, and left. Mr. O'Dwyer saw it, grasped the oddity, looked at me inquiringly, and I blushed. I said nothing. What could I say? "Oh, my father's embarrassed because he thinks I'll try to persuade him to leave his actress and come home"? Or "Oh, my father's embarrassed because he doesn't want to talk to me on account of what I know about him and he thinks now that he can never get away from me"?

I saw and heard the car pull away. Within the space of minutes, and one by one, Mollie May Holmes, Kitty Cleary, and Joan Hogan walked through the door. The first two whispered to me, "Is he here?"

I whispered back, "He came, didn't vote, and left."

Joan Hogan had seen him and smiled. " 'Tis the car he's after." Which made me laugh—from relief, because a crisis had been averted.

47

The 1932 general election made history. Mr. de Valera gained a substantial number of parliamentary seats on his main rivals, Mr. Cosgrave's party, and became the biggest group in the house. Though five seats short of an overall majority, he had enough support from minor parties to declare that he'd govern. We didn't know how the wind was blowing until the end of the week, and we had to wait until the Tuesday of the following week, the twenty-third, to read that the government had decided to go into opposition and give Mr. de Valera "a free hand," as they put it.

Our election day in the village turned out as expected. We had no trouble, as other polling stations did, no fistfights, no threats with guns, no assaults on election staff (for which I was grateful).

My own high point came at four o'clock, when Mother arrived—accompanied by Joan Hogan, to whom Mr. O'Dwyer said, "Voting again, Joan?" and she replied (she wasn't a petite lady), "A woman my size needs two votes."

Joan, I would learn, had behaved as though nothing had happened and had called upon Mother, who behaved impeccably and, I thought, with something of a flourish. She had dressed with great care and I hadn't seen her look as well since the Catastrophe began. I asked for her name, and she addressed me as "sir"—which meant that some kind of energy had returned. Or that she was putting a brave face on things.

She didn't linger; she voted, pressed the paper through the slot in the old black tin box, and left with a smile to Mr. O'Dwyer and me. Was she acting? Who can say? I was by now so generally pressed that I hadn't had the time or the energy to scrutinize her on my visits home; I was exhausted.

And when I went home that evening I found a situation that puzzled me. Mother had a kind of acolyte, a girl from Kilross named Mary Lewis, whom I knew slightly, an insincere hanger-on, with a calf's nature and—I have to say—pretty as a flower. Mother spoke of her with notable warmth, and Mary Lewis often hung around the house.

When I came in from the yard, I found Mary Lewis sitting in the porch. She rose and stood in the doorway. Something about her bothered me; she had a listless nature, she half-sauntered, half-slouched, but once or twice, I had seen her when she thought nobody was observing her, and she had a much swifter, brisker demeanor.

One morning in particular, when I was at my window—this was long before my father had left—I overheard her below talking to Large Lily, who told her that Mother was down in the garden. Mary Lewis said that she'd wait—but as I looked down she took a mirror from her purse, groomed her face and hair with a sharp purpose, and then walked more purposefully than I had ever seen her do.

From my window I can see all the way down to the garden walls, although the hedges conceal anybody on that path from any other view. Mary Lewis walked like a soldier until within ten feet of the garden gate, when she slowed down and resumed her coy saunter.

Billy Moloney hated her.

"D'you know her crowd? Flockin' liars, the whole flockin' family. Her oul' fella—he'd plámás the hind end off a flockin' donkey." (*Plámás,* the Irish word for "sweet-talk," is pronounced *plaw-maws.*)

"Don't you like her, Billy?"

"No, I don't flockin' like her. Nor her father—he has a filthy mouth on him. And I'll tell you somethin' else. Lily don't flockin' like her, and Lily knows flock-all."

He flung some more manure into the cart. My father said that for

Christmas Billy gave Lily a perfume named "Dung." And Mother said that Lily wore it.

Soon I came to dislike Mary Lewis too. Late one beautiful summer morning, I'd heard her argue with Mother in the orchard. The ground wore a carpet of blossom and I could still see the cobwebs of the night reaching in jeweled swags from branch to branch. Mother had gone down to tell the bees that Matty, the aged dog, had at last died. (We kept three beehives and we observed the ancient tradition of telling the bees everything that went on in the family. I never found out whether she told them of my father's antics. Billy Moloney was barred from going near the hives because bees dislike bad language.)

From where the pear trees bunch too closely, I heard voices. One was Mother's: "Mary, I gave you a lot of money last week. Now where did that go? H'm?" And the "h'm," with its rising inflection, told me of Mother's annoyance.

I went cautiously forward and saw them. Doe-eyed, fluttering, voluptuous Mary Lewis had her arms around Mother's neck. Mother seemed awkward but not as awkward as I wanted her to be. I stepped back several feet and called. By the time I reached them, the two women stood well apart and Mary Lewis simpered at me again, as she did all the time.

Now, as I greeted her in our porch, Mother overheard and emerged from somewhere.

"Mary's going to work for that Mr. Kelly down in the cottage," she said.

I didn't like that at all.

That encounter took place, as I say, on election night. I didn't stay to talk; after some food I went to bed and slept until nine o'clock next day. I didn't ask if Mary Lewis had stayed the night—I didn't have to; Large Lily told me.

"That one is gone," she said, as she slammed down my breakfast. "Good riddance to bad rubbish. Her and her face. You'd think butter wouldn't melt in her mouth. Nor anywhere else on her and she a walking strap."

Here's the translation: "Her and her face" means "She thinks she's so pretty." The butter reference signifies pretended innocence, and in this case, morality. A "walking strap" is a prostitute; Lily didn't like Mary Lewis either.

During the voting I had taken the occasional idle few minutes to map out the rest of my week. Nobody expected a conclusive result soon, but some constituencies put on more vote counters than others. North Cork, in which Mr. Kelly and Blarney were candidates, expected to declare early.

I resolved to be there, assuming that my father would put in an appearance. With the usual frantic exhortations coming from Mother, I packed my suitcase and would have felt much wearier had I not been so interested in the election.

And I wanted to find out more about Mr. Kelly. Think of the circumstances; here he was, now living on our land, and my father had run off with the man's granddaughter. All kinds of alarm bells were ringing in my head; and when I added Mary Lewis to the picture I began to feel that we had opened our doors—in my father's absence—to people who shouldn't be trusted.

That was Wednesday, the day after voting; the headlines said, QUIETEST ELECTION DAY ON RECORD followed by REMARKABLE RUSH TO THE BOOTHS. By "quietest" they meant "most decorous," because, as they went on to suggest, this was the largest turnout in history—they estimated a 90 percent poll. The newspaper believed that "the mood of the people was in keeping with the glorious weather conditions that prevailed."

They were counting the votes for Mr. Kelly and Blarney in the town of Fermoy, on the lovely river Blackwater. The Daimler told me where the count was going on; I saw it outside an official-looking building, the only car in town until I arrived.

I parked the Alvis out of sight, several hundred yards away, and walked back to the town hall. Inside the door I met my father; he sat on a table, with a suitcase beside him. I knew what I was looking at—he was in charge of the dummy.

I've never liked clowns; they trouble me, and they're not funny. And I used to dislike ventriloquism dolls, found them unsettling too. Nor did I find it very dignified that my father, my well-respected father, to whom so many farmers came for technical advice on grain crops, on which he was thought something of an expert, and who was known nationally when it came to caring for dairy cows, should be sitting here in a small town forty miles from home looking after a wooden dummy.

When I see a ventriloquist at work today, or when I speak to people about the phenomenon, I often uncover fear.

Is it the highly painted face or the hinged mouth or the leering eye or the smart-aleck demeanor—or the combination of them all? I think that it also has something to do with this grotesque object being given our gifts and then looking superior to us.

The doll, you'll note, always knows more than the master. Have you ever seen a ventriloquist whose dummy was, well, dumb? I haven't, nor do I expect to, not that I seek out ventriloquists and their dummies—I am, in fact, finished with that sector of the world and hope never to be obliged to revisit it.

But my acquaintance with Blarney sent me tracing his origins. Here's another Very Brief Digression. Let's call it Relatively Important.

Ventriloquy has an ancient, shamanic root, and one of its most powerful exercises took place in Greece's great pre-Christian shrine of Delphi. There, a priest ascended by a hidden stairway into a hollow statue of the god Apollo. In answer to the prayers of the multitudes, he spoke as though he were indeed the very voice of Apollo. In other words, the voice was used to trick people, to generate belief, to cow people into thinking that a god was speaking—in other words, trickery.

I dug further and found out a great deal as to how "throwing the voice"—ventriloquy, speaking from the belly—was used in other religions. It even had a satanic connotation in the Middle Ages.

All of this is knowledge that I acquired many years after the fact, essentially when I began to put this entire story together. Slowly but surely I came to understand how appropriate it was that a ventriloquist's dummy should run for political office. And perform the other stunts that I saw from Blarney.

My father looked embarrassed; he knew that I'd seen the suitcase, and he shifted to try to obscure it with his bulk.

"Very-very-very exciting, isn't it?" he said.

"Have they started counting?"

I'd begun to detect a change in myself—I was developing irritation with him, anger. Serious matters that have no reasons bring dismay, and I hadn't yet found sufficient explanation for his behavior because I hadn't yet spoken a word with the object of his madness.

The door from the hall opened and Sarah appeared. She smiled when she saw me; she lit up like the sun coming out, stepped across the hallway, and took me into her arms.

Boys of eighteen in the rural Ireland of those days didn't get hugged by ladies. Not at all, not even by their mothers. Mother hadn't embraced me since I was little—after puberty she certainly kept her distance. And I didn't have any older sisters, among whose friends such huggings might have arisen.

That morning I felt like a man who had fallen into a fabled pool. I'd never touched the bodies of others except in the contact sports of school and parish—our game of Gaelic football combines elements of rugby and soccer; our game of hurling looks as though it mixes hockey and homicide. My experience of the body of another had never been anything but hard and muscular; in fact, I had hugged more animals than humans.

Every part of me that was touched by Sarah's hug resonated. My cheek, where she'd pressed her face, glowed like a fire at sea. Down the length of my frame, instant life sprang up, and new memory faculties came into play, to hold on to what had just happened. My body would retain forever, I believed, the sense of that tall softness pressing into me. And my nose would never be the same after that aroma of far-off lands.

She stepped back and looked at me as a trainer looks at a racehorse. She wore a necklace of diamonds hard and bright as the Arctic.

"Harry, he's a beautiful young man," she said to my father. I held her gaze—I don't know how, but I did. The process, as I now know, had begun—of drawing me in, and then in further. It escalated within seconds—because next through the door came Professor Fay, small, fat, and sweating, even though it was still only the middle of February.

"Professor, isn't Ben beautiful?"

By now Sarah, as she did when I first met her, had folded her hands over mine as though I were a saint and she a supplicant. To this day I relish that moment. Inconsistent of me, I know, but I loved every sensation of it then; I love it even more now.

Sarah looked at my father again. "Harry, I suppose you have to stay here?"

She turned back to me, and spoke a deal more respectfully than she'd spoken to my father.

"The professor and I mean to have an early lunch. You'll come with us, Ben?"

48

They led me to a hotel just down the street; I didn't have enough discrimination to say whether it was a good hotel. People thronged the bar and the hall. We sought a quieter place, so they took us to an upstairs lounge.

I asked for steak; Sarah flattered me by saying, "That's a good idea," and ordered the same, as did Profesor Fay. He also ordered a cognac. For the waitress with the open mouth he had to yield and say, "Brandy."

Professor Fay leaned back and said to Sarah, "And of course Ben has met your esteemed father."

"Oh, my goodness!" said Sarah, not unlike what I was thinking myself. "How did you get on with him?"

Professor Fay butted in. "Famously by all accounts. Famously. By all accounts. Your father loved him. Your father loved him."

Sarah said, "At least he was born in this wonderful country."

"But so were you, my dear, so were you."

"My father and mother came back here so that I'd be born Irish," Sarah said to me. "I wish I'd done that with Venetia"—and thus began my first instruction in the lives of the Kellys; that's when I heard about the mythic New Year birth in the blizzards of New York; "She sprang from the womb and waved to the crowd."

Whatever the subsequent awfulness, I look back on that meeting as magical. Sarah, with no self-consciousness that I could observe—and I was staggered by her lack of what Mother called "essential modesty"—said to Professor Fay, "I wish that you could have seen me when Venetia was born. D'you remember what Venetia looked like about ten years ago? I was even more beautiful."

"Of course you were, of course you were."

What does one do about a man with halitosis? Every time Professor Fay said anything I had to lean back in my chair. No wonder his sister sucked mints all day long.

We ate our food. Sarah and Professor Fay talked to me as though I were massively important. I remember thinking, *They want to get me on their side,* but I dismissed the thought. For what possible reason could they have needed me?

Oh, the naïveté of the young!

After almost an hour, their attentions were interrupted by the arrival of the show—or some of them. First came Michael the acrobat, thinner in real life than on the stage. I thought, *There isn't enough room for him to turn a cartwheel in here.* When he spoke I understood why they gave him so few lines onstage; he had a girl's voice.

"I detect vittles," he said; I never heard him speak again.

Behind him came the neckless man. Dressed in aged corduroy, he held his waistband to his body by means of a striped necktie. He looked all around the room as he spoke—in other words, never off the stage; he had the voice of a grave and considered patrician.

"We are well met here, are we not?" he said. I didn't have the faintest idea what he meant; I never would understand anything he said.

No sign of my father; would he be the next to arrive? Not that it mattered; at that moment Venetia appeared. I, as taught by Mother, stood up. This caused a delighted outcry from Sarah: "The manners—oh, my!"

Venetia again wore a scarf that day, but only around her neck, and in that first instant I saw every particle of her face. The light eyes held mine; I, naturally, caved in first and looked away—to where I can't say. My mind froze.

To this day I never have met anybody who has looked at me in the same wonderful way.

"Ben," she said. "Isn't that your name?"

I stood there, nodding stupidly. We had collection boxes in pubs and churches where the saint bobbed his head in gratitude when you slipped in a coin; I nodded like that.

What happened next? I suddenly felt crowded out, and somewhat overwhelmed. Thanking Professor Fay for the food and offering to pay for mine, I left almost immediately—but not before Venetia had said to me, "I'm visiting your cottage on Sunday."

The day had the texture of spring. I stumbled down the hotel stairs, sure that I'd made a graceless departure. My face was hot and I didn't know why. In the great and unexpected sunshine I saw the river and a path beside it. For the next hour I walked that path, fighting with thoughts that flew at me from all directions.

So that's what she's like, my father's obsession. She's much older than me. Much younger than him. Tall. Eye level. She looked me in the eye. At eye level. Gray? Light blue? White? No, nobody has white eyes. Can't see her eyes from the audience. Gray-white like the Daimler. No, light blue. Her hand—she didn't take it away when she shook my hand.

The first birds of spring dipped and swooped in the bushes near the river, searching early for places to nest. I calmed down and remembered my quest. Back I went to the hall where I'd seen my father guard Blarney. At the door I took a deep breath. This time I would speak it plain: *The election is over. Come home with me today.*

It didn't happen; I found that he'd gone. Damn! And worse—I met King Kelly, who strode the hall watching his votes being counted.

"It'll be like the Battle of Waterloo, damn close-run thing," he shouted at every person he met. Including me, at whom he boomed, "The very man! Come over here."

Long tables beset by frowning people ran the length of the room. Piles of paper kept growing as the tin ballot boxes kept arriving.

"We're counting every box," he said. "Not just every vote, every box. Boxes have gone missing before, you know." He added, "Politics attracts a lot of crooks."

I wanted to know how the votes were for Blarney, but I had enough sense not to ask him. Mr. Kelly moved away to talk to somebody else and I whispered my question to a counter.

"I wouldn't be surprised if he's elected," the man said.

"How's Mr. Kelly doing?"

"It'll be between him and his grandson."

"Who?"

"Blarney," said the man and grinned.

I left the hall with the count still going on. Think of my problems. No nearer to persuading my father to come home, now I couldn't find him. Worse than that, the object of his affections had disturbed me profoundly—and she was about to make an appearance on my family's farm. How could I tell Mother? Should I say anything?

In what culture do we find the proverb "When the student is ready, the master appears?" Is it Buddhism? The Hindus possess wonderful sayings, as do the Tibetans. And I've heard an Eastern legend that I've been unable to trace—of a man, a magical teacher and guide, who emerged from a stone at the moment of the hero's greatest need.

It was at that moment, on the stone bridge over the river in Fermoy, that I met James Clare.

As you might by now have come to expect of me, let me tell you the story of James Clare. He came from the County Clare, where he was born in 1872, making him sixty years old when I met him. But 160 in wisdom; he was as sage as a prophet in a cave. By the age of ten he could play with the musicians in the local pubs. His father had a special set of pipes made for him, with a smaller bag than the adult instrument—James didn't grow fast physically until he reached fourteen, and even then his arms remained too thin to power a full bag under his elbow. It turned out that as a child he'd had tuberculosis (at that time the Irish national disease), hence the early puniness, hence the wheezing when he cycled up a hill.

He wanted to teach music—"so that I could learn it all the time, that's what teaching is, teaching is learning." Poor boys had no means of getting into a music academy, but at the age of twenty he did win a scholarship, and became a teacher at primary level. And that's where and how he discovered his love of story. First came the effect—the rapt faces of the children. Then he expanded the cause; he went in search of tales.

He lived near the village of Doolin, in as magical a countryside as you'll find in the world. To his west lay the sea, the Atlantic Ocean. To the east stretched the white moonscape of the Burren. North and south of him he could find megalithic tombs, castles, the ruins of ancient churches—every field, it seemed, had a legend attached.

At first he specialized—he talked to the fishermen, and the men who went out to the lobster pots. From them he heard stories of great tragedies, shipwrecks, drownings of handsome men and beautiful girls.

They told him of a woman north of there, who lived on an island in Galway Bay; they were no more specific than that. She'd lost seven men to the sea, her husband and six sons, and the seventh son had promised his mother that he'd never again go out in a boat. But one day, the horse that he was leading along a cliff path reared up in fright at the force of a high breaker hitting the rocks just beneath them, and he dragged the young man off the cliff down into the waves.

"And that, as you know," said James Clare, paying me the compliment of being well read—which I wasn't at the time—"was where John Millington Synge got the plot for his play *Riders to the Sea.*" In which Sarah Kelly had once starred at the Abbey Theatre.

James Clare began to write down these stories, but he didn't do so in front of the narrators. Instead of making them self-conscious or halting their flow, he went back to where he lived and wrote them down that same night, often working until four or five o'clock in the morning. At the end of a year or two, he had transcribed, he said, tales of mermaids, golden towers on the horizon, ghost ships.

He told me too the origin of the word *mermaid*—it had been "merry maid," an ironic term, since their singing was designed to lure mortal men to their green, tendriled lands beneath the ocean.

I asked him the foolish question "D'you think there's ever any truth in the stories you hear?"

He considered long and hard and said to me, "The first lesson I learned about a story was—there's always some truth in it. A mermaid could have been a seal seen at a distance. Or a manatee that had strayed a long way from her native shore; a manatee can look very like a human. The golden towers of Atlantis—they could be icebergs, lit by the sun. Ghost ships? Well, we know they exist—because we've seen them. But don't confuse the words *truth* and *fact*—they mean different things. A truth is the meaning the story can give you. A fact—like, did it happen? That can't give you much, unless you make something of it with your own imagination. And that then becomes the truth of it. So, a fellow saw a seal or a manatee off in the distance—and his imagination turned it into a mermaid, because he needed a mermaid at that moment in his life."

The man who spoke those words became my teacher, my adviser, my leader in life, and my closest friend. That morning in Fermoy he also became my guide in the immediate circumstances of the Catastrophe.

Paying no attention to the world around me, I had walked across the bridge intending to get to the car and drive to Mallow, the next show venue. I didn't see the man in the black coat leaning back, watching the world, his elbows on the parapet. But he certainly saw me, and as I drew near, my head down, brisk and focused, I heard the broad voice that would become so dear and familiar.

"Stop for a minute and talk to me. The man who made time made plenty of it."

That was James Clare's opening gambit for everybody; that was how he got his stories. I stopped. His face, open and warm, the crinkles, the wrinkles, the great shock of snow-white hair—how could I not trust him at once?

"But would I know where to begin?" I said.

"Try the middle," he said. "The beginning is often too daunting."

"I've just met the girl my father has run off with, and I think we're about to have a ventriloquist's dummy in our government."

He didn't laugh; he nodded and said, "That sounds to me as if things are sitting about right in the world. Do you know this river at all? You can see why it's called the Blackwater."

We looked down at it together. And we saw our faces side by side, as we would many a year after that.

"There's a place along the bank," he said, "with a bit of a seat on it. We can get hold of the sun."

I followed him down the path, not knowing what I was doing, watching the shiny wheels of his beautifully kept bicycle. On the back sat two elegant, polished black leather panniers; in another basket on the handlebars sat a similar black leather briefcase. Who was this man, dressed head to toe in black, with a white shirt and black tie?

As this story proceeds, James Clare will play an important part. For the moment, let me just tell you—that day, he extracted from me the entire story of what had been going on.

When I had finished, he did a most interesting thing—he told the story back to me, but as if he'd heard it in legendary or mythical form. This is how it sounded; I'll remember it forever.

Once upon a time, there lived a man who loved the land that he worked. He was an anxious man, as all red-haired people tend to be. And he was a kind man, but he was prone to a little madness now and then. Usually this madness didn't affect people much; he'd get up in the middle of a moonlit summer night and walk his fields in his nightshirt, looking to see whether his crops continued to grow in the dark. If he got cold he'd go over and lie down with his horses where they were sleeping under a tree.

Now this man had a wife and a son, and to them he looked for wisdom, because this man had one great fear in life—that he'd do something crazy one day, and never be able to recover. They, though, looked to him for wisdom, and in the back-and-forth they never stopped to think that he thought them wiser than himself.

One day, a Princess came by. She was an unusual young woman, different from the rest of the world, and she had wonderful gifts—gifts of speech and illusion, gifts of compassion and intrigue, gifts of excitement and praise, and she looked at this man and he looked back at the Princess. With no more than a few words, he put down his farming tools and followed the Princess across the country. When he met her mother, the Queen, and all the court, he stayed with them in their land of gifts.

The man's wife and son, good people, didn't know what to do. Eventually, after some days of debate and worry, the wife asked her son to be like the heroes of old—to undertake a quest. He—again like the heroes of old—did so unwillingly, and, as in all good legends, he failed and he failed and he failed.

One day, he met the Queen, and soon after that he met the Princess herself, and he began to understand why his father had so suddenly disappeared into this magic world. These were different people, these royal travelers; they were like the gaudy caravans that rode through the deserts, stopping at each and every oasis to dance and sing and playact.

The young man was disturbed by them, and was especially shaken to find that they had in their midst an old and wicked King, who threatened danger to everybody, while at the same time offering words sweeter than combs of honey.

On a sunny morning, however, the young man took the first step toward completing his quest. He stopped on a bridge to look down into a river, and he saw there a face, an ancient face, and he called to it. He called, "Tell me what to do, old face in the river."

A man arose from the water; he floated up from the flowing current and walked up onto the bridge. He wore a long black coat and miraculously it was bone-dry—as was his hair and his skin and his shiny, shiny boots.

"Yes, I'll tell you what to do," he said. "Follow your own power."

"Follow my own power," said the young man. "What does that mean?"

"Only you can know that," said the man from the river.

James Clare halted there and laughed in delight—probably at the bemused expression on my face.

"That, as you'll gather, is the story so far. What do you make of it?" I was embarrassed to say what I felt, and he picked that up. "Go on—say what you feel."

I said, "It's—exciting. When you tell it like that."

"It might make it easier to handle."

And then I laughed, because I didn't know what else to do.

Yet I had immediate and very difficult problems. The woman with whom Father had run away would be on our farm this coming Sunday, within a few hundred yards of Mother. I told this to James Clare.

He said, "Do you need advice?"

"Oh, God, I do!"

"See whether you can send your mother somewhere for the day. Go to the gathering. Then use your own power. Your father won't be there."

I must have looked puzzled.

"Of course he won't be there. He's too much of a gentleman to do something like that."

James Clare and I arranged to meet in Fermoy again on Monday morning.

"By then," he said, "we'll know how the country is going."

51

Symbolically, almost, the days became glorious as the voting results came through. My own story grew more dramatic. As the country changed direction, so did my life, and it too was lit by a sun that seemed to have leapt forward from May or June. That day, I acted upon James Clare's advice to the letter—as I would do all my life. I went home, and, abominably, but powered by my own feelings for her, told Mother a lie—that my father had gone into the west, and nobody knew where he'd gone, but that he was expected back next week. I also told her that I needed a rest, a break from the incessant pressure—and that so did she.

With good maneuvering I arranged for Billy Moloney to take her to her sister's house in Kilkenny, where she could stay for the weekend; I would collect her on Sunday night.

Such fortunate timing; almost as soon as they drove out of our yard, Mary Lewis appeared—inviting us on behalf of Mr. Kelly to come to the cottage on Sunday for a victory celebration.

I wanted to ask, "Is he that sure he's won?" but I kept my powder dry.

Not yet had I revealed to Mother the identity of King Kelly. In the few days since the election, she'd shrunk a great deal, I thought, her spirits lower than ever. Years later she revealed to me that she had hoped the election and its results would bring my father back home.

"As if all the nonsense had now ended," was how she put it to me.

I began to debate with myself the kind of equations Mother must have been making in her head. *De Valera in office and my father home: politics as a securer of family stability. The turmoil of an election campaign: a disturber of the marriage bed. A predatory woman as an indicator of Fascism. Therefore I've judged accurately not to tell her yet of the King Kelly connection.*

Luckily the glorious weather continued on Sunday. I finished all the chores on the farm early (how I loved being back in working clothes!) and I prepared for the luncheon party. From Christmas I had some gifts of shirts not yet worn, and a new necktie; I also had new shoes. I can see now that I was preparing like a bridegroom.

By the time I got to the cottage, about twenty people had already gathered; I'd never seen most of them before. The fine weather had drawn everybody out of doors—and then I saw her. I hung back for a moment, relishing the sight of her in the sunlight.

Tall as a statue, striking as a princess from a James Clare legend, she stood like some wonderful lighthouse, mingling with the others, yet apart, though they swarmed around and about her. Of Sarah I saw no sign, but her father was dominating the occasion; from hundreds of yards away I could hear King Kelly's voice booming out across the fields.

Professor Fay saw me. He called me over and introduced me to a gentleman called O'Duffy, whose name would become very familiar in the coming year.

"Ben is one of us," said the professor, and I had no idea at that time what he meant. King Kelly then greeted me with a crushing grip on my shoulder, and told Mr. O'Duffy that I showed "great promise," and that he was "delighted to have me on board." Promise of what I could not say; on what or whose board I had no idea.

For many minutes I stood with those men as people came to our group, greeted us, and went off to talk to others. Young enough to be their grandson, I was bewildered, but sufficiently anxious to keep my wits about me. No sign did I see of the man with the gun and the shiny black hair. Nor of Miss Fay, which disappointed me. What struck me most about the place was the lack of mirth. Were this party at our house, the laughter would have blown across the parish like a gale.

The ingratiating Mary Lewis appeared with food, and once more I saw her in a different light—she had a competent edge to her. Therefore, despite my immaturity, I'd always been right—she had long been deceiving Mother. She saw me looking at her, and it didn't faze her at all; in fact she came over to where I stood and said, "A new side to me, Ben, right?" and winked.

I especially didn't want to be winked at by Mary Lewis, so I went at the food—egg sandwiches, mostly, and some ham sandwiches. Mr. Kelly put a drink in my hand and insisted that I taste it; I didn't like it and said so and ate another egg sandwich.

"See," Professor Fay almost shouted. "See how forthright he is. Forthright."

All this time I had only one intention—to meet Venetia. She who came to fetch me; I knew when she was standing behind me—that's how strong a presence she had. When she joined our group, all fell silent.

"Hello again, Ben," she said. And to the gentlemen, "Excuse us."

She took my arm and led me toward the path by the river.

52

You'll have observed that I haven't speculated on the nature of my father's relationship with this young actress. Were they lovers? That would have been anybody's question. Not mine; I knew nothing of such things. However, Sarah's embraces when greeting me had caused a change in focus—I was now thinking about dark and exciting matters of which I only dimly knew.

Venetia said, "Tell me where to meet you. We can't talk here."

I pointed. "Go along the path. Up past the wood, where you'll see a well in the middle of the field. I'll be there."

She said, "Give me half an hour."

It became the longest time in my life.

I had no experience of girls. None whatsoever. Nil. Zero. I hadn't even come a little close, no female cousins of my age, no sisters of school friends—that was my sheltered life. So, instead of the more natural wondering what should or might happen between Venetia and me, I thought of her and my father.

Should I ask her? Should I say, "What goes on between you?" Should I ask, "Is my father in love with you?"

Love I knew from the cinema and from books. Kissing I somewhat understood. Of the other things I had no concrete impression as to what took place; animals in the farmyard, the necessary trips to stallions and prize bulls, cats, dogs—I'd seen all of that, and the exciting, spontaneous behavior of my own body, but it gave me nothing by way of insight into human behavior. Thus, as you can understand, I had myself churning in some turmoil by the time I reached the wood.

Life is an ambush, by and large. None of the questions in my head became relevant that day or ever again, because events turned out very differently.

They're mostly beech, those trees (they're still there) and some ash, sycamore, and most of all hazel. The summer canopy offers an almost totally closed shade; look up and it feels so green and exotic that you'd expect to see parrots. I've tried to get back there every year; it calms me more than anyplace I know.

James Clare used to say, "Everybody should have a sacred place."

In winter, and noticeably that day, the trees reach up to scratch the sky. Their trunks are cold and a little dank, but they've always welcomed my touch.

That afternoon, the well always in my sight, I went from tree to tree, and back again—that side of Wade's Wood stretches to about a hundred yards or so. Eventually, as I was always going to do, I stayed at my favorite tree—a great beech.

This was the tree of all my childhood; this was the tree I used to climb, and then swing down to the ground on one of the stoutest branches. The branch would naturally snap back up into place with a thrilling *whish!* Now I could reach it anytime I wanted and swing from it. Over the years, as I grew bigger, the branch didn't snap back quite as fast or as fully.

I was hauling on it when I saw Venetia, picking her way like a gray stork, up through the grasses of the field to the well. A memory of something I didn't quite grasp flooded into my mind and I started in alarm.

Do you recognize that uncomfortable feeling? Some call it déjà vu—"what you've already seen." Meeting her mother, Sarah, had given me a slighter jab of the same dart; this one, however, jolted me hard.

I went through the trees to meet her. Some clouds had encroached upon the sky, lighting the grasses where she walked, and shining on the river behind her, while casting the trees near me into shadow. She kept her head down as she approached, watching her step. Keeping pace, I aimed to reach the well at the same time as she did.

Venetia looked up, saw me, and waved. I tried to place her in the world—the same age, perhaps, as Mother's cousin who'd married and had a baby all in the same year? A few years younger than Large Lily (but so, so different)? A good deal older than irksome Mary Lewis? My range could stretch little wider than that; I couldn't guess the ages of women or girls—I still can't, and I think it's mildly indecent to do so.

As she drew closer I had to keep swallowing.

"This is the well," I said.

"Will you get me a drink from it?" I hadn't seen her smile like that before.

Kneeling down on the cold flagstone, I did what I could and brought up my cupped hands full of the brilliant water cold as lead. She steadied my hands and drank from them, then wiped my hands on the hem of her ankle-length skirt. Then she headed for the wood; I followed and walked beside her.

I remember thinking, *She's completely at one with this place, she likes it, she likes what I like.* Fifteen, maybe twenty yards into the trees, in the deepest part, she halted, turned to me, and took my hands.

"I'm so sorry, desperately sorry for what's happened to your father."

If that didn't take me aback, her next move did; she laid her head on my shoulder.

I kind of patted her hair, thicker than hay, smoother than satin. What else should I do? She didn't move, not even when she said, "And I'm even more sorry for what's going to happen to him next."

"What? What's going to happen next?"

There was a hesitation in her. She checked, she held back. She edited what she meant to say. I saw the change of mind, change of direction. And then she lifted her head from my shoulder and said, "This." And she kissed me.

Other than by my mother on the cheek or the top of the head, I had never been kissed. Nor have I ever been kissed again like that. It was so simple. She laid her lips softly on my mouth and kept them there, never moved them, just stood at equal height to me or, so it felt, her mouth lying on mine.

No movement came from her lips or tongue—nothing, just a soft lying there, her eyes closed. I didn't even know that it's good manners to keep your eyes closed during a kiss.

Possibly I exaggerate when I say that we stood like that for five minutes, and then she put her head on my shoulder again. I'm not young anymore, and memory distorts things into what you want them to be until they fit you—everybody knows that. But my bones tell me that it was the longest kiss I have ever experienced.

As to time—we then stood with her head on my shoulder and my arms around her, supporting her, and I can be objective about that period; the sun moved right around the sky, as it always did in the early afternoon, until the wood grew shadowy and cold.

Stiff in our limbs, we drew apart. She lifted the silence.

"I need to talk to you," she said, "in a quiet and safe place where we'll not be interrupted. I don't want anyone drawing conclusions. Not yet."

Going to our house was my idea, and I never stumbled or hesitated at the thought. I knew that the fire in the parlor was set, ready to light; and I knew that nobody was there.

Although we didn't speak as we walked up through the fields and into the grounds, I knew that I had never met anybody like this, nor did I know that such people existed. She looked at everything; she stopped and scrutinized a stone or a burst of grasses. Once, she halted and gazed at the sky, turning a full 360 degrees.

"I love clouds," she said.

Inside the house, she walked around as though in a church. She admired everything, touched objects here and there, sometimes with her tongue. When she saw me looking at her tongue on a glass bottle, she said, "Fingers have limited ability." She spoke candidly. "I've heard so much about this house. I feel I almost know it."

"Does he talk about it a lot?"

"He mostly talks about you."

While I made tea she roamed the hallway and the downstairs rooms; above the roaring in my ears I could hear her footsteps. I might as well admit that it was tremendously exciting to see her there, even though guilt and other difficult feelings pressed in on me. She came into the kitchen, picked things up, took things down, scrutinized things.

"Oh," she said, "I recognize this." Meaning the large mug with the black horse, my father's when he drank tea anywhere out of doors. "He misses it, he says."

"How much has he told you about us?" I said, but I meant about Mother.

"I wish," she said, "I had a father who spoke as fondly of me."

When I brought the tray into the parlor, the fire had taken, with lovely flames and the smell of wood smoke. Venetia sat on the floor in front of the fire, near enough to my chair to lean on my knees.

"Where shall I begin?" she said.

I was about to reply with the obvious remark "At the beginning," but she spoke again.

"But why am I asking? I know where to begin. With you."

What? said my mind.

"The true loving—and that's what's going on here—is from me to you. Not me to your father. I've come to you. I've come for you. He was the pathfinder. But he doesn't know that yet."

I was mute—with shock, and with what turned out to be hope. And I stayed mute, as she told a story that had a beginning, middle, and would soon, as far as she was concerned, have an end. She knew what the end would be; it just might take time to achieve it. As briefly as I can, I'll recount what she said, and I promise not to dwell on the immense, almost unmanageable conflicts that attacked me. Contrary to what you might think, this was no romance, like in films or books.

My father, on his way back from Galway some years earlier, had stopped in Ballinasloe to visit some friends. They, on their way out to see Venetia Kelly's Traveling Show, persuaded him to come along—not much pressure needed, I imagined.

As they sat in the hall they told him that the girl at the core of the road show was the daughter of the renowned Abbey actress Sarah Kelly. My father told them how, when he was a younger man, he'd seen Sarah Kelly with J. M. Synge, walking the red roads of Ballsbridge in Dublin.

That night, as my father watched, Venetia played the scene from the end of Act One in *Macbeth* where Lady Macbeth goads her husband into getting Banquo killed. For me, by the fire, she spoke—she performed in miniature—some of the lines: "Was the hope drunk / Wherein you dress'd yourself? Hath it slept since? / And wakes it now to look so green and pale?"

Even though she tossed the lines off almost casually, she matched the flames from the logs. The light of huge energy danced in her face.

"Your father was stricken to the heart, and he wrote a note asking to see me; he was staying at Hayden's Hotel. I didn't reply; I receive many such notes from men. We traveled on—to Tullamore, and he was there that night too, in the front row, and he wrote again. I'm afraid that his second note landed as fallow as the first—but after that he wrote to me every week. Eventually I wrote back, and said that I'd meet him in Callan one night."

I remembered my father going to Callan, and I remembered his high spirits next day; that was about two years before he finally decamped.

Venetia said that my father "sounded" her that night in Callan. "He asked delicate questions as to my 'status.' I told him, No, I'm not married, nor do I have a 'swain.' Don't you love the word? He told me it means a country lad who woos."

If I needed to know whether she was telling the truth, I knew from that moment—I recognized the word "swain" as my father's. And all through her narrative I knew that she was telling the truth, because the language she attributed to him was so recognizably my father's.

He went away—and some weeks later wrote to her again.

"It was a long and careful letter, and it was a declaration of profound love."

Now I felt deep shock. But I held my counsel (as my father would say) and listened on.

"I told nobody, not even Sarah, and I agreed to meet with him. He told me that he was prepared to give up everything for me and travel the roads too, protecting me, financing me, caring for me. I turned him down flat and he wept salt tears" (a term of Mother's, this—how my nerves jangled).

Above and beyond her gifts as an actress, Venetia was a magnificent storyteller. Yes, I know the tale she told was about me—but nobody could have told it better: the voice, the delivery, the perfectly timed and appropriate hand gestures, and from a less than advantageous position, sitting on the floor.

"When he wept, my heart was touched—and when my heart is touched, I believe that I must look beyond that to find meaning. I began to believe that your father had been sent to me for a purpose. And I came to the conclusion that you were the purpose."

"Me?"—my only interruption. The fire crackled. "That's wood from an old apple tree," I said.

Venetia looked at me, paused, and nodded her head a number of times.

"Yes. I was right about you." She continued. "Here was the meaning I found. During the meeting, he talked about you, his son, his only child. And he talked so touchingly about you that when next I saw Sarah I told her the entire story. Sarah told me not to dismiss your father, that a follower of such ardor would be difficult to find, especially a man of substance."

By now I had picked up many of the story's threads: my father late back from the Galway races; his disappearances on nights with his unusually late homecomings; the visit to Callan; Mother's comment that he had been "following" somebody for years. Everything made—unpleasant—sense.

Venetia listened to her mother's "strong advice" and accepted my father's attentions. "Sarah isn't a woman you can argue with. And her father, my grandfather—he has a great influence on her, and he kept pulling some strings that I couldn't quite see."

She reached up and took my hand. "I went along with it—but I didn't do so on Sarah's recommendation; actually it was more of an instruction. I based my decision on the way your father spoke of his son, Ben, his only child. That, I figured, was the life to which I wanted to belong. And I felt—in some almost magical way—that I was utterly right."

It was, as James Clare said, "an unusual but understandable interpretation"—but it left me wondering whether I was in some way to blame for everything.

She finished telling her story. Difficulties loomed like mountains. Venetia had wanted a father, but Harry had hoped for a lover, and in due time a bride. She told me all of this in a clear and important way. Her voice, her bearing, the urgency in her shoulders—we weren't dealing in trivial matter.

I look back now and I see the room so clearly, and I see the two people in it—one young, the other younger, both vulnerable, one less so than the other, and you'll be surprised to know that I was the less vulnerable. After all, I'd had my father's unalloyed tenderness for eighteen years, and Venetia had had it at that stage for no more than three weeks.

The flames danced from the cords of wood, a bird outside called to the powers of evening, and not another sound could I hear, except the breathing of the girl sitting on the floor gazing into the fire, the strange, half-cheerful young woman who had just brought her crucial tale up to date.

As often happens in such circumstances we both began to speak at the same time, and then went, "You first. No, you first."

She anticipated my—so obvious—question.

"This is what happens. Harry, your father, travels with me. Always. He looks after all my things, my costumes, my boxes, Blarney's suitcase, everything. All those stage needs. When a show finishes—or in the mornings, if we're not traveling that day—he and I talk. He tells me about farming. And about you. I tell him about the stage. I—well, I *perform.* For him. And him alone. We manage to get a lot of private time. He says that I entrance him."

Suddenly she turned to me and put her head down on my knees. She continued to talk.

"I know that I must tell you something else and you may not like it. Sometimes I perform for him while I'm not wearing any clothes. He looks at me with such feeling. And he knows that he mustn't touch me—he's not allowed to." She all but muffled her words. "Are you very shocked?"

I remember this thought crossing my mind: *This girl is also the voice of the jeering dummy Blarney.*

We stayed as we were, silent and close, until the fire began to sink. She raised her head and said, "I must go."

"Why—" I said. "Why did. Us. This. Why now, why did it happen, why did this happen, today?"

In certain circumstances incoherence has its own eloquence.

She looked at me. Every man in the world, every man, woman, and child deserves to be looked at like that. Just once would be enough; I still live off the fact that it happened to me.

I walked her back toward the cottage.

At the point just before we could be seen together she stopped and kissed me again.

"You'll know what to do," she said. "And I won't let you down."

53

The more I thought of that bizarre afternoon, the more I began to wonder whether it had truly occurred. And—not the least of my worries—had Venetia merely told me a version of events? I reeled back to the house, my mind refracting, diffusing. In the science room at school they showed us what happens when you put your finger down on a drop of mercury; it shoots off in a number of smaller but identical blobs.

Colors from that episode leaked across my life. Over the years that followed I interpreted it—or believed I did—in so many ways. In this, I was helped by James Clare, who viewed everything as a legend. When, a long time later, still seeking meanings, I narrated the events of that afternoon to him, this is the story he told me.

The King of Munster, Brian O'Brien, was out riding one day, on a hunt in County Waterford, and he lost track of his companions. He was such a good horseman that he had outridden them all. Although he waited on hillsides and he waited in glens and he waited on the banks of the rivers and lakes, they never caught up with him.

Night would soon fall, and he thought of heading for home, but he had by now ridden a great distance, and there was no moon and in the darkness the bandits of the countryside might not recognize that he was a king.

Besides, he liked to visit his subjects and he didn't often visit that part of his kingdom; Waterford being a law-abiding county, it needed less attention than, say, wild Clare or rebel Cork.

Up ahead of him he saw a low, wide gate across an entrance. He could see no house but the gate had such a clear and strong appearance that he put his horse to jump over its five wooden bars, and then he galloped up the driveway.

Now the King had been recently widowed, and was still a very sad man. He had put behind him the traditional Irish mourning period of a year and a day, but he hadn't yet the heart to begin looking for a new wife. He certainly understood that he needed to; a king requires a queen to help him run his kingdom and to provide leadership and example for the women.

And this was a young king, in his mid-thirties, though of course, nobody would ever dare to ask a king's age; a king is deemed ageless until he departs for his next kingdom.

Most important of all, he had no heirs. And he had quarrelsome brothers. So this, as you can see, was a king who needed to marry again and marry a young woman. And marry her soon—for he was a warlike man and there was much fighting among the tribes of Munster in those days. We're talking now about the year 995 or thereabouts, Anno Domini.

As he rode up along this strange avenue, he was struck by two facts: the length of it—and he knew full well that only well-to-do people could afford to live that far in from the road—and the lavish trees and shrubs, which confirmed for him that these were substantial people who lived here, whoever they were.

And indeed he arrived at a substantial house. Not a castle, more of a manor house, a tidy-size mansion—and this told him that they were also respectful subjects and hadn't built a castle—only the King was allowed a castle. He rode up to the front door.

A hound came out to greet him, a tall, hairy hound with a smiling face. Behind the hound came a woman of great beauty. She stood in the doorway, looked up at the King on his horse, and then greeted him. He dismounted and bowed to her, and she invited him to come in.

The King entered the grand hallway of this fine house and asked her name. She told him that her name was Ishka, that she was named for the water in the river that flowed clear and sparkling, and for the water in the lake that sat still and clear, and for the water in the sea that rolled and tumbled, and for the water that fell from the skies to make the crops grow, and soothe and cool the faces of troubled people.

As the King was about to introduce himself, she held up a hand and asked him not to tell her who he was; she said that she'd like to try to find out.

Some servants appeared, and she ordered food and drink for the King, and a basin of water, and linen towels to wash and wipe his weary face and hands. When the servants had finished ministering to the King, they guided him to a large room with a stone fireplace so wide that half the trunk of an old oak could burn on the fire.

And indeed half the trunk of an old oak was burning in the fire, crackling and spitting and throwing up lovely colors and shadows that danced down the room.

Ishka sat there, on a great couch covered with the furs of beautiful animals, and the half-light of the fire made her seem even more beautiful.

The King, feeling much better now that he had washed his face and eaten good food, sat down where she indicated, on a great chair on the other side of the fire. He was about to speak when Ishka held a finger to her lips.

She told him that he'd passed two tests so far, and that she was about to find out who he was from his reaction to some remarks she would now make. He was not to speak, but to nod his head if he agreed, and shake his head from side to side if he did not.

The King, amused by the instruction, but still alive with questions—Who is this woman? Does she own this place?—waited, never taking his eyes off her. Her smiling dog sat by her feet, on which she wore gold sandals. Then she spoke.

First of all she said, "When the dawn breaks I look to the east and praise the sun for rising on yet another day. Do you agree that I am right to do so?" The King nodded his head.

Ishka then said, "When the wind comes up the river and raises little feathers on the water, I think it not a good time to seek fish. Do you agree that I am right to think so?"

The King again nodded his head.

Ishka said next, "When I tell a tale, I must seek to enchant my audience and put them under a spell in which they think they are living within the tale. Is that how you believe a tale must be told?"

And again the King nodded his head.

Ishka fell silent. Then she spoke once more.

"I think that you must be a king. And I think so because you entered my house without fear, you accepted the ministrations of my servants without surprise; those were the first two tests. Then I saw that you understand the magic of each new day that dawns, you know the life of hidden things such as the fish in the river, and you believe that few matters in life are as important as a well-told tale."

"Madam," said the King, "I am Brian O'Brien, King of all Munster, and I must know your name and your state in life."

She said, "I know who you are. I sent for you."

And she told him that she was the daughter of parents who had come from the spirit world, who had placed her on the earth, had lived with her in mortal life for long enough to be sure that she would meet and marry a man of noble birth. Her parents had but recently returned to the spirit world. She had remained behind, and when no man came to claim her she used her magic to send for one, and now he had arrived.

And that is how King Brian O'Brien found a wife, and she was the mother of the greatest king that Munster ever had, Brian Boru himself.

54

Mr. de Valera won the election by persuading the country that the sitting government was too cozy with the English. By implication he almost gave the impression that if Mr. Cosgrave was elected one more time, he'd come close to inviting Britain back in. Nonsense, of course—"blarney," if you will—but enough mud stuck.

As for the other Blarney—the dummy didn't get elected, but he polled arrestingly well. Normally the crazies in an election will get maybe a few hundred votes; Blarney polled a few thousand—enough to give King Kelly the shakes for a day or two. With hindsight, the message in Blarney's vote might have been saying that none of the other candidates was very much better than a wooden doll.

On the Monday, with most of the national results still being verified, I went back to Fermoy. That was February 22, three weeks now with my father still "at large," as Mother put it, as though he were a criminal. When I collected her on the Sunday night after Venetia had gone, Mother looked rested, but when we were alone in the car she asked me immediately, "Any news?"

The phrase meant only one thing: "Have you found your father and is he coming home?"

That's why I went back to Fermoy next day—as I told her, the show was booked there for a week. And I lied with that remark, a lie of omission; I was also going there to see Venetia. Almost as though standing outside myself, I wanted to see what would happen next.

To reach Fermoy, I had to slow down to a crawl for the last ten miles, because the car's tank had sunk so low and I hadn't refilled the spare jerrican. Filling up in those days had a haphazard nature to it; garages with pumps hadn't yet proliferated—no need to, little demand.

Humiliated by my incompetence, and further humiliated by the fact that children along the way could keep up with me as they ran alongside, I finally reached the town and got filled up.

At the count, I met bleary-eyed people. They had by now come down to seventh and eighth preferences. In the proportional-representation system the count goes on until every seat is filled without any possibility of argument. Sometimes, the candidates will hit the quota early and everybody can go home. That year, in an election so charged, and in that constituency with a personality as large as King Kelly, and an even larger one in Blarney, nobody would take any chances.

Within about fifteen minutes of my arrival, the Kelly entourage appeared. He came in first, booming and waving his cane. Some hanger-on had clearly reached him to say that his moment of glory might be here. Behind him came Sarah, willowy, ethereal, very Sarah-like. Next came Venetia; she carried Blarney as though he were her baby, and everybody cheered.

To the hall now packed with people, the returning officer began to make the announcement. Again and again he had to ask for quiet so that he could be heard.

The candidates assembled beside him on the stage—King Kelly, who was the government nominee for the seat; Mr. de Valera's candidate, who was a prosperous and handsome farmer; my man in the leprechaun hat, wearing a placard that read, under a huge arrow pointing to his head, THIS IS THE FELLOW TO LEAD YOU; then came two more—independent—candidates; and at the end of the line stood Venetia with Blarney.

Somebody nudged me; by my side stood my father.

"Isn't-isn't-isn't this great?"—and he pointed to the man with the leprechaun hat.

We stood together as the returning officer did his work. Mr. de Valera's candidate headed the poll, by a huge majority; behind him everybody floundered. The announcements are made in descending form, the highest number of votes first. After the Dev candidate came a man from one of the two independents, and he was elected to further loud cheers. One seat left now, and to whom would it go? It went to King Kelly; the shouts of the government faction drowned out the returning officer, who waited.

To my astonishment and everybody else's, the next highest vote went to "Blarney Kelly." A wooden dummy had come within a thousand or so votes of winning a seat in the Irish Parliament. Laughter rocked the place. Blarney had even beaten my leprechaun, who wasn't elected that time around. Not only that—Blarney had come very close to defeating King Kelly.

Now came the speeches. Dev's man spoke straightforwardly of "a new nation for a new people, a rising ambition for a risen people; the new force in Ireland will be the Soldiers of Destiny."

King Kelly promised to take back the power at the next election—and then said, mysteriously, "And who knows? Maybe before then."

My father, standing beside me, said, "Uh-oh."

The third speaker promised intensive opposition on behalf of the Irish people, and committed a delicious gaffe when he said, "No turn will be unstoned."

As he stepped back into the line of candidates, a call began to rise: "Blarney! Blarney! Blarney! Blarney!"

Nothing in Ireland should ever surprise one; anything can happen in this country and usually does. We can't be satirized, because in any vein of behavior we're always well ahead of the satirists.

Venetia walked forward—and so did my father—and so did I. Not even at that moment did I anticipate what was to happen in the weeks and months ahead. She hoisted Blarney and patted his head.

"Well done, Blarney. Congratulations."

"On what?" he said, his voice like an angry hinge.

"You did very well," said Venetia.

Blarney looked up at her. "You think so?"

"I do."

"You think I did very well?"

"But you did. You came fourth."

Blarney replied, "And the Lord said to Moses, 'Come forth, come forth, and Moses, he came fifth.' "

"Blarney, you were voted into fourth place."

"Yeh. I was. Behind three rank fools. Why is that congratulations?"

I gasped. By now the other candidates looked uncomfortable, especially King Kelly, and the audience laughed more and more.

"Would you run as a candidate again, Blarney?"

"I will. I'll run next year."

"But, Blarney, there won't be an election next year. It'll be five years before there's another election."

"No," said Blarney, in a flat contradiction. "The Long Fella won't have a big enough majority, and he'll call another election inside the year."

"How do you know this, Blarney?"

"He told me."

"Mr. de Valera told you?"

"Yes."

"When did he tell you this, Blarney?"

"Last night."

"Last night? Where last night?"

"He was down on his knees polishing my boots and he lifted his head and he looked straight up at me, the glasses winking in the light, and he says to me, 'D'ya know what, Blarney? I'll have to go again next year.' "

When my father stopped laughing, he nudged me and we went outside. Again, we had a lovely sunny day, and we strolled down the street to the bridge.

"We could go home now," I said. "I filled the tank in the car."

"Wasn't that great?" he said. "Fourth place."

"Mother isn't doing well."

"He was nearly elected. I wonder-wonder-wonder what would have happened."

I said, taking a deep breath, "There's the money."

"Ben, you should go on home."

I said, "What are you going to do about the money?"

"I don't-don't-don't know yet."

I said, "Will you come home with me? Even for the day?"

"I'm going to stay with this girl. Ben, she's-she's-she's like a great dream that goes on and on. At my age, that's like, that's like Heaven."

I said, "But the farm? And everything?"

"She's, Ben, she's a wonder altogether."

I said, "My instructions from Mother are to follow you until you come home."

"She tells me these wonderful things, she transports me."

There are moments, aren't there, when you think that the person with whom you're conversing has gone mad—or has been mad for some time and you simply haven't observed it?

We'd both been leaning our elbows on the parapet. He stood up straight and looked into the distance like the captain of a ship or a mariner from a legend of the sea.

"I'm where I want to be. I'm where I want to stay."

I said, "And what about—" I struggled and came out with "Miss Kelly?"

He didn't answer, because he had seen something. Toward us came Venetia, still holding Blarney. All my father's systems sprang to the moment; I'd seen him like this only when a horse won a race.

Venetia reached us, and I went on alert too. There we stood, on that bridge over the Blackwater, the best salmon river in the country, as the February sun looked down on us, a lemon in the sky.

My father shook Blarney's hand and spoke to him.

"Congratulations. A fine showing, Blarney."

Blarney looked at me and said, "Of course you know Miss Venetia Kelly—but say, 'How-d'you do,' to her anyway."

I turned to Venetia and said, "How d'you do, Miss Kelly?"

Were we all mad? Were we crazy?

She said, "I'm very well, thank you. I'm so glad you came to see the votes counted."

Blarney interrupted, "Blazes, girl! He came to see you. Are you blind in one eye and can't see out the other?"

And we laughed—including my father, who chortled in delight.

Venetia said, "We all want to go back to Charleville. Including my grandfather. Somebody's waiting there to drive him somewhere." She turned to me. "Will you come, Ben?"

Venetia turned and walked away. My father followed her—and then stopped abruptly, turned back, and addressed me.

"To-to-to answer your question—Miss Kelly will do what I want. She'll do what I say."

My poor father.

How much I learned in that one year—in that one day! Some things were not good; some were wonderful—and one was a lesson for the rest of my life. I'll address it first; the others, the good, the not-good, the wonderful—they will become apparent.

Here's the lesson: We're born—forgive me for stating the obvious—of birth parents, our blood, our kin. By the act of bringing us into the world they're charged—or are supposed to be charged—with the task of steering us across our early lives so that we, like them, can go and do likewise, bring children into the world and perpetuate our species.

By and large our blood parents do that, or at least they did so in the society into which I was born. True, we were having at that time a massive aberration in our family, and it was having a great and difficult bearing on the bringing up of me; that is also self-evident from all you've learned so far.

In Fermoy that Monday, I learned that "other" parents exist. The world knows that they exist too, but it doesn't often acknowledge them. It makes a halfhearted effort to do so by, in some societies, giving us godparents. But those sponsors at the baptismal font amount to no more than a nod in the direction of which I speak.

The alternative parents whom I have in mind come from the spirit world. "Extra," or "additional" parents, whatever you like to call them, they're often preferable to your birth parents. And, whatever their spiritual origins, they can be practical and very present if you allow them to be.

If we find and identify them, they guide us, they tell us things that no other parent would dream of telling us—because they know things about us that no blood parent can ever know. How do they do it, how do they know? That is part of the mystery—they know it instinctively.

I found my new parents that day. They parented me for years and years, for as long as they lived. Their presence inside me parents me to this day, no matter what my age as I tell you this. In fact I've decided not to disclose to you the age I am as I write this down. It's irrelevant, because I'm using their energy, the force they gave me, to tell this tale. Therefore my calendrical age doesn't matter.

You can probably guess who they are—well, one of them anyway; the other had been offering herself as such for some time. In my general agitation I'd forgotten to mention to James Clare the name of Miss Dora Fay, who had often said how much she wanted me to meet him.

They were lovers at the deepest level you'll find on this earth, in that they cared for each other more than they cared for anything else—except for the work they gave to the world, and that was a kind of loving anyway.

I almost fell down when I saw them together. In those days, a kind of tearoom existed in Fermoy. It is long gone. The woman who owned it ran away one day in 1935 with a sailor who swaggered in, took a look at her, and said, "Will you come with me to the coast of Africa?" And she did, a woman with straight hair and curly teeth, and she closed the door and never came back.

I met her that day—she was named Molly Barrett and I look at her in my mind's eye and wonder where such a plain and ordinary woman hid her dreams of romance, the dreams that took her to the coast of Africa. (See? Another Digression; I can't seem to break the habit.)

So, I parted from my father and Venetia (as I looked after them I saw Blarney hoisted high, looking back at me and waving, and I know that my father never saw Blarney doing that). The morning—it wasn't eleven o'clock yet—had me ravenously hungry, as all emotional perturbation still does.

I asked a man at a street corner, an old soldier in his army tunic, ragged pants, and broken shoes, where I could get a cup of tea, and he said nothing, just looked into a distance that would never be available to him. He was like all those old soldiers who stood on those street corners, shell-shocked from the World War, and would remain so all his life. A woman overhearing my question pointed me to Molly Barrett's tea shop.

The door had a bell that jangled—and so did I. At a table by the wall sat James Clare and Miss Dora Fay—my new parents, according to the mystic and mysterious systems of the world. Though deep in conversation, they turned their heads as one person. As one person they held their hands out to me. And as one person they smiled.

That is why I believe in a life beneath our lives, a system below our consciousness, a world of half-thoughts and memories of times in which we've never lived. Never in my life up to that moment had I needed help so much, never had I needed somebody to slow me down and make sense of all that had been happening.

Indeed, my intention had been to sit in the tearoom and list out and look at all that had already happened. A formidable list, you'll agree, and changing all the time; my father gone from home, and now beyond recovery; the woman who was the object of his affections attaching herself to me; her grandfather associating with sinister men, and having sinister intent; Mother holding herself up in the world after a collapse so steep that John Milton couldn't have written it. If ever a paradise had been lost, Mother's was.

And me, myself—torn in all directions at once—ringing, ringing, ringing with the moods and feelings induced by Sarah's embrace and Venetia's kisses, and not having the beginnings of a notion as to how to handle all this; and worried sick about Mother and faced with the prospect of endless weeks and months, maybe years on the road, and no solution of any kind in sight anywhere.

I had a lot to think about. When I sat down, I knew I was close to tears and unable to look at either adult. Miss Fay shook my hand—and held it for just a moment. So did James Clare.

He said, "I didn't know until this morning that you're the young man my friend Dora told me about so long ago. How are you?"

Naturally, I told them. Everything. They listened in silence; that's one of the great gifts that alternative parents can give—they listen without comment and never make judgments. I expected them to home in on my worries regarding Mother and money and everything of that nature. Instead they became greatly excited about the relationship—so far—that promised to arise with Venetia.

They kept on exchanging what are called "significant glances." If my parents did that as I was telling them something, it always bothered me, made me anxious. Here, though, I took it as a sign that they were on my side and were thinking between them as to how they might help.

I don't know how I received that impression; I certainly didn't imagine it, because that indeed is what they were doing—silently figuring out a way to help without actually intruding. And with the first words they spoke they showed me how much they were on my side.

"Ben," said Miss Fay; she had that slightly lisping speech you find in all people with prominent front teeth. "You know, don't you, that you're caught up in very fantastic circumstances."

(One of the things that I always liked about Miss Fay was the way she attached the word "very" to many of her terms, even to her superlatives. The milk I brought to the cottage was "very delicious." A rainbow was "very wonderful." Eggs were "very brilliantly nourishing.")

James Clare added, "That's a bit of what I was trying to say to you the other day."

Miss Dora Fay said, "And you've probably been wondering whether you're exaggerating the way you feel about it all."

Again I nodded; there wasn't a lot else I could say.

She patted my arm. "It's very impossible to exaggerate it all. I've never heard of such a thing as you're immersed in."

James said, "And you're wondering what you're going to do? Well, the first thing you're going to do is what you should always do—have a cup of tea and a bun."

As I would discover, James's solution to most difficulties was a cup of tea and a bun; it's now my solution too.

They sat back in their chairs. Molly Barrett came over. She said to them, "And this is your son, I suppose?"

"In a way," said Miss Dora Fay. "In a way."

I was introduced to her; she came back with tea and a bun that had currants on it, and a cherry on top.

"Get yourself outside that," said James.

As I ate my bun and drank my tea, Miss Dora Fay said to me, "Now, Ben. Let me guess which is the matter that most besets you." She reflected for perhaps half a minute and said, "The matter of your father's young lady? Am I correct?"

I nodded; nodding was still a high priority with me, and anyway my mouth was full.

"Is she lovely?" said Miss Fay.

James blurted with crumbs, "Oh, Dora, wait 'til you see her. She's like the moon—silver and mysterious."

"And it seems," said Miss Fay, like a scientist analyzing a problem, "that she's choosing you."

"Why shouldn't she, why wouldn't she?" said James.

"Then that's what will be," said Miss Dora Fay. "The world knows its own mind."

"D'you remember what I said to you last week?" said James, his face alight. "Use your own power. Isn't that what's happening?"

56

Miss Fay, for all that she looked like an ostrich with glasses, possessed useful social gifts. She knew, for instance, when to bring a conversation to a close—as she did now.

"I've arranged to meet my wretched brother here in Fermoy," she said. "What a lousy trial he is to me."

James said, "Have you continued your story—I mean telling it to yourself?"

This time I didn't nod. I shook my head; my range of nonverbal communication was evidently increasing.

He drained his teacup. "Now when will we three meet again?"

Miss Fay looked at me and said, "Remember?" and quoted, " 'In thunder, lightning, or in rain?' "

I smiled.

"It's bad luck," she said, "to quote from *Macbeth.* And good luck is what we need."

Although no agreement had been reached, and no advice had been given, I parted from the two of them with a strong sense that they wanted me to go to Charleville, to the house, to Venetia.

I offered lifts in the car—to anywhere; they declined, and I looked back to see them standing side by side looking after me like real parents—or, rather, in the way that we hope real parents will look at us when we're walking away from them; standing close together, smiling with warm pride, giving little waves, hoping that you'll be safe, and longing for the day they'll see you again.

Of course the trouble with additional parents—especially if they're like Miss Dora Fay and James Clare—is no matter how good you believe your real parents are or have been, the new parents make you realize what you've missed.

The door to the house in Charleville stood open—mystifying, given how cold the house always seemed to be. I rang the bell and called but nobody answered. What must I do now? Stand and wait, ring the bell again.

A woman next door, wizened as a broom, said, "They're not up yet, they don't get up 'til 'tis late, they're very like that."

I was about to argue that I knew some of them were up, I'd already met them, when I heard the voices. So I followed them. I went into the house, along the passageway I'd first been drawn along by Sarah, and I heard the voices more loudly with each step—Venetia and her mother in an argument. Of my father's voice, or any male voice, or even Mrs. Haas, I heard nothing.

At the foot of the stairs I stopped; that's where the argument came from—the room directly above. No argument this, but an outright fight, with voices rising all the time. I still couldn't hear what they were saying—and by now I didn't want to, so I called, "Hallo? Hallo?"

The voices stopped. Sarah appeared and said, as though never in an argument in her life, "It's Ben, dear Ben. Ben, come up, let's see you."

Venetia appeared, her head above her mother's shoulder—and from the way she looked at me I knew that my new parents had judged everything right. This was the direction to follow.

I climbed the stairs. "Is, ah'm—"

"Is Harry here? No, Ben," said Sarah, "but you are."

When I reached the landing, both women took my hands, as I had seen them do with my father. This produced the eeriest possible feeling in me—and at that stage in my life I didn't even know about *Oedipus at Colonus,* and the death of the king. They led me along the passageway, which was at least as long as the one downstairs, to a small and what Miss Fay would call a "very marvelous" sitting room.

Sarah went into the room first; Venetia squeezed my hand and I followed her. Given what I've so far told you, given the maelstrom of my life, why did I feel that I had come to some different but infinitely truer kind of home?

I sat with Sarah and Venetia. They were unquestionably the two most beautiful and exciting human beings that I had ever seen, and they made me feel that I was the center of their lives. But I reminded myself that it was my choice to feel so.

When I was about ten, I asked Mother if she'd ever heard anybody say anything about me. She said, yes, that her friends talked about me. Mollie May Holmes said that I was "as demure as a girl"; Kitty Cleary said that I was "a sweetheart." When I protested these troubling observations, Mother turned them into compliments. I never saw it like that. What boy could, especially if he was saving the world?

In that very marvelous sitting room those descriptions came back to my mind. *Is that how these people see me? Demure? A sweetheart? God, I hope not.*

We talked—no, they talked, I listened. They told me about the house, about making films in Killarney—that's when I first heard of Esmeralda—about the Abbey and Mr. Yeats and Mr. Synge. I don't think the sun moved around the sky that afternoon; I believe it stood perfectly still high above me, as did time itself.

My idyll ended when my father came back. We heard him call from downstairs. The arch of Venetia's eyebrows told me to go. On the staircase, he and I shook hands like friends, not father and son; I left the house edgy at my ousting.

Had I been less irked, I might not have exploded when I reached home. "Demure"? That vanished like the coward that it was. No sweetheart I—not at all. I, who had never raised my voice in anger, who wouldn't say "Boo!" to a goose, screeched and screamed, rampaged and roared. I kicked the floor. Mother recoiled; her friendly dog had suddenly developed rabies.

"*What,* Mother?"

She waved a document. "It's only a piece of paper."

I now think there may also have been self-destruction and revenge in it. And a hastening of fate, as though sick of worrying as to how she could keep the farm going, she relinquished it.

"It's a mortgage, Mother."

When it came down to it, none of us had the power to digest what had happened. We had no preparation for such an event. We were emotionally quiet people. We had no training in relationship drama. How could we have? Our farm was like so many others. We had the usual scruffy backyard, never clean enough, with cows parading in and out twice a day, leaving their calling cards in great flat plashes a few feet from our back door.

We had a pigsty on the wrong side of the wind, so that winter and summer we had no choice but to be aware of what Mother called her "second family," long, pinkish, snouted folk whose quick intelligence and easy responses delighted her. She was so fond of them that she scrubbed them with a yard brush. "The only woman in Ireland to wash pigs," Large Lily said. "There's people who don't wash their children as often."

And yes, we had a couple of good horses, and yes, an excellent motorcar, and a small truck, and yes, one of the first tractors in that part of the county—but that all came from management, not style.

But we had no "style" in the international-traveler, glossy-magazine sense of the word; we were what we seemed to be—an Irish farming family with no pretensions to glamour or sophistication.

Now, however, we were nothing, and I was the only one in the family who knew it—Mother certainly didn't know.

"But mortgages are never cashed in."

"Yes, they are."

Now the screaming began. I'd had too much—too much for any grown man, let alone a boy fresh from school, waiting to go to college. I remember thinking, *If only I could cry.* And I remember thinking, *Why do I know this is dangerous? Because it is.* And I remember thinking, *Where's Billy Flockin' Moloney when I need his language to describe this stupid woman, my mother?*

She fetched the "piece of paper"—a Deed of Agreement nine pages long, every sentence a stick of dynamite, every page a minefield.

"Did you read this?"

"Mr. Horgan will read it"—Leonard Horgan, whose law firm had been our family solicitors for five generations.

"But you've signed it. It doesn't matter who reads it."

"I think it's all right. Mr. Kelly is a very remarkable man."

For what reason I don't know—call it survival, call it instinct, call it James Clare and his talk of "power" and "story"—I ran to my room and came back with pen and paper.

"Now, Mother, tell me everything, and I'm going to write it down, what he said, what he offered, and what he said you were signing."

For the next half hour, with me pushing her and pulling her, she told me the story of—call it by its right name—the confidence trick. Professor Fay was in on it, that little greased pig, and he in some ways did the most damage, because Mother had known him and had found him and his sister trustworthy in their dealings.

In essence, King Kelly had vaulted into Mother's broken heart off Professor Fay's shoulders. A low position to jump from, I know, but it didn't need a big leap in those days to get into Mother's heart.

My pen grew a blade. No sword was ever as mighty. The nib almost ripped the paper. Blobs of ink fell like buboes from the plague. I had fantasies as I wrote.

Had I known the word "scrotum" in those days, it would have joined "twist," "shred," and "wrench" in the language my mind was screaming.

Had I been less "demure," I would have written only four-letter words. Had I been less respectful as a son, I would have been screaming wild epithets with "stupidity" and "imbecility" in them.

The writing helped me to find the calm that lives in the heart of rage, and I got everything down, every sentence, every dripping cajole used by King Kelly. It filled six pages of my notebook.

"Read it, Mother."

Mute as stone, she took it from my hand.

"Is it a true and accurate record?"

She nodded, afraid of me.

"Then write the words. 'A true and accurate record,' sign it underneath, and put in today's date," and I called, "Lily!"

The floor shook as Large Lily thundered in.

How did I know to do it? How did I understand that it needed a witness to Mother's signature? How did I make sense of it all? I have no idea. Sometimes my mind leaks like a colander, sometimes it fills with sand, a silt piling up, and I have to tilt forward to get a clear view of my own floor. But sometimes, like a silver javelin coming at me, I see the truth, I see the right thing to do. I wish I could see that javelin more often—thick, shiny, sharp-pointed, and rotating slowly in the air as it aims at me; I still look for it.

"Mother. Listen to me."

"Yes, Ben. I'll listen carefully." She had lately taken to saying this. She said it, I felt, out of defeat, as though by listening to me she could persuade the world to revive her and stand her on her feet again. She looked at me with the sad eyes of an ill-used dog.

"Understand this. Mr. Kelly has taken a mortgage over our property. It means that at the end of the month, if you haven't paid him back all the two thousand he has loaned you, plus the interest he has declared, then he can evict you and move in here."

"But the interest rate is very, very decent."

"Nothing to do with it, Mother. How much of the money have you still got?"

"Well, Ben, I had bills to pay. I had to pay Billy and Lily."

I sat back and so did she, and we both knew what had happened.

"Can you do something about it, Ben?"

There are some looks you never forget. Passion. Slyness. The sudden giveaway downward glance of somebody who's manipulating you. Entreaty—that appeal that asks, "Can you do something, because I can't?" Which was what I now saw in Mother, added to the chagrin, the "I'm so stupid" look, and in her case, the "My husband has left me" look.

So that you know—that was the moment when "demure" no longer applied. Timidity vamoosed, to use my father's word. I can call up that "entreaty" look of Mother's any time. For the purposes of telling you this story, I've just gone to a mirror and called it up, and I saw it reflected in my own eyes. I hope I never have to recall it again.

59

I'm fond of the word *hero.* James Clare and I talked about it often, and I made him laugh when I described how, as a little boy, I used to stride through our woods as I thought a hero might—long steps and emphatic footfalls. He loved it.

"But that's how they walked," he said. "That's how the gods strode the mountaintops. How do you think Finn MacCool went across the Giant's Causeway from Ireland to Scotland? Think about seven-league boots."

I love the idea of seven-league boots—a league is three miles; therefore you travel twenty-one miles with each stride: perfect.

That hero stride came back to me when I left the house, with Mother numb in the parlor. God, I had seven-league boots! I was about to descend on Mr. Kelly and Professor Fay and crush them with my giant boots. How dare they?!

If you'd been there, you'd have seen my stride—a "here's-my-head-my-legs-are-following" sort of aggression about me. It used to make Billy Moloney laugh.

"There'll be flockin' trouble now," he'd say.

I headed like a beast for the cottage. This had to be sorted out. Not for a day longer could that mortgage be permitted to exist. I didn't know what I was going to do; all I knew is that I intended to do something.

In those woods, where, as I've told you, every tree is my friend, there's a clearing. It's far from the paths but I know it well, and I've always loved it. Mother took me there first, and told me that she used to lie on the grass in the pool of sunlight during the months before I was born.

I often meant to ask her whether I'd been conceived there. It became my true childhood refuge, my place when I was confused or lonely, as I was without a sister, brother, or often even a nearby friend. Hazel trees rim this clearing, decent with branches; it's like a big circle of peace.

Buying time—I think I was trying to establish whether my timidity really was evaporating—I headed for the clearing, intending to go on from there to the cottage and see Mr. Kelly or Professor Fay or both. As I got nearer, I heard noises—metallic sounds and voices raised.

In my clearing? What the hell!

The ferns stood shoulder-high and no Mohican ever reconnoitered like I did. I got forward to the hazels without disturbing a frond. Through the greenery gleamed something incongruous—a strong color blue. And a gunmetal gray. And a man in a loud check suit with a big, unlit cigar. And a sweaty little man beside him, pompous as a gamecock.

The blue came from the shirts worn by thirty, forty, maybe fifty men; the gray from the barrels of the guns they sported as they drilled up and down; the loud voice from a white-haired man older than my father. He also wore a blue shirt as he put the armed men through their paces as though he were drilling a secret army. Which he was.

Very Important Digression: We had Fascism in Ireland. It wasn't called that—but Fascism is what it was. Very suitable, in part, to the Irish temperament; if we want to settle an argument, observe how often we use our fists. Avoid doing it if you can; it's a bad idea. Extend such a tendency upward into the national body politic and you can easily see that there are many ways in which we'd have been pals with Hitler. Communism would never have worked for us—we're too envious. Climbing up by standing on the bodies of those you've killed—that'd work.

Let me explain the root of the word *Fascism* to you, because you'll already have come across it very often. I find that I understand more in life—and more clearly—if I go by the language.

Here's what I understand by *Fascism,* one of the filthiest words in the world.

In some form, it originated within the Roman Empire, where, as a symbol of military power, legions carried an ornamental, tightly bound set of *fasces,* the rods of authority. These were bundles of short staves held together by leather bands, and when an order wasn't obeyed, the officer carrying them brought them crashing down on the head of the offending soldier.

Eventually they gained ceremonial status, and in the Roman Senate, when somebody wanted a debate to end, he reached for the ornamental rods and raised them—to signify that there would be no more discussion.

Don't trust me necessarily on this; place no bets. My authority, our English teacher, Mr. O'Toole, also told us that you determine the sex of chickens by holding a needle on a thread above the chicken's private parts, and if the pendulous needle swings up and down in a straight line it's a boy chicken, and if the pendulum describes a wide circle it's a girl chicken.

When Mr. de Valera won in 1932, a number of his opponents contemplated the Fascist route back to power. This is what happened: Six days before the election, a bunch of men (fascists always move in bunches) met in the Wynns Hotel on Abbey Street in Dublin. It became a notorious meeting, at which many of those attending, including several army officers, understood that they were participating in a "might is right" debate. And it wasn't the first such meeting—it's merely the most famous.

By then guns were available. To cut a long story short, within a year the militia that they founded had begun to appear across the country. They didn't wear brown shirts like Hitler's bunch, or black shirts, like Oswald Mosley's mobs in England—they wore blue; and they had the straight-arm salute. I don't know if they ever worked out a Gaelic equivalent of *Sieg Heil!*—but I remember them in towns and villages, and they looked sinister.

What I saw in my little clearing in the woods must have been one of their very first musterings. Years later, I heard that they'd come together very quickly, because their eventual leader, the man I'd met named O'Duffy, then the country's chief of police, had substantial organizational talents.

That afternoon, as I peered through the ferns, they seemed very pleased with themselves. With them stood the man with the thick and sleek black hair who had had the gun in the cottage. End—for the moment—of Very Important Digression.

60

I lingered and lurked, hidden in the ferns. The men had little skill, and only a few knew how to handle and present a rifle. They marched like rookies, but hard and determined; if zeal wins wars, we were lost. Hands slapped on the guns as they presented arms; bolts clanged in the sunshine. When the "Stand at ease" order went up, I ducked back through the ferns and got to the cottage before anybody returned.

Through the window, Mary Lewis saw me arrive and came to the door. Her smile of welcome had too much of the gloat in it for comfort.

"How's Mammy?"

I hated that parental term—syrupy, gooey, and too common; children all over Ireland used it, and I knew married men who addressed their wives as "Mammy." To this day, it makes me inclined to retch.

"Is Mr. Kelly here?"

"That's a very nice coat." Mary Lewis stepped too close and fingered my sleeve. "I s'pose 'tis as well you got it while your daddy could still afford it."

"When will Mr. Kelly be back?"

"Did you know he has me permanent?" She looked at me like a

slug—but I felt like a bird. "And great wages. How much is Lily getting from your mammy?"

I looked hard at her and she retreated.

"You should see the French wines they have here. And a ton of cheese."

I turned to go and she said, "He's not far away—d'you want to wait?"

We called it "the cottage" but many people raised families in smaller houses. Mary Lewis had a fire burning, and I could see why the Fays liked the place so much; cozy and quiet, full of what Mother called her "warmth colors"—browns and soft greens and mustard cushions.

Mary Lewis disappeared into the kitchen at the rear, and I stood in front of the fire trying to make myself feel proprietorial. I had no anchor. Up to then, when faced with anything, I asked myself what my father would do. But that sense of authority in me had been undermined—by him. No anchor—and no rudder. Difficult to be proprietorial.

Now, at the moment when I needed the authority and its strength, I couldn't muster it, but I managed to produce the next best thing—silence, or something close to it. Not entirely by will, though—when King Kelly arrived, my tongue stuck to the roof of my mouth.

All his affability had fallen away.

"What can I do for you?"

Oh, those glittering eyes.

"The mortgage," I said.

"You left us early on Sunday, eh?"

My brain was rocking like a boat in a storm; my eyes, damn them, watered.

"The mortgage you made my mother sign."

Behind him appeared Professor Fay.

"What's this? What's this?"

"He's muttering about something."

Little sweaty Fay had the decency to flinch. His pitted skin had black pigments like those of a coal miner. He said nothing.

I stepped away from the fire and made for the door. What I now know is that, despite my terror in the moment, my silence frightened them.

"You're not leaving us, are you?" said Professor Fay.

King Kelly picked up the warning and became the cheery host again.

"We're famished. And young lads are always famished, aren't they?"

"They are, Tom, they are, Tom."

King Kelly called. "Mary!"

She appeared, smarmy as a courtier.

"Mary, Mary, quite contrary, will you make us all a sandwich. Not the one sandwich for the three of us. Make three."

By the time they'd finished their false laughing I'd sidestepped King Kelly and swerved through the door.

Not clean away, however—he called me.

"D'you know about the Golden Rule?"

I turned, in midstride (by now I was a giant again), and I think I held a pose, as I quoted from our Christian-doctrine class in school.

"Yes. Do unto others as you would have them do unto you."

"What?" King Kelly looked at me as though I had just grown an additional head. "What the blazes are you talking about, boy?"

"The Golden Rule. Moral reciprocity."

"No, boy. The Golden Rule is—the man with the gold makes the rules."

61

This is the point where I think perhaps you'll begin to dislike me. Feel free—because I did many despicable things. Sin is falling short of your own standards; I discovered that fact at the age of eighteen; I didn't know what it was before then. In which case I sinned. On a grand scale. Don't rush to judgment, though; my sins may not be what you think they were. Did I cause them? Or did they "happen" to me? The telling of this tale determines and identifies them.

Here's my first offense: I ran away. Appalling. I ran away from Mother and left her to stew in her own gravy—in fear, in dread. After my giant strides (in which I'd accomplished nothing), back to the house I went; in my father's little office I found the cashbox, took a chunk of money, tiptoed out to the yard, and drove away.

There's a place where the driveway bends, and you can look back and see the front door, and I looked back and I saw her. She stood there, not beckoning, not waving, just bewildered.

That decent, good woman—how could I have done it? How could I have abandoned her like that? At the time when she most needed me?

And I knew that she had nobody. Mother had too much pride to ask for help. I had been her lifeline, I knew that, and now I had shredded the strands of that rope, whose threads were already thin.

Worst of all, I knew what I was doing. I knew I was abandoning her to the dreadful life that had just fallen on top of her and—be shocked by this—I enjoyed doing it. Yes—a part of me relished it. Somewhere inside me, a grim creature spoke, larger than an imp, not quite as big as an ogre, a creature who had not previously existed.

It said, "Hee-hee, you're getting away from it all; that's right—run. Why not? It's the best thing for you. Therefore it's the right thing to do."

The sun that day shone like the face of beauty. Birds had come back to the fields after winter. A new government was sliding into power. Life was opening up. I was never going home again. "Demure." A "sweetheart." Not now, not ever again, no more "obedience" and "conscientiousness" and "responsibility," the watchwords of my childhood—I'd had far too much of all that.

The moment when we do things that we shouldn't is also the moment when we least and most see the truth about ourselves. That has been my experience; maybe it's different for you. As I drove out through our gateway I thought, *I'm not carrying this burden anymore.* That was me seeing the least truth of myself. And the most truth at that moment? Simple. I had discovered kissing, and that was what I was going after.

Kissing, and some notes thereupon, as we take this now-familiar journey to the house in Charleville, on roads empty save for creamery wagons and an almond-eyed goat here and there.

Once again, go for the language: Here you'll find a disappointment; I've been able to trace few linguistic roots for *kiss.* Mind you, there's a limit to the number of people of whom one may inquire. In her later years, and when I was older too, I asked Miss Dora Fay.

"It's onomatopoeic. Every culture had a ritual kissing gesture of some kind. And the lips when employed in kissing make a sucking and blowing sound." And she smiled. "Terrific, isn't it?"

One afternoon, not long before he died, I contrived to lead my father to the word.

"Osculation," he said immediately, and also quoted verbatim one of

his gods, the aforementioned Mr. Bierce; " 'A word invented by the poets as a rhyme for 'bliss.' " He grew somber. "Don't ever give in to a pity kiss."

He never told me what he meant.

How surprising kissing felt. I didn't know that excitement could have such a dry, cool feeling.

And—that kissing on Sunday, was that all there was to it? What do I do if saliva escapes? When I'm excited I burble a little, some foam is loosed. "Say it, don't spray it, MacCarthy," Mr. O'Toole used to say to me when I was standing up in class.

I've mentioned eyes, haven't I? Meaning, I didn't know whether to keep them open or closed. My instinct had been to close them—to concentrate on the enjoyment. Yet I also wanted to see her eyes, guess what she was thinking.

And—what are we supposed to think about while kissing? I found myself thinking, *What about my nose—how do I keep it out of the way? And where do I put the rest of myself?* And *Is there anybody I can tell about this?*

Breathing too—what to do about it? I didn't want to blow a gale into the poor girl's lungs; kissing wasn't the artificial respiration they taught to lifeguards—at least I knew that much. But if I breathed through my nose wouldn't she feel my nostrils dilating? And—wouldn't it be only a matter of minutes before I was heaving like a dragon? Yes—there were things I needed to know here.

Tightness of embrace? Now we get into the difficult and confusing stuff. When kissing Venetia I felt certain softnesses that I knew to be bosoms. *Not bosoms like Aunt Anne's rock-hard prow. Am I supposed to feel more of them with my chest? Am I supposed to stand back? Is there a recommended stance for all this?* I doubted it, because there was also lying down to be considered—eventually.

62

You can imagine, can't you, the clashing sounds in my head as I slowed down the car in Charleville. At least I knew where to find everybody. The pickings had proven so rich in this part of Munster that the show decided to work every small town in the counties of Cork, Limerick, Tipperary, and Waterford. I was to learn that Sarah had decreed Clare too poor and Kerry too sharp-witted: "In the one there's little financial reward, in the other there's only emotional defeat." Meaning that the Clare people wouldn't or couldn't spend the money, and the Kerry people knew every line of every Shakespeare play, and knew them better than anybody in the company, including herself and her daughter.

I hadn't worked out a plan as to how I should address my father. Certainly I must tell him about the mortgage—or must I? Wouldn't that only drag me back to the problem I was fleeing? He'd want me to deal with it. That was my guess.

He had found his bench again, across the street from the old Market House, and he had company—the neckless little actor. I strolled over, not as calm as I tried to appear, and the neckless one, whose name was Graham, first made room for me with a nervous smile, and then stood to go. *Do these people know all about this situation?* The thought angered and embarrassed me.

"No-no-no need to go, Graham. Ben's good company—" But Graham went. "They've started the prosecutions," said my father as I sat down. "A fellow in Dublin got two months in jail. And there were twenty others who tried to vote early and often."

I said nothing and he shook out the newspaper, went to another page.

"Happy-happy-happy Birthday this week to the Countess of Athlone."

Again, I didn't bite. He flipped another page and a new note came into his voice.

"Have you got any investments in British government securities? Everybody seems to think they're doing well."

Sarcasm. I didn't hear it often from my father. He used it on the workmen: "Billy, did you leave the gate open to let air into the field?" And, as you know, he had used it on Missy Casey—but never on Mother or me.

My father, I think, sensed the pressure from me. He looked nervous. The rapid turning of the newspaper pages—that wasn't typical; he usually read every page from stem to stern.

He stopped at a page. " 'For your throat's sake smoke Craven A—the cigarette made specially to prevent sore throats.' "

"Stop," I said. "Stop your nonsense now."

He didn't look at me. With great care he folded the newspaper, rose and walked away down the street; I watched him out of sight. Another unseasonable day of sunny warmth—and something was taking place, some kind of reckoning.

From inside the open front door of Sarah's house, I heard a voice rising and falling, in recitation, not in song. I went indoors, treading heavily after my knock had gone unanswered. Nobody heard my step; I reached the kitchen unintercepted. As usual, clinical tidiness everywhere, with no sign of Mrs. Haas. Who was reciting and where?

I returned to the hallway and heard the voice clearly. From upstairs, and with great power it came, and although I couldn't hear the words I recognized the cadence.

With one foot on the lower step I waited, fully aware of what I wanted to do. How long did I stand there like that? Perhaps two hours, perhaps a minute or so. Already it had become that kind of day.

I looked down at my excellently polished shoes and the home-knit yellow socks, and I still felt no pang of remorse about having abandoned Mother. My hand on the newel post felt strong and dry. With my foot firmly on the stair tread and my grip on the round cone of the newel, I had become a hero to myself once more.

The voice stopped. All sounds from the outside world ceased too. I heard only what echoed inside my head. A kind of bell, was it? Not necessarily a bell, but the same quality of sound, the clean peal of a clarion. I made ready to move and squared up my heart and mind to be as one.

Up the first step. And now the second. And next the third, to the little platform, the small, low landing from which the staircase turned left and climbed its full length upward. These were slow, heavyish, deliberate steps.

I looked up—to where I had previously seen the heads of daughter and mother, the younger above the older. Now I saw no head, and I heard no voice.

Then the voice began again, lower, still in a reciting lilt. If I climbed some more steps I might make out the words. I softened the weight of my footfall, not to creep or lurk, merely to dim the noise and hear the verse. The voice proved too soft.

I thought I detected the word "Netherby," and my heart leapt. Young Lochinvar stands among my greatest heroes. He carried away—stirring verse—the bride of Netherby because she should have married him in the first place. I climbed on. "Halfway up the stairs is the stair where I sit," but I didn't sit.

The voice stopped and the door opened. She said that it wasn't so much that she heard me as that she felt my presence. My presence? I didn't even know what that was.

My presence. For months, for years, I hugged the words to myself. I hugged them when elated, when depressed. What's the difference between those two states, elated and depressed? None. They're both liars.

"Some people are like that," said Venetia. "They have a force in their spirit that announces them."

She stood aside to admit me to the same small sitting room. The colors seemed brighter than before, probably because the sun had begun to stream in. She stepped in behind me and I walked straight to the window.

Not a soul to be seen down there in the cut-stone street. I saw a pony and cart with its silver churns. The pony looked listless, and I guessed that the owner had gone into a bar across the street. A small bird flew by, a sparrow. His movements were like my thoughts—small, but for him, huge, with much flickering and whurruping.

Venetia stayed where she'd entered, her back against the closed door. She said that she'd been rehearsing a poem she wanted to introduce into the show soon. And she said that I, in my being, had reminded her of the poem. It was "Lochinvar."

I felt the compliment, I felt the thrill of it. And I felt the thump of it: Was this a manipulation? Was Venetia manipulating me? But I didn't care; I took it for what it felt like, and now I was a giant again, now I was a hero. A tongue-tied hero, perhaps, and my legs were shaking a little.

Turning away from the window I looked at her. Definitely I can say that this was the first time I'd ever looked at a girl with such intensity. Not curiosity—I had done that; I had done that with the occasional girlfriends of Large Lily when they called to the house, girls who were wild and drab all at once. And I had looked—yech!—at simpering and false Mary Lewis. But I hadn't truly known why I was looking at any of them at all.

I knew, though, why I was looking at Venetia Kelly now. It had nothing immediate to do with the fact that she was daughter of Sarah, the wicked queen, and granddaughter of the evil King.

Every time I feel heat from the sun on my shoulders it's the sun that came through that window. Every time I look out of a window from an upper floor, I'm looking out of that window. I didn't know then that I would go on to have so much of me formed by that moment. But if you'd been there and if you'd asked me, I might have sworn an oath that yes, I would remain like that all my life. And I have done—taking every reference point of serious awakening from those few seconds of sensation.

The curtains had a willow-branch pattern, long and climbing. I've ever since liked willow branches. On the sash bar sat a perfect little porcelain knob for opening the catch. My heart lifts if I find one in a house or hotel today. The window had shutters too, folded back, just the same as in my room at home.

My coat had a herringbone pattern. I know because I now studied the sleeve as intently as an archaeologist looks at a shard. The air felt light. Perfume somewhere? Too early for flowers. My feet on the wooden floor felt solid and comforting.

Her voice was telling me that she knew I'd come back for her, and she even wondered whether that was the reason she had been rehearsing the poem. The sound in my head, the bell that wasn't a bell, rang more beautifully now, and each stroke, each tolling ring, came from somewhere I'd never been.

You think I exaggerate? I do not. This was the beginning of the passion by which I now live, and by which I began to live that day. I knew it from the moment I turned around and saw her arms open wide toward me and heard her say the word "Welcome."

Whatever tragedy followed has been of my doing.

We didn't embrace. Instead, she took my hands and looked me directly in the eye. She said that we should sit down, and she arranged us on the sofa. Directed by a gentle push from her, I sat back and she sat up, on the edge of the couch, where she could look at me. A blind spectator would have grasped the gravity between us.

"Why d'you think I haven't married or settled down?" she said. "And I'm nearly past the age of what's seen as marriageable. Ben, we could search the world. We might find partners with whom we could have good and even excellent lives. I don't believe in that. For me it's always been the idea of one and one only whom I'd recognize the moment I saw him."

In my newfound sense of purpose, I went straight to the point I most needed to have answered.

"My father believes he'll be with you for life."

"I've already told you—he was the path to you."

"But he lives with you?" No matter how I tried, I couldn't get rid of the burning hurt that he didn't live at home anymore.

"I've told you what goes on between your father and me." She paused.

I thought, *I've never seen anybody I like as much. But I've never met an actress before; I hope that's not the only reason I like her.* That's true to this day. Just "liked"—I liked her deep down the way I ordinarily liked my father, and I liked her the way I ordinarily liked Mother—that is to say, feelings of great warmth, together with a profound interest in their best well-being, and what I could contribute to it. The word *love* has had a bad time. I myself am not much good at defining it. But I think it begins with "like."

The same impulses as I'd always had for my parents flooded all over me now. Were I wealthy beyond planets I'd spend it all on this girl's safety and comfort.

Venetia went on. "I didn't want your father to leave his home. And farm. And wife. And son. As you know, he'd been following the show for months. Each night he'd come around to the back, and we'd all go off and have something to eat and drink and he always paid. Not that we couldn't afford to—we have plenty of money, especially when my mother's traveling with us. Not to mention my grandfather. And we'll come to him soon."

I tried to enumerate the questions in my head. Immediately I had the fear that I'd never get to ask them all, would never get all the answers I needed. Yet Venetia, beside me, looking at me, had suddenly, at one stroke it seemed, become a permanent part of me. The importance of my questions was fading.

"When your father first declared himself, long before he began to travel with us, my mother and my grandfather urged me to accept him. He's young enough, they said, the age gap, twenty years, that's nothing. And he has money. Yes, there's no divorce in Ireland, but there is in England and in the United States. He can get a divorce somewhere."

"Divorce"? She might as well have said "murder." Although I'd never heard of anybody in Ireland who was divorced, I knew that it had the worst associations, not just illegal but evil. I saw Mother shudder when she heard the word—which wasn't often.

And I had my own shudder. Mother. Grandfather. Was a plot emerging? Worse—was she part of it, this girl to whom I had already committed myself, even though I had as yet no idea of such a concept, nor a language for expressing commitment?

There isn't a term comprehensive enough for the kind of commitment I entered into that day. All I knew is that the world could now go on safely about its business, because I could stop worrying about the rest of my life; I was feeling the safety that's embodied in commitment, no matter how heartbreaking it may be.

The floor had a rug woven with the scarlet, orange, and gray mysteries of Afghanistan. It didn't reach to each wall, and the boards in between had been painted gray-white.

"I like your father very much indeed. No, I should say I love him. I do. He's a dear and wonderful man. And because he's like that I've let him into my life. We aren't lovers, if you know what that means."

She looked at me and she knew I didn't know, except perhaps by dim instinct.

"Never mind. We travel together to the towns where we have shows. He watches me. Did you know that he's a wonderful critic?"

I said, "He reads a lot of Shakespeare."

"And," said Venetia, "he tells me that you're better on Shakespeare than he is. Instinctively, he says."

"That can't be the case," I said.

"He brings you into every conversation."

"You told me that," I said, and shook my head. I didn't think that my father talked about me to anybody, but when she told me I believed her.

Venetia said, "It's 'Ben this' and 'Ben that'—and it's not all easy either."

I must have looked alarmed because she leaned forward and stroked my face.

"No, no, I'm sorry, I didn't mean to upset you. What I wanted to say is this—he talks about the anguish of loving you. He says there's no pain like the pain of a father for a son."

On the wall hung a painting of an old stone bridge, with a high curved arch and black water tumbling beneath. And now I must have twitched, because she took my hands to her lips and kissed my knuckles.

"I know what you looked like as a baby. I know that you didn't speak your first words until you were almost two, and that you then spoke perfectly. I know that all who meet you consider you strong and generous and funny. In return, I tell him about the loves I know—Shakespeare's women, Lady Margaret and Cordelia and Ophelia and Juliet. When it ends, he kisses me on the cheek. That's all."

In the silence that followed, both of us heard a sound. I listened. From somewhere outside the room a little creature was sawing—a steady, rasping sound, quite faint but distinct in the still air of the day.

Venetia whispered, "Audrey's room is across the way."

Mrs. Haas had her shoes off.

64

We stood up. Venetia told me that my father would soon return, that they had an "appointment"—to fill a number of hours free before she had to travel to that night's show. I made no comment; my mind had ceased working.

She said, "Come back tomorrow. At two o'clock."

I met my father on the staircase. He didn't look alarmed or surprised, but he did look different. Had he changed? Oscar Wilde greeted somebody one day: "Oh, there you are—I didn't recognize you because I've changed so much." Had I changed so much? No. That's fanciful, isn't it? Or—is it? He definitely looked different.

I said, "I've had a long talk with Venetia."

Maybe a shiftiness came into his eyes. Maybe he looked uncomfortable—but if he did, it was fleeting and minuscule.

"The-the-the new routine for Blarney is great," he said.

"Do you know about Mother?"

Now little shadows did gather in his eyes.

"She didn't write to me or anything."

James Clare once told me that I have what he called a "burly" mind, meaning that I too often attack problems with mental force, hammer rather than scalpel.

"Where would she write to you?"

"Is she all right?"

"Except for the mortgage."

I heard my harshness and was dismayed by it. What had happened to me? My father heard it too.

"That's no way to talk about an act of decency."

"How do you make that out?"

He said, "Mr. Kelly has his family's interest at heart. In this case his granddaughter's."

"And the guns?"

I expect that you've never had the experience of looking into the eyes of an adult male to whom you have looked up all your life, whose welfare has been of the dearest concern to you, whose well-being you have plotted inside yourself insofar as you could, and suddenly seen something different there, a complete lack of competence, a crude ignorance.

What a chastening moment. Except—be careful here: This is all hindsight. I thought none of those things at that time. I do know this, however; I had enough presence of mind to be shocked at myself when I found my hands curling into tight fists ready to punch my father hard in each eye. Even more shocking—I knew it had little, or even nothing, to do with what he had put Mother and me through. That also was what James Clare meant by a "burly" mind.

If I'd known where to find him I'd have gone looking for James Clare. I needed to steady myself; such little self-knowledge as I had told me that much. My father continued upstairs and I heard him knock, then enter the room where I had been sitting with Venetia and close the door behind him. *He'll now be sitting on a couch still warm from me.* The thought gave me a shiver.

I was ravenously hungry. My food savior appeared—Mrs. Haas, and I thought, *She's going to make me one of those great sandwiches.* But she didn't; instead, with a worried face, she made a shooing gesture, flicking the back of her hand at me, and mouthing the word "Go."

How strange can all this get? I thought. I wish I'd had a voice inside me saying, *You ain't seen nothin' yet.*

No James Clare, no Miss Fay, no food, no nothing, no nobody. I didn't want to eat in the town—that is, if I could find somewhere to eat, which didn't seem likely. Not thinking where I walked, I found myself beside the car, climbed in, and drove away.

I had no place to go. My father didn't want me near him. Venetia did seem to want me near her—but not yet. Home offered no option; I had left there. The show had gone to Adare, one of the prettiest villages in Ireland. No harm in going there. And anyway my father had alerted me to a new routine by Blarney.

Minutes later, on the outskirts of Charleville, I passed a sports field; above the walls I could see the tall uprights of the goals. I also saw a number of bicycles leaning there, perhaps twenty in all.

A game of football was beginning, a pickup game, no formality, no jerseys or other kit, just a bunch of fellows and a leather football in the middle of the day.

Important Digression: Our "football" in Ireland refers to Gaelic football, a game that looks a little like soccer, and a little like rugby, and nothing like either. It is played with a round ball and fifteen men on a team, and a player is allowed to handle the ball but not throw it; bounce it, but not too often; run with it, flipping the ball from hand to toe (considered an exercise in great skill); field it—the higher the better; and kick it as far and as accurately as possible. End of Important Digression.

I played it in school, and (excuse the immodesty, but you need to know this) I was the star player and became the senior team captain, playing at midfield—which is where the traffic of the game gets controlled. These players, in their everyday clothes, seemed about my age, and I asked to join in.

For the next hour or so I had a good time. The confusion of encountering my father dissolved; the hero returned. It took me a few minutes to warm up, and I had to decide how much clothing to discard. Sunshine or no, the air still had a nip in it, which gave the exercise a sharp edge.

It's a violent game. When you leap to field a ball coming from on high, you make yourself vulnerable from the fingertips down, leaving the length of your body open to attack by a shoulder-charging opponent running at you. But when you're up there, your feet three or four feet off the ground, in a leap that you've achieved by running into a takeoff, and you feel your fingertips touching and then closing on the leather of the ball—there's no feeling like it. Also, it's almost impossible not to do it elegantly.

How I played! I had joined an ordinary, casual game of football, dragged together by lads from the town and nearby countryside, all of whom no longer went to school—some were apprentices or clerks—and who played like this, weather permitting, every week.

Like a bird, or a salmon at the weir, I rose above the others, fielding impeccably. Nobody reached me up there, nobody rose as high, and when I came down to earth I strode among them like the giant I had become.

The ball went where I sent it—to the hands of a player on my team or between the goalposts. When I made a run, it came from my toe to my hand as though connected by elastic string. My shoulders went into challenges fearlessly. I ran as fast as I'd ever done.

Energy, energy—that's all I was, a mass of energy, heat, and speed. And urgency—I wanted to spend energy, I wanted to put force about me, to send force from me out across the earth, to express strength, to see what power was. That afternoon I could have done anything I wanted.

At the end we took our farewells. The exercise had been exactly what I needed. They asked me back, they asked me where I lived and if I would play for their team. But I avoided disclosing whence I came.

The boys gathered around the car and for ten minutes or so I had to tell them all about it. Like monkeys, they poked here, picked there, sat in the driver's seat, the passenger seat, the rear seats, touching it, stroking the leather, turning the wheel.

One boy, red-haired, asked me if I'd give him a lift home, that he'd love his father to see the car; he had been the other outstanding player in the field. He sat beside me, we drove away, and that's how I came to eat my next meal.

They had a good farm, not as clean as ours, and not as modern. A horse and a pony did their work—the horse for the heavy fields, the pony for lighter jobs such as taking the churns to the creamery or the family to Mass on a Sunday morning.

Many children and their mother came out to see the car. When the husband and oldest son came in from the fields, they had to see it too. Inside the house, I was given full plates of food—and an unpleasant shock.

Having eaten, the children scattered. The father, when I told him, roughly, my address, asked me if I knew "that immoral fellow who was after running away with some dirty woman."

I said I knew nothing of it; his wife spoke words like "scoundrel," "scandal," and "disgraceful." As soon as I could, I left the house, trying not to look hasty—but hurt to the core.

65

En route to the show I got lost in the maze of small roads around Ballingarry. Not all signposts had been reinstalled since the War of Independence, when local people removed them to confuse the British soldiers. By the time I got to Adare, the show had begun; I paid my ticket to somebody I'd never seen before and squeezed into a tight standing space at the back.

Portia had just begun the "quality of mercy" speech. How odd to see her onstage again, and how thrilling. On account of my height I had a clear view; I hoped that she could see me, but I wasn't close enough to check whether her eyes found me. Nor could I see my father, but from that I deduced nothing—impossible to find anybody in so packed a hall.

Other than the Shakespeare, they had revamped the repertoire a little. Michael had a new tumbling act, and it required the entire stage, because he rolled across it like a wheel with spokes. The rude lovers had again become a milkmaid and her randy farmer, with much chasing around a wooden cow. And, as I'd hoped, "Lochinvar" appeared—Venetia's next starring piece.

So daring in love and so dauntless in war,
Have ye e'er heard of gallant like young Lochinvar?

She told it like a story almost, yet never failing to hit the rhyme and keep its ballad shape, and she extracted from it every drop of romance. I don't care what the audience thought—I know it was meant for me, and I know that it was about me. That's what life is like at that age, especially for an only child.

I found the show much improved—or was my heart so engaged that my objectivity had dissolved? Yet the audience bore me out, shouting and stamping their feet. And then came the biggest cheer of the night—Blarney.

This time he arrived sitting like a monkey on Venetia's shoulders. She sat on a chair, brought him down, and plonked him on her knee. Now the wooden horse stood nearby—I'd first seen it in Cashel.

"Whassup with you?"

Venetia looked at him, puzzled. "What do you mean, Blarney?"

"Why aren't you on the horse?"

"I'm resting him. He has a race on Saturday."

Blarney peered around her, twisted his head in a cunning leer at the audience, and looked up at Venetia.

"He. Has. A race. Is that what you said?"

"Yes, Blarney."

"He—races?" Doubt hung in icicles from his voice.

"Yes, Blarney."

"But he's wooden." And just as Venetia was about to retort, he warned, "Don't say it."

The audience loved it. Blarney winked at them. Then he sat back, his head against Venetia's upper arm, and looked up at her.

"Venetia?" His voice sounded plaintive.

"Yes, Blarney."

"Venetia, do you love me?"

"Yes, Blarney."

"Say it."

"I've just said it."

"No, you only said, 'Yes.' Tell me you love me."

"I love you."

"You do?"

"I love you, Blarney."

"That's good, Venetia. And do you love only me? No, don't answer that question." Blarney sat up in alarm and stared wide-eyed and open-mouthed around the audience. Then he cocked his head to one side and looked up at her. "Give me a hug, Venetia."

"Of course I will, Blarney."

She coiled an arm around him and pressed his face to her bosom.

We heard him saying a muffled "I can't breathe," and she released him. He spent some time getting himself to rights on her knee again and looked out at the audience.

"If I tell you a joke will you give me a kiss?"

"I will, Blarney."

"It's a joke about drinking."

"Yes, Blarney."

"It's a joke about the Irish and drinking."

"Yes, Blarney."

"An Irishman walked out of a pub."

He paused. Venetia looked down at him; he swiveled his head from the audience and looked up at her.

"Go on, Blarney."

"That's the joke. An Irishman walked out of a pub."

The crowd began to get it. Venetia pretended not to, and he explained.

"No Irishman would ever walk out of a pub. Even if they wanted to, most Irishmen wouldn't be able to walk out of a pub. They'd fall out of a pub."

He got a huge cheer.

"Where's my kiss?"

Venetia kissed him on the forehead and Blarney pretended to swoon. He sat up again and composed himself.

"Venetia?"

"Yes, Blarney."

"Do you love me?"

Venetia looked away, a little miffed. Blarney banged his head against her arm. "Do you love me?"

"I told you I do, Blarney."

"Would you ever love somebody else?"

"I might, Blarney."

Blarney turned his head into Venetia's bosom and began to sob; the audience said a huge "Awww . . ."

"Blarney, it's all right. There's nobody like you."

He lifted his head. "You have the look of somebody in love with somebody. Are you sure 'tis me?"

"Blarney, I love you."

"Venetia, what's wrong with you?"

"What do you mean, Blarney?"

"What kind of a woman are you?"

"I don't know what you mean, Blarney."

"A fine woman like you loving a wooden dummy." And he cackled.

66

I didn't attempt to meet anybody after the show. Venetia had been so emphatic, so specific about our appointment next day, and I didn't want to breach her arrangements or jeopardize my own interests. Which, by now, had become considerable. I thought of nothing but her, I imagined nothing but being with her. As to how it might work out regarding my father—I had no idea what to do, and it didn't seem to be troubling me very much.

Anyway, I had a more immediate problem—I had no place to stay. Having got lost on my way to the show had left me without a chance to find a place for the night. I can best describe my state and attitude as "light-headed"—not quite irresponsible and wild but getting there fast. Yet for all my feckless mood I didn't want to sleep in the car—so I reversed my earlier decision and decided to sleep at home. That's how consistent I was!

I knew how to do it without being detected. If I cut the headlights before rounding the corner, I could leave the car parked on the driveway; I could even face it back toward the road for a quick dawn getaway.

All went according to plan. I tiptoed from the parked car onto the grass verge and walked along to the yard, then slipped through the back door. With the flashlight I had taken from the car I found bread, cheese, and milk, and ate in the kitchen.

The house had an uneasy feel, but I couldn't say why. Things seemed to have been put back in wrong places; the bucket of spring water for the kitchen (drawn every day from the well, usually by Billy, Lily, or me) always lived on a small wooden platform inside the scullery door; now it had been moved along the wall to a more inconvenient place. Two empty mugs sat on the table, something never allowed by Mother, who liked all surfaces clean and clear. The aprons hung on a hook in the scullery, and not on the rear of the main kitchen door.

I headed upstairs, feeling disjointed. And—shock! I found my bedroom door locked. I stopped and listened—not a sound anywhere. Again I tried the doorknob, and pressed the door hard in case something had jammed. No, this door was locked. But it had never been locked; there was a key; it lived above the door on the lip of the frame—but I'd never seen it used in my life.

We had four bedrooms—my parents' room, mine, and two guest rooms. I tried the two empty rooms first—all doors locked. No keys anywhere, nothing on top of any doorframe. I figured that I had to brave Mother, so I knocked on her partly open door. Had she been locking these rooms for a reason? I needed to know. No answer. I knocked again, slightly louder, then I beamed my flashlight and tipped open the door an inch at a time. And found an empty room.

The bed remained as impeccably dressed as she left it every day. I lit the large oil lamp on my father's night table and looked all around. Some decision had been taken about this room. It felt abandoned. Everything might have seemed normal—but there's more to a room than the way the furniture is arranged.

I then lit her lamp, and the two together gave me a very full light. Walking here and there, I looked at this and that, uncomfortable at the hugeness of the sinister shadows I made—but that wasn't what disturbed me. Something here was very wrong; I had come home to an empty house.

Everywhere I went, I found the same impression—although things seemed more or less normal, they also felt different. Downstairs, some chairs had been moved around in the parlor; the settee in the hall had been dragged a foot or two along the hall and no longer sat under the painting of Connemara; no coats hung on the racks in the porch.

I opened the front door and walked out—a frosty night and the stars doing their best to light the world. With heavy footsteps I made deliberate noise as I walked into the yard—but no bark. In the first loose box, Bobbie Boy lay asleep. In the second box, the pony stirred—but what was going on? Where was the dog? And Miss Kennedy, the cat?

Typically we took the cows in during November, and they stayed in the cowshed until March or thereabouts. Saint Patrick's Day, the seventeenth, always had significance for dairy farmers, because by then we probably had enough new grass to let them out—though we had to be sure of having enough hay scattered in the fields. The cows were fine; they turned their heavy heads to look at my flashlight. One or two lumbered up in alarm.

That's where I should have slept that night—with the cows. Instead, I lay in my parents' bed—and on my father's side. If you assume that such a deed might have given me gyp, you're right—a very odd feeling indeed. When I lay down, I saw that my legs reached longer than my father's did. On how many past occasions had I seen him in this bed? Since early childhood, for instance, when I'd climb on top of him in the morning and insist on his getting up.

And this had been the bed of my parents' wedding night. Their honeymoon had been delayed due to some international tension or fracas somewhere, and they cleared the house of all the people, so that they had their first night alone together—in this bed. Shouldn't that remembrance have made me queasy in some way? It didn't. I'd never heard the word *taboo* and I didn't know I wasn't supposed to have such thoughts.

Perhaps you're finding this strange—but I knew nothing whatsoever about what we call "the facts of life." Not a thing. I had no anatomical knowledge; I had no emotional knowledge.

None of that would feel surprising to any man or woman who grew up in the Irish countryside during the early twentieth century. Who was to teach us anything? Certainly not our parents—because all of that was only to be learned within marriage. What a crash course! Outside of marriage any discussion of sex was a sin. In short, we all knew there were taboo subjects without knowing the subjects, or their language.

So I lay there, on my father's side of his marriage bed, and wondered what to think about—I mean about him and Mother in this bed. Instead I began to think of Venetia—again. These were romantic thoughts. Rivers came into it, and misty valleys, and flowers and snatches of poems and songs, and possible gifts, and once again the idea of making great riches so that I could shower her with beautiful things. I fell asleep.

Next morning I woke up early. The clatter of buckets in the yard felt so normal that I forgot the oddities of last night. Yet, there I found myself in my parents' bed. I turned my head, half-expecting to see my mother—a weird moment: The relief that she wasn't there surged through me. Can feelings get any more confused than that? I came close to laughing.

The house, though, disturbed me even more in daylight, with its atmosphere so different from normal. I dressed quickly—still half dark outside—and headed downstairs. Too early for Lily, but from the yard came the noises of milking. Not many cows milk all through the winter, so I wondered which of the two men would be here.

Ned Ryan, little Ned, had taken charge that morning. He saw me as I saw him, and he turned away so rapidly that I thought he couldn't have seen me. I followed him. He dropped the empty bucket and ran into the cowshed. I ran after him and we had a ridiculous chase—ridiculous because he could never get away from me; he was three times my age.

When I cornered him at last, down the driveway, near where I'd parked the car, he wouldn't look at me. Nor would he speak to me.

"Ned, what's going on? Where's my mother?"

He kept his head turned away, his face downcast.

"Ned, is she ill?"—of which I'd been afraid.

Now he turned completely away and I assumed the worst.

"Where is she?"

"She's at her sister's. There's nothing wrong with her. But, Ben, get outta here, go on, go on."

Now I made a great error—or did I? I did what he had suggested; I climbed into the car and drove away. My reasons are perfectly simple—I wanted nothing to interfere with the promise of the day and the crucial appointment that I had to keep that afternoon.

67

How any young man of my day ever fell in love I simply do not know. Correction: How any young Irishman of my day conducted the business of falling in love remains a mystery. Without language, without knowledge, without schooling—what did we have? Instinct, I suppose, and in my case that's more or less what I used.

My thoughts as I drove away from our gate don't show me in a good light. I behaved recklessly; I pursued only my own immediate interests. It was disgraceful. Or was it? The events of that day brought about redemption, even if it did take some time.

Not far from our house, a hill sits high above the river. I know the place very well; I often return. The river bends as it approaches the hill, and through a quirk of geography widens to its broadest point in its one-hundred-mile journey to the sea.

I've seen that bend in all weathers—when the sun shines on the flat waters; when the wind feathers the stream; I've even been there in snow, but that hasn't happened often.

That morning I went there too late to see the moment of dawn. In mid- to late February the sun begins to reach the river bend a little before eight o'clock. It had come up red, meaning rain later. And it had come up wonderfully, slowly coloring the stream and bringing a red-gold tinge to the bare, overhanging branches.

I tried to imagine the day ahead. *Will we walk? Will we talk? Where will my father be?* I felt no pang of guilt about him; instead, an ever-deepening annoyance had settled on me, lit by ever-brighter flashes of anger. *Look at the trouble he has caused.* And then my thoughts returned to Venetia. *Will we hold hands? Will we kiss again?*

That was a curious kind of excitement—I haven't felt it since. Although I was riven and thrilled at the prospect of meeting her—especially as she had been so particular in making the arrangements—I felt patient; I could wait, almost like eyeing a delicious food one has saved for later.

The sunlight came down the river like a miracle. Soon the surface of the water became too bright for the eyes. I got out of the car and stepped forward to the clearest view. Cold, yes, and the morning had some damp in it, but this channel of red light seemed to have leaked through the floorboards of Heaven.

The sun fleshed out the morning, and now I was hungry. I made my plans—food, a newspaper, pace myself through the day until two o'clock. At breakfast in the Royal Hotel, in an empty dining room, I scanned the newspaper, and I know now that I was seeking to establish the size of world events too, and weld them to my own life.

In China, the Japanese were denying a major victory being claimed by the Chinese. Astounding rows were taking place in the German Parliament, where the Chancellor's denunciations of the Nationalist party "aroused the Nazi deputies to violent outbursts of rage." In South Africa a man who suffered a fractured skull in a mining blast was able to walk to his doctor's surgery.

And at home, Mr. Cosgrave, the defeated leader, threatened that if de Valera's policies went through, "England would come back here with all their force, and immediate and terrible war would be the result."

I read the newspaper from cover to cover. At half past eleven I left the hotel—150 minutes to go. The barber had opened; my beard hadn't yet become an issue, too fair-skinned; nevertheless I had a shave and a haircut—that took me to one o'clock.

At just before two o'clock, after an hour along winding roads, some no bigger than farm lanes, I drove into Charleville and parked around the corner from the house.

Unexpectedly, I found the door closed. When I rapped the satisfying lion's-head knocker, I heard immediate footsteps. Venetia opened the door wide and gestured me in. She closed the door, bolted it, and put her arms carefully around me. Then she led me by the hand upstairs to the very top floor, to a room I had never seen, a large and airy, bright place shouldered by the sloping mansards of the roof. Outside it had begun to rain.

She took my coat and, as though handling a golden cloak, hung it in a closet. I sat down where she directed, and she lay on a chaise covered in raspberry-pink velvet. She wore a long, loose shift of dove gray, and as I attempted to speak she put her fingers to her lips and indicated that I must say nothing, adding that we should simply look at each other.

All my inner awkwardness disappeared. In her company I felt assured and easy about myself; I've never known that feeling with anybody else. To illustrate how composed I was—I never flinched when, after some minutes, she stood, removed her robe, and lay down again on the chaise, completely naked.

With her hands she indicated that I must look at her all I wanted, and she raised herself a little, this way and that. But now you have, I feel sure, recalled how I reported interviews with Sarah, in which she described the relationship with Mr. Anderson.

I didn't know about that until long after this February day. Not that it would have made a difference, because after many delighted and fascinated minutes of my scrutinizing her, Venetia again rose from the couch and said, "Now it's your turn."

Looking back, I marvel at my own boldness. Think of the leap I made—from virginal farm life to this. With no shyness, I undressed. She rose, took each garment from me, folded it, and laid it like a vestment on a chair. I lay down as she had; she looked at me as I had at her; she closed her eyes in delight and pleasure as I had, and opened them again to gaze.

After some length of time—it might have been twenty minutes, it might have been an hour, it might have been three minutes—she rose from the chair in all her glory, took my hand and walked with me to her bed. A wide bed, more like a sultan's couch, cushions everywhere, and, on the wall above, a framed portrait of an Elizabethan gentleman with a beard, whom I recognized as William Shakespeare.

We lay down facing each other, and the world as I knew it came to an end and a new world began, the universe I have lived in—to varying degrees—ever since.

The human spirit knows how to suspend matters—some things weigh too heavily to be experienced in full at the time. And shock comes in many forms. I know one old gentleman who told me that he exhibited all the symptoms of stroke the day after his wedding night. The effects of great emotional moments often have to be deferred in order to manage them: grief; success; love.

Did I defer my fullest responses? It wasn't like that. My deferrings came much later and for different reasons. I took to love like I took to breathing. No angst, no depressed or worried feelings, not a hint of sadness; I was never anything but delighted and happy with Venetia.

It had to be like that; it felt as though we were one person. We clanged together like a couple of magnets and we stayed deeply, deeply united, in every imaginable way from that moment until—well, you shall see.

The rain poured down on the roof, inches above our heads, and made the experience even more delightful—a couple of children hiding from the storm. We scarcely talked, too busy. She took pains to establish how identical we were in experience; I didn't know how to tell anyway.

The softness of her skin remains my abiding memory—and the shock of how beautiful I found her to look at. Naturally I had seen illustrations of the undraped female form—in art books at home, and in what the boys at school called "nudie pictures" that somebody's brother had brought home from England.

And the scent from her skin—no picture can convey that. And the stillness—we had silences, and we had sounds. My mind filled with images of hunting.

Here, I wish to stop; I have no words that I want to use; there are some memories that must never be shared; if you rob the nest, the bird won't come back.

Let's leave it with Miss Dora Fay's words. Of my relationship with Venetia, she said to me long, long afterward, "My word, wasn't it all very complicated and wonderful?"

68

That evening, as we drove to the show, I found myself in a new experience—clarity. The air seemed clearer; I could see farther, hear more keenly, feel more sensitively. And I could think with a new and powerful brilliance, and in thinking so, I understood what I had been evading since that morning—the farm was gone. Mother, exhausted, fearful, tearful, had handed it over. The mounting anger at my father rose up inside me afresh, and built into a new kind of rage—unfamiliar and very hot. I had enough control to say nothing. Venetia sat beside me in the car, her hand always touching my knee or my arm. We rarely spoke, didn't want to; anyway, they weren't quiet cars like today's models; easy speech was a problem with the wind whistling in everywhere, and the engine roaring like a dragon.

Isn't it disappointing, when we look in the mirror, that we can't see instant change? Isn't it a shame that we have no means or mechanism by which our faces, our eyes can record what has just happened? I'd just had the experience of seeing my mother develop a grayness on the skin of her face—a color that hadn't been there before.

Yet, I'd have given a lot if, that afternoon, as I looked in the mirror before leaving the house, I'd seen something of the massive change that I felt had taken place in me. I didn't and was disappointed.

It feels clichéd, doesn't it, to discuss a loss of virginity in terms of "becoming a man"? And anyway that's not how it felt at all. Yes, I was changed profoundly—but it was a change deriving from having found another human being who was the other half of myself. And knowing it at the time, and knowing it would be true for all time. As it has been.

And for her? This is what she said.

"You're the antidote to the bad parts of my life. I can be as odd as I like and you'll think me normal."

I didn't go to the show that night. She didn't want me to, didn't give an explanation, and said, "One day you'll understand." I expected to feel hurt; I didn't want this girl out of my sight, but my compliant nature—as it always had been—accepted her wish, and turned it into something positive.

Instead, I enjoyed waiting, standing outside the hall and listening to the cheering. I could tell who was leaving the stage—or indeed who was onstage—by the force and length of the applause. Oddly, it felt as though her own solo appearances excited people just as much as her stint with Blarney—though the laughter for him hit the highest notes on the night's scale.

My feelings about Venetia as I stood there, leaning against the venue's wall? No guilt, no confusion, no anxiety—how could I? I didn't know enough. The excitement almost drove me. I wanted more, more, more. Part of it was physical, that softness, that comprehensive embrace—I'd never known anything like it; I still haven't. I wanted to see her every second of every minute, wanted the feel of that skin, the look in those eyes.

Then the abiding emotion arrived, clearing its way through everything else, through the urgency, the desire, the sheer "everything-ness" of the experience—responsibility. That was what I mostly felt, responsible for this woman, this "girl," as I thought of her. I wanted to care for her, protect her, simply look after her every minute of every day.

It must be the case, mustn't it, that I learned that behavior. I must have seen it in my father's life. I've already told you how attentive I'd always seen him—the cups of tea, the rescues from depression. Learned behavior—that's what produced this sense of responsibility. It felt good too; I felt powerful—even though I didn't have anything like the language to express it that way.

The feeling of responsibility also enabled me to cope with not watching the show. When she emerged later I would be able to swing into action and begin my intended project of taking care of her. We had already established that I would take her back to the house in Charleville, and that from now on I would spend every night in the same bed with her.

I know it seems fanciful to look back after all these years and insist that those were my feelings—that driven sense of responsibility. But I assure you—I've given it intensive and extensive thought, and that is truly what I believe I was feeling at that time.

And as I stood there, a figure walked toward me, the maker perhaps of that responsibility gene—my father. Not saying a word at first, he patted me on the shoulder and leaned against the wall right beside me.

We stood there for long minutes, smiling and chuckling at our separate—but I'm sure not very dissimilar—thoughts, as we heard the laughter and applause coming from inside the hall.

During a lull he said to me, without turning his head, "I-I-I often do this. I often wait here so that I have the pleasure of looking forward to seeing her."

I had been thinking the same.

The likely problem facing me hadn't yet surfaced. I was so lost in my new, white-hot, tumbling emotions that I never focused on any difficulty for long. Nor did I when he made that remark—"the pleasure of looking forward to seeing her." Nor did I say to him, as I was supposed to, "When are you coming home?" or "Please come home." I said nothing, not a word.

He said it again, in different words. "It's such a joy to be with her when the night ends; she's always so tired and I can look after her."

And I wasn't even jolted by this. Nor did I give any thought to the next moves of the night, which were now approaching, because we could hear Blarney's voice from inside, and we could hear the laughter, and Blarney was always top of the bill—meaning the evening would end within half an hour or so.

I stood there with my father in what I now see was a most unreal situation. He closed his eyes, a smile on his face, and settled back to enjoy the laughter.

"Oh, by the way," he said suddenly. "Could you come over with the car tomorrow? I want to go to a funeral."

"What time?"

"Your uncle Denny is dead. In Kilmallock." In an instant I saw him again: *the man under the lamplight, the affable host, the much beloved, walking weakly home.*

Loud applause, loud and louder—the show was over. My father pulled his shoulders off the wall and bounded away like a colt. Now the reality rode in. I stood there, not knowing what to do, and fending off the idea of what might happen next. Instinct is the oxygen of love. I remained where I stood.

The crowd departed in the usual glee, laughing and reminding one another of the evening's highlights. I moved a few yards around to the front of the hall, to stand in the light coming from the open doors. As I did so, I saw Venetia jump from the stage and run down the shabby hall between the chairs. At the door she grabbed my hand and led me away, running from the place. I had parked the car out of sight, to keep the curious from pawing it; we left town within minutes.

"He's staying with the company," she said.

I looked at her; she had fixed this. *Should I ask how?* I didn't.

Sometime before dawn we fell asleep. Our last remarks to each other had to do with how much better could this get, with how much older than eighteen I seemed to be, and with the future. The future—ah, yes, the future; it and its possibilities became the subject of challenge while we were still asleep.

69

I heard the knock. Then I heard the door open. I'm a light sleeper. Somebody looked in and I saw a disappearing arm, a woman's. Venetia woke too, took no action, and went back to sleep. I lay there, wide awake, and now the implications sailed in like menacing ships. I didn't own a watch in those days and always guessed the time by the light of day—not more than eight o'clock. Once again the noises floated up of a small town waking—a door slam, the clang of some utensil somewhere, a cyclist whistling, the clop of a horse's slow hooves: sleepy sounds, but important in their assuring-ness. Typically they'd have lifted me into the morning; I had no intention of leaving that bed, not that day, if I could help it.

Venetia slept for another hour, and I lay there, shifting between the delight of recent memory, anticipation of the imminent, and fear engendered by the implications.

We didn't rise until late. She sent me downstairs first, and the darkness of the day under heavy overcast, gave us night at noon. Ravenous, I went straight to the kitchen, Mrs. Haas's exclusive domain; I had never seen anybody else in there. She'd heard me coming and stood in front of the black stove with its driving flames seen through the grid. As I walked in she clasped her hands in front of her like somebody receiving an award.

"Oh," she said, and said it again. "This is so good, so good."

I mustn't have been quite sure of what she meant, because she crossed the floor and stood close to me.

"She is a lovely young voman and I am pleased, pleased. This is the right way, not the other way, the other way was bad and wrong, this is good. Oh, yes, and I am going now to make you such food."

Mrs. Haas, when she first met me, told Venetia that the fates had intervened and that the "right man" had arrived. Apparently, those two spent most of their lives discussing the possibility of a loving life partner for Venetia. When my father showed up Mrs. Haas had wondered at first if this was indeed the direction that the world had chosen—but then decided that my father had been only the pathfinder, which is where Venetia got that idea.

She turned and marched back to the stove, beside which she had arranged all her pans and ingredients, and once again I heard her noises, this time a small song, almost beneath her breath. As she began to cook she looked at me again and winked, then went on arranging pans on the stove. I stood and watched—and she turned, looked gravely at me, and said, "Run away. The two of you. I don't know how you vill do it. But run away."

Mrs. Haas stood over me as I ate the bacon, the eggs, the potato cakes—the mound of food. Now and then she muttered, "Strength, strength."

I felt some undercurrent; I couldn't say what it was. If I'd known enough, I'd have said I was being oversensitive, that all my senses were now heightened and everything magnified. If I could sum up what I felt—Mrs. Haas was showing an unseemly sense of triumph, and I knew not why.

When I finished the first batch of food, she strode across, took my plate, went to the stove, renewed my plate, and came back. I didn't protest. As I began to thank her, she looked away at something else, and began to step backward; her face had turned white as a gravestone.

I looked where she stared. Three people, one behind the other, blocked the wide doorway of the kitchen. Nearest me stood the man with the black hair oil, from the cottage, from the secret blue-shirted drilling. He was holding a rifle with a shining wooden butt and he had pointed the gray-blue barrel straight at me. Behind him stood King Kelly. And behind him, holding her face in her hands as though expecting something awful to happen, stood Sarah, Venetia's mother.

Everybody froze. The tableau stayed rigid for maybe ten long seconds. I felt some food coming back up my throat into my mouth, a sign of intense fear. My stillness—which came from fright, nothing else—may have persuaded them that they were dealing with somebody of a cooler and braver temperament. King Kelly spoke.

"Go closer," he directed the gunman.

"No," said Mrs. Haas, who began to scream.

You have never heard a scream like Mrs. Haas's. She opened her mouth just as the gunman put the muzzle as close to my left eye as he could without actually impaling me on the gun.

The muzzle touched my eyeball—I swear that when I blinked, my eyelashes brushed the metal. Mrs. Haas's scream rose higher and higher. I had the thought: *Has she trained as a singer?* She didn't take a breath, and if you can imagine something between the howl of an aged wolf and the dragging of metal along a road, you'll get close.

The scream distracted everybody standing in the doorway, and then I heard the footsteps on the stairs. The gunman's finger tightened on the trigger. I saw it and felt it, and the gun moved a fraction, touching my eye again—I pulled back my head and the muzzle followed me. The scream continued—it rose like a shriek in a nightmare of terrifying fogs and shapeless beasts.

Somebody said, "Stop, stop." Sarah's calm voice, it transpired—and then Venetia's, asking, "What is it?"

She told me afterward that she'd heard her grandfather's voice, then heard Mrs. Haas screaming, and thought me dead. As Venetia reached the bottom step of the staircase, Sarah moved to block her. But Venetia knew that her grandfather could be there—as she later said—"for no good reason."

By now the noise had grown huge, because a loud argument broke out between Sarah and Venetia. Sarah wanted to keep Venetia out of the kitchen, and Venetia had guessed that something wrong had come my way. And the man with the gun moved the black hole of the muzzle to my left temple, and King Kelly told me, "Stand up, boy."

When you look back on extreme circumstances in which you may ever have found yourself, try to remember what you did with your body. It's illuminating and very instructive. That day, I stayed very still. The time was by now close to one o'clock in the afternoon and I held myself like a creature in a web. In fact, I rose to a half-crouch before I stood to my full height.

Did I do this because I knew that the man with the gun was very much shorter than me, and that he might have to make a sudden—and therefore perhaps dangerous—movement to compensate? Who can say? I can't; but nothing would surprise me.

Now freeze this tableau for a moment: Stop all the movement. We have Mrs. Haas with her mouth open wide, and I can tell you that her teeth were pointed like a saw all the way around, the Sierra Haas. I'm standing nine tenths upright like a tall lobster, my hands on the edge of the table. The man with the dense dark hair, so oiled that I can see a yellow tidemark on his forehead, is holding a gun to his shoulder and sighting along the barrel as though he were lining up a target, which in fact he was.

I see King Kelly: Again a contemptible brown suit, and a check waistcoat, and the nest of hair in his nose and ears—his mouth is open too, in mid-bark of an order. Behind him I see the back of Sarah's head turned to her daughter—Sarah is wearing some peach-colored garment that falls in large soft rolls around her neck.

And there is Venetia, suspended in mid-struggle to get into the kitchen; her hair is wet; she has a towel over her shoulder, she is now wearing the long white nightdress that she wore briefly last night.

Action again—Venetia breaks through and the noise of her movement alerts the very jumpy man with the gun.

Whatever you've read, whatever you've seen in films, nothing is ever what you expect when you're faced with something like this. The hero is not free at a swift leap, nor is the villain vanquished. Nobody overpowers anybody else. That is how tragedy is born—expecting heroism where none is possible.

Somehow I knew all this, and yet I was driven by my sense of responsibility, by my private, intimate connection, to protect this woman. So, I was the one who moved.

Mrs. Haas is still screaming the longest screams that I or anybody else have ever heard—I bet she auditioned for *Lucia di Lammermoor.* The man with the gun jerks up the muzzle ever so slightly—a tiny movement with the menace of a shark.

King Kelly says, "Make him march. Never to come back."

Sarah is saying, "Venetia!"—who is saying, "Let me in."

And I? I say nothing. Instead I step back from the gun. One step—the muzzle is now a foot away. A second step—another foot. The third step takes me a yard away, and I can see the puzzlement in the man's eyes, dark eyes, dark as a Latin. *Is he Irish? He could be from Galway, a descendant of the Spanish Armada.*

One more step takes me much farther away in the sense that I have now stepped around the corner of the table—and my plate of lovely food lies there beneath my eye. If this is to be mended it's not going to be by anything I say. Another irrelevant question rolls loosely about my reeling brain. *Is there a past tense of "mended"? Could it be "ment"?*

I step farther and farther back, and now the man with the gun adjusts his aim—we're still talking about a distance of less than ten feet, about the maximum distance for accuracy in an old and beautiful gun such as this one was.

It ended. Venetia came through, and at the sound of her voice the gunman, on a tap on the shoulder from King Kelly, lowered the gun.

"I'm trying," King Kelly said, jovial as a clown, "to turn this young man"—he pointed to me—"into a soldier who'll fight for his country."

Now, of course, I sagged. Would they have killed me? I don't doubt it—given what I now know. They certainly meant to frighten me and ideally to run me out of town; King Kelly's time in the American West had shown him things.

It hadn't worked, and now it was never going to work. With not a word to anybody, King Kelly and the gunman, whose name was Alec (and he *was* from Galway, but I didn't discover that for years), turned away and quit the house through the open front door without a word to Sarah, who stood by, overwrought.

Mrs. Haas grabbed the edge of the table and took many deep breaths. Venetia looked at me, held up five fingers, and then pointed upward (she was a wonder at signs and gestures), and steered her mother to the staircase. I closed my eyes and began to sway. Mrs. Haas grabbed me and opened the back door of the house, which led into a little garden. Outside she put her hand on my waist and bent me double several times.

If she intended that I throw up, she made a mistake. In my life I can never remember vomiting—food is much too important to waste like that. I did accept her glass of water—and then I came back indoors, sat down, and finished eating the second plate of food. To give you an idea of how long the incident lasted, the food hadn't cooled at all.

Mrs. Haas began to mutter: "Dreadful man. Dreadful man." Looking askance at me, as though unable to face me full on, she said in the same low mutter, "You don't know what's going on, you don't know what's going on." And in her concluding remark before she rose and left the kitchen, she said, "Be brave, oh, be brave."

I finished eating all the food, and went back upstairs to the little sitting room. There sat Sarah and Venetia. When I went in, Sarah reached out a hand to me and held it.

She said, "I'm so sorry. And you were so cool, Ben. I can't believe that you're so young."

"Have they gone?" I asked.

Venetia said, "I've told Sarah that you're now part of the company."

Sarah looked into a distance that didn't exist in that small room. Venetia rose and said, "I have to dry my hair," and she beckoned to me with her head.

I followed her into the room in which we had slept, and as she closed the door behind us I heard Sarah outside sigh, rise, and go away.

70

And so, at gunpoint so to speak, I became a member of the company of Venetia Kelly's Traveling Show. That very day, I took to the road. Even though I only carried spears or led a wooden horse or cow onstage, I became a traveling actor, part of a great tradition—the strolling player, descended straight from the troubadour, the minstrel, who wandered Europe singing roundelays beneath the windows of beautiful ladies. Shakespeare belonged to traveling companies. And perhaps I was descended from an even more wonderful figure: the strolling bard, the storyteller who came to the castle gates and that night, after the feast, entertained the King and his family and his nobles and his warriors with long and absorbing tales.

I have to say that Venetia Kelly's Traveling Show may have been a little different. I was introduced to them all, and they were more numerous than I had expected—she had a company of more than a dozen, yet it seemed to me that I'd seen only a total of perhaps six. There was Cwawfod, and he hadn't appeared onstage; Graham, the neckless one; the old man who played the tuba—his name was Derek, and he had a staggeringly posh English accent that got ever more exaggerated when he drank, meaning that it got very grand indeed. You've already met Michael, who played Bassanio, with many tumbles, in that "loose interpretation" so beloved of Miss Fay.

The girl who played the milkmaid and other saucy roles—she came from Dublin and had run away to escape a family that made her go to Mass every morning and, as she told me, "I'm a bit wilder than that, like, ya know, I like the romantic life. And yourself, are you romantic at all?"

Some of them rarely appeared onstage. Nasal Cwawfod, for instance, had no more than a factotum role; he drove vehicles, put out chairs, helped with scenery, such as it was. Behind the scenes also worked a man and woman—a husband and wife, Venetia told me, Martin and Martha.

They never spoke, at least not in my hearing—they never spoke to anybody, not even each other, that I ever saw or heard. They came from Belfast, one was Catholic, one Protestant, and they'd had to leave their homes because of their love affair and subsequent marriage. Long afterward, I found them—at least I found Martha, and discovered that both had been severe alcoholics.

And then there was Peter, the temperamental one. At the time I joined the show I had never seen Peter onstage—because Peter, though a very experienced actor, rarely went onstage.

"Temperament," Venetia told me, smiling.

Peter, it transpired, believed every role beneath him, apart from, say, Hamlet or King Lear or Prospero or Othello.

"I simply cannot see the point of treading the boards in puny characterizations," he would declare, when the company had assembled to put together the stage for a performance. By February 1932 he hadn't made an appearance for more than six months.

And we had Timmy, three or four years older than me, rescued from a life of habitual imprisonment, and a gifted magician. Timmy had a pickpocket act that audiences loved; "art imitating life," Venetia called it with a dry grin. Timmy could remove a man's wristwatch, necktie, or shoelaces without the man knowing. Ladies returned to their seats having been onstage, and as they sat down Timmy gave them back their necklaces. Timmy had a red face for one so young, and a ferocious body odor—to this day I have no idea how he achieved it; he must have built it up in layers, like shale.

These "men and women merely players" were my new life.

As I look back over this document I realize that I may not have given as clear a picture of Venetia as I have of Sarah. That hasn't come from any wish of not wanting to portray her, no selfishness of holding her to myself—it comes from inability; I simply can't. The subject is too embedded in my heart, and I don't wish to chisel it out; not from any lack of generosity—I'm simply not objective about her, not even now, so many decades later.

I can tell you—and already have to some degree—what she looked like, I can tell you how her skin felt, I can tell you how she walked, but I can't describe her essence. I can tell you how she looked at me—as though I were the dearest person ever born, as she was to me.

Perhaps she'll appear clearer to you through the company's reactions. I observed them all when I became part of that group, and I've since then searched for and found as many of them as I could. They helped me to deepen and copper-fasten the impressions of Venetia that I can convey. And they confirmed for me how unusual she was; "quirky," some said; "lonely," said another; "a gift for doing the unexpected," said somebody else.

They pointed to her diligence, the assiduous learning of her lines, her passion to please her audiences. For instance—and I later saw this myself—when playing a new venue, she'd walk through the town and pick out some detail about the place to include in the show that night. It could be a statue, a notice of an auction, a local band. Blarney might then have a reference in his act, or one of the others would mention it in a jokey exchange.

I've assembled their impressions, and fed off them for years; here's a sample. First, the men in the company. Now they were, in any language, misfitting and rough. None of them had gifts of hygiene or stability; they all stank to a greater or lesser degree, and they all had weeping fits or drinking jags or some other kind of outburst.

If they had anything in common with Venetia, it must have been a deep love of performance, and a relish of fine language. I stood with them many a night in the wings, and watched the starry beginnings of tears in their eyes at a wonderful Shakespeare line. I heard them murmur phrases from "Lochinvar" or *The Rime of the Ancient Mariner* or "The Passing of Arthur" or whatever poem Venetia was using at the time to hold the show together—which is how she saw the function of that particular reading. It always came near the middle of the evening—this was a show without an interval—and it always proved a kind of emotional rallying point for both cast and audience.

And these men, these rough men, outcasts from their previous lives—they always stood up when Venetia walked in. They deferred to her; they fetched a chair for her; they poured her some of their truly awful tea—they themselves called it "the urine"—they'd say after some exertion or other, "A dose of the urine is needed." And then, as she sat and sipped the tea, they stood around her like a ramshackle household guard, listening to every word she said as though she were their empress, which she was.

Many, many years after it all came to an end, with the show long folded, I found Peter, the temperamental one. He lived in a convent home run for indigents outside Waterford; when I met him he'd become immobile, but his personality remained intact.

He recognized me the moment I walked in—and he began to cry, Which took me aback, until he said: "I'd always hoped to hear from darling Venetia. Is she with you?"

I tried to explain, saw that he couldn't cope with such a difficult burden, and instead asked him for his impressions of her.

"She took me in as though I were the brightest star in the theatrical firmament. I was on the heap, old boy. Rubbish. Useless. Over. On the skids. Every opportunity I had—and I knew the greats—I pissed away. I offended every manager who hired me, I was too grand, they were beneath me, I was too temperamental to act. I was an Actor."

As I recalled it, he hadn't done much acting for Venetia's company either, and I put that to him gently. By now I was maturer and better able to couch things.

"No, old boy. And she knew why. She knew I was afraid, too worthless. So she gave me the job of being her Shakespeare coach. And I often chose the repertoire with her. I would never have had a life without her."

Now the women. Mrs. Haas adored her, no need to remind you of that. Sarah, as you know, considered her daughter mythical. From the company, Martha, when I met her, told me that she herself had had two miscarriages on the road. All the medical arrangements—made by Venetia. The doctors—paid by Venetia. The emotional aftercare—Venetia.

"Before the house that you knew in Charleville, she had another house. She sent me to that house to recover, and she gave me a housekeeper to look after me. D'you remember her? That Mrs. Hiss? Terrible bitch, she treated me like I was a fool or a convict or both. And then Venetia'd come over to see me and everything'd be fine again. Did you know that the mother was dead jealous of her? She was an actress too, the mother."

For a woman who never spoke when in the company of the show, Martha made up for lost time. I asked her whether, as a woman, she had liked Venetia. Martha thought, frowned, took her time, spoke slowly.

"She was two people, like. There was the warm side to her, that we all saw, I mean, friendly-like. And there was another side, distant-like, I don't mean cold, no, she wasn't cold. But she was away out of things, like. Yeh, distant-like. Yeh, cold, maybe. But we'd'a done anything for her." She paused. "That distant thing. I think she was lonely-like."

72

That day, as she dried her hair, Venetia and I shook our heads in horror over the gun incident. She thought it no more than what she called "a stupid jape" by her grandfather. I believed that he meant something else and something stronger—but I hadn't formulated my thoughts. Vaguely I felt that it had something to do with Mother and the farm, but I'd resolved not to discuss the matter of my own family's problems with Venetia; I didn't want to trouble her with them, and I'd decided to wait until I could talk to Sarah.

Drying her hair, preparing her face, getting dressed—that day I witnessed a sight to which I became addicted. In galleries around Europe, where any such painting exists, I look for portraits of ladies at their toilette. *What is its enchantment? The absorption? The concentration?* With Venetia I didn't speak—I watched.

Part of my silence—our silence—may have been recovery from the fracas downstairs, that combination of menace and bullying that so came to identify King Kelly for me. Part too, however, came from Venetia's simple wish to complete her preparations, and my simple wish to watch.

Mrs. Haas arrived with a sandwich for Venetia. We learned that Sarah had disappeared with King Kelly and the hair-oiled man. I now had so many things whizzing around in my head that I needed help, and I asked the simple question of Venetia and Mrs. Haas, "What's going on?"

"Not yet to tell," said Mrs. Haas.

"We're not quite sure," said Venetia.

"His father," said Mrs. Haas, pointing to me. "He knows."

Now, at last, the real world came in. Venetia knew it too, and stood up. "Then we need—I need—to do something."

I said, "I'm about to take him to a funeral."

"Yes," said Mrs. Haas.

"How do you know?" asked Venetia.

"He's downstairs waiting," said Mrs. Haas.

Venetia made for the door and I stepped across to block her way.

She persisted. "I have to do it. Then you come down."

Mrs. Haas, the unlikely champion, went with her. I heard Venetia say, "Harry?"

My father replied, but I couldn't hear it. I stepped out onto the landing, and kept out of sight; then I heard everything.

"Is-is-is it true? That's all I want to know. Is it true?"

Venetia said, "It is true, Harry. It's true."

"But he's my son."

"That's probably why."

My father then repeated himself. "Is it true? Is it?"

"Yes, Harry. Yes."

"But—he's my son, my lovely son."

"As I say—that's probably why."

"How could you?"

Venetia said, "I have no idea."

My father's speech hesitation now disappeared—as it did when he was under extreme pressure; I've often wondered why the precise opposite wasn't the case. His voice rose.

"Where is he?"

"He's upstairs. About to take you to a funeral."

"To my own funeral, that's where he'll be taking me. To my own funeral."

"Shhh, Harry, easy now." She handled him beautifully. "I will always love you."

"You can't! How can you? Oh, my God, my own son!"

"You mean a lot to me."

"My own son. My son. You can't love two people."

"Yes, you can, Harry. You can love any number of people."

I moved. They heard me. I walked down the stairs.

"Oh, Jesus God!" said my father and lowered his face.

Perhaps the light did it, a dull sunlight through the glass of the hall windows in that old house. Perhaps my mind exaggerated it—but I had never thought of my father as old before. Now he looked not merely old but haggard.

"What time is the funeral?" I asked, and walked past him.

I'm bound to say that I felt myself swagger, even if—as I hope—I didn't show it.

We drove to a place called Kilcoran, to a little graveyard up on the hillside. In the car neither of us said a word. *Will Mother be there?* I wondered.

Venetia had patted us both good-bye. In the car my father sat on his hands, he retrieved them, he bit his knuckles, he bit his nails, he sat on his hands again. He opened his window, put out his head, inhaled huge gobbets of air, closed the window, opened it again.

As we were leaving, Venetia had murmured to me, "Say not a word. It will be difficult—but don't say a single word."

"Difficult"? Oh, yes it was. He tried to open the conversation in a number of ways and I, who had never disrespected or disobeyed my father in my life, had to keep my mouth shut.

He began with "This is a foul thing you've done. You must really hate me." When I said nothing, "You must hate me. Do you hate me, Ben? I've always been good to you. Do you? Do you hate me?"

I couldn't put together this man with the farmer I saw astride his harvest stacks of straw and hay, directing his workers, the dust smoky in his red eyebrows.

When he received no answer he lapsed into a kind of muttering. "Yes, that's it, you hate me. This is an act of hate, I know that. This is hateful. Hate. Full. That's what it is."

Then he fell silent. And then opened up again.

"What was it? That you wanted what I had? The very thing that's so dear to me? Is that it? Is that it, Ben? Just because I had it you wanted it, is that it? The young bull jealous of the old bull? She'll drop you anyway, I know that, you're too young for her, she'll drop you like a stone."

For some time after that outburst he sat silently, except for the shifting of the hands here, there, and everywhere. He opened the window again, stuck his head out, and whoozed in mouthfuls of exaggerated air. Then he attacked once more.

"I know what it is," he said, triumph ringing from him. "I-I-I know what it is. You decided to usurp me so that I'd go back home. That's it. A ploy. That's it. Your mother put you up to this."

By great good mercy we had arrived at the graveyard when he came out with this. Amid five other cars, myriad bicycles, and a long chain of pony traps and horse-and-cart rigs, I drew to a halt, got out, and breathed.

I knew Mother wouldn't face it. She couldn't. Others made up for her—cousins consumed with interest, who looked at my father and me as though at a zoo. My father greeted his sister, the widow, with great kindness—and as though his own life were as smooth as a lake. To my delight I saw James Clare across the little hilly burial plots.

I shall keep this brief; it's unpleasant. With prayers and the thoughts of his family, his close relatives, and a wide variety of friends and acquaintances, my uncle Denny went dust-to-dust. About three hundred people attended, their presence a compliment to the man's decency. The prayers went by quickly and we began to disperse, picking our way through the graves.

I wanted to speak to James Clare—but he made a sign that he'd be outside, and I thought I'd better wait for my father. In our part of the country (this was about twenty miles from my home), the gravediggers often don't fill in the graves until the funeral drinking has ended. My father lingered until everybody had gone—and I waited for him, down the path, fifty or sixty yards away.

He left the graveside slowly. Deep in thought he made his way to where I stood. By now everybody else had gone from the little cemetery, and we were masked from the road by trees and shrubs. He wore a coat that I'd never seen until that day, a gray coat, somewhat military in appearance, with epaulets and a belt. In no hurry he took slow steps through the green mounds until he found himself on the level pathway, much nearer now to me. He walked head down, still deep in thought.

As he reached me, and just as I was beginning to walk beside him to the road, he grabbed my arm.

"Come on. I'll fight you for her. Come on."

I stood back, still determined to say nothing.

"Come on! Put up your fists."

I shook my head and again tried to walk. He hopped ahead of me, like a comical rabbit, and blocked my way.

"Fight-fight-fight for her. Settle it now. Fight for her."

In the distance, over my father's shoulder, I saw James Clare walking back into the graveyard. He had attended to whomsoever he'd needed to see and had come back to find me. As I looked, he stopped, watching.

I tried to get past, through, or around my father, but he stopped me—and this time he swung a punch. I got my head back out of the way—barely; his fist grazed me. He swung again—I evaded again. This time he held my sleeve and landed a heavy punch on the side of my head.

Never had I intended that anything like this should happen. He hit me again, this time a stinging blow that made me reel. When I looked past him, James Clare had come closer but seemed to have no intention of stopping us.

"Don't tell me you haven't the guts to fight for her. That's-that's-that's why you won't get her and I will."

The brawl began; I broke all the taboos in the world and fought back. In school nobody ever fought me because I was the biggest in my class. Outside of that, my life had been so sheltered that I hadn't been exposed to violence. The only fight that I'd ever seen had been the Prizefight between my father and Mr. Kane, and that had perturbed me for months.

Its memory came back now, vivid, sharp, and frightening, and I said to him, "I'm not Mr. Kane. You've no reason to hit me."

My father said nothing but he grew more violent, his punches stronger, harder, and delivered with more venom. How could this ever be repaired?

I too have red hair—not unrelievedly so, more a deep, dark red, close to black. If red hair causes ignition—that can also help to explain how the brawl progressed. I began to defend myself, and then I fought back. My first punch landed on my father's right cheekbone and hurt my hand—but not enough to stop me. I saw the surprise in his eyes—he hadn't truly expected me to respond. He saw the shock in my eyes, I think, at the fact that I had struck my own father, and he retaliated—with his fiercest punch so far.

Now we went at it like two sailors in a bar. It became a savage and dirty fight, much worse than could ever have been anticipated. He bit my ear. He tried to gouge my eyes. I kicked him, I stamped on his ankle, I kicked his knee. We breathed heavily, each of us, we muttered at each other; the main sound, though, was a series of grunts and scuffles. I grappled for his arms to stop him, he kneed me close to the groin—in fact, I remember that he had avoided a kick by twisting, and I did the same, by instinct, I think.

Under Heaven how can it have looked? Two otherwise decent men, father and son, locked in an ugly brawl of filthy intent in a sacred place. The fight ended when my father fell and I stamped on his neck and throat and kept my boot there. In that moment I aged twenty years, and I had my first taste of that bitter thing called remorse. Awful, truly awful.

I removed my foot, stepped away, and sank to my haunches, in dreadful anguish. My father scarcely moved, but he talked to himself and that is how I knew that he hadn't been injured. When he rose he had bruises across his throat, and on his face, livid red patches that began to turn blue. I had no idea how I looked but my face felt hot and sore—like my spirit.

He walked away, brushing past the watching, waiting James Clare. I continued to squat; the pain in my heart had spread to my stomach and I felt that my bowels would split apart. No urge to weep, strangely—though I fancied that my father had begun to as he walked off. My abiding feelings can be summed up by words such as "ugliness" and "disgraceful" and "appalling." I felt lower than low—my beloved father, my own beloved father—the disappointment, the shame, the loss.

The footsteps that I heard approaching on the gravel path belonged to James Clare, and I stood up. My mouth had the salt taste of blood; I had a lip that was split on the inside, nothing serious. Small, watery blood came from my nose; my upper jaw hurt, as did both cheekbones, one eye, and the side of my head. But my soul hurt most of all.

"Stand back here for a minute," said James. "Rest yourself against the wall."

"Do you know who that was?" My voice had that snuffle you get as a child half an hour after you've been crying at the injustice of the world. "That was my father."

I found the wall and put my hands behind me at hip height to steady myself.

"I know," said James Clare. And then, this earnest, wise man said with great approval, "Do you know what you've done?"

"Fought my own father."

"As the gods did."

73

Now I'm exhausted by that memory, so I'm going to digress a little into the politics of the day again. I had managed somehow to keep abreast of all that had been happening in the first days after the historic vote. Mr. de Valera had taken power, or was about to—he would become the prime minister or taoiseach (pronounced *tee-shock,* meaning "chieftain") early in March, when the new Parliament assembled.

I still think it was the most important moment in modern Irish history. It showed in more ways than one that we had come to maturity. Indeed, you could argue—and many did—that the government changed because we (a) were now a nation unto ourselves, and (b) therefore got buffeted by the harsh economic winds blowing across the Atlantic from the Depression in the United States.

Certainly Mr. Cosgrave's outgoing government had been the victim of the hard times, but at the same time he hadn't managed to come up with anything that would inspire the electorate to keep him in power. So the feared Mr. de Valera had triumphed; the Risen People had risen further.

I knew that it was going to be a fascinating year. When it became clear that a decisive parliamentary majority hadn't been elected, many politicians continued to campaign. They held if not rallies, meetings; they roamed their constituencies if not exactly canvassing, pressing the flesh, as it's now called.

And had I not been so caught up in my own drama, I should have been enjoying this ongoing tumult every day. Had my father and I been at home, living a normal life as once we had been, the comments would have been stimulating and often funny. Instead, my home now had its interior doors locked against me; Mother had gone away; the life of the farm seemed near imminent collapse; and I had brawled with my father in an unseemly fistfight. Had all this turbulence stemmed from the tumult in the countryside? It's tempting to look for blame elsewhere—but it doesn't work for me.

James Clare and I stood there for some time, mostly not talking. How shocked I felt, how dismayed. It seemed a very bad development indeed. He, getting the full story out of me, took a different position—a view that something major had taken place in my life and the life of my family, something fundamental and brave. I couldn't reach that conclusion with him, so I let it sit in a realm of respect. We made an appointment to meet some weeks thence, and parted company. I kept that appointment and so did he, and by then everything had changed again, this time cataclysmically so.

No sign of my father; I looked far and wide; I drove down lanes and up side roads; he had vanished. *How is he going to get back to the show, still in Abbeyfeale? Has he disappeared again?*

When I gave up looking for him I took a new decision. Perhaps conflicted on account of my state of shock, I needed a feeling of home. It's perhaps also true that, with my blood still on fire or at least smoldering, I wanted to see whether I could get to the bottom of what had happened in the house.

And my abandonment of Mother now began to kick in. With my father "defeated," or "dethroned," or whatever epic word James would someday come up with, somebody had to look after her. And I was no more than twenty miles away.

The gate was locked—by which I mean not shut, which it rarely was when we lived there; it had a padlock on it. Not a huge padlock—in fact small enough to tempt me. But the car contained heavy tools for wheels and suchlike, and I broke the padlock so hard the flying metal almost hit my eye; that would have been all I needed. I pushed the gate back and replaced the heavy stone that propped it open.

As I rounded the bend in the driveway, I had to stop. Ahead marched twin lines of about twenty men, parading, shouldering weapons, presenting arms, all wearing blue shirts. They halted when they saw me, and their officer, as he turned out to be, made his way to the car. I'd never seen any of these people before.

"Who are you?"

I got out of the car and said, "I live here."

"With Mr. Kelly?"

"Is he here?" From where was I acquiring this cunning?

"He had to go to Dublin. As you know, he's been elected."

"I had the pleasure of congratulating him." My goodness, I had grown up fast! "I need to get some things."

The officer divided the men and I drove through. As I walked to our—open—front door, Mary Lewis came out and looked at me in some alarm.

"What, Ben?"

"Where's my mother?"

"They'll go mad if they see you here."

"Who's in the house?"

"Mr. Kelly's gone—"

"Yes. To Dublin. Who's in my room?"

"They locked all the doors, Ben. I didn't do it. Honest, I didn't."

"When you tell me who you mean by 'they,' I might believe you."

She turned away and tried to close the door. I stuck my foot in it and she backed off, then ran toward the kitchen.

The hallway, so carefully ordered by Mother, had been changed. My ancestor's portrait (nobody knew anything about him except that his name was Hopkins) had been taken down and replaced with a framed election poster blaring the name Thomas Aquinas Kelly. Blank rectangles showed where other pictures were missing. The small chaise longue that Mother loved had pairs of army boots piled on it. Several rifles leaned against the wall, in groups here and there. Two of the floor tiles had been broken as though something heavy had fallen on them.

When I went to the kitchen door, Mary Lewis had locked herself in—no chance of forcing any doors in that old house. I went to the back stairs and found that door locked too; and when I finally got to the two upstairs landings, my parents' bedroom door was now locked. Inside my own house, where I'd roamed free as a young bear since I could crawl, I now couldn't move.

Think, don't feel. Cunning, not emotion.

Look—I have no cunning. One day I hope you'll find that out about me. In fact, I dislike it as a quality, even though I acknowledge its necessity at certain times and in certain situations. But I find it hard to quarry from within myself, and I found it hard to uncover then. Whatever I found in me, cunning or instinct, I went to the cottage, and there I found the truth beginning to unfold.

Mother sat there, alone, in the cold, like a woman stunned. From time to time, I've visited old people in hospitals up and down the country, old people who've sent for me because they have a story to tell. As I walk through the hospital wards and corridors I glance through doors and I see people in different states of emotional condition. Some are lively, some recovering, some engaged with the nurses or their visitors, and some look into the distance, knowing that they have nothing to see.

That's how I found Mother. She still wore her coat as though she had been somewhere—I learned that she'd returned some hours earlier from her sister's. And she hadn't taken off her gloves.

In those few weeks when I had come home she'd always looked up at me with immediate hope. That day she didn't; she stared at me, said nothing, and her dull, hopeless expression didn't change.

The cottage seemed clean and neat, more than I could say for the house. I did what she always did in a crisis—made a pot of tea. Said nothing. Moved normally. Made, yes, a large pot of tea. When I had poured her a cup, and one for myself, I sat down in front of her and said, "All right. Tell me."

"We've lost the farm. And the house. They're allowing me to live in the cottage. Until I find somewhere."

"They?"

"Professor Fay's doing the talking. They just marched in."

"How many people are up there?"

"Ben, where am I going to live?"

"Are you sure about all this? Where's the deed, the mortgage?"

"Mary Lewis has been told to come down twice a day with food."

No wonder Mother looked insensible. And I had no answers.

"Do you want me to stay here?"

"Can you get him to come back?"

Maybe I haven't been very firm in my various resolves across life. By returning that day I had just broken one promise to myself—for which I have forever been grateful; how would I have felt if I hadn't come back for months and it would all have been too late?

"It might be a couple of days," I said. "But I'm bringing him back. Do nothing. Sit still."

I thought, *As though you're capable of anything else.*

74

Our government in Ireland (this isn't a Digression) operates through introduction of legislation, followed by parliamentary debates, leading to the execution of statutes. The law can also be changed by court judgment, setting precedent. Many countries across the world operate similarly. Or say they do. To obtain the maximum debate, every such Parliament has its committee systems, to which a proposed law is referred, and where it is then debated—the "committee stage"—by a representative selection of all parties.

Membership on such committees becomes a prized matter, because the selection indicates the standing in which the members are held by their parties and by others, their strategic importance as elected representatives, their personal acumen, their power. Members often bribe and graft their way onto such committees too. Thomas Aquinas Kelly, newly elected to the Irish Dáil as a member for the constituency of North Cork, was about to become an Opposition member of the Finance Committee. That was power. From there he could change Ireland.

After seeing the disaster that Mother had become, I returned to Charleville, had some food from Mrs. Haas—Venetia and I sat at the kitchen table—and spoke little. A downpour had begun; the street outside the front door had become a small river; the town's drainage needed improving.

I looked up during eating and saw Mrs. Haas and Venetia exchange glances. Let me tell you now how Mrs. Haas loved Venetia. She had been there at the birth, had delivered her, had washed her. Unconditional love governed that relationship—both ways. When I began the first of my interviews with her—those awful, frightened exchanges—which would lead to the compiling of this story, I asked Mrs. Haas to tell me about her life with Venetia, not with Sarah, not with the Kelly ménage in general, not as the anchor to the show.

"Ve vere all things as vomen to each other," she said. "Do you understand me? She vas my daughter and my granddaughter, and my sister and my mother and my life. I stayed mit the Kellys not for Sarah, who, yes, I loved too, but for Wenetia. You may not think so now, but Wenetia was frail."

Mrs. Haas then began to weep. "And you so kind. And she so good. Do you know that she bought all my clothes for me? Since the age she was fifteen. A girl. She gave, gave. To everybody. But not to herself."

I have to tell you that I abandoned the interviews for some time after that, seeing the distress I was causing and being caused.

Now back to that significant look. They saw that I caught the glance and both seemed awkward.

Mrs. Haas said, "Wenetia, do it. Go get it ready. I tell Ben some things."

Venetia left the room, planting a slow kiss on top of my head as she left. Again, I reeled slightly under such unexpected and unprecedented attention. They had bathed my bruised face, put ointment on my gashed hands. When she had gone, Mrs. Haas cut a giant wedge of apple pie and said to me, "You must ask some questions. Wenetia—she is preparing the answers. You must not mind how she has the answers told to you."

"Things are very bad in some of my life," I said.

"I am trying to tell you, Ben. Ve know. Ve know that. But you vere sent as the champion. That is vhat I see. Now go to Wenetia. And take her in your arms."

She must have seen the awkwardness in my eyes.

I said, "Fine, fine," as though I were a mature gentleman, an officer perhaps, or a lawyer, a man dealing with a situation to which he was well accustomed.

"She needs to be held and hugged, that girl. Do you know about holding and hugging?"

I looked alarmed. "Oh, certainly, yes."

Mrs. Haas nodded so hard that her head might have fallen off. "Doing it is all you need to know."

Venetia stood by the window, looking down on the flooded street—such rain we'd had. She had arranged a table near her and, to my surprise, on the table sat Blarney. When she came offstage at the end of a performance, Blarney went into that special suitcase that she'd had made for him. I'd seen her do it—packing him in, arranging his floppy arms and legs, and talking to him when she did this, shushing him, saying, "Not another word. You were wonderful, Blarney, you slew them. Now get some sleep," and with her soft fingers closing his eyes.

I walked across the room to her and held out my arms. We stood toe-to-toe for long ages, the difference between that and our first embrace being that I was the one in charge. When we separated, she indicated that I sit on the sofa while she picked up Blarney and went to a chair opposite me that she had prepared.

Blarney spoke first—in fact Venetia never spoke, not until my conversation with Blarney had ended, and she and I lay side by side again.

"Ben?" Quite rough, though not so raucous as onstage.

It had always been ridiculously difficult for me to associate Blarney with Venetia. A tribute to her skill? I suppose so. My failure of perception? Definitely—or else from the first time I saw her I rejected any possibility that she might have been giving voice to what he was saying.

"Ben?" Blarney said again, and this time in a tender voice.

"Ye-es," I said.

" 'Yes,' what, Ben?" By now I almost didn't recognize the voice.

"I—I don't know what."

" 'Yes, Blarney,' " said the doll, his eyes giving a little hopeless look to Heaven.

"Yes, Blarney," I said, trying to get a conversational tone.

"Ben, it's very nice to see you. Venetia thinks such a lot of you."

"I think a lot of her too."

"Do you, Ben?"

"I do, Blarney."

"Good." He paused and cast his eyes down.

"Ben?" He looked at me again.

"Yes, Blarney." I was finding it easier.

"Do you love Venetia?"

"I—I haven't ever kissed anybody before."

"Tell me what it's like, kissing Venetia. Because I like it too."

"I get very excited, Blarney."

"Does it make you feel that you'd do anything for her, Ben?"

"It does, Blarney."

"And Ben—when you're lying down with her, and you're each kissing and touching each other's skin, what's that like, Ben?"

By now I had engaged and had no way back.

"Blarney, I want nothing else for the rest of my life."

Blarney paused, looked down, swiveled his head, and looked up at Venetia.

"Ben?"

"Yes, Blarney."

"I asked Venetia the same question and she said the same nearly as you."

"Did she?"

"Yes, Ben, she said that she'd been looking for years to know what to do with her life. Now she knows. She knows she wants to spend it with you."

I didn't glance at Venetia through all this, and I could tell that she looked mainly at Blarney.

"Blarney, I'm very pleased."

"Good. I'll tell Venetia that. Do you know why Venetia wants to spend her life with you, Ben?"

"No, Blarney."

"Ben, Venetia finds that you balance her. You're steady on the ground. She spends a lot of time flying through the air—and she knows that you know what I mean. You're strong; she's different from anybody she knows, and she finds that very hard to cope with. And you don't seem to mind that she's different."

"Blarney, I think she's the best."

"Now, Ben, I've been asking all the questions. I bet you have many questions—about all sorts of things."

When I look back on it now, the ploy appears obvious. Venetia, with the collusion of Mrs. Haas, had been watching everything King Kelly was plotting and saying nothing. Both women had grown desperate to try to tell me, yet felt that it belonged outside their concern. Or feared Sarah and King Kelly so much that they dared not say anything.

And I can presume that Venetia wanted me to know that she had had nothing to do with it. We'd never talked about the farm, the mortgage, and all of that. I sat back. Where to begin?

"How do I get our farm back?"

"Talk to Sarah," said Blarney. "That's how you'll get the farm back. It won't be easy and she won't give you any answers. But Sarah's unhappy that you've arrived, and you'll have to find a way to frighten her. So that she can then scare her father. And it'll have to be a big scare."

"When should I do it, Blarney?"

That I found none of this incongruous shows how desperate I must have been, how disturbed—despite my joy—how thrown from post to pillar, the post of misfortune and disgrace and sadness to the pillar of passion and confusion.

"You'll have to wait, because Sarah's gone off to America to make a film." He pronounced it in the Irish way, "fill-um."

"When will she be back?"

"Months, Ben. You'll have to hold the fort."

"But, Blarney, my mother won't have anyplace to live."

"Explain, Ben."

I told him—about the farm, the cottage, the soldiers, and Mother's desolation. He turned his head right away from me, unable to look at me, as it were. I added, to give him a jolt, "And she has no protection, Blarney."

He said, "And you can't be there, Ben, because you now have to go on the road with Venetia."

I nodded, just an acceptance, no need to comment. And I looked at Venetia; she wouldn't look at me.

A silence fell; then Blarney spoke again.

"Now, Ben, listen to this. I've been watching your father for the last few years on the nights he came to the show. And I've been in this room as he sits listening to Venetia. Sarah told Venetia to invite your father to join the show. And Sarah told Venetia that she was to entertain your father. That was easy for Venetia, because she's very fond of your father. And you should know that Sarah was put up to all this by her father, Venetia's grandfather—this was all thought up months ago, but Venetia didn't know why. It was all about money and land. And it was Sarah who told Venetia to behave as though one day she and your father would be like you and Venetia. But that isn't happening. And won't happen. And never would."

Another pause: "So now, Ben, you know what to do. With your father. Don't think about it; just go and do it tonight. After the show."

75

Venetia and I had some hours together before I faced up to what was now a difficult and melancholy task. Some hours in which the only talk was in whispers. Some hours in which we felt our first mutual sadness. Some hours in which we learned how to convert that sadness into calm and optimism. Blarney went back into his case, and we lay down. No more than that do you need to know.

I paced outside the hall that night. Got my feet wet in the puddles. My shoes ruined in the mud. I paced and paced. Logistics for the time ahead: clothes; money; home; life. I decided to ignore them for the moment; I had my hands already full.

As the last applause roared I went to the rear door of the hall, the smelly hall, where the paint peeled like scabs, the dowdy hall, with the broken chairs, the drab hall, still hung with flitters of colored streamers from some Christmas long ago.

First I saw Cwawfod, who looked at me, I now realize, with a new and subdued respect. Then I saw Graham, who said, "Good evening, young squire." I saw Venetia's back and bare shoulders as she returned to the stage to take her bow. And then I saw my father. He saw me at the same time; the bruises on his face had become livid; mine had faded.

I beckoned with the air of a man giving no choice, and I turned away. He followed; I knew that he followed, and I walked to the car. For a moment he hesitated, and I looked back at him.

"This is serious," I said.

He climbed in and I drove. Not a word did we say to each other along those roads of puddles and pools. Not a glance did we cast at each other, along those lanes of high shrubs and bare hedges. We shivered, each of us, in the cold and the emotion.

There is a lane that leads to the cottage without going near the house. No gate, just an opening, and that night mud, mud, and more mud. The high wheelbase of the Alvis helped. When it threatened worse we climbed out and walked the last hundred yards or so to the cottage, our way illuminated by the car's headlights.

No lights, no candles or lamps; Mother had gone to bed; the time was about one o'clock in the morning. She had locked the doors, back and front.

I pounded. From inside I heard a door creak open and her voice inside the front door.

"Who's there?"

I nudged my father, his face blue with cold.

He said, "Louise, it's-it's-it's me. Open the door. It's all right."

76

I left them to it. The moment demanded utter privacy. In the car, I had a brief and intense flash of curiosity, almost turned back, thought it unseemly, and drove on. I had no idea what transpired between them that night after I'd gone. Years later, I did find out, because I asked each of them. They told me different stories.

Mother said that she thought a trick was being played on her. When she grasped that my father was real, and stood there, and looked as though he had indeed come home, she grew angry. For a moment she thought that she might hit him across the face; indeed she stepped back to stop herself from doing so. She led the way into the cottage, where a fire's embers still glowed. He added some logs and they sat there until almost dawn, seven o'clock in the morning.

"I never asked him if he had a mouth on him," she said. "Maybe I'd so lost the habit of feeding him. How can you lose such a long habit in such a short time?"

What did they talk about? Did she ask him any questions? How did he explain what he had done—if he explained it at all?

"I told him what had happened, the mortgage and that. And I asked him about our money. I told him we were now poor, that we had nothing. He said it wasn't right, it was criminal trickery, but he didn't know what to do about it. And I said that neither did I."

His story differed. And possibly had more accuracy.

"I-I-I said I was sorry. I've been saying it ever since. Neither of us heard the other that night."

I asked him what that meant. "Neither heard the other." He hesitated, and then spoke like a man telling everything.

"We-we-we cried a lot. The whole stupidity of it. And we cried because we didn't know what was going to happen to us. We didn't know then that we had a savior."

When the door had closed behind my father, I went to the car and turned off the headlamps. For long minutes I stood there, looking at the dark cottage with the glimmer of light from my mother's candlestick.

It could have been a scene from a legend—the little gate, the garden, the thatched roof so lovingly kept in repair. The stars gave out enough light to touch the thick white walls and the straw roof with a little silver glow.

Was my job done? No—and I knew it. These people had been reduced to almost nothing; such diminishing had to be reversed. Did I think that they could do it, could take control? Not at all.

I turned to the river and wondered how to get them back what they had lost—indeed whether I could effect anything. The black, sleek waters slid by with a small gurgle, and at once I knew my pathway to the advice I needed—James Clare.

First, though, I needed comforting. It strikes me now that knowing I needed comforting showed how much I'd grown up.

Venetia lay awake. She heard me at the front door and I found her kneeling up in bed. I told her what I'd done.

"Has anybody praised you?" she said.

I had no sense of achievement that night until she told me. I had no understanding of the night's significance until she pointed it out. I had no grasp of the night's meaning until she underlined it.

"You've reunited your parents. You've done your mother's bidding. You've acted like a grown man."

She had a way of speaking to me that made me feel safe. With her by my side, no problem would have been too great. How I could have cared for her, would have cared for her. And did, as far as I could, in the months ahead, which were so often glorious.

Next morning, lying in an afterglow, we made plans. She wanted to take the company away from Charleville.

"Genuine touring—from town to village to hamlet. And get rid of the damn vaudeville. Ben, how much depth can country audiences take, do you think?"

"We all did Shakespeare at school. And Milton. And Dryden."

"Benedict MacCarthy, I'm going to build a new show."

In the meantime, I told her, I had to find somebody—by whom I meant James Clare.

He had told me how to go looking for him. When he traveled, he used the post office as his base—to cash his government paycheck, keep his savings, and set up forwarding addresses. If I needed to contact him, I was to hand in a letter addressed to him, and the post office knew the town he was visiting next. He would then reply to me via the post office through which the inquiry had been made. Everybody who wanted him came to use this method. Simple, yet clever and countrywide—just like James himself.

It took me no more than three days to write and receive a reply. He hadn't gone far—to the village of Hollyford, at the foot of the Silvermines Mountains. I got there in a morning.

James had stayed overnight in the house of a well-known farmer.

"This family," he told me, "have stories oozing out of them."

We sat in their parlor, conducted thence, with tea and cake, by the farmer's wife, a small live wire of a woman who spoke so quickly that I couldn't make out what she was saying.

James, seeing my bemusement, said when she'd gone, "She's not from around here"—which is Ireland's catchall excuse for every human frailty.

He had long set the ways of his life. I later came to know and navigate them. If I broached a topic with him, I had to wait until he had narrated some other, seemingly unconnected tale. As I got to know him better, I understood that he was buying space to think before he gave an answer to my question.

After my first sip of tea, I told him what had happened. I delivered it like news headlines and sat back.

James said, "They have a brick of silver in this family, an ingot, that they say was mined in the hills you saw on the way in."

"Well, they're called the 'Silvermines,' " I said.

"This man's aunt," said James, opening another topic, "she was famous around here for having a baby at the age of sixty. And the child was healthy."

I'm a good eater—and always have been. But I've never been anything like James Clare. He could put away food like an eating machine, and he remained as slender as a plank. That morning we finished half a large fruitcake between us, and would have eaten more. Then James sat back.

"D'you recall what I did in Fermoy?"

How could I not? He'd told me the story of the recent events in my life as though he had found an old tale.

"I think of it often," I said.

"Can you do it now?"

He knew I couldn't, but in kindness wanted to give me the opportunity. I shook my head, and he began.

"The Queen knew from an early moment that the man had a son. And the wicked King knew that the man had left his son and his son's mother unprotected. But when the Princess—not the Queen—when the Princess saw the man's son, she knew what the gods had decided. And when the wicked King saw the man's son, he grew afraid. He tried to get the son to join him, to lead his army—"

James broke off and said, "How is this sounding?"

"What I need to know is—what do I do next?"

"In something as important as this," he said, "you first of all have to establish what you know, how much you know. Telling it as a story should make it clearer."

I didn't want to hear more because I felt uncomfortable; I should have known to take this as a sign of the story's accuracy.

"But—"

"I know, Ben, I know. What do you do next?" His advice surprised me. "I'd say—do nothing."

"Nothing at all?"

"Leave it alone. Live day to day. Meet me in the west; I want to show you the ocean. Your strength is in the power of others."

For the few weeks following that meeting, I reordered my life. I wrote to my parents and said that I'd be away for some time. In the note, I told my father where I'd left the car—in Cashel. He must have known that now I had the big, high-ceremonial Daimler; I wonder whether it hurt him. My actions, to an outsider, would have suggested that my life had been altered permanently—which it had been, but the greater change was internal, a maturing at top speed. At that moment, I assumed a new role in life—that of partner to Venetia in every waking moment of her existence.

We had peace. And a surprising amount of it. The members of the company intruded not at all. Apart from the nightly—and sometimes afternoon—involvement with the show on the road, we saw only Mrs. Haas.

Sarah had gone to New York, and from there to Los Angeles. Of King Kelly—not a sign; his new parliamentary life had taken him to Dublin.

Mrs. Haas behaved as lady-in-waiting to a bridegroom and his bride. She ostentatiously put herself at our disposal—handmaid and housekeeper, cook and controller of our home. She changed bed linen and towels every few days, created special mealtime atmospheres with candles and perfumed air—plus sumptuous food.

I look back on that time now as I recall some dreams, and indeed it all had the texture of dreams, the vague and airy sensations, the basic peace.

Real life intruded rarely. We went to Limerick because I had no clothes; Venetia bought wardrobes for me. She found a doctor for my badly affected knuckles where I had struck my father. How was it that I hadn't killed him? The thought still makes me shudder. We saw a lawyer in the city of Cork, because Venetia wanted to make a will, and she insisted that I overhear it because I was to be the sole beneficiary. And she took me to a garden that she loved, the garden of a great house whose owners were away.

This mansion sat on the same river, Blackwater, that flowed through Fermoy. In the car Venetia carried letters from a number of owners who had such houses and gardens. She knew these people from Dublin, from her days in the Abbey Theatre, and had been given introductions by letter.

We walked between rows of trees.

"Planted," she said, "to commemorate the British victory at Waterloo."

And I said to her, "Did you know that the schools on both sides, British and French, teach Waterloo as a victory?"

Her method of talking still intrigues me. She managed to give the impression that she said little, yet she talked all the time. I was the silent one—because I wanted to listen. I had no wish to speak, especially if it was going to curtail the time in which she might have something to say.

And she had plenty. She loved gardens and showed wide knowledge of trees, flowers, and especially flowering shrubs.

"If I could," she said, "I would do all my rehearsing in a garden. A large garden, with bowers, and a lake and fountain—not too noisy a fountain, because I wouldn't be able to hear my lines. And it would make me want to pee all the time."

I often walked behind her as she high-stepped through the gardens we visited. She always walked with respect, never straying off the paths, not even when a tree intrigued her. That afternoon she stopped by a hedge of honeysuckle, which we had growing at home.

"You've got this at your house, haven't you? I saw it when we came up from the woods." Then she stopped and narrowed her eyes. "D'you know what I'm doing, Ben? I'm trying to imagine what it's going to be like here when May comes. We'll come back and see."

She collected things—tiny pebbles from the gravel; odd shapes of fallen leaves or little sticks; feathers, the tinier the better. From one bare shrub she took a bird's nest from last year.

I asked her questions. She told me that she had no friends, not even in the theater, that all her time had been spent with her mother.

"If I talk to you too much it's because I've never been able to talk to anybody like this. All my companions have been older—my mother's friends."

We'd reached a pocket of tall hedges, where the sun made strong heat. She felt the stone of a bench with her hands and we sat down.

"Do you want to marry me?" she said, grabbing my arm.

I didn't have to think, but I wasn't quick enough to reply.

"You will, won't you? You will marry me? You're the only person I've ever known whose company works for me; I'm safe with you. You'll let me be what I am. It's right for me—is it right for you?"

"Completely," I said.

"I'll be no good without you. My mother will be furious."

"When," I asked, "will we do it?"

"Do you have to be twenty-one?"

Neither of us knew—but we walked from that garden as married in our minds as most people ever get at their weddings.

The pleasure of being with Venetia surpassed anything that I had ever known or imagined. It still does. I hadn't been a dreamy boy, at least not the romantic sort, but I'd had my share of fantasies—I've mentioned it already, the usual stuff about heroism and conquering the world.

But I'd never daydreamed about being in the company of someone lovely, appealing, interesting, and calm, someone thoughtful, entertaining, talkative, and warm.

When I lay it out like that for you now, you can see that my parents, each of them, supplied quite a few of those qualities, and from both sides. To find, at the beginning of my adult life, the same—and more—in one person, and that person a beautiful and talented woman, and somebody who felt close to me in age despite the calendar's evidence—I could have reached for the word "miracle"—if I'd known enough to think like that.

All I knew is that I was having feelings that I'd never known existed, and I wanted them to go on and on, and it seemed very much the case that they would.

We shared everything. I came into her world as though it had always been my intended place. Without comment, without feeling unusual, we settled down in Charleville through the last days of February and all through March, and as Venetia prepared a new repertoire for the show, I observed and interjected and contributed. It was a paradise. The world left us alone.

Sometimes one or two of the other actors came to discuss her choices. Of these, Peter, who never acted, made the best contribution, had the best taste. When Venetia wanted to try something, she gave readings from the play or poem. If we were alone she asked what I thought; and I gave my opinion on how it affected me. When others gave their views, she always turned to me in the end.

In the long term I came to think—especially after it had all ended—that I had been flattered by Venetia and the others, until I found Peter in his old folks' home. He changed my opinion.

"You know," he said, "we couldn't grasp one thing. We couldn't understand how a country lad—which is what you were to us, a bumpkin, a farmhand—how a rural lout could have formed such taste. We used to get so annoyed. When I got blind drunk, as I often did, I could hear myself swearing your name out loud. What was it, old boy? Instinct? Wish I'd had it. My taste was all acquired. Winchester School and Oxford."

I avoided going home—too much, too much. By the middle of May, Venetia had a whole new show. We took to the road in the first week of June, playing the west coast from Dingle up to Donegal, and on the first of July she went to a doctor in Castleisland and was told that she was "carrying a child."

Time for an Important Digression: Throughout that spring and summer, the new Irish government was coming into being. The first assembly of those elected in February didn't happen until March. Anybody interested in politics at any level would have paid good money to get behind the scenes before they all met in Dublin; in fact Mr. de Valera could have sold tickets.

He had such horse-trading to do. The election had involved four distinct and registered parties, and fourteen independent members. To get anything passed, to make sure that he outnumbered them all, Dev needed ten clear votes. He'd won a total of seventy-two seats, an increase of fifteen on the previous Parliament. Mr. Cosgrave had fifty-six, the Labour party had seven, and the Farmers' party three. Add up the smaller parties, and the Independents, and the Speaker (always returned unopposed), and they came to eighty-one.

You can probably tell that I had now taken to reading the morning newspaper like my father, who was after all the only husband I had ever seen. I scanned every day in deep detail, and that is how I ascertained that King Kelly was making a lot of noise and was indeed going to sit on the Parliament's Finance Committee. He might even become a major player on the Opposition benches, challenging de Valera's policies.

My heart sank; how could one ever challenge that power? End of Digression—but there will be more.

Venetia touched the clouds in her joy. Everything about her became dual—at times she could barely speak in excitement, and at times she chattered nonstop, to everything around her, including me; she wanted to dance and she stood still as a statue; she laughed and she wept.

And I, who hadn't known the word *virgin* except in a religious context, who knew nothing of procreation except in the animal world, I took to my new status as a duck to a stream. My protective instincts doubled, of course, and I didn't even know why; I did no more than respond to my feelings.

The night that we knew, Venetia gave performances far beyond anything I had yet seen. She even thought so herself. She was building this new repertoire gradually. Already she had expanded her range, and had put together a "medley"—her word—of Shakespeare's speeches, mostly heroines, although she did include two of the soliloquies from *Hamlet,* and continued to follow the requirements of the nationwide school curriculum.

I loved the fact that some of these words echoed in the shabbiest buildings I had ever seen—to people who sat packed shoulder to shoulder, some of them following the words of every speech with their lips.

She'd also chosen what she called "tougher stuff"—she gave them glimpses of *Antigone* and *Medea,* setting up the chosen speech with some plot narration, either her own introduction or something very orotund spoken by Peter (now back onstage) or Graham.

The company loved the changes, and admired the skill with which they were being phased in. Few of them missed the "funnies," as they called them, and they relished being given the chance to do what they called "true" acting.

Cwawfod, in particular, found his reward. Far from not being allowed to speak lines, he was converted into true character acting. Where a role needed to be exaggerated on account of its brevity in an excerpt, Cwawfod was used to considerable effect. He was comic, touching, sinister, hopeless—whatever was needed—and Venetia brought out of him depths that nobody had even suspected.

He gave up drinking, and when eventually the show folded, he became a not inconsiderable minor character in films, and made money.

Ireland had always loved a traveling show. With so little transport available, the world had to come to the people, who repaid with attendance and appreciation. Strolling players had long been a part of countryside life and tradition. Venetia's forerunners had brought to the villages the melodramas of the nineteenth century, and the classics, and the specially written local dramas, often based on famous tragedies or mysteries.

In the years after Venetia, other distinctive companies toured with troupes of experienced actors—and they also bred actors who went on to great fame. Harold Pinter, for instance, before he made his name writing plays, appeared with companies that toured Ireland.

As with Venetia, a basic economic principle underpinned them all—the opportunity for students to hear the play they were studying, and now, in her revamped repertoire, Venetia included longer and longer excerpts. It was her intention, I knew, to build up to entire plays.

The current season of engagements arranged from the Charleville base still had to be played out. Our life on the road became much more delightful—nothing nearly as grim as those weeks when I was pursuing my father.

Sarah and King Kelly, I was learning, had had strong fingers in the traveling-show pie. With them out of the way, Venetia also changed the way she conducted business.

The audiences for this more serious material grew larger than anything she had known. Priests and teachers began to approve, and in most towns she had to do two shows a day. In effect the income more than doubled, and she plowed it back into the show. She bought an extra car for the others; she hired carpenters and painters to make new scenery flats; she spent money on costumes.

The players responded by working harder than ever, and showing her an increasing devotion. On those occasions when we played a town for a week, Venetia found fresh flowers in her dressing room, such as it was, on opening night (I think the actors raided local gardens). They brought her little gifts; they gave her performance notes; they found new material for her.

For instance, Peter and Graham persuaded her to perform the Tennyson poem "The Lady of Shalott"; it had also been on many curricula. They wrote an introductory script for her, in which she connected the poem and its origins in an Italian folktale with the legend of the River Shannon's name, where the princess Shannon, also dead and in a white robe, flows mystically down the stream like Ophelia. Venetia brought the house down with the story and the poem.

Now and then events might have delayed a performance, such as the election rally in Kilmallock did, but being shrewd, she simply held back the opening of the show and attracted a huge overflow from the other event. The money poured in.

She looked after her company even better than before. Every player saw a doctor; if the town had a hotel, they stayed there, booked in advance by writing; all of these arrangements were looked after by silent Martha, who, by all accounts, wrote in a beautiful copperplate hand and an elegant letter.

Where a town had no hotels, advance research revealed good bed-and-breakfast places or pubs with rooms overhead, although Venetia favored those less than any kind of other accommodation. "We have enough problems with pubs," was her dark reply when I asked.

And so we went from town to village to little crossroads hall. We were becoming celebrities. The local newspapers wrote anticipatory notices and gave us departing reviews—always praise, never a negative word. If those notices happened while there was still time for people to see the show, we had to put on extra performances.

None of this bothered Venetia; the more she performed, the more she bloomed. She even gave some free performances in schools, and from the faces of the teachers and the students, it looked as though a comet had decided to come to earth and light up their lives for that hour or so.

I watched everything she did; I was near her all the time; I saw every bit of material. There was a sense in which I was deliberately "learning" her—after all, I scarcely knew her, conventionally speaking. Nothing ever grew less; in everything we did, we increased and intensified.

The watching, the constant observation of her onstage, led me to analyze her art, her skill, her craft—I still don't know the appropriate word, perhaps all three. My abiding impression has to do with how little she did, not how much. Silence governed everything, stillness, often a motionlessness; time after time I watched her walk onstage and for an astonishing number of seconds do nothing. Maybe a small move of the head, maybe a folding of the hands—and then, before she spoke, a slight shift of posture, perhaps a foot forward, especially in the classical pieces.

Also, she carried that same holding mood into the delivery of the words. There's an exercise I'd like you to think about. When next you hear a major singing star performing a song that you know and love, and have sung often in the bath or the shower, follow the words silently. See how the the singer holds back. Note how he delays the phrase. Observe how he waits to deliver the freight of the line.

That's what Venetia did. She understood—and I think it was by instinct—how to keep an audience waiting without the audience knowing that it was waiting. And she understood that acting is mostly reacting. I used to watch her "reading" the audience, as she called it. She didn't appear to be looking at them; it always seemed that she was not of them at all; for example, I never saw her making eye contact—or so it seemed.

But she saw them, all right—she told me so. She never referred to it as "the whites of their eyes"—she loved them too much to say that—but that's what she was looking at.

And she reacted to what they loved. Not that she allowed herself to be steered by them—not at all; she just wanted to make sure that they were getting the full value of what she had to offer. When she had divined what they were enjoying, she gave them more—and more.

And every night, as I stood there in the wings and watched her, my pride grew. And every night she not only never disappointed me, she made me even more proud. And afterward I got to hold her in my arms, sometimes all night.

If I woke up and didn't get back to sleep, I often tried to imagine what lay ahead. Would Venetia go back to the Abbey—or had King Kelly fouled the water in that well for all time? I wouldn't have wanted her to, especially if Sarah intended to continue playing seasons there; mother was not good for daughter professionally, no matter how much they loved each other.

My belief now is that we would have gone on to do what she dearly wished—establish a theater in a country town, and give it a touring company too. In between she'd play roles in the great theaters of the world—and we knew she would because scouts came to see her, and offers reached us all the time.

In particular, though, she so wanted to go on bringing these beautiful words, these time-honored emotions to the people in the countryside, who lived by "the rules of nature," as she put it. She understood that they had grim lives, mostly—they did hard, scrabbling work with the rewards few.

79

The night after we heard the doctor's good news we decided to tell nobody. Except Mrs. Haas. I had to establish the legal age for marrying, and the means of doing so. At the same time, we had a major distraction, a new member of the company; his name was Cody.

A smallish man with a hooked nose and a broad Irish accent with a slight whine, Cody walked into our lives one night as a performance ended. He seemed more than respectable, but his suit, when scrutinized, had shiny patches, and his shirt had been in a war or two.

Cody carried a briefcase, and he said that he'd worked in England for some theaters and traveling companies, and had what he called "tremendous experience" in managing the finances of people who worked on the stage.

He didn't steal money; that may be your initial suspicion. Nor did he fracture the company's economic structure. On the contrary, Cody helped us in many ways.

For instance, we had problems in the amount of cash we had to carry—all our takings from, often, three shows a day, at least two performances on most days—average fourteen shows a week. Cody set up a relationship with a bank that enabled us to draw money in any decent-size town. A worry evaporated.

He also identified, for future purposes, the towns where our income had been greatest—on account of venue capacity and so forth. Not that we'd ever have abandoned the little places that only held fifty people, and another hundred and fifty peering in through the doors and windows, and on one occasion in Kilcallaghan, hanging from the roof beams.

In short, Cody eliminated the need for us to keep such a close eye on the financial end of things and allowed us to concentrate on the repertoire and the logistics.

Venetia checked Cody's work with a rigor that surprised me. Every week she examined the books that he kept, and reconciled things with every bank we visited. What she couldn't check was what we didn't know—that Cody had no intention of hitting our pockets; his intent, a strategized effort, had much greater damage in mind.

We married in the depths of the summer. Venetia wore flowers in her hair. It wasn't a conventional wedding but it was legal. We did it in Galway, which was my idea; I took a leaf from the book of Mr. de Valera's life.

As we strolled the docks a ship sat at anchor about half a mile out. I asked a dockhand where she'd come from, and he told me New York. This happened before Cody had streamlined the cash and the banking arrangements, and we were carrying in her purse and my pockets a considerable amount of money.

I told Venetia my plan, she got some flowers, and I hired a boatman to take us out to the ship. We called up to a deckhand, who sent for the captain. They dropped a ladder, we climbed, and the captain (for a consideration) married us. He had to weigh anchor to do so, because the law required the ship to be under way. The persuasion eased when we told him of the expected baby—he had nine children at home in New Jersey.

Mrs. Haas wept, and baked a small wedding cake when we went back to Charleville at the weekend. We swore her to secrecy. By the time Venetia's condition became obvious we would have worked out how to tell people. Mrs. Haas loved keeping the secret.

Only one other person knew about the pregnancy and the marriage—Cody. We had to tell him on account of banking papers and signing authorities, and we swore him to secrecy too. We didn't know that there were no conditions under which he could keep such a confidence; he was pulled by other, more powerful string masters. If ever I meet Cody again, I will end up in jail.

And so the year 1932 wound on. I never missed my daily ration of politics, and with this newfound maturity I began to see things in a much clearer light. I watched the posturing of our leaders; I watched how they arranged to be photographed with church dignitaries who came into Ireland for the giant Eucharistic Congress, an international Catholic Church assembly in Dublin to celebrate worship.

And I watched the rise of King Kelly too. He did indeed become a member of the powerful Finance Committee. And he did indeed sit in the Opposition Front Bench, as it's called, where he was the shadow spokesman on finance—which meant that he shadowed the finance minister. Which meant that if Mr. Cosgrave ever got back into power, King Kelly would himself become the country's finance minister, the second most powerful job in the land.

I made no contact with my parents. As James Clare had advised, I did nothing—not least because I still hadn't unwrapped the meaning of his final remark to me: "Your strength is in the power of others."

James had said, "Meet me in the west; I want to show you the ocean." On the day after the wedding, I went to the post office to find a letter for me; James knew that in a matter of weeks we were coming to Sligo, and we'd meet there.

Knowing that James could keep a secret, I resolved to tell him that I'd seen the ocean, and tell him how and why—that Venetia and I had married onboard a ship. I longed to hear him tell the next chapter of the story.

You must visit Sligo one day, Yeats's town—for me his shadow stalks the place. Here are his two magic mountains: The body of Queen Maeve, the most ancient and most famous of all Irishwomen and the most warlike and the most fearsome, lies in a stone cairn on Knocknarea's peak. Across the country from her sits the magical table mountain of Ben Bulben, and the people of the netherworld fly between the two, but you have to be quick to see them and you have to be able to see in the dark.

I'm repeating more or less accurately James's words to Venetia, as we walked around the town. She enchanted him, and he delighted her. He told her stories that made her clap her hands in amazement; he taught her scraps of ancient poems; he explained the structure of the old world to her—who the "Little People" were who lived beneath the ground of Ireland.

We came to rest on that first day in a public house in the outskirts of the town, where, James said, the landlady would make us a meal. He added that he had a surprise for me—and he had: Miss Dora Fay. She went to Sligo for a week every summer, and she and her old friend James tried to coincide there.

I was delighted to see her and she was staggered—and thrilled—at our marriage. Never had I seen her so excited; she said over and over to Venetia, "But, my dear, you are lovely, lovely." And then said, "And what a young man you've found for yourself, what a guy."

She and James came to all the night performances of the week; they knew that the program changed with each show. Miss Fay knew every word of every scrap of drama; I could see her from where I stood—she was mouthing the words and smiling in all the right places. James sat back, proud like a man at his child's school play.

In the new repertoire, Blarney's role had changed. He still had a solo appearance with Venetia, and he still did "political commentary"—but she also deployed him in the play extracts. He did Fool from *King Lear;* he was young Gobbo, and Autolycus, and most touchingly of all, Ariel, the wistful but dangerous sprite from *The Tempest.* Venetia had arranged costumes for him, and he electrified the audiences—and the players—in his new colors.

On the last night in Sligo, we had arranged for our hotel to put up a late meal for us with Miss Fay and James. By now we'd met on a number of occasions, and it was clear that for them our marriage amounted to a gift. At a moment during the meal, Miss Fay said to me, "How are your parents?"

She said it with some caution, her face down somewhat.

I said, "I've been on the road since late February."

Venetia, always quicker than me, said, "Should Ben go to see them?"

James said, "The nothing time is over." He smiled and explained to the two women, "Something I said to Ben when we last met. There is always a time when to do nothing is to go forward."

We all agreed to meet next day and say our farewells. Venetia and I walked upstairs to bed; her condition didn't yet show; the baby wouldn't be born until December. In the room I took the Blarney suitcase off the bed and she said, "No. Open it."

She took Blarney from the case and sat down. Blarney began to speak.

"Ben, you like stories, don't you?"

"Yes, Blarney. I like stories." What was this? Venetia ignored my raised eyebrows.

Blarney went on. "Ben, there's a story I can't tell you yet. But I will one day. You'll probably find it out before I can tell you. All I want you to know is—it's no part of my story. You know that, don't you?"

"If you say so, Blarney."

"Do you mean—you don't believe me?"

"I think you're a tough little fellow, Blarney."

"Ben, I'm hurt. Will you believe me if I tell you that Venetia has nothing to do with that story either?"

"Is this a bad story, Blarney?"

"It is, Ben. It is."

"Then I know that Venetia had nothing to do with it."

Blarney lowered his head and Venetia looked away. Then they both recovered and Blarney said, "You should go to visit your parents, Ben."

"I don't want to leave Venetia."

"Venetia understands. Don't you, Venetia?"

She nodded and Blarney said, "And go soon, Ben."

Next morning we made arrangements. James and Miss Fay were taking a train to Dublin that evening. I decided to go with them; much easier to get down home from Dublin than from Sligo, whence I could find no direct route. Venetia came to the station. She seemed unusually somber, and I put it down to the fact that we had never previously parted. I boarded the train, and waved from the window.

As we left Sligo, James began to point out the landscapes of Yeats's poems and recite from them.

" 'I will arise and go now, and go to Inisfree.' "

Miss Fay and I chimed in. " 'And a small cabin build there, of clay and wattles made.' "

The two adults began to talk about the poet. For all of my young life, from the time that I began to read as a pastime and not merely as a school necessity, the figure of Yeats stood in the Irish landscape like a huge tree. The analogy isn't mine. Friends who are authors and poets and dramatists have often said to me that any Irish writer in the early twentieth century found it hard to get the warmth of the sun in a shadow as great as that.

My lasting image of Yeats has as much to do with his physical appearance as with his verse. I saw him many times—a big man, bigger than my father, and much heftier. Unlike my outgoing and smiling parent, Yeats always wore a preoccupied air, as though pondering great things.

Perhaps he was—but as I've already hinted, I've since learned from many people who knew him that he was a calculating man who judged carefully the image that he wished to present to the world.

None of his shrewdness, though, or his attempts to conceal it, impinged upon his poetry, and if his large frame in his cloak and wide-brimmed hat dominated my mind's eye in my teens, twenties, and thirties, his poems became my sound track—and the nation's.

James then remembered a story that he had told Yeats.

"He sat on the edge of his seat like a child. His eyes were round and wide, and his mouth open like a bag. He was hanging on every word."

Miss Fay commented, "It must have been a wonderful story, and therefore you have to tell us."

He began; this is what I recall of it. As James told it, and as I see it written down now in my own words, I understand that the language was as important as any of the narrative drive. And as ever, James was using it to teach me about life in general.

There was a man one time and he knew many things. He knew how to grow beautiful ears of wheat and when to take the new potatoes out of the ground. He knew when a horse was ready to be taught how to jump a ditch, and he knew when to bring his dairy cows in for the winter. He knew how to take care of his family, for he had a wife and a son, and he knew how to hire good men and send bad men away. This was a man who knew how to get himself liked, and how to like people, and that is one of the greatest gifts of all.

Above all he was a man who knew how to conduct himself decently, and to keep himself on a safe and steady path. If he felt sorry for himself, he never allowed anybody to know it, not even his dear wife. If he felt sudden bursts of gladness, as we all do, he knew they were dangerous things too, and he kept a lid on them most of the way, like you'd keep a lid on a pot, with just a little bit open so that the water doesn't boil over.

The people who knew this man well, who saw him every day, saw that he was a man who understood things. He understood how the sun rose, followed by the moon. He understood why hares danced in the fields at certain times of the year. He understood why grain had to be harvested at an exact moment in its ripeness, and people used to send for this man and ask him to come and rub the ears of their wheat between his fingers and tell them if it was ready to be cut.

There were many other things he understood—like the moment to stand in the river and catch a salmon with your hands as it leaps northward over a weir on its journey to the spawning grounds. Or not to cross a male donkey with a female pony, but to do it the other way 'round; otherwise you'll get an animal over which you'll have no control, your only reward will be biting and kicking and bucking to beat the band.

This was a man who understood why the stars are brightest on a frosty night, and why a shout can be heard for miles across a lake. And why milk turns yellow at certain times of the year, and as a consequence, the care to take when feeding cows that have calved. And why a man will look you in the eye during the making of a bargain, but you should always look at his feet, because if his feet shift you have a liar on your hands.

Now this man was also a successful merchant, and he practiced his merchantry in great style. He sold barley to make ale and he sold pitchforks to make hay. He sold polish to make boots shine, and he sold cards to make men gamble. He sold pipes to smoke tobacco and pipes to make music. And he dispensed all these things with always the good word, always the willing piece of advice.

"Mind, now," he'd say, "that you don't let the dog lick the polished boot for he'll get dizzy. And mind, now," he'd say, "that you clean the inside of this basin with cold water, else the milk'll turn sour when the moon rises. And mind, now," he'd say, "that the stone for that knife is kept wet for an hour and a half before you come to sharpen—otherwise the stone won't like the blade. And mind, now," he'd say, "that you give your good lady a ribbon for her hair to match her eyes—otherwise she won't know that you think her a beautiful woman."

This was also a man of learning. He had learned what other men will take by way of orders, and what they won't take. He had learned that some trees have to be cut down in a particular way, because he was also a man who sold timber. He had learned the names of all the old gods, because he knew that a day might come when he would need to speak to one of them. He had learned the lessons of the old sages because he understood that wisdom, if there is such a thing, takes three hundred years and three hundred days to be worth anything. And he had learned one of life's most important lessons, which is when to talk and when to fight.

So, as I say, this was a man who knew a great deal of things about a great deal of things and was generous with his knowledge and his advice and his observations.

Like Yeats, Miss Fay and I, in the train carriage, listened like small children. And I had a wonderful idea—why not have Venetia turn Blarney into a storyteller? She had already gone a long way to reduce his sinister qualities by including him as an actor in the play extracts.

We never heard the end of James's story—because the train slammed to as sudden a halt as it could manage. We had run into a new drama. On the side of the track—we'd halted by a small village—a house blazed.

Men jumped from the train to see if they could help. The villagers were running too. Flames licked from the windows—a poor enough, two-story dwelling.

I could see the men asking questions of a woman, trying to ascertain whether all people had quit the house. The woman had gathered four children around her, and she kept shaking her head. She evidently assured the questioners that nobody remained inside, because, working in teams, men went in and brought such furniture as they could grab out onto the street.

Then, however, beams began to fall, and with each crash the sparks rose in ever higher showers, causing the children to recoil farther each time. They wailed and danced in anxiety.

I stepped out too, but James suggested that nothing could be done. Such a sight! Sparks flying to the sky, faces turned to the flames, children not knowing whether to cry, the woman distraught, the train like a long green creature stretched and curved down the line, shining in the fire. I don't know what became of those poor folks after that night. With the rain pouring down, I climbed back on the train and saw the flames reflected in the windows.

From the outward signs it seemed that James visited Miss Fay's house often. He had what looked like a permanent room there, where he kept some papers, and the notes for the book he was writing on traveling storytellers. I learned all that during supper, and was then shown to a room that I would use for many years. Miss Fay lived in Rathmines, in a tall brick house, with a pleasant smell of old carpets. She had a retainer who lived in the basement, Allie, who shouted rather than spoke. Every room on each floor had collections—masks, birds' eggs, small animals in glass cases, umbrellas. The room in which I slept had shelves of old engineering and geometry instruments—ivory slide rules, dividers, and protractors—and I felt protected and safe, I who had at that time slept in so few houses in my life.

I've said that James and Miss Fay may have viewed me as a kind of surrogate son—but I never felt less than the same age as they were. They delivered their remarks as to an equal; their advice took the form of debate. Today I know that I was witnessing perhaps the last practitioners of eighteenth-century manners.

In anticipation of my visit to my parents, they asked what I expected to find. We discussed many options. It became clear that Miss Fay knew of my parents' removal to the cottage—and the likelihood that they would still be there. I sensed her embarrassment, but she fought it, and joined in the discussion.

They concluded that I must keep calm no matter what I found, that above all I must attend to my parents, establish what they needed, and see how I could help their lives.

"Imagine how they're feeling," said James. "Just think on both positions—your father embarrassed beyond description, your mother torn between delight and despair."

"When I'm in a bind," said Miss Fay, "I like to walk very slowly because it helps me to think deeper thoughts."

My train journey next day had no fires, and no stories. All the way from Dublin the sunlight beamed like glory through the windows. I walked from the train station to our house, a distance of four miles.

On a fine morning, with only a light suitcase, it almost felt pleasant, especially as the road from Dundrum Station passes through woods, and on the last stretch to our house I walked along and above the river. Once again I found our front gate closed, and once again I opened it wide and propped it open with the stone that had been there since before my father was born.

As I rounded the bend in the driveway to the point where the house first appears, two sentries in blue shirts barred my way.

"State your name and state your business."

"My name is Ben MacCarthy and I've been sent by Mr. Kelly."

"Have you a letter?"

"My parents live here."

"Nobody's allowed on this property without written permission."

They made me leave my own driveway—my own ground, where I knew every pebble on the gravel, every plant in the hedgerow. They made me turn my back on the white fence snaking up the field where I'd seen the great and shapeless Animal in the Incident. They made me turn away from the sight of my own doorway, with the stained-glass porch windows throwing colored petals on the floor inside.

To think slowly—walk slowly: I held on tight to Miss Fay's advice and decided to outwit these armed men. No sentries barred the old road that led to the wood. By now the sun had heated the countryside, and a strong wind blew feathers along the river.

No sign of life in the cottage—surprising on such a beautiful day. I knocked on the closed door.

"Give the password," called my father's voice.

"It's me. Ben."

He opened the door—he looked twenty years older. Behind him stood Mother, haggard and scared.

"They told us we're not to open the door to anybody," Mother said. "How did you get in?"

"They tried to block me."

Like fearful people—which they were—they hauled me in and closed the door. Both vented relief—and excitement that I had come home.

"If you can call it home," said my father.

They told me a dismal story. An officer, whose name they didn't know, had taken charge of them and said he had orders to keep them indoors. New housing was being arranged for them, perhaps in the United States, and they remained on the land at Mr. Kelly's pleasure.

"It's like house arrest," said my father.

When my puzzled face asked why, Mother said, in a whisper, "We think there's something big going on."

My father said, "I got talking to one of the fellows. In a few months there's going to be a big announcement of a new political party. These fellows here will be its army."

"Why are they wearing blue shirts?" I asked.

"Why do Hitler's fellows wear brown shirts?"

Mother said, "They're drilling and marching and handling guns. They told your father that this is the biggest secret in the country."

Once I sat down with them and we began to talk, my parents became for a time much like their old selves. The previous months had cut furrows in them. Equally, they had no idea what was going to happen to them, or what they would live on. In the cottage Mary Lewis brought them food twice a day, but they weren't allowed out under any circumstances.

"She's so nasty to us," said Mother.

"No surprise there," I said. I looked like a young man flourishing in his life—which I was.

"We've been the victims of a confidence trick," said my father. "And it began a long time ago."

Strange to say, I've never been more impressed with my parents than at that moment. Despite the pain for both of them, my father told the story of how he was—as he saw it—drawn into the web. He loved the show; he'd long known who Sarah was—and he met her at a performance that one night when he delayed his return from the Galway races.

She charmed him, he said, and he now realized that she extracted a great deal of information from him—where he lived, the size of the farm, his station in life, all of that. On the next visit, he met Venetia, who captivated him. Then, and with great skill, it seemed to me, Sarah drew him into a web at whose center sat her daughter.

Soon he had met King Kelly, who told him of Venetia's "financial plight." My father began to give what Sarah called "loans"—and I ascertained, because it was crucially important to me, that Venetia had never had a conversation with my father about money.

Not long after that, the trap was ready to be shut. When my father complained that he had no more money, Professor Fay moved in. We all three felt that this plot had been long in the hatching, that King Kelly had been looking for some prime victims.

For hours we sat there, talking back and forth, back and forth, inspecting every wrinkle, every twist in the story. My father spoke openly—and often with apology—of his role and how he had been fooled. Mother never, not once, made him feel bad. As we talked they expanded, and apart from the physical wear and tear, they began to sound like my parents again. We went over the story from every angle, until we were satisfied that our version of the story was what my father called "a true bill," his verdict of authenticity.

Next we discussed strategy. Getting the farm back, we agreed, had to be our prime thought. We debated the legality of all that had gone on—and we agreed that we needed to see Leonard Horgan. Getting there might be problematic; the men with guns had taken my father's car.

We plotted this: I would stay the night, and at dawn slip away, cross the river down at the ford, where the trees gave me the greatest concealment, and get to Cashel and Mr. Horgan's office. Having outlined the story, I would get his opinion and bring it back to my parents.

Mother confided to me that my father had almost ceased eating. And sleeping.

"You never saw such fretting."

"What about you?"

"At least I eat something," she said.

Both ate hearty meals that night. He made some jokes, they had second helpings, and they shared some wine from King Kelly's stacked cases in the little kitchen. The "theft," as they called it, bucked them up like children.

I worried that they would turn to me and ask questions. How much had my father told Mother? About Venetia? About the fight? How did he feel—the question I hadn't dared confront—about being ousted from his love by his son, his only child, his heir?

I didn't ask those questions; it would be years before I could. It seemed, by the way, that he'd said little or nothing to Mother about Venetia and me. A long time later I established that he had told her that I'd replaced him as a member of the company, no more than that.

Nor did I tell them that I'd married—I didn't know how to do that, and I didn't know when I could. Think of their connection to Venetia—my father's love, my mother's hate.

Besides, the atmosphere militated against it. No matter what the jollity among the three of us, we still spoke in hushed voices. Once or twice, one or the other stopped at a noise outside—and we all froze.

Before retiring to bed, we talked it through once again. My father said that he thought he'd known of a similar case, a "land swindle," he called it, up the country somewhere, but the details wouldn't come back to him—except that he believed it might also have involved a politician. And as the next words began to pour from his mouth, Mother and I chimed in, "The conduct of public affairs for private advantage."

However, as he said, "It makes it all the more difficult. He's where the power is now."

I'd intended to slip away close to dawn and without waking them. Instead I found Mother up and about, with breakfast ready.

"He's thrilled you're here," she said.

"I wondered if he'd be cross at me."

"At you? Ben, he couldn't be. Your name is the only light in his face since he came back."

It was impossible to dislike Leonard Horgan, a man who doubted everything. Head like a greyhound, sleek blond hair, he breathed as heavily as a fat man, yet if he stood sideways he'd have had no shadow; I've never known a thinner man. Nor a quicker mind; he grasped our story before I'd told it. And then he quizzed me.

"What's the level of shame at home?"

"Has your mother forgiven your father?"

"Will he stay with her?"

"These Kellys—do they like your father?"

High, but being handled well by both parents.

Yes, I'd say so.

Without a doubt. He'll do anything for her now.

Yes. They do like him.

"Not only that, Mr. Horgan." I paused.

He looked at me, green eyes. "Oh, Christ, no."

That's how quick he was. I dropped my eyes; it wasn't that I was embarrassed—it's just that I saw how this could complicate the matter.

"Tell me one thing. Tell me that you'll marry her."

"I did."

He clapped his hands. "Problem solved," he said. "Does old Kelly have any other family?"

I said, "But—there's worse. He's using the house—well, the place is full of men with guns."

I described it and he grew embarrassed.

"Well, I can't do anything about that. That's none of my business."

He looked uneasy; he shifted his feet in their black shiny shoes. Here's the thought I had; here's how fast my mind was working: *He belongs to the same party as King Kelly. He may not know about the guns, but he knows something and wants nothing to do with it. He's looking for an easy way out.*

"Mr. Horgan, can you tell me—if we went to court—if we took an action . . . ?"

He looked again at the mortgage document that I had brought with me—and handed it back.

"Not a sou. Not a cent. Not a chance. Your father, your mother—free will. Any judge would throw it out."

"Have you ever heard of a land swindle like this?"

"Ben, you've to be very careful with your language. Calling it a swindle—that's slander." He softened, recovered his composure. "Prevail upon your bride to have her grandfather make over the farm to her. At least it'll keep your parents there. As to the other business—all these things pass."

At the door I said to him, "Mr. Horgan, the men in the blue shirts, the guns—are they Fascists?"

He stepped back. "Christ, Ben, you use strong language. You'd be best off saying nothing to nobody."

And so I had no elevating news to bring home, but I saw one good thing, what James Clare would have called "an omen." Workmen had begun to tear down the old hall in Cashel where my father had run off with the show. Mixed feelings for me—I had first seen Venetia there, but it had occasioned bad times in my life, and it was never good enough for her anyway.

It crossed my mind to get a souvenir. Beside the door a little plaque had been inset showing the year of construction, a curly and ornate 1842, and a workman excised it for me.

We sat up late again, we ate well again, we debated back and forth again.

My father confirmed Leonard Horgan's politics and said, "He was almost a candidate in the 1927 election."

I didn't tell them his advice—how could I? The poor report notwithstanding, we relaxed even more than the previous night. They hadn't seen anybody all day—except Mary Lewis, who'd asked if they had "any news of Ben." We reasoned that the sentries must have made a report.

"She's a snake, that one," said Mother.

At last! An accurate character judgment from Mother—progress!

I asked them whether they minded if I went off and tried some things.

"If anyone can fix it," said my father, "it'll be you."

Next morning I left before dawn; my note on the kitchen table said, *Back within days.*

82

I went back to Dublin by train. For all the time that I knew her, and that was many years, I trusted Dora Fay more than anybody. She gave out a calm air, and yet I knew from James Clare that it came from a troubled soul—an excellent combination, because it showed that she had overcome difficulties in her own life. That evening in Dublin I told her first about my journey—people carried geese, toted hounds on leashes, small children roamed, and impossibly packed baskets and cartons blocked the corridors. Every town, village, and crossroads seemed to have its own station or halt. Nor did the train seem bound to any schedule that I could interpret.

Next, when the laughter had died, I told her about my parents' circumstances. This is what she said—James Clare was listening, with that shrewd look on his eyebrows:

"My first response is embarrassment, for all the known reasons. My brother is a louse in the locks of politics. My second has to be an attempt to rationalize everything we know."

I said, "I want my parents to get their farm back. To sleep in their own bed again."

Miss Fay pursed her lips and, as though thinking aloud, said, "From what I know, the law will not help you. And you have discovered that yourself. But law in this country is made in many ways, one of which is precedent."

I had to have it explained—and she continued.

"So if this has happened before—then at least you have moral law on your side."

I waited. She remained silent for what seemed like long minutes of my life, her face contorted as though in pain.

"I love my brother, I do, he's my twin. How am I going to get over this?" She turned her head. "Can you help me, James?"

James said, "In every legend, at a very important moment, the hero receives help from somebody wise."

Lips still pursing in anxiety, she asked, "If I write it down, then I'll not have spoken it. Will that do, James?"

He nodded.

"And, James, tell us more of what happens in legends. That might help Ben too."

James grinned, and cranked up that voice of his, a voice that went on to tell an entire generation of schoolchildren what he explained to me that night. To them he gave the examples; to me, the theory.

"It's as old as the hills. Ordinary life. A hero, always a young man. He's given a task, usually by his king or queen. To save a realm or right a wrong. Great forces will try to prevent him and he has to defeat them—by strength, but that can also mean strength of character. He has many setbacks, but as long as he keeps his heart pure, he wins and comes back in triumph."

I needed to hear no more; the parallels felt uncomfortable; I asked only one question.

"His heart pure?"

"That means seeking nothing for himself," said James.

Miss Fay retired to her writing desk, and James told me more—about the characters that heroes meet on such quests: the scheming queen; the evil king; the wizard; the princess; the gatekeeper

"If this is a legend, what are you?"

He laughed. "You won't know that until it's all over. But—and this is what I've been trying to do with you—you'll be able to see it all as a legend. And boys, oh, boys, that's a powerful cure."

Miss Fay reappeared and handed me an envelope.

"Now," she said, "I've handed you a weapon. God forgive me."

Time, the pressure of it, and the concern over my parents' circumstances, forced my hand. I should have researched everything. Instead, I went at the problem headlong. It took one day to locate King Kelly, and another day to come face-to-face with him. Dublin, most cities, confused me; I knew fields and riverbank pathways and trout pools, not long rows of tall houses. Country cuteness—our term for cunning—travels well, however. I used my experience of talking always to everybody, and despite my confusion in the streets and lanes, I gathered the information I needed.

While in Dublin, King Kelly lived in an apartment at the top of his sister's house, where Sarah and Venetia had stayed when they first came to Ireland. I went there.

Gretta, Aunt Kelly, looked askance at me (she did in the later years too, when I went back to question her). No information of any kind would she impart about her brother. Nor would she "send the fool farther"—that is, give me a clue as to how I might find him.

A doorman at the Mansion House had more specific news. Mr. Kelly would be attending a meeting tomorrow morning of his party's elected members—in the same Mansion House on Dawson Street. The meeting, set for ten o'clock, would go on until noon.

Next morning, I stood there from nine o'clock. They began to arrive at about half past, King Kelly among the first. He saw me and had reached the door before I could get to him. I waited. On the way out, two hours and more later, he tried to walk away very quickly—until I said, "I'm going to follow you everywhere."

Turning like a cornered rat, he fumbled in his vest pocket, handed me a card, and said, "Be at this address this evening at six."

I mostly recall the staircase, winding and elegant, and the white stucco details—relics of empire. He had a large office, and when he opened the door he hustled me in.

"What do you want, boy?"

"I'm married to your granddaughter, Venetia."

"Ah. A handout? Is that it?"

I didn't even know what a handout was.

"My father's farm. Put it in her name."

The cigar. The brown suit. The veins on the face. The nose hair. He plucked at his crotch like a banjo player.

"You cute little bastard. That's why you married her."

"Why should my parents have to suffer like this?"

"You're too young to understand stupidity, Ben. But you will, you will."

"Did the Morans in Ballymore—did they understand it?" I didn't yet show him Miss Fay's piece of paper.

He walked to his desk, sat behind it, and pointed to a chair. I walked to the chair, thinking slow, deep thoughts.

"I was right to pick you. You were wrong not to come with me."

"My parents."

"What about them?"

"Give us back our land. And the house."

"Ben, who told you about the Morans?"

"Isn't it well known?"

He sighed and sat back, as thoughtful as a judge.

"I see where you're headed. When are you going home again?"

"When I get an answer from you."

"Oh?" He looked amazed.

"I'm going to follow you everywhere. People will start to ask questions."

"God," he said. "You mean it."

"It's our farm."

"Go home to your parents. I'll work something out."

"The men there. With the guns."

"Leave that to me too." He glanced across at the clock on the mantel. "But I'll have to hurry."

I said, "I'll take the morning train."

Then came the moment that I described at the outset of this tale, what I called the "Beginning of the End." As I've said, I saw my father standing at the door of the cottage, cheek by jowl with a man I'd never seen before. Now that I look back on the scene, I should have guessed from the demeanor of both men that my father had been instructed to look out for me, and that the other man was now hustling him with some force indoors.

If I'd known—would I have gone ahead to the cottage? And been grabbed by the throat? And seen my parents terrorized? And my father hammered on the car with a gun butt?

When they released me and pushed me into the center of the room, they should have had more men there. Four proved insufficient, especially if you immobilize two of them with heavy kicks to the knees, a trick that I saw dirty players use on the football field.

Bizarre, isn't it? For a moment I hated using that piece of foul play. It paid off. I elbowed the third in the ribs, deflating him, and ran so heavily and fast past the fourth that he couldn't catch me. And in such a small room he didn't fire at me—that was my gamble, which paid off. They couldn't now kill us all, they couldn't now erase the family; my parents would be safe; I was an escaped witness.

If you ever have the misfortune to become involved in a piece of violent contact, know three things. First, it's faster than you think. Second, it's nastier than you'd ever anticipate. Third, no matter how well you acquit yourself it leaves you feeling lower than you've ever known. After the fight with my father I couldn't smile for days; after this fracas, I felt smeared with slime.

And yet some kind of new feeling had gripped me. I can best describe it by saying that I behaved almost as though I were acting a part. At this far distant remove in time I've been able to see that I'd thrust myself into the story of my life; I was acting my own deeds. And believing them. Once again I was striding like a hero; once again I wore seven-league boots.

In those boots I took my next steps. I felt sure that my parents wouldn't be harmed. And I also felt sure that King Kelly had no intention of restoring our property to us. I'd need greater force on my side.

My newspaper reading had informed me of an event about to take place in Ennis, the principal town of County Clare. That, I felt certain, and I don't know why, would ensure my success—after which I would go to join Venetia and the company in Donegal, where I could read the newspapers, and watch for the fallout.

83

With a new assurance I asked all the right questions in Ennis. I was directed to be at a certain place at a certain time. Be there early; get up to the front; be the first through the door. Have my question ready; ask it succinctly; ideally have my name and address on a piece of paper; don't waste time.

Powerful men have a singularity of purpose about them. When they look, they look only at you. When they focus, they focus only on you. I saw and felt all of that when I went to Clare and met Mr. de Valera in the room where his constituents came for his help. Most elected members held a "clinic" or "surgery" once a week; he, given the demands on his time, could do so only once a month; acolytes and party managers did the rest.

The queue formed early—eight o'clock for his arrival at ten o'clock; I'd been there since six. He stepped from the car and walked up along the line of people, shaking hands, until he reached the doorway. How tall he was, and how forbidding—and yet a flash of good nature, because as he shook my hand he said, "If you're the early bird, I must be the worm."

He had no idea what I wanted—I presume he expected help with a grant, planning permission, or, given my age, a scholarship to some college.

When I, his first supplicant of the day, was shown into the room, he was sitting at a table, a statue in remoteness and authority. Men hovered, and at his side a woman sat with a pad taking shorthand notes.

"Tell the Chief your name," said a hovering man; I had no piece of paper.

Too nervous to accept the great handshake, I blurted, "Sir, there's a private militia, wearing blue shirts, hundreds of them training with lots of guns on the farm that was swindled from my father."

It wasn't a face you could ever forget. I've used the word "hawk" before; after that encounter I prefer "eagle." If Ireland ever had a Mount Rushmore, there would have been room for only one face. Not only that, I seemed to see it all at once—the dark and fierce eyes, the long nose, the longer jaw.

Did I feel comfortable? Oh, God, no! I felt that my body had been strung across wires. It got worse. He stood up—he was much taller than me—and put his hands on my shoulders.

"This, young man, had better be the truth."

"It is. Sir, it definitely is. I've just come from there. To tell you."

"Who's in charge? Who brought them together?"

I'd rehearsed all of this. "Sir, the newly elected member for North Cork, Mr. Thomas Aquinas Kelly."

De Valera beckoned to a hoverer and whispered something. I was escorted, neither kindly nor unkindly, from the room and taken in the official car down the street to the Old Ground Hotel. There, I was asked to wait in a small meeting room at the back. A minder hovered and a waitress brought me tea and toast.

At just after noon de Valera and his entourage arrived, including the woman with the shorthand pad. I rose, trembling again with anxiety. He gestured for me to sit, and took the chair beside me.

He questioned me like a policeman—not a flash of warmth, not a kind look. He asked the same questions over and over—the first time the men arrived, the first time I saw a gun there, the number of men. He asked me again and again, "Are you sure of Mr. Kelly's identity? What you're saying is very serious."

At the end of it I saw why he had become a leader. He softened his attitude and thanked me so warmly and with such respect that not only would I have followed him out of a burning house, I'd have gone into one for him. As he rose, I heard him say to one of the men, "Sooner than I thought." Then he turned to me and said, "I don't think there's anything I can do about the farm. But you should keep up the pressure."

I never met him again. Not face-to-face. I saw him many times, at rallies, functions, national events. The ferocity seemed never to dim; the aloofness never broke down. When people hated him, they couldn't say it temperately. When people loved him, they idolized him.

I stood at neither extreme—fascination was my response. This was a man who had been alive since the beginning of the world—or so his sheer force suggested to me. In that encounter I believe that I matured by several years.

84

Exhaustion swept in like the seventh wave, which, they say, is the biggest of the tide. I felt that I should leave Ennis as soon as possible and get to Venetia. A complicated journey—I had to take a train to Galway, and then to Sligo, and then a bus to Letterkenny—slow trains and bad roads. I stayed that night in Galway and reached Letterkenny late evening. To find a surprise—a closed and dark hall; no show was playing.

I knew where they were staying—and found nobody. The engagement had been canceled, the hotel told me, and Miss Kelly had changed all her plans. In those days we didn't pay deposits in order to book some of the venues; touring companies kept to their agreements—otherwise they'd never work. They said that she'd gone back to Charleville. And the company? Nobody knew; nothing had been said. Had everything seemed all right? Oh, yes. The de Valera encounter had jangled me to the marrow. I told myself, *You're worrying unduly.*

Nevertheless I set out next morning, urgent as a storm. In the hotel the previous night I spent an hour squeezing everything I could from the map. Buses, trains—yes; but if I had to, I'd walk. I made a hectic journey, in assorted ways. They included a ride in a hearse, a motorbike pillion, a delightful pony trap, and, at the end, a drive in a constantly-breaking-down Morris car from Limerick.

No lights in the house; no open door; I had no key. I peppered the windows with pebbles from the gravel on the street; no answer. All along the route, my heart had beaten faster—and for no reason that I could discern. Sheer anxiety? Perhaps. Premonition? I thought so, particularly when nobody came to a window.

The house had a small garden; I'd walked out there on the night of the gunman. A wooden door led into it from a lane at the rear. Easy to climb and, as I'd hoped, yes, the kitchen door hadn't been locked. I lit the lamp, found food—and an unsigned letter addressed to me. On official government writing paper, in a brawling scrawl, it said, *The damage you've done. And you've destroyed everybody's chances.*

I knew who had written it; was he in the house?

Across the street, life continued in the public house. The summer night had led one or two people to drink outside. I opened the front door, lit the lamp in that hallway, and, seeing people fifty yards away, felt safer.

From above came sounds—feet on the floor. By now I recognized them. Yet I still thought my heart would stop when I saw her dear face peep around the edge of the baluster. She said nothing; she hurtled down without a care. I held her with the deepest sense of relief that I had yet known.

Venetia had been asleep; so had Mrs. Haas, who now appeared, beaming like a toothy sun. You'll not be surprised to learn that she prepared food—her answer to everything. I used to think that if an earthquake opened a fissure in the ground, Mrs. Haas would throw food into it.

We sat, and I discovered the reason for the cancellation. For the past few days, fire officers had been closing shows after they began—"the crowds," they said; "safety," they said; "too many people," they said. Not yet did I put together this development with my visit to King Kelly's office.

However, I must have sensed something, because I chose that moment to show Venetia the unsigned letter.

"He spent the afternoon here."

I recoiled. "What did he say?"

"Nothing. He left that letter on the kitchen table—and just sat there looking at it."

"Do you want to know what's happened?" I asked.

She shuddered, as if I'd flung a slew of cold water over her. "Not yet. And maybe not at all."

I said, "Are you worried? About the show?"

"Not yet. We have plenty of money. And Cody's coming here next week to show me everything. We have time to make plans."

Regret touched me—I'd been so enjoying the shows. I much preferred the new seriousness; the disappearance of the bawdy and low-grade material had given every performance a better texture. Their original "lowest common denominator" policy had come from Sarah—urged on by King Kelly himself.

Until three o'clock in the morning we sat and talked; Mrs. Haas had long gone to bed. Venetia seemed exactly the same as when I'd last seen her. I told her about the fire, and Miss Fay and the train and Miss Fay's house.

"Dare I ask about your parents?" she said.

"How much do you know?"

At that moment she hooded her eyes with one hand stretched flat—and reached for me with the other hand. An actor's gesture, it also had huge trouble behind it.

"I don't know what to do. My family—there are awful things. Can we ignore them for a while? Is it all right if I tell you when I'm ready to talk about them?" She smiled—the sun again. "I'll be an honorable wife, I promise."

We spent the rest of that week in loose bliss, sleeping late, staying up later. We explored what it was like to be silent in each other's company. We played the games we had known since childhood—what she called tic-tac-toe, I knew as noughts and crosses; we both had rock, paper, scissors.

She wanted to see other gardens, so we went to Waterford. She wanted to buy jigsaws when she heard of mine, so we went to Cork. She wanted to find a good doctor—she had a midwife in Mrs. Haas—so we went to Limerick. We had picnics, and late-night suppers in the little garden of the house in Charleville—the weather had become hotter than usual for Ireland—and during the day we found old public houses where the owner's wife would make us a sandwich in the kitchen.

Venetia said she never read newspapers, didn't like them, a habit born of disliking reviews. And so she missed, on the Tuesday of that week, the announcement—broad headline—that King Kelly had resigned his seat. He made the statement "from his constituency," said the report, and "with great regret," and "for health reasons."

I took three things from the news—that Mr. de Valera had acted with fast brutality; that I now knew what the scrawled letter meant; and that King Kelly wasn't far away.

The Blueshirts didn't disappear at that moment—in fact they hadn't yet appeared in public. De Valera might have spiked King Kelly's guns, so to speak, but there was more than one forerunner. By then, the organization was taking firm shape. To give you an idea of what I had stumbled upon—or had thrust upon me—this is what had begun to happen.

Before the 1932 election, many people felt that if Dev came into power, he would use the Irish Republican Army, to which he had so long belonged, as his armed militia, and effectively declare a dictatorship. They still had caches of guns, they still carried out an armed attack here and there. Learned papers have been written, and were written at the time, discussing the suitability of Ireland for such a development—a banana republic without the bananas.

Mr. de Valera, however, had as much to fear from his own armed republicans as from anybody else, and he also knew that their swaggering existence encouraged other would-be power brokers—such as King Kelly. Indeed, clashes had long been taking place between the republicans and the men who would later wear the blue shirts—who first appeared in public, in force, in 1933.

The white-haired man I had met at the cottage was the same O'Duffy who then became the leader of the Blueshirts when Mr. de Valera dismissed him as police chief in 1933. But O'Duffy had proven inept politically, unstable almost, and Mr. de Valera buried the movement within a year.

Was it Fascism? Hitler with his Brownshirts, Mussolini and Mosley with their Blackshirts: I suppose in Ireland we should have had green.

It's important to me that I now write down as many details of that week as I can bear. Mrs. Haas knew of King Kelly resigning—Mrs. Haas knew everything—and in a whisper, she suggested not telling Venetia. I didn't. We spent five more days in each other's company, to the exclusion of almost the entire universe. From time to time Mrs. Haas entered our lives, always with comfort, usually with ever more wonderful food. We met other people too—gardeners and waiters and people we stopped to talk to, or who wanted to admire the car. Other than that, we lived in the same shell of life, turning always and only to each other. They say that perfection between two people is impossible, the philosopher's ideal. The "they" who say this are wrong.

We rode a train, from Limerick to Cork and back again, just for the joy of it. We climbed a mountain, Galtymore, and looked down on the wonderful plains. We drank water from fresh streams. We walked for miles on deserted roads, and by rivers and into bog lands. We lay in the green aftergrass of meadows from which the hay had but recently been harvested.

Plans—that's what we talked about, plans and children. We agreed to put aside time the following week for discussing problems, for facing matters that would then need attention—such as whether and how many of the company to keep on. Such as telling my parents that we had married. Such as facing Sarah when she came back at the end of the year to a show that had been completely altered. Nominally she had a director's role; in practice she had forced, cajoled, or persuaded Venetia to put and keep together the program that I had first seen.

When I first began to tell you Venetia's story, you'll recall that Sarah had been effusive to me about her love of her daughter, the auspicious birth, unicorns, and so forth. From that you might have assumed a deep, close bond between the two women. Sarah, when I interviewed her down through the years, continued to give that impression.

I, rather cruelly perhaps, allowed her to go on doing so—not least because I wanted to hear Venetia praised. And because I wanted to confirm over and over Sarah's duplicitousness. The truth from Venetia's side had long been known to me—everything she told me about Sarah's demeanor toward her suggested a deep and rivalrous envy.

Still, I might never have met Venetia had it not been for Sarah's competitiveness. Venetia had so begun to top the Abbey Theatre bill in Dublin that Sarah engineered a row over earnings—by the simple expedient of asking King Kelly to negotiate for Venetia. He generated a mighty fracas with Yeats—persisted in calling him "Yeets"—and Venetia was forced out.

That's how she came to have a traveling show. Sarah encouraged her, put up the money. It took Venetia off the Abbey stage, out of Dublin, where she'd also starred in society, and away from the public eye.

"Tell me about Sarah, about the family. I mean, in New York. Who were the Kellys?"

She said, "My grandfather's mother went to New York from County Cork and I know this story."

Venetia told me, with all the drama and the accents, a story that encapsulated the Irish experience, the journey from desperateness to the first good plateau—and a story that would have a terrible reverberation.

Her mother, Sarah, knew a Dutch family who lived down the street. Bankers and cloth merchants, they had wealth and comfort. They owned warehouses on the Hudson River in New York City, and into the basements they crammed Irish immigrants off the ships.

Why Irish? Because, said these practical Dutch people, the Irish were so desperate that they would take on any kind of work, live in any kind of room.

And so this Dutch family got all its workers from these arriving immigrants, whom they "stored." The men worked upstairs in the warehouses or on the farms up along the river, and for a pittance of wages. Their women also worked in the warehouses for an even smaller pittance or in domestic service, like so many arriving Irish women and girls.

In fact, so prevalent was the Irish female in American domestic service that in some cities a maid was known as a "Bridget" or a "Bridie." A "Bridget" was fresh-faced and innocent, straight off the green fields of Ireland; whereas a "Bridie," also Irish, had been in the United States for some time and been hammered into a tougher woman. And now the focus of the story narrowed.

In the very early 1800s, a girl, from the wide fields of Cork, went to work for the ancestors of this Dutch family. On the day she started there, she said to her sister—whom they also hired as a servant—"This is what we'll do. We'll work like fire. And we'll watch everything. And wherever we get the chance we'll teach them something they don't know—so's they'll take more notice of us. And no matter what they say to us, we'll be as nice as pie to them all the time, and we'll make them laugh."

The girl's name wasn't Bridie or Bridget—she was Nora Tobin and her sister was Eileen, and they made themselves so amenable, so indispensable, to the Dutch family that they changed how that Dutch family perceived the Irish immigrants.

Then Nora showed her astuteness. She watched how the rich Protestants believed that from great wealth must come great charity. And she observed how the head of the house, the Meister, supported churches and other Protestant organizations in Manhattan.

One Sunday morning, after he'd had a good breakfast and had been to a rousing service, Nora went to the Meister in his study. He was sitting there reading his newspaper and smoking one of his long, dark cheroots. Ash had fallen on the carpet and Nora swept it up, tut-tutting at him quite bossily, an attitude that he liked—as she had noticed.

The Meister laughed and said, "Nora, you are like a headmistress"—which he often said to her.

She, expecting that he would say that, replied, "Well, Meister, now that you say it—"

And she asked him there and then for money to start a school for immigrants.

The Meister laughed, but was arrested by the thought.

Nora said, "Do you find me and my sister clever?"

He thought about it and said, "Well, yes, I do."

"And does your wife?"

"Now that I think of it, she often says so."

"Well." Nora stood with her hands on her hips and said to him, "And we're not the cleverest of us Irish, not at all. If you helped me to open a school, I'd secure for you the best clerks for your bank."

The Tobin sisters went on to open a school, and indeed did give the Dutchman brilliant employees for his bank—but they and many other Irish teachers also gave New York the clerks and civil servants that ran the courts, organized the city's systems such as transit and roads, and provided the civilians and the uniformed men in the police and fire departments.

In this fashion, the Irish population in New York began to raise itself out of the hovels to which it had been consigned when it landed. It would take many years; the stigma clung.

Like Nora Tobin had done, the Irishwomen looked around them, saw their incumbent predecessors—the Germans, the English, and especially the Dutch—observed the fine houses, the starched linens, the children at excellent schools, and by a combination of literacy and religion, went after the same for themselves and their families.

So earnestly did they pursue this collective ideal that by the time Sarah was born in the late 1870s, the legions of Irish-American women who formed societies and clubs in New York and elsewhere across the continent didn't refer to themselves as "women"—they called themselves "ladies."

Venetia finished her story—but I could see that there was more.

I applauded and said, with a grin, "Go on."

She said, "My mother left out some details when she first told me."

I waited.

"She left out the fact that Nora Tobin was my grandfather's mother. And guess where Nora Tobin came from?" Venetia pointed down to the ground at her feet. "Here."

In other words, Sarah had descended from the poorest of the poor—her grandmother was an Irish maid plucked from a rat-infested cellar on the dockyards of New York. That was why King Kelly could run for office in North Cork—he had been born here. And he had also lived here—which led to the sinister part.

86

Venetia had a deep-grained obedience in her; I recognized it—it's not uncommon in an only child. After the fracas at the Abbey Theatre, in which she had been an innocent, she'd done as she'd been told—just as I had eventually obeyed Mother when she sent me after my father. Venetia formed the traveling company and bowed to Sarah's experience in choosing road and repertory material. Now Sarah had gone away, creating a long breathing space, and the company, for the moment, had come off the road.

Given all that, you can understand why we wished to delay any discussion of the problems King Kelly might pose.

The glorious weather continued and King Kelly didn't appear. In fact we had idyllic privacy. I knew a lake in the mountains where we could swim unseen; Venetia took off her clothes and floated. "I'm the Lady of Shalott," she called. A garden near Adare had a lily pond; we placed coins on the lily pads for luck. We befriended some horses, took them apples, and got drool on our sleeves.

On the Sunday afternoon, because it rained, we went to a film in Limerick; we saw Loretta Young in *Beau Ideal*—and I had read the book by P. C. Wren, and its two companion volumes, *Beau Geste* and *Beau Sabreur,* and we talked over dinner afterward about the French Foreign Legion and being film stars.

We went home to Charleville in the dark, and found a note to say that Cody had arrived. Next day, when we went downstairs to the kitchen, Cody sat in the kitchen waiting for us—as did King Kelly.

Now we have our hands on the chain of events. Now I must handle the icy cold links, one by one, and follow them, fingering them and feeling their chill. Now I must force myself to bring everything to the eye, to redact as faithfully as I can everything I saw and heard over the week that followed.

No matter how objective I am, no matter how calmly I try to view, to assess what happened, I remain shocked, and that's why I've waited so long to tell this tale. It's true, I know it, that such things don't easily take place in people's lives, no matter what we read in the newspapers. It's true, I can vouch for it, that treachery is indeed treacherous, that triumph is indeed triumphant, and finally that terribleness is indeed terrible.

They sat in the kitchen, one tall and heavy, a slug with frightening eyes and a big cigar; the other, narrow and scrawny, a rat in a suit, with the cold, uncaring eyes of Death. Amiable conversation had been going back and forth between them; I later ascertained that.

Venetia and I walked in, close to each other in height, an erogenous glow surrounding us like a benign fire. King Kelly's hands lay on the table, two fat and hairy weapons; Cody sat in a slouch, his hands between his knees.

"The honeymooners," boomed King Kelly, and Mrs. Haas rebounded like someone hearing a sudden, loud noise. Cody stood up; King Kelly didn't—but he held out his arms and said, "Have you a kiss for your grandfather?"

"Hello, Grampa," said Venetia, and went to him; he pulled her down onto his knee, put his hand around her hips, and flicked me a wink with more dirt in it than a slum.

"I was there before him, wasn't I, child?"—and he pulled her face down to kiss her cheek.

Revolting; that's how I recall it; that's how it was—those monstrous paws, with dirty fingernails. He wore a canary-yellow bow tie. And he hadn't taken off his brown hat.

"How's married life?" He leered like a bandit.

"What are you doing here, Grampa?"

"Cody, tell her what I'm doing here."

"Hello, Cody," said Venetia; she had better manners almost than Mother.

"I hope I'm not too early, Miss Kelly," said Cody, who glanced at me as though the cat had dragged me in from the street.

"So, are you happy now?" said King Kelly to me, a hand tightening on Venetia's hip.

"Ow, Grampa."

I said nothing, but I felt my body coil.

"I have to talk to your bridegroom," said King Kelly. "Cody, look after my granddaughter—not too tightly now, mind you." All beasts have a natural habitat; King Kelly's was the sewer. "You too, Shark-face," he said to Mrs. Haas. "Out."

She averted her face from him as she walked past his chair.

Everybody quit the kitchen; Venetia planted a kiss on my jaw as she went. King Kelly sat back until they'd gone. With the pleased face of a tourist, he looked all around—then swiveled back to me. It wasn't a big room; twelve feet between us, perhaps. I stood with my back to the door.

"Come closer," he said. "I'm shortsighted and I want to see your eyes."

I stepped forward. He had a heavy walking cane, made, I think, of hickory, with a brass ferrule, and a brass dog's head. It rested between his huge knees. He lifted it, hefted its weight, held it by the head, and wagged it at me.

"I could crack your skull with this," he said. "And maybe I should. You crooked, scheming little bastard. You and the Long Fellow. Happy now? Are you, are you?"

He poked me in the chest with the stick. It hurt. I winced. He poked again.

"Are you happy? I've lost my seat, thanks to you." He poked again. "Well, I'll make you happy, you wait and see."

The ferrule dug right into my sternum. If I spoke, my breath might sound caught—but I took the risk.

"I'll be happy when my parents get back what you stole from them."

He pulled back the stick to poke harder, as if to stab me, and I caught the stick and wrenched it from him. I broke it across my knee—it wasn't easy, but I snapped it. It cracked into three pieces, one of which, no more than a shard, flew through the air and landed on the floor. Where I now threw the other two fragments.

He half-rose. I held out a fist.

"The last time we met in this house—you had a man hold a gun to my head. Move now and I'll drop you. I flocking will."

Thank you, Billy Moloney! Though I didn't use the euphemism, you understand.

"Why are you persecuting me?" he said.

I looked at him. The nerve!

He pressed it. "Come on. What have you against me? I have to go back to Dublin now and answer impertinent questions. Because of you. You've destroyed my career. You and that Spanish crook." I had never heard Mr. de Valera called that. "Why? Why are you doing it?"

"Give my parents back our farm."

He twisted in his chair, exasperation his only tune.

"I've resigned my seat because of your lies. You and yours will never live there again. If your stupid father came to me tomorrow with cash worth ten times that mortgage I wouldn't let him redeem it. That's done. That's over."

King Kelly rose to go. He stopped, wary that I hadn't moved.

"What you gonna do now, slug me? Use force where you can't persuade? Who's the Fascist now?"

I stood aside. He bent down to pick up the broken walking cane, decided against it. Just for mischief I made a small and sudden move as he walked past, and had the gratification of seeing him flinch.

As he opened the door into the hall, I heard the footsteps scurry upstairs—Venetia. She must have heard everything at the slightly ajar Georgian door. Cody emerged from the little sitting room; sitting in the dimness, the room cool with drawn curtains, he too had been listening.

One by one they came back to the kitchen—Cody first, Mrs. Haas second, Venetia a slow last. Nobody said anything; embarrassment hung everywhere, stale as the smoke from King Kelly's cigar.

"I'm hungry," I said.

"He is gone?" said Mrs. Haas.

"When did you travel?" said Venetia to Cody. "Are the others here?"

He didn't answer her and I observed that fact; it was one of those moments when you know you've seen something without quite knowing what you've registered.

We all sat around the table, including Mrs. Haas, who never sat down when we were eating. The room took on a subdued mood. I watched Cody. He separated his food ingredients from each other—the ham from the egg, the eggs from the sausage, the sausage from the mushrooms.

I didn't like the way he looked up using only his eyes. I didn't like the way he held his knife and fork, like spikes he was driving into the plate. I didn't like the way he sucked his teeth. I didn't like him.

When we had eaten, which helped us to recover, Cody, Venetia, and I went into the little sitting room. He had placed his bags there, and his accountancy books. Why did I so recoil from him?

We sat down and he said to Venetia, "Now we can go over everything, I've spent the week extracting all the information." He looked at me sidelong and added, "Is it all right if—" and he broke off, and looked at me again.

"If Ben is here? Of course," said Venetia. "It's Ben's business now too."

I took Cody's snub for what it was. And I answered it by asking many, many questions. We had plenty of money, enough and more to pay everybody until Christmas, which would buy us time to find an existing theater or a premises.

That night, Venetia told me the story of her life. She recalled the ship that brought her to Ireland; she even remembered, she said, being swung out of her cot by King Kelly and the bristles on his face. She told me the story of her grandfather giving her Blarney. And she told me the story of the boy and the talking animals.

"I lived by that story when I was little. With no friends or playmates, there was always the chance that the cat would chat to me. And so I made friends with Blarney—who could and did."

I introduced the idea that I'd had on the train.

"Why not turn Blarney into a storyteller?" I said, and I told her about the seanchaí, who still roamed the countryside telling stories.

"What's the word?" she said.

"Shan-a-kee. It means 'One who tells old tales.' They're still around. We had one at our house years ago. They still work in Kerry and West Cork and up in Donegal and in Scotland."

She grew excited and I expanded—how the storyteller would arrive in the evening, be given a meal and a drink, and afterward take pride of place at the fireside. There, for the evening, sometimes into the small hours of the morning, he would tell a tale of long ago, and the flickering of the flames lit the stage of his face.

We planned—we would have James come and stay, and he would instruct her.

"Can't you do it, Ben?"

"I have no talent," I said.

"Oh, but you have. You just haven't gone looking for it yet. Or you haven't been forced to find it. Do you know any stories? James told me some."

Although I'd been bold with her in love, now my shyness was visible matter—and she had the sensitivity not to press me; she knew I couldn't do it. Not then, anyway.

We spent the next day making notes, calculating distances in Ireland, guessing at the sizes of towns, figuring out where we might find or open a theater. As a team, she and I scarcely needed to speak aloud—over and over, each of us interrupted the other with the same thought. Again, we had a perfect day, and I thought that we'd shrugged off the shadows that hung over us.

87

I'm still gripping the chain of events; I can still feel the cold, cold links. Without my need to know and perceive it, my life growing up on the farm had given me the concept of perfect days—no disturbances, a rhythm of the seasons, a wheel of life. In that light, you can see what had changed and you can also see the contrast with the system that had been mine. How could it have become so exotic so quickly—though not all for the best? On the simplest, most outward level, there I was, driving one of the few motorcars in the province of Munster, a great ghost of a machine, sitting up behind the wheel like a red-haired young grandee, Alexander the Great in corduroys, now a young bridegroom and a father-to-be and a slayer of dragons. Mystifying—in part, anyway, and I could begin to grasp the sense in James Clare's view of life as a myth. Now consider what came next, and feel the chill of the chain.

That night, Venetia, at bedtime, said to me, "I want to arrange a surprise for you. Give me some time."

I heard the sounds of furniture being dragged around upstairs. I sat in the living room and tried to net, as though they were butterflies, the thoughts flying about in my head. I kept returning to the problems that had to be solved. And I also found comfort in summarizing them—and my life.

When at last Venetia called, and I went up to our room, I found that she had used curtains, sheets, clothing, and all kinds of props to create a miniature theater, much more elaborate than the previous exercise when Blarney had asked me if I loved Venetia.

She sat "center stage," with Blarney on her knee. He greeted me.

"Hello, Ben."

"Hello, Blarney."

She had changed his costume. No longer an Irish farmer, or King Lear's Fool, he looked like an old man; he had a white mustache and a battered hat and a black garment that might have been an overcoat.

"Ben, I'm learning to become a storyteller."

I hadn't yet interrogated the presence of Blarney in Venetia's life. Once or twice I almost raised it—I wanted to know the training, the interface, how her personality and spirit belonged in his persona and stage act.

Reticent, awkward, she said, "I wanted somebody to speak for me. To say the things I wanted to say. To utter my rage."

But she veered away from any discussion as to whether she viewed Blarney as a separate person. If I had to guess now, I'd say that she did—as evidenced by what now took place.

"I think you'll be a very good storyteller, Blarney," I said.

Blarney replied, in a sober, almost sad way, "Let me try out a story on you."

"Good man, Blarney," I said. "Vote for Blarney."

He closed his eyes at the inappropriate levity and turned away his head. When he was ready, he spoke; and I sat down. This is the story that Blarney told me; although I'm now telling it to you in my own words, I'm content with its accuracy.

A long time ago, in a village not far from here, lived a young and clever girl. She went to America and started a school there and married. When she found that she was expecting her first child, she came back to Ireland so that the child would be born Irish. As indeed he was. Not far from here.

And so, the child grew into a young man who spent his time between New York and North Cork, because he often came over to see his grandparents, and he was always welcome in these wide fields. In time, he married a girl from Connecticut—she was from an Irish family too, and had also been born in Ireland. And when she was expecting a baby, they came back here so that the baby would be born Irish, just as the young man's mother had done.

But the young man had a poor character, and he involved himself with bad local people. With their help he got a farm, but he got it through trickery and devilment.

His young wife with her young child didn't like this. She said it to him, and told him that if he didn't make amends, she'd go back to her mother in Connecticut.

A coolness sprang up between them, and the young wife made arrangements to go back to America, because she was afraid. And she took another precaution—she told somebody her story. She told a local policeman, a young fellow by the name of Luke Nagle, living in a place called Coolnagle. He, a clever and observant man, wrote down the story, and told of the young wife's fears.

She never went back to America. They found her body floating in the reeds in the lake named Lough Gur, not too far away from here. At the inquest the coroner recorded an open verdict, meaning that nobody would attempt to say how she died. The husband sold his farm and took his small daughter back to the United States. And the young detective has spent the rest of his life holding that story to himself in his house out at Coolnagle, where he reads books all day. He's an old man now, and his daughter sells eggs to people here in the town. And that's the end of my story.

This was the time to weep. For all of us. I had the thought *If Blarney sheds tears, will his paint run?* In the silence I heard a door close somewhere. I helped Venetia to dismantle the little "set," we stowed Blarney in his case, we lay down, and I can't say who held whom the tighter. In the darkness I whispered to her, "You know, don't you?"

Her head nodded at my chest.

"And you know what I'll now do?"

Her head nodded again.

Luke Nagle and I became friends. I visited his house many times. In his late seventies when I first met him, still a steel rod of a man, straight as a pike, he had hair that stood up as though he'd had a fright. And he had some kind of second sight, because the moment I walked through the door, he knew why I'd come.

His daughter made tea.

"No, Rose, give the young fella a drink."

"He's underage, Dada, he won't be able to hold it."

"He'll hold whiskey."

"No, he won't and it'll take that lovely gloss off him."

How she spoiled her father—patted him, fixed his woolen cardigan, checked that his tea wasn't too hot, smiled at him all the time. She winked at me.

"He's a lovely man, my dada."

Luke Nagle opened the furrow, so to speak.

"Did you see that resignation?"

I nodded.

"A thunderbolt," he said. "A political thunderbolt."

"They're reeling from it," said the daughter.

"He should be in jail," said the father. A bead of milky tea hung from his mustache.

"Can we put him in jail?" I said.

"Will I get it, Dada?" asked the daughter.

"Rose hates him," said Luke Nagle.

She went away and came back with an envelope.

If you yourself read what Luke Nagle wrote—and I hope one day that you will—you cannot doubt what happened. King Kelly murdered his young wife, Sarah's mother. My guess is that he held her facedown in the water of the lake, and then dragged her body through the shallows along the bank of Lough Gur to another spot, the place where she was found, so that no traces of a scuffle could be linked with the discovery of the corpse.

Irish official writing has always been large and looped, every word as clear as elocution. In a vivid recounting, Luke Nagle, the procedural policeman, had listed the days and dates of the young wife's visits to him, and had kept a detailed record of their conversations. At the very least it would have cast a shadow over the young husband.

"Is this the only copy?" I asked.

"No," said the daughter. "The authorities, they had one, I don't know if they still have. And we have another."

"Can I keep this?" I said.

"Only if you're prepared to use it," said this feisty little man; no wonder we became such friends.

I sat back, read it again, drank more tea.

Rose said, "You can tell that it's true, can't you?"

Luke Nagle said, "I never tell lies."

Rose ruffled his spiky hair and said, "Except about how many drinks you have with Tommy Heffernan."

I said, "What was she like, the woman who died?"

Without having to think he said, "Tall as a statue, and she had the nicest nature, sometimes quiet, and sometimes she'd chat like a sparrow, and as kind as good weather."

Rose said, "She was blondy-haired a bit, wasn't she, Dada."

"I wasn't married then, but anytime she touched my arm—I'd have married her for that alone. And I'd have been better for her than him. That animal."

"She was a dancer, wasn't she?" said Rose. "Over there in New York."

Luke Nagle shook his head in sorrow, and I rose to go.

He shook my hand. "Did you ever hear the saying 'Patriotism is the last refuge of a scoundrel'? Well, it isn't. Politics is."

88

It's not a big lake but it's lovely, in placid and welcoming countryside. The deep breast of the Knockfennel hill reaches down to the reeds. Woods line the other shore between the water and Bourchier's Castle. You won't find many places in Ireland with as much depth of antiquity. People have lived here since thousands of years before Christ. I often go there now and walk in the stone circles and touch the rocks that the ancient men lifted into place for their rituals. Ireland is a small country, with an ancient gene pool, so these were my people, and perhaps Venetia's. Pagans then—and pagan enough still; her grandmother won't have been the first beautiful woman who got sacrificed in the horseshoe lake.

For transport, I had the white Daimler. I shouldn't have taken it down that long narrow lane to the lake, but it stood up well.

I had the thought *What is wrong with me? There's a myth everywhere I turn.* And I changed that thought to *No. What is right with me? How did I get such good fortune?*

With one last look at the thick and silver-sheened water, I drove back to Charleville, where Venetia held up her hands in a warding-off gesture.

"Don't tell me. Not yet. Can you do—can you do what you have to do, everything—can you do it so that it's all over?" Today was one of those days when she flew through the air high above us all, remote and swirling, turning this way and that.

Another challenge. "I think so."

I was used to challenges now. She put a note in among the clothes in my suitcase. All it said was, *Dear Ben.*

King Kelly recognized the car. Not many cars on quiet Dublin streets anyway. You know—he was frightened. He stood back against the railings, scared.

"Don't come near me," he said. "You're after putting a curse on me."

"The farm," I said.

"Go away."

"Give it back."

"Leave me alone."

"Give it back. We can go to a solicitor's office and do the papers now."

"Aren't you after ruining me enough?"

I stood there, not saying a word, staring at him. He tried to hold the silence too, but couldn't, and erupted.

"What?"

"The farm."

"Go away. Forever."

He began to walk down the street. I expected that he was catching a tram into the center of the city, and I walked beside him.

"Do you ever go near Lough Gur these days?" I said.

I hadn't expected him to stop. And he didn't—until I pulled the handwritten pages from my pocket.

He directed me and we drove to a gathering of shops and offices.

"Stop here," he said.

I parked near some sidecars, used by visitors as sightseeing transport around the city. On the short journey, King Kelly had been subdued beside me; not a word, not a gesture until "Stop here."

He led me through a doorway to a legal office above a greengrocer's shop. I stood back, near the window, as he had a whispered conversation with a man in striped pants and morning coat. This man kept looking at me over his spectacles, looking at King Kelly and back at me.

Through the window, the rows of cabbages and pails of potatoes smiled up from the stalls below. The smell of farming came to me, and I grew passionately vigilant about the transaction that was supposed to take place across the room.

It didn't seem to be moving fast enough. I walked across to the desk and said to the elderly lawyer, "This document has to be short, clear, and unchallengeable."

"These things take time—"

"No. I'll dictate it. Now."

"All right, all right," he said, and I thought he had relief in his voice.

"No, no," said King Kelly.

"Tom," said the lawyer, his voice inflected with warning.

I had long had it ready in my mind and I said, "I, Thomas Aquinas Kelly, do hereby give back to Harold and Louise MacCarthy their farm at Goldenfields. I cancel any mortgage that I once had on that entire property, and I state that at no time in the future will I ever try to state or reinstate any claim of any kind to it."

The lawyer said, "Well, God knows, that's clear."

I repeated it, he wrote it down, called in a secretary—a woman who walked sideways into the room, and sideways back out, and sideways in again, with several typed sheets, the original and copies. She—standing sideways—witnessed King Kelly's signature.

"Give me the other paper," said King Kelly.

"No, give it to me," said the lawyer.

As I handed over the Luke Nagle report, I asked King Kelly, "The men on the property. Where are they?"

"There's only Mary," he said, as sour as a quince.

The rest of the proceedings took two days to complete. Two wonderful days, they were, two days of incomparable rejoicing, two days of relief and restoration. Without boasting, I can say that I did it all, I organized everything, and I sent a telegram to Venetia: ALL WELL. HOME SOON.

You may find my first act surprising—my first act after driving down home, that is. Not wanting to hurt my father's feelings, I hid the Daimler.

Near our entrance stood an old ruined farm building, down a kind of awkward and overgrown lane that ran parallel to part of our driveway. Through grass as high as the door handles, I nudged the Daimler toward the old ruin, turned it around so that it faced the direction I had come, pulled aside the branches that covered where there had once been a stable door, and backed the car in. Then I pulled the branches back across the door—perfect concealment.

Nobody stopped me as I walked up our drive—no soldiers, no blue shirts. The house looked deserted, although I heard sounds from the yard, some barks, some whinnies.

Our car, the Alvis, was parked to one side and looked as though it hadn't been used. I knew why—it was too well known locally and any driver other than my father or me would have raised questions.

I walked in. My house. My home. My place of birth. I knew that I was going to do this right.

Mary Lewis heard the footsteps and came from the kitchen. She looked terrified.

"Don't hit me, Ben, don't hit me."

The insult! As if I were like that!

"Mary, I need you."

Never did she work as hard. And probably never would again.

"Two things, Mary. You're to clean this house from top to bottom. And you're to speak to nobody. If anybody asks you a question, you're to say only that you're not allowed to speak." She nodded. I felt like a young commander, barking orders. "Where are Billy and Lily?"

"They haven't been here for weeks, Ben."

"Who's in the yard?"

"Only Ned Ryan, Ben. And the dog. And Bobbie Boy, Ben."

I left her to her terror, told her I'd be back later, and drove off in the Alvis.

My next port of call brought cheers and shouts.

"Flock! Flock! Flockin' great out!"

Large Lily almost swore too, but Billy dominated. He wouldn't stop shaking my hand. "D'you know what, Ben, you're flockin' cat, that's what you are, flockin' cat."

Though I never got to the bottom of that Irish term *cat,* it means marvelous and wonderful, and I was flattered by it. Speaking of which, when they'd left our house, they had taken Miss Kennedy, who now rubbed herself against my legs.

Billy told me that everybody in the locality hated King Kelly. "Even them of his own flockin' stripe. You should hear Davey Treacy, the vet; he said to me, 'Billy, I wouldn't give that Kelly fella the flockin' time of day, he can flock off with himself.' "

Since Mr. Treacy had the mildest manner and the cleanest mouth in the county, I had some adjustments to make to get a clear picture.

Billy and Lily and Miss Kennedy sat in the car with me as I made three more visits—to Mollie May Holmes, Joan Hogan, and Kitty Cleary. They behaved, those three women, as though I had garlanded them with flowers. Such excitement!

For the rest of that day, we all toiled. Billy hadn't been in the yard for several months, not since King Kelly had thrown him and Lily off the property. He fumed at the lack of care evident in Bobbie Boy. Large Lily began to order Mary Lewis around like a slave.

And I—I slept in my own bed that night, and helped Lily put my parents' room back to rights. When I opened my bag I found the note from Venetia: *Dear Ben.*

Washing, ironing, polishing, cleaning—such a surge of effort; the gratification! At noon next day, I fetched the three women. It proved difficult to fit them into the Alvis because they had prepared so much food.

And at five o'clock, with the sun still in the sky, I walked down to the cottage holding in my hand the lawyer's piece of paper, signed and witnessed.

The range of human emotions isn't always wide enough. Or we can't—or daren't—expand on it. I watched it in my parents that evening, and I think the word *daren't* applied. Neither took it in fully; they delayed its digestion. This time at least, I found the cottage door open.

They never heard me coming, and each started in fright at the big shadow that loomed in the doorway. Both rose, and my father pushed his spectacles back on his head, saying, "Well, look who's here."

Mother said, "Did you travel far? Have you eaten?"

I said, and I couldn't hide my smile, "You'll need to be sitting down."

They were my children now. Just for that afternoon and evening. Like toddlers they sat obediently in their chairs, looking at me, not knowing what was to come.

I pulled the piece of paper from my pocket and began to read from it: " 'I, Thomas Aquinas Kelly, do hereby—' " A little overcome, I had to stop and start again. " 'I, Thomas Aquinas Kelly, do hereby give back to Harold and Louise MacCarthy their farm at Goldenfields. I cancel any mortgage that I once had on that entire property . . .' " I stopped.

"Show me that," said Mother.

I handed it over; he looked over her shoulder. She took his hand and they couldn't look at me, but I was fine with that.

Mother had a saying that I loved—because she said it with such satisfaction. She said it everywhere, around the house, in the garden—she even used it to potty-train me. Now she said it again as she looked at me.

"Job done."

They walked up to the house, arm in arm. I went ahead, just by fifty yards or so, to tell everybody that they were coming. A long table had been set out in front of the house, as we sometimes did on fine summer days. White linen shone in the sun—and piles of food glistened.

In a row behind the table stood Lily and Billy—no sign of Mary Lewis—and Mollie May Holmes, Joan Hogan, and Kitty Cleary. They didn't applaud or anything like that. It wasn't their way. The most they managed was "Howya?" and "Welcome back."

My parents shook hands with everybody. Mother looked at the food and began talking about recipes, and my father asked Billy to bring around Bobbie Boy.

Nobody left that table until ten o'clock that night. Billy, who had been off the drink since my father's initial departure, didn't touch a drop. He drove the women home.

My parents, Lily, and I tidied up. Mother inspected everything, the rooms, the floors, she ran her fingers along high edges looking for dust.

All she said was, "Is this your doing, Ben?"

They went to bed. Lily walked home. I sat alone in the porch. There was a moon that night, and it lit the white railing that needlessly divided the field, and down along which the Animal had galloped in the Incident.

I left a note for my parents: *I'll be away for a while. Expect letters from me.*

The driveway in the moonlight stretched as clean—I thought—as the life ahead of me, and as I strolled I sought the honeysuckle that Venetia had admired. I stopped to savor it, and taste the moment, and then, a hero again, I strode on. The car wasn't seven leagues away; I reached it in minutes.

89

Do you remember how I described the first night that I drove in the dark? That dank and awful night, with the goat's greenish-yellowish eyes on the roadside? This night bore no resemblance to it. I didn't drive; I rode a magic carpet. Isn't it wonderful what happens when you're driving under a full moon? It appears, it's gone, and then, like a child playing a game, there it is again, above a new hill. *My friend the moon,* I remember thinking, *my friend the moon. And tomorrow,* I thought, *my other friend the kind old sun.*

With a flourish I parked the Daimler outside the house. Midnight. *Minuit,* the French call it. The witching time.

The witching time? Why did that sinister phrase from *Hamlet* cross my mind at that moment? " 'Tis now the very witching time of night, / When churchyards yawn and hell itself breathes out."

I stepped from the car and kicked something. A head. A head lay in the street. Blarney's head. It had been hacked from the neck. Inside the front door, which stood slightly ajar, I found his torso, his arms, his legs.

90

They took Venetia away. And they took Mrs. Haas too. Nobody saw it happen. They left two significant traces to tell me a story. One was the death of Blarney, the brutal slaying. I gathered the pieces, I saw how he'd been hacked—so savagely that I was surprised not to see blood. His head had been attached to a long "neck," a thick tube that went down into his body, where Venetia could reach in through his back and turn his head with a lever. They had sawn the head from the neck just below the chin. His feet had been cut off halfway up the calf, the hands at the wrists. That was the first message to me.

The other trace told me who had done it—Cody. Cody knew that we had a suitcase of money in the house. He'd brought it down from Donegal, and we were deciding how much of it to bank, and how much to use in cash bargaining for rent or property. And Cody knew where we were hiding that money, in a closet upstairs, covered over by boxes. He had taken out the suitcase but he'd taken only some money, not much, and left the rest there, out on the bed, in the suitcase.

It must have happened minutes before I got there. Everything had a fresh feeling—the teapot in the kitchen was still warm.

Do you know that moment, that suspended, almost happy moment when you know that something awful has happened but you're still thinking that it hasn't? That night, in that house, I had that feeling, and it seemed to last for a time. When it ceased, I screamed. I ran all over the house calling out Venetia's name, yelling for Mrs. Haas.

And I knew that nothing would come of my shouting, I knew that something so bad had happened that I had no mechanism to address it.

I also, without much effort, knew the truth. Cody had been planted in the traveling show by King Kelly—which explained their familiarity with each other. And Venetia's disappearance was my punishment. Cody, probably with some henchmen, and almost certainly at gunpoint, had taken her away in the middle of the night.

Charleville had a police station down the street, and I walked to it; but not a light showed in its windows—or anywhere in the town. I walked back, falling apart. My brain kept veering to the worst, the dark water at Lough Gur. I walked all around the town's two main streets like a madman; I had no idea what to do. The house repelled me; I couldn't go back in. Not safe to drive the car either—even at this remove in time I can tell how badly I was disintegrating. In truth, I didn't have a coherent thought in my head, yet I knew, I somehow knew, that I would have a difficult task to persuade anybody of my worst fears.

Which is exactly what happened. At first light I waited outside the police station, beside the old and half-concealed ROYAL IRISH CONSTABULARY sign. As yet, not every physical conversion had been completed, and many stations, such as Charleville, had posted a temporary sign with the symbol of the new civic guards over the old insignia.

A man inside saw me waiting and opened the door.

"Y'all right there, huh?"

What words could I choose that would make the most impact? I'd tried all night to think of some. By then my appearance spoke for me. I threw out my hands and the man, still in his shirt and suspenders, said, "Come in, huh?"

My mind registered, *Why is it that policemen always say everything as though they're asking a question?*

"I'm from Rosewood Cottage," I said. "Down the street."

"The actor crowd? D'you want to sleep it off, so?"

"Something bad. Something—bad—"

I couldn't speak—I've replayed this moment all my life.

"Are you an actor yourself?"

"No."

"What are you? Are you after doing something, huh?"

"No. Somebody's vanished."

"Is there blood?"

"No, no, I mean—there's a doll cut up."

He looked at me. "Is there anybody over there now?"

"That's it, that's what's wrong, there's nobody there and there should be."

He leaned close and I figured later that he was trying to smell my breath.

"Is there damage to the property?"

"I want you to come look."

My agitation produced his effort—sort of. The policeman went away, shaved, ate breakfast, dressed, and came back. How do I know? He hadn't already shaved, he hadn't been fully dressed, he was gone for nearly an hour, and when he came back he had a flake of yellow egg near his mouth. And he was sucking crumbs from his teeth. He applied his cap to his head and we walked to the house.

I, as bidden by him, stayed in the hall as he went through every room with elephant plods. It took him many, many minutes.

When he came back downstairs he said, "There wasn't a robbery, was there? All that money, huh? Is that yours—I s'pose it must be."

"But something bad's happened." My voice wailed.

"Who's missing?"

I said, "My wife."

Odd, isn't it? The first time I used the term in the outside world was the night I lost her.

"Is that all?"

"The housekeeper. Mrs. Haas."

He looked at me and looked all around. "We'll leave it a bit. If you don't hear from your wife or Mrs. House, I s'pose we'll have to do a report. People go away a lot. Did you have an oul' row or something, the two of you, huh?"

I shook my head, miserable, destroyed. He coughed.

"I'd say, I'd say—she'll be back. I mean, the money, huh? You know, like, you know—women. And money."

He touched his blue cap, walked out of the house—and that was it.

92

Now I shall tell you the awful story of my searches, and what became of me after Venetia's disappearance. I had nowhere to go, nobody to whom I could turn that day. This matter couldn't be aired at home to my parents—and James Clare would take three days to contact. I thought about going to Dublin and Miss Fay, but I felt that the burden of it might be too heavy for her, and I felt that I should stay in Charleville in case anything happened. When a moment of calm arrived I understood that I had an empty house, a car, a suitcase full of cash—and a terrible, problematic loss.

All that day I wandered around the house, going mad fast. My wife—that proud phrase again, *my wife*—had gone missing. I feared her dead, I knew that. I feared her and our unborn child murdered.

Next raft of thought: *The policeman believes that she walked out on me after a row, and that our housekeeper went with her. Missing persons, not murder.* I disagreed in my heart.

Third level of, as it was by now, despair: *I can do nothing. She might still be alive somewhere, not yet killed, and I can do nothing; I can't save her and I can get nobody to help me.*

Fourth, and worst, level: *This happened because I blackmailed her grandfather and cost him his prestigious job. I killed her.*

You think that was a bleak day? It was—but I would have bleaker.

Toward evening, after hours of fitful sleep and mad food consumption, I rallied. I still had some things on my side. The company was on its way down from Donegal after a vacation paid for by Venetia. If nothing else I would now have a team to help me search. And search is what I intended to do—search the world, if necessary. I rallied myself with one central thought: *Don't think of yourself, Ben; think of Venetia's safety.*

When I awoke next morning, the bed—our bed—looked as though it had been bombed by massive ordnance. I must have twisted and turned, rolled and tumbled. Mother had insisted since age six that I make my own bed every day—two minutes was my record; this took ten. I washed with great care, trying to impose order upon myself, and mapped out my day.

Downstairs I forced myself to eat, and I walked slowly from the kitchen to the hall, from the hall to the kitchen. *Walking slowly is thinking deeply; thank you, Miss Fay.*

Outside, no rain, some light overcast—the daylight helped. At ten o'clock, the hour that I had observed Charleville usually woke up, I went from door to door and asked the same question:

"The night before last, just before midnight—did you hear or see anything unusual?"

(You can tell, can't you, that I was a widely read boy? Adventure stories contain good basic lessons.)

Nobody saw anything. Two people, close to the house, heard what they called "a lorry," but they had gone to bed and didn't get up to look. They timed it identically: "About ten before midnight."

Everybody wanted to know why I was asking; I said, "I can't say yet."

They all found out within days because they told the policeman that I'd been asking questions, and he told them that my wife had run away.

"Actors," I'm sure they said. "Them bad morals."

If they only knew.

I had intended visiting Luke Nagle anyway, to tell him the whole story. His diligence all those years ago had brought off an excellent result: In at least one mighty infringement King Kelly had been nailed, a wrong corrected; I knew he'd be pleased. Now I sat in front of him and told him in sequence what had happened—the lawyer's office, my parents, the farm, all of that.

"But," said he with a raging blurt, "that animal! He did the same here; that's how he got his first farm—he hoodwinked an old couple. He should have been strung up."

The interruption over, I told him about Venetia, and who she was and what had now happened. Here's why I liked him so much; he didn't gild life—he took it on straight, headlong.

"The lake isn't very deep," he said. "You could drag it easy enough."

"Dada," said his daughter. "Slow down."

"False hope is no hope," he said. "Always best to know what's happened as soon as you can."

Though I admired him for his words, they crushed me. When I recovered as much as I could, I told him the missing-persons dilemma.

"Kelly should be behind bars for the rest of his life. They won't hang him now."

I asked, "What are you saying?"

"Go after him."

"I'd get nowhere."

"Good Christ, let me into court. I'll witness that fellow through the gates of Hell."

So began the first phases of my search. I would climb two more levels, including one national and very public plateau, and in between I would sink lower than I ever want you to think about, much less feel. The final stages—they occasioned this account that you're now reading.

In that first phase, I waited for the company from the show. My calculations told me that they'd arrive at the end of the week. I could scarcely wait; I'd grown to like them so much, and to trust them.

I assessed who among them might give me the best, the coolest assistance. Would it be Graham? He had a certain distance to him, and he read more than the others. Peter would weep and get blind drunk. Cwawfod might get hysterical. Michael would rage over the "death" of Blarney, and kick things (and maybe turn somersaults). Martha might be useful; she had an energy the others didn't, and she worshipped Venetia.

As I sat there, at the kitchen table, helpless as an infant, I tried to make sense of it all. I couldn't. My wife was dead, my bones told me. And

I was sitting here. Doing nothing. And life wasn't allowing me to do anything. There was nothing I could do. Nothing.

I know now why people in solitary confinement become unhinged. But at least they can see and come to grips with the forces containing them. I had to do something.

Again I went to the guards. The same man. Sitting, this time, reading the newspaper. He looked at me and went back to his reading.

"Hallo."

"Yah."

"I was—the day before yesterday. I was, ah'm, here."

"Is she back?"

"I want to make out a missing-person thing."

"Three months."

"But—"

"You've got to wait three months. If we made out a missing-person report for everybody who ran way from their husband, we'd catch no criminals."

I wanted to ask, "How many do you catch, you yourself?" Instead, I asked, "Why three months?"

"As for men who run off from the missus, 'twould be like the Red Sea deluge."

As I walked out, he called after me, "Hang on to that money and she'll be back. Women don't run away from money."

The company never arrived. I never saw them assembled again. For days I waited. I knew where they were meant to stay for their holiday; I knew because Venetia had discussed it with Cody, who had made the payment.

And then of course I knew that there probably had been no holiday; that Cody had paid them off and disbanded them, had told them some story about Venetia being pregnant and giving up the traveling show—that is what I speculated when the truth came to me, when they didn't arrive. Time proved me right on that one, but I didn't know it for many, many years.

Now, despair picked me up by the hair and dragged me across open countryside, across deserts and scree, and tore me up. I went nowhere, I saw nobody, I went down to the dregs.

Grief, I discovered, operates in different ways. It can begin protectively, by not letting you feel too much. And then it can scorch you and chill you all at once, like the winds of the Arctic do. Those days brought me into the first bad stages of such grief. I didn't wash, I didn't sleep, I didn't eat what could be called food—an egg, stale bread, nothing of any taste or use.

Here's what surprised me most: I had no coherent thought—about anything. All I could say, think, or feel was *Venetia, the baby, the baby, Venetia.*

My mind's eyes were filled with blood; I knew they had killed her horribly. Would they now torment me further with some evidence of this? And when I moved on to thoughts of Mrs. Haas and how they must have killed her, I went further berserk.

Enough of that now; I've made it clear how bad it was. It did get worse but not as dramatically; it turned into a long bleakness "dropping slow," as Yeats said of peace. I'll come to that bleak time later; let me finish the Charleville phase.

One afternoon, as I hit my worst patch (Oh, how can I say what my worst patch was? It was all dreadful, and the shock of loss made me shudder every few minutes), I heard footsteps in the hall. The knocker had been banging, and I had ignored it.

Into the kitchen, calling exploratory cries, came Rose Nagle, daughter of Luke, followed by a man as wide as a shed.

She looked at me and said, "Go and wash your face. This is Petey."

I went upstairs, washed my face without looking in the mirror (that's another thing: Grief doesn't allow you to look at yourself), and came back down.

"Petey is a detective in Cork," said Rose. "I'm going out to get milk."

Some men break chairs when they sit down; Petey could have done. He had the biggest shoes I had ever seen—he must have paid ground rent.

"Howya doin'?" said Petey.

"Don't talk to me if you're not going to believe me," I said. Or—I thought I said it but I must have screamed it.

"Hey, whoa, boy, hould on here, like."

Which I did. He pointed to a chair; he was in command.

"Come on now. From the start." He said "shtart"; they all do around there—"shtart" and "shting" and "shtagger" and "shtruggle," my word of the moment, because I struggled. I struggled to tell the story in a linear way; I kept jumping ahead, being pulled back, going sideways.

Rose came back with milk and eggs and bread. The talking went on for hours—the questioning; the retreading old ground; the new ideas, which, no matter how wild, he wanted to hear. It's a clear enough picture—he leaning forward, never taking his eyes off me, not making notes, me blabbing and blathering, and rampaging across the story and back again.

He told me to come to Cork two days on. By then he'd have "talked to a few people," and he'd have "an idea how to proceed." And he told me, "Calm down, keep your head cool, like."

I'll go straight to the upshot: Petey found that the company road show's holiday had been canceled, and that they had scattered to the four winds. They'd left the cars parked in Salthill; of the big van no trace—the police found it in Galway near the train station, with all the scenery in it.

In Cork, furious discussion had opened up in the police station—was this a kidnapping? Would a man kidnap—or have somebody kidnap—his own granddaughter? Some argued, "This man would." They'd all read the Luke Nagle paper. But would a judge think so? There the arguments began to founder.

Petey, aided and abetted from a distance by Luke Nagle (who also wanted Petey to marry Rose), got permission to reopen the Lough Gur murder. They brought King Kelly in for questioning, and they used the occasion to ask him about his missing granddaughter.

I never heard what he said about Venetia and me—but I read it many years later, in the police record. He didn't go as far as to say that I'd raped her, but he portrayed me as a stagestruck fortune hunter, and proceeded to tell them the story of my father and Venetia.

"So the young fellow comes in, the young bull, and he elbows the old bull out of the way. And he comes to me, and he asks, straight out he asks it, that the farm, which I acquired by legitimate transaction, he asks that it be made over to him and his wife—my granddaughter. He's after marrying her illegally on a ship in Galway Bay. I mean, look at it, look at the facts. Now tell me whose side you'd be on."

Every which way they tried to shake him up, but he never shook. The art of illusion: He gave the impression that he was the downtrodden one, who had lost his granddaughter, and his housekeeper, to whom he was devoted. Perhaps, after all, he was the best actor in that family. Or he knew how to tell the Big Lie. Like Hitler.

He almost cracked one morning; I was there; I watched him. Petey had wangled permission from his superiors to drag Lough Gur. A confidential operation—nobody to be told except King Kelly and me, and my focus changed horribly that morning.

Petey the detective told me that they still wished to connect King Kelly to the death of his wife all those years ago, and would drag the lake for further evidence. As I got there, it also struck me that they intended to drag for other bodies, more recently put there. Swallowing my throat almost, I went forward to the point where everybody had gathered—including King Kelly.

Since then, methods have advanced—for which, be thankful. Today we have divers—they used to be called frogmen—with breathing equipment. We had no such facilities in 1932, hence what they called "dragging." They attached weights, hooks, and grapnels to long lines and went out in a boat. Do you have any idea how sharp the hooks are, how piercing the grapnel? I thought of Venetia's neck, her breasts.

Did I say it out loud? Beside me, Luke Nagle, glittering in the early sunshine, said, "Imagine the damage them hooks'd do to a body."

King Kelly heard and turned away, coughing. Luke Nagle, old as he was, spry as he was, walked the few paces to King Kelly and said, in a voice that he wanted everybody to hear, "See them ropes? I'd hang you here now with one of 'em."

The boatmen pushed off. They took some time to settle the hooks and grapnels on the bed of the lake and began their first drag, a sweep all along the bank. Would a body—her body—would it lie softly on the bed of the lake? Had they attached weights?

Up along the first curve of the horseshoe they went, the lines snaking out behind them. We began to walk after them, Petey, Rose, Luke Nagle, and I, stumbling in the wet grasses along the bank. King Kelly stayed behind, watched over by a uniformed guard.

The boat stopped abruptly, yanked back a little by something in which the line had snagged. Along with the others I gasped.

"Oh, Jesus," said Rose. "We should be saying a prayer for her."

Her father, ever the policeman, said, "I hope we get an arrest out of this."

The men in the boat hauled and grappled. A large shapeless mass came to the surface slowly. Two of the men—they all wore thigh-high rubber waders—jumped out and attended to it. They hauled and scrabbled and poked.

"Weed," shouted one. A dense web of weed and algae had wrapped itself around the grapnel.

They took half an hour to untangle it. The sun pushed the early-morning nip from the air. Birds corresponded from every tree. Far away, tiny black-and-white cows flooded back into a high meadow through a gate from a lane. And over all of us hung the thoughts of two lovely tall women, one the granddaughter of the other.

The boatmen reset themselves and went on. They had predetermined their path—their sweep would go all around the lake a few yards outside the deep fringe of tall reeds. Some of the sedges wore startling, acid-yellow bonnets. I asked Petey about searching the reeds too.

"We did that, boy."

Luke Nagle said, "They were out here with pitchforks this past two days."

I nearly fell over. Instead I turned away.

Lough Gur isn't a big lake and they had dragged their mapped perimeter in a few hours. Now and then they hit more weed, not as serious as the first, not as tangled. They came ashore for lunch, and little was said.

King Kelly sat by himself; I had been unable, almost, to look at him. Now I walked over and sat down on the grass beside him. I handed him a sandwich; he all but knocked it out of my hand with his brusque shove.

"Look at you. Look at you."

Was it the words that made me uncomfortable? I had so much distress in my arteries that I couldn't define a new onset. But the words did disturb me; where had I heard them before and with that inflection: *"Look at you"*?

"What happened?" I said. Don't ask me how I kept my voice from cracking; I don't know how. "Just—tell me what happened. You of all people know how lovely she was."

He didn't, wouldn't, answer.

"Come on. She loved you."

Not a word. He kept his head turned away.

"Have you told her mother—does Sarah know?"

He moved his jaw like a man chewing, but said nothing.

"Sarah'll go crazy," I said. "Or does she know you killed her mother?"

Not a single word did he say. Not a word. He turned his head farther away, then rose to his feet. And walked away. He had a new walking stick, not as posh as the old one.

"I might break that stick across your head," I shouted. "They should hang you. I should do it myself."

Luke Nagle, Rose, Petey, the other police—all turned their heads. Petey strolled over.

"Listen here to me, boy. He could ask me to caution you and I'd have to ask you to leave, right?"

The point was made, though it cooled me not at all.

Soon, the boat set out again, this time to drag up and down, up and down, the middle parts of the lake. They found nothing—some old sacking, more weed, a rusty wheel, nothing else. King Kelly walked to the police car and waited. Petey went back to Cork with his colleagues, and I drove Rose and Luke Nagle home. We talked into the small hours, and I began to feel a little calmer; I stayed in their house that night, and next day I braved the house in Charleville.

What am I left with? Anything? And what now? What next?

Those and similar thoughts took me into the hallway and the kitchen. I got practical—I recommend it. Checking everything, I made a list—food, milk, eggs, the rest. I counted the money, close to three thousand pounds—a fortune, a hundred thousand and more in today's values.

At the bank I confirmed the signing permissions on the bank account; I had complete access. Now all I could do was wait until the prosecution of King Kelly played out. If they found that they had enough evidence to charge him with anything, then they'd search for Venetia and Mrs. Haas.

When they went to pull the files from the drowning of King Kelly's wife, most of the documentation had gone missing. No medical report, no autopsy report, even the coroner's proceedings—all gone.

The scrutiny of Venetia's disappearance gave them even less material to prosecute him. King Kelly never spent a night behind bars. He had a few days of discomfort, and that was all.

I filled in a missing-persons report; in the circumstances they allowed me to break the three-month rule by six weeks. Newspapers picked up the story, but not very energetically. A few sightings were reported, never of two women together. A man said he saw Mrs. Haas on the docks at Cork, then said he wasn't sure. In Dublin, a maid said that Venetia had stayed in a hotel room; questioned, the description only fitted Venetia in that the woman was tall and alone.

Overall, though, hung the notion that Venetia and Mrs. Haas had gone away of their own volition. One newspaper observed the closing of the show and the fire precautions. My name never appeared.

Then began the rest of my life. Then began the slow, slow acceptance. Then began the shaping of the life that took so long to shape. It would lead me to places in my soul that I never knew existed. It would lead me to landscapes barer and colder than that of the moon. It would lead me to make an interpretation of this calamity, an interpretation that turned into a life.

And it would lead me to embrace the most powerful emotion in the world. That, you say, would be love, wouldn't it? No. The most powerful emotion in the world is hope. I should know.

I reached for James Clare. I reached for him through Miss Fay. I reached for her too, my first step to my own salvation. By the time I went to her house, I had come to believe that the rock bottom I had reached was where my life would be lived. I locked the Daimler in her garage and, as it turned out, left it there for many years: When I took it out again, it had become a vintage curiosity.

No answer to my knocking or bell-ringing; I sat on the bench in the front garden until she came home. Her housekeeper, Allie, whose shouting always irked me, was deaf, and had never heard my calls.

When they perceive their friends in trouble, good people say nothing. They draw them into their own lives, and see that as the best way of taking care. Miss Fay greeted me with not much more than a shrewd up-and-down look, and led me to the room in which I had slept last time.

"I have some work to do, not for long—make yourself at home."

"Is James here?"

"I'll drop him a note."

In my room, among the engineering instruments and souvenirs, among the mechanical artifacts of precision, I began to learn that I had to put away the wonderful life I had glimpsed. Trouble was, I didn't know how to build a new life, a new anything. Venetia had, in a short time, become my certainty, and all certainty had gone.

95

Here now is an account of how I lived the next several years. I spent most of the first year in Dublin, hiding in Miss Fay's house. I had failed at something deep and ageless—I had failed to guarantee the safety and comfort of my wife. I failed, therefore I hid.

It opened the healing process, though. Under that roof, the first new skin, not much, began to form around the wound. It began slowly. I mean—I did things so basic, so childish; for instance, I drew pen-and-ink pictures of every mathematical and engineering instrument in that room. Miss Fay's idea—line drawings of attempted precision for precision artifacts; I saw the self-control that she wanted me to acquire, and I went along with it.

Each morning, therefore, I had a task facing me. Miss Fay said that she wished to give the instruments to the National Museum and needed to have a record of them; I became her recorder. Barely sentient, or so it felt, I drew all day.

She left the house each morning just before nine o'clock, and came home each evening at just after half past six; she was, herself, a precision instrument. Over dinner she told me about her day, her academic work, her meetings, her colleagues. After a week or so, she brought home a newspaper, and that's how I got through the nights. I can almost quote to you from *The Irish Times* for the second half of 1932 and the first half of 1933.

Fortunately for my healing process, Mr. de Valera did indeed call an election, for January 1933. With bitter sighs I recalled how Blarney had predicted it. And Mr. de Valera at last got the majority he wanted.

Actually, not quite; he got exactly half the number of seats in Parliament, an increase of four, tying the vote, but the convention is that the Speaker votes with the government, so he was clear.

Miss Fay and I lived like that, uninterrupted for a number of weeks, an aunt with a brokenhearted nephew—indeed, a mother with a destroyed son. I came to know her very well. Grief, and in this case, frightened bemusement and a terrible sense of failure—these can, in time, heighten powers of observation.

She was a thoroughly decent woman. I never heard her raise her voice; she allowed no drama into her life; everything remained on a steady keel. How perfect an atmosphere for a recovery such as mine.

It also worked because, for all her seeming diffidence and spinsterhood, she understood emotion. To grasp that, you needed only to see her with James Clare. He was, in fact, our only interruption, if you could call it that.

On a day that he was due to arrive, she came home early, cheeks alight. Her step quickened, she laughed louder—this woman, so level, so seemingly dry and academic, this shy woman, became excited.

As did he when he saw her. She always took part of the next day off after his arrival, and breakfast lasted until noon.

Then I had him to myself. He made me talk and talk. He asked me over and over what I needed. He made me say words such as "funeral" and "mourning" and "loss."

In the eleven months that I was there, James came to stay four or five times, sometimes for a weekend, sometimes for a week. He too had business in the city; he had to go to his employers, the Folklore Commission, and hand in his most recent notes and collections, and discuss his next—self-made—assignment.

During one visit, he and Miss Fay stayed up especially late, and talked into the night. Next day at breakfast—this was now late June or early

July, and we had the windows to the garden open wide, and everywhere I looked I saw Venetia's face and the flowers in her hair the day we married—James, with Miss Fay's round eyes watching, aired, as he called it, "a notion." His sister, who was married to a farmer in south Donegal, needed a "civilized" man to run the place because her husband had to have a surgical operation.

96

Healing stage two: In Donegal I became quieter than I'd ever been—call it morose. But I worked so hard, day and night, for this couple whose children had grown up and left home, gone to Scotland and Canada, a typical Irish tale. I had to do everything—cattle, sheep, pigs; I even did some building, and discovered that I had skills I never knew I possessed. All those years being everywhere with my father and Billy Moloney, and all the others who came and went—now I translated the deep-seated and well-remembered information into action.

I slept in a separate building, a room over a cowshed, and at night the warm smells and the warmer snufflings soothed me; Mother's stories about her cows came back to my mind, and comforted me.

James Clare visited every few months. He had a circuit that took him all around the country in a most regular way, and he could always tell roughly where he'd be on any date of the calendar. In a man who had no constraints on his movements, I found this sense of organization impressive.

My grief notwithstanding, I was by now, and unknown to myself—certainly unnoticed in my state of mourning—learning how to live a life out in the world. I had to get up at the same time every morning; others, including animals, depended on me.

Brutally, I had to look back on my time with Venetia as dreamlike, which, as you will recall, is how I described it. And I knew that I couldn't stay suspended in this half-dream, whole tragedy. If I wanted to honor Venetia I had to become a functioning human being; the greater the functioning ability, the greater the honor.

Those were not my words or ideas; they came from James. On a late October evening of the third year that I'd been there, when the weather—as can happen on the west coast—had gone all Mediterranean for an entire week, he invited me to walk out to Kildoney Point.

He said, "I like looking at the ocean. It tells me what the human spirit can encompass."

His sister's husband, a pale and likable man, had now fully recovered, and although they wanted me to stay with them for the winter, they no longer needed the help.

"They're very fond of you," James said. "But they worry about you. You're too quiet for your age."

I said, "I suppose so."

"If I could wave a magic wand, Ben, what would you want me to do?"

I thought for so long that he had to ask me again. Then I said, "In the legends that you love so much, what does a hero do if he's lost somebody?"

James quoted first a snatch in Gaelic, and then the translation.

"He searches north and south and east and west, but they're the north and south and east and west of his soul. He searches up and down and in and out, but they're the up and down and in and out of his heart. He searches back and forth and hither and yon, but they're the back and forth and hither and yon of his spirit. And then he finds what he seeks."

"But," I asked, "he only searches his heart and his soul and his spirit?"

"Take it as metaphorical. They're the four corners of the earth. They're the sun, moon, planets, and stars. They're the four winds."

"And," I asked, "at the end—is he healed?"

"Always."

James and I sat looking at the sea at Kildoney Point, and I knew that we would go on sitting there until I answered him and his magic wand.

"What I say might surprise you."

He laughed. "A surprise is as good as a meal."

I took a deep breath and said, "I think I'd like to be a spalpeen."

He didn't flinch. "All over the country?"

"The four corners."

James said, "Wait 'til the fine weather comes in. And we'll make sure we meet on our travels."

I didn't ask the terrible question "Does the hero find what he's looking for?" because I had long known the sad answer.

Or thought I had.

We walked back from the point. As we reached the house James said, "May I ask you a favor?"

I looked at him. "If I can."

"Try to stop drinking."

97

I hear you asking, "What's a spalpeen?" Let me give you some context. Outside that farm in Donegal, that room above the cows, that house and those decent people, the world still turned. Looking back on it now with some (not much) objectivity, I was at least engaged by the politics. The new Parliament was up and running in Dublin because of Mr. de Valera's talks with the members of smaller parties. His absorbing horse-trading had continued.

In Scotland they have a good word, *outwith*—meaning "all things considered," or "notwithstanding." Outwith the turbulence in my own life, I knew things had changed nationally—and everybody in the country knew, whether they liked to admit it. It continues to fascinate me that something that seems as megalithic and remote as government machinery can have so intimate a reverberation.

Though serene at the fact that he was back at home, I missed my father. With his gifts of explanation, and his instinct for involvement in momentous things, he could be at his best at a time like this. I needed somebody to explain to me why I felt that the entire country had changed; in other words, that it wasn't just me.

People still walked about the streets. Farmers continued to take their milk to the creamery. Housewives went on shaking the bread crumbs from their tablecloths out into the world. And yet—things were different.

Perhaps the newspapers had something to do with it. They were alive with politics. Every speech, every utterance of every tinker and tailor, every Tom, Dick, or Harriet who had any political thought in his or her head was reported. You may think that the endlessness of political comment today is new. Not at all. Page after page of the newspapers reported from every one of the country's thirty constituencies and 153 seats.

What was it, that powerful interest in how we might govern ourselves? I've seen this country at ground level and I think I know, and it's an inspiring story.

To begin with, a large percentage of the Parliament members now representing the people of the country had come from nothing. From less than nothing. Is there a word *abjectitude*—meaning a state of being permanently abject? If there isn't, let's make one: *abjectitude.*

Abjectitude in Ireland meant, not many generations ago, mud huts. Deep in fields, masked by mounds and hedgerows, people lived, raised families. They cut sods of turf from the ground and, the grass side turned out, built igloos for themselves. Inside—earth above them and earth below them, raw, brown soil, always damp and dank, always unhealthy.

On the level above these mud caves, some families lived in houses. But that's all they did—"lived." A wretched existence it was too; we had them in our village. In one family, the food, to use Mother's word, "rotated"—that is to say, not everybody in the household ate every day of the week.

Clothing rotated too; when the children all stood within the age brackets that required them to go to school—from ages four to fourteen—not every child could emerge from the house every day, because such clothes as they had needed to circulate.

Dole. Social welfare. Child support. None of that existed or penetrated. The rural Ireland in which I grew up had permanent strata of poverty. If you looked you'd see it, the deep, wide band of gray-and-black grime just beneath the brighter surface of "normal" society. Except that there wasn't a normal society. What's "normal" when you have families who might eat a full meal on Friday or Sunday, or might it be Tuesday? With scraps in between.

They didn't wash—no soap and no knowledge of how to wash. My father often told how, when Billy and Lily first came to the yard, Billy had to be shown how to wash his neck; he had never done so. When she saw on Mother's dressing table that other shapes, scents, and varieties of soap existed, Lily began to cry. Such soap as she had seen came in thick yellow bricks, and always smelt of damp newspaper.

Nor did they know anything about forms of clothing. For years Mother badgered my father to tell Billy about underwear. My father went carefully on the subject—he knew that Billy, when he grasped the concept and the hygiene it implied, would blush red as a radish for days, and not speak to anybody, and swear even more than he usually did. Once, late in her life, I asked Mother about Lily and hygiene.

"Don't," she said, so pained and anxious that I never raised the subject again; I was interested from a folklore point of view.

As to behavior—my father had to slow down or otherwise make intelligible many of the workmen from around and about the place who came to our yard, especially the migrants. And now, in my roundabout way, we've come to the word *spalpeen.*

In those days we still had a spalpeen system. From early childhood, the spalpeens fascinated me and also wrenched at my heart; I knew even then that they warranted deep compassion, if not outright pity.

They were migrant workers, wandering the countryside, especially at the heights of farming seasons, looking for work. Haymaking, grain threshing, picking apples in County Armagh, harvesting potatoes in the big market gardens near the cities—they drifted on and on, often returning to the same farmer year in year out, a place where they'd been treated well before.

Many of them had families—somewhere, anywhere, and I remember trying to ask them about their children, and getting sparse replies not much above the grunt level. My father could translate; he took them slowly, as he did the local men, and he often said to Mother that he hoped, when they went back to their homes, they would pass on to their children the slower, clearer methods of speech he had tried to impress upon them. Some of them, native Gaelic speakers, spoke poor English.

I remember one spalpeen, though, who spoke clearly and rather beautifully. He came from Mayo, a county of great and longstanding poverty, but he seemed not to have a western accent, nor indeed any notable speech influence. I'll call him "Tom"—a man older than my father, or so I thought. Many years later, to my astonishment, I discovered that Tom, when he first came to our house, was no more than twenty-five years old; he looked fifty.

Over Tom hung a cloud of great sadness. His eyes seemed moist all the time; he had a sonorous tone, tending to the somber. Every year Tom left home at the spring season and came down to the south or went east from Mayo, drifting from farm to farm, doing without food if he hadn't found work, sleeping in ditches if he hadn't found lodging—and I know that cold spring wind, I've mentioned it before: Ireland's whipping scirocco.

Every year too, for many years, he left a pregnant wife behind him in a house that was no more than a shed—I've seen it—a lean-to, with a corrugated steel roof. And every year when Tom returned, expecting to see a bonny pink infant, he found that his wife had miscarried again. Nine times she went to various stages along her term, nine times she failed to give birth.

On the tenth pregnancy she died, and when Tom went home they had buried her and her stillborn baby in a pauper's grave. He then showed them the biscuit tin that he kept hidden in the wall of his cottage for a decent burial for his wife, should they ever have needed one, and he'd never told his wife it was there in case she got upset.

Here's the point about all this and that 1932 election: The previous government had undoubtedly an elite clique at its head, merchants and city men, who came from comfortable lives. Now, and for the first time truly, these people from the mud huts of the past, and the houses where food and clothing rotated—they had representatives. Many of the men who now spoke in Parliament, some still in the Irish language that had so long been criminalized—they knew the lot that they wished to improve.

They knew it because they came from it themselves. Poverty had burned into them. It had changed the pigment of the skin all over their bodies. Like fire victims it had scarred them forever, and they had sworn profound vows to change it in each and every way that they could.

Along the way, as is human nature, they would feather their own nests first. The sea beneath all the boats that rise on the tide of democracy is as full of filth and sludge as of clean water.

We saw Tom for only one year after his wife died. He never came back again. The spalpeens continued to appear in time for the haymaking in July, the grain in August. They didn't know one another and we'd gain nothing by asking about Tom. We assumed that he'd taken a job somewhere or gone to England or the United States.

All of us agreed that he'd do well wherever he went. Another definition of the word *spalpeen* has connotations of roguery, slick and underhanded dealing, probably because, when they were on the road, the itinerant workers often stole out of sheer hunger. None of that ever touched Tom.

And so, a few days after the election, a photograph appeared in one of the newspapers of all Mr. de Valera's new governing party, the seventy-two winning members, or "deputies." In the third row, third person in from the left, stood "Tom"—I looked and looked, got a magnifying glass; there was no doubt. Later I verified it easily—because his maiden speech in Parliament addressed "The Problems of the Migrant Rural Worker."

Isn't it clear to you why I became a spalpeen? For all its intensity, my mourning was incomplete. I had none of what today they call "closure." No corpse, no wake, no funeral, no grave—none of the essential comfortings of death. And I had three deaths to mourn: Venetia; our unborn child; and poor Mrs. Haas. Now I could visit every place where Venetia had performed, I could ask about her everywhere, and ask everybody I met whether they had ever seen her.

I had a photograph of her; I'd taken it from the house. How it stayed in one piece God only knows. I showed it in the four corners of the country. To my delight—short-lived but no less real—some people said, "Oh, yeh, I remember her."

They spoke of the show, and how they loved it and laughed about Blarney. In halls of all kinds, in shanties and shebeens, in castles, cabins, and cottages, wherever I worked, wherever I heaved a forkful of hay, or milked a cow, or shod a pony, I brandished this picture. It also kept me close to her—some might say too close.

Nobody had ever seen her since. There must have been times when I seemed demented, a wild-haired young man with a photograph of his missing wife. They all said the same: "What about the police?"

And I'd shake my head and say, "They never found her body."

I went everywhere in Ireland. The years I spent on the road, the years of draining the grief from my system, I worked for gentlemen and bullies, I worked for widows and women of means, I worked farms that had two hundred acres owned by farmers who wouldn't work them.

The frost in the mornings bit my hands and my ears. The rain in the day stung my face and my neck. I built a hay shed in County Monaghan, I repaired a mowing machine in Kildare, I herded sheep on the coldest headland in County Mayo, and I'll never do that again.

But I know how to do it, and I know how to get a horse to calm down when she's foaling, and a sheep to go easy when she's lambing. And I can teach a child to milk a cow, to squeeze and pull at the same time and never too hard because the cows don't like it.

What a time it was, wonderful in many ways and lonesome in most. It also contained atonement—for the sins I had committed, of blackmail, harassment, and that time I ran away from Mother, and the brawl with my father. And losing my wife and child.

I should have atoned. After all, I had cause. And so I atoned. On every freezing hill, in every damp bed above a barn, under the voice of every abusing farmer, lashed by the tongue of every harsh farm wife—I atoned. In the process I tried and tried to grant James Clare the favor he asked, to keep my promise. It did not go well.

And then one day, when it finally got too lonesome and I was very, very tired, and I had taken myself down as low as I needed, where I touched the base of my grief, I went home to my parents.

98

Perhaps you've been thinking me callous—that I haven't mentioned them, or talked about seeing them. I often wrote to them; I wrote to them when I was at Miss Fay's, explaining that I wasn't feeling well. Miss Fay had also written to Mother, of whom, as I've said, she was particularly fond. My parents knew what had happened; my father read the newspapers; he put two and two together.

If anything, they'd grown closer. He deferred to her more, Mother touched him oftener. No outward appearance could have given the slightest hint of the drama that had gone on here previously, the Catastrophe. The farm throve and Billy Moloney had grown larger.

When I walked in, he was working in the yard.

"Hah! The big flockin' man himself! How're they hangin', Big Ben?"—a good job Mother didn't overhear that little squib.

Had it happened, had it all really happened? It had. That first night at dinner—Mother insisted on the dining room—they spoke of it.

"It was all a deep plan, wasn't it?" and "Such an old crook." It was from my parents I learned that Professor Fay had taken a job at a college in Scotland.

"I hope never to meet him," I said.

They marveled at my appearance—windblown, sunburnt, and much, much older-looking than when they had seen me last. As Mother said, "You actually have lines on your face."

"Without you," said my father, "we probably wouldn't be alive today. We'd have died."

I said, "It was my job. And I wouldn't have known that but for Mother."

In different ways, and at separate times, each asked me, "How are you, Ben? Are you all right?"—meaning, *We know what happened and how on earth are you managing?*

My father said, "Jesus God, she was wonderful, wasn't she? And her mother. And that bloody old crook is still alive."

"Where is he?"

He laughed. "Would-would-would you believe it? He bought land a few miles from here. Paid for it this time. You should go to see him. Rattle him up a bit."

"What's Sarah really like?" I asked him. "Is she as bad as her father?"

"In-in-in his thrall," said my father. "Did I ever tell you I saw her once, long before you were born? She was with John M. Synge. They were walking in Dublin. He'd have made some play out of all this, wouldn't he?"

And Mother and I—at another moment we sat on the window seat, looking out on the huge beech. Never had I seen the branches so naked, so gaunt; at the last moment of autumn, the gales had come in and done their annual work of stripping the leaves and sending them down to fertilize the earth. I made some remark about the tree's fingers, and its very bareness, and its age.

Mother, not looking at me, said, "The things you know, Ben, don't you? And you knew them so young."

James's story began to echo. *There was a man one time and he knew many things. He knew how to grow beautiful ears of wheat and when to take the new potatoes out of the ground.*

I tried to kill the echo; it persisted.

He knew when a horse was ready to be taught how to jump a ditch, and he knew when to bring his dairy cows in for the winter. He knew how to take care of his family, for he had a wife . . .

Excusing myself, I rose and walked away. I was that man. Or, I could have been. Had I still a wife.

99

In due course James Clare pulled strings and made me his assistant. Such a wing as he took me under. When James retired, his poor respiration finally immobilizing him, I took over and became a folklore collector in my own right, permanent and pensionable, paid by the government. In my travels I had to come back often to Dublin, where, as you know, I met Sarah many times. I went to see her perform at the Abbey, and visited her dressing room between afternoon and evening performances. Or, as I told you earlier, I went to have tea at her house, where I had many interviews that included her husband, Mr. Anderson.

I also did as my father suggested—I went to see King Kelly too. At my first visit, he nearly fell down his stairs when he saw me in his doorway. Thereafter, I saw him more times than I would have liked. I listened to his stories, as I listened to Sarah's. And as I've indicated, I also tracked down the members of the company, and I've talked to them—some of them many times.

It took a major effort of will to see Sarah. In truth, it happened partly by accident—a gift, a free ticket to Synge's play *Riders to the Sea,* at the Abbey, where Sarah reprised her famous role of Maurya. One of my reports had included stories from the aged daughter of the woman on whom Synge had based the story, the woman who had lost her husband and all her sons to the ocean.

I have to say that Sarah took my breath away. The newspapers had been reporting her "magnificence," her "stupendous performance." When she uttered the famous line "They're all gone now and there isn't anything more the sea can do to me," I thought that the audience would break out into a wail. I certainly wailed, inside me. Was I looking at Venetia?

I didn't know how—or whether—Sarah would receive me. But I should have known—Sarah "Incorrigible" Kelly, serene as linen, posed by her mirror, one hand on the rail of her gilt chair.

"Ben! My beautiful boy—no, not boy anymore—my beautiful man. Look at you!"

At first we talked more easily than I'd expected. Does it say something poor about my character that I liked her so much? Not only did we talk, we made arrangements for lunch. But—she controlled me. Again.

"God, I miss Venetia," I blurted.

She burst into a weeping so powerful that I had no recourse. Waving a hand, deep in her grief, she gestured for me to go. As I stood, and her sobs came under control, she began her deflections—come to the house, you must meet Mr. Anderson, and so on. It took some months before I found the courage.

We sat in the garden; it was the first time I visited her house, and the first time I met Mr. Anderson.

"Sarah," I said. A child would have known that I was desperate. "What happened to Venetia?"

Again, she burst into tears and Mr. Anderson asked me to leave, and please not come back if I meant to upset his wife.

I didn't, not for months—but when I did, we had an amiable conversation, all three of us, about the Waldorf-Astoria and the New York stage and all of that.

And then I heard, as I was leaving, what I thought was a noise of scratching.

I stalked the place—and two days later I ambushed Mrs. Haas when she was shopping. She nearly died of fright; we had to hide down a lane lest she be seen. How she had aged—almost unrecognizably. She told me as much as she knew. We met again and again.

"Her father, Mr. Kelly—he sent Sarah, the mother, the cable—'Come back. Urgent.' She come back and they had the big conference. And my Wenetia, she scream and scream and I'm told to go avay and not to listen at the door. But I heard. The mother, Sarah, she told Wenetia, You must go, or they kill Ben."

"What?!"

"Ben, do not tell that you've met me, not even to say that you know Wenetia is alive."

"Where is she? Where is she?"

"I do not know. Sarah, the mother, she goes away somevhere, tvice a year."

"Is there a child?"

"They tell me nothing, Ben."

"Do you think they meant to kill me?"

"Ja. The gunman in the kitchen, the old Mr. Kelly's attitude. Ja, they vould kill you. Think. He, the old man—the lake, Gur, his young vife, all that."

"You know about that?"

"I tell Wenetia. The shop man—he bought eggs from Mr. Nagle's daughter. Wenetia tell Blarney. Poor Blarney."

King Kelly promised Venetia that if she went away for a while they wouldn't harm me—which he and Cody meant to do. Then they found that they daren't—on account of the police investigation. With the dragging of the lake and all that, I was prominently linked in police thinking to King Kelly and it would have looked too obvious. Some months later, Sarah told Venetia that I was dead, killed in an accident.

"Ben, is the vord—*implore*? I implore you. Do not tell you met me."

"Can I find Venetia?"

At our last meeting, Mrs. Haas ran away, and I didn't stop her. Couldn't. I didn't want to endanger her. I didn't want anyone hurt on my behalf ever again.

The members of the company had limits to what they knew—or know—but they confirmed sufficient details for me. Their best information had to do with the closing of the show.

"That bloke Cody," said neckless Graham. "He was at the root of it.

Money, I'd say. But he did tell us the jig was up. We didn't know what the jig was."

Martha said, "I don't believe them. I think they killed her. They're only telling you she's alive so's you won't go looking for a body again. 'Cause if you find one—well, they're murderers, aren't they?"

Peter wept. "My poor Venetia, my light, my shining angel."

I believe that Venetia is alive—or was taken away alive. In time, King Kelly more or less told me so; that's why I went to see him so often, because I suspected that he'd relish the opportunity to torture me. And I believed that Sarah confirmed it—Sarah, turning her figure this way and that, with alluring smiles; and Mr. Anderson, wintry Mr. Anderson, in his black suit and his shirt of unreal white, smiling his thin smile at her. They held me captive, and still do.

It's a simple story. King Kelly wanted land, but for very little money. He'd worked the mortgage stunt once or twice; he'd learned it in Montana on the land rushes—and he was always looking for vulnerable targets, widows, innocent people, those in distress.

Afraid to risk his political future, he wanted nonetheless to own someplace near his future (as he hoped) parliamentary constituency. Professor Fay shared the same Fascist persuasion—let's call it what it was, Fascism, aimed at right-wing dictatorship—and they'd met at a political gathering in Dublin.

Fascists destabilize—that's what they do, in order to gain power. When my father showed such an interest in Venetia, King Kelly tracked his identity, and found that Professor Fay knew him. They began an elaborate scheme of further destabilization. I was, to them, collateral damage.

Strange how pieces fall into place.

"Look at you," said King Kelly to me more than once, "look at you."

"Look at you," said Sarah, when I went to see her in her dressing room. And she said it the next time too. By now, she knew that I suspected the truth of things. "Look at you," she said again.

I thought, *Where have I heard those words before?*

In her mirror I saw something behind me and I turned around—a Kinsale cloak hung on the wall. By now I was challenging her openly.

She laughed and said, "It was foolish, it was stupid, but you have to admit—it was imaginative."

"But it harmed me," I said. "And it harmed your daughter."

I went back to see King Kelly.

"I believe that I know the whole story."

"Have you any land to sell?"

"Where is she?"

"You'll never find out."

"But—she is alive?"

"Go away. And stay away."

I never did. Bit by bit, he told me more. Cody took Venetia away. The person who had seen Mrs. Haas on the docks at Cork—he had indeed seen her; she had put Venetia on the tender that took passengers out to ocean liners.

Bit by bit, I went back to Sarah too, and I added questions.

"Was a child born?"

Behind Sarah's chair, Mrs. Haas nodded furiously. Sarah wept, and Mr. Anderson said, "I think we should close this conversation."

100

My parents retired from farming in their late seventies. Few farmers took retirement, but I had no wish to take over. They fetched an excellent price, bought a house nearby with a spare bedroom, and when I wasn't staying there, Miss Fay was—or so it often seemed. James Clare had taken to "living in Dora's house," as he put it—essentially they lived together. And I had the wonderful good fortune to see each of those four people safely into their next worlds.

The men went first, led by James. He couldn't speak at the end, he so lacked breath. In his last weeks he wrote me little notes, in his small, neat hand, telling me where all his researches lay, his address books, his sources. I inherited all his papers, and, as I say, his position. In the end he stopped breathing, almost as a decision, and he left his life in the way he had occupied it—with grace, still inquisitive, and a thoughtful look on his face.

My father got a stroke, lived four days—long enough for me to get home—and got another stroke, which took him. Before he died, the side of his face had dropped; he could speak with difficulty.

"I'm all to one side," he said, "like the village"—a taunt hurled at our native heath by rival villagers. He died with Mother sitting on one side of the bed and me on the other.

She said later, "I think he looked at you more than at me."

"No, Mother, he didn't."

She herself didn't want, she said, "to make old bones." I've always believed that she chose when to die—on what would have been my father's eighty-fifth birthday. She went suddenly and without a word, clasping my hand as she sat up in bed to take a cup of tea from me.

And Miss Fay—cancer: a long, slow time.

"The dreadful thing is," she said, "I enjoyed every little gasper"—her name for cigarettes.

These, my four parents, for all their faults and failings, garnished their lives so well that they afforded me the opportunity to be with them at the end. As you can see, we may be barbarous over in this part of the world, but we are caring people too.

I'm done now; the story as it stands is over, with all people reckoned for; Billy and Lily are still alive—they're not much older than me. Sarah Kelly died in a Florida hospital; the Irish newspapers carried long obituaries. I don't know what became of Mr. Anderson and I don't much care—he colluded. Mrs. Haas died in a fall—or was she pushed? I've never known, and all I hope is that I didn't contribute in some way to what happened.

And so, I'm left with only one person—the person for whom I wrote this account, the person I've been addressing all the way through—the "you" to whom I've been writing this very long letter.

Who are you? Are you a boy? A girl? Are there two of you, twins? In those days we had no means of knowing in advance.

I've tried every means I can think of to search for you. Not willing to afford a private detective to follow Sarah onto an ocean liner, I have found the trails necessarily short. (In essence, I want to keep the money that I have for you.)

I mean to go on searching. This narrative will poke out between the bars of my cage and somebody will read it, somebody who knows you—maybe you will read it yourself.

If you do, come to find me, in the care of the Irish Folklore Commission, or ask for me at almost any house in the Irish countryside; they all know me.

Also know this, my son or daughter—although I have never met you, I can say without fear of being contradicted that you were born of something special. Few women have been loved as your mother was—fewer still by a father and son. My father may have done something unsteady and foolish, but he did it with a heart full of admiration for a most remarkable woman.

And if she's still with us (I tremble in the hope that she might be), and she reads this document, then she'll know that everybody in all of this is long forgiven—forgiven everything. I have largely forgiven myself too, and that has taken some doing.

Where are you, anyway? Under what kind of sky do you walk? What voice do you have? Is it a bell like your mother's? Or something of a flat drum, like mine? Are you a brittle flower? Your mother had a broken petal or two—and therefore was all the more loved. I'm certain that you must be tall, like your parents.

If you find this, you'll now know the story of your own life before your life began. In other words, you'll have your very own legend. Not many of us have that; as James Clare taught me, we must often look to other stories in order to tell our own. But not you.

ABOUT THE AUTHOR

FRANK DELANEY is the *New York Times* bestselling author of the novels *Ireland, Tipperary,* and *Shannon,* and his nonfiction work *Simple Courage: A True Story of Peril on the Sea* was selected as one of the American Library Association Books of the Year. Formerly a judge for the Booker Fiction Prize, he worked for many years as a broadcaster with the BBC in England, where he also wrote many fiction and nonfiction bestsellers. Born in Ireland, he now lives in the United States.

ABOUT THE TYPE

This book was set in Garamond, a typeface originally designed by the Parisian typecutter Claude Garamond (1480–1561). This version of Garamond was modeled on a 1592 specimen sheet from the Egenolff-Berner foundry, which was produced from types assumed to have been brought to Frankfurt by the punchcutter Jacques Sabon.

Claude Garamond's distinguished romans and italics first appeared in *Opera Ciceronis* in 1543–44. The Garamond types are clear, open, and elegant.